Praise for the Cape Cod Foodie Mysteries

"This is one of the freshest, funniest murder mysteries I've ever read. Amy Pershing is a wonderful and clever author."
—Elizabeth Gilbert, *New York Times* bestselling author of *City of Girls* and *Eat, Pray, Love*

"LOVED it! I literally walked around trying to clean my house with the book in my hand! I couldn't put it down!"
—Deborah Crombie, *New York Times* award-winning author of the Duncan Kincaid/Gemma James novels

"Amy Pershing writes with a fresh, fun voice that will delight cozy fans."
—Krista Davis, *New York Times* bestselling author of the Domestic Diva mysteries

"A delightful sleuth, a complex mystery, and lovingly described cuisine: a winner for both foodies and mystery mavens."
—*Kirkus Reviews* (starred review)

"Amy Pershing's debut mystery will leave you longing for a sea-side vacation, complete with fried clams and the next book in her charming series."
—Lucy Burdette, national bestselling author of the Key West Food Critic mysteries

"Amy Pershing delights and thrills with this debut cozy mystery set on iconic Cape Cod. This book is a must-read."
—Edith Maxwell as Maddie Day, Agatha Award–winning author of the Cozy Capers Book Group mysteries

"This series is quickly becoming one of my top favorites."
—Cinnamon and Sugar and a Little Bit of Murder

"Five stars, a perfect escape."
—Escape with Dollycas Into a Good Book

The Cape Cod Foodie Mysteries

MURDER
Is
NO PICNIC

A Cape Cod Foodie Mystery

AMY PERSHING

BERKLEY PRIME CRIME
New York

BERKLEY PRIME CRIME
Published by Berkley
An imprint of Penguin Random House LLC
penguinrandomhouse.com

ISBN: 9780593199183

First Edition: June 2022

Printed in the United States of America
1 3 5 7 9 10 8 6 4 2

Book design by George Towne

For Nick and Quinn

You have to love a nation that celebrates its independence every July 4th, not with a parade of guns, tanks, and soldiers who file by the White House in a show of strength and muscle, but with family picnics where kids throw Frisbees, the potato salad gets iffy, and the flies die from happiness.

—Erma Bombeck

ONE

"LADIES AND GENTLEMAN, I have an announcement," I said grandly.

My friends paused from wolfing down various decadent desserts and glanced at one another skeptically. They were not used to me saying anything grandly. Usually my pronouncements began with "Um . . ." or "Yeah, but . . ." This time, though, it would be different. This was an historic moment.

"My search for a blueberry buckle worthy of our upcoming Fourth of July picnic is finally at an end," I said, still in grand mode. "This"—I paused dramatically—"is the world's best blueberry buckle."

I waved my fork at the deceptively simple wedge of buckle on the plate in front of me. My gaze invited my fellow diners to admire the dense, almost cookie-like cake studded with tiny berries and topped by a rich, crumbly brown sugar streusel. To call this confection a coffee cake would be technically correct but would diminish its rich, buttery deliciousness. And besides, it was being served as dessert, as evidenced by the rich dollop of whipped cream on the side, so it was a confection. Serve anything with whipped cream and it automatically becomes a dessert. Everybody knows that.

As one, my friends reached toward my prize, forks at the ready. I picked up the plate and waved it out of their reach.

"Oh, no you don't," I protested. "There is no 'we' in blueberry buckle."

The five of them sat back, sighing audibly. I grinned at them. I love my friends. I love my organic farmer friend Miles Tanner, who looks like a gay Paul Bunyan. I love my best friend from childhood, Jenny Snow Singleton, who has three rowdy boys and is married to a high-powered lawyer but is growing her own videography business like the tycoon she secretly is. I love Jillian Munsell, who manages the local nursing home with immense efficiency and warmth and who is the best baker I have ever known (and as a one-time chef, I have known a few). I love Helene Greenberg, my sixty-something next-door neighbor and the town librarian, who wears T-shirts that say things like "I do a thing called what I want." I even kind of love my friend/boss, Krista Baker, the editor in chief of the *Cape Cod Clarion*, who, when I complain that she can be a bit overbearing, dismisses me with a quick "I'm not bossy. I have executive leadership skills." A reply which, I might add, she got from a tote bag my mother gave her for Christmas. Thanks, Mom.

So, yeah, I love them. Even Krista. Sometimes. But at that moment, I loved my blueberry buckle more.

"No fair," Jenny protested. "We always share when we go out to eat." Jenny can be a real Greedy Gus.

"We share when I'm doing a restaurant review," I pointed out. "Not when we're out as friends. You all wanted fancy stuff like chocolate soufflé and strawberry pavlova. I ordered the old-fashioned blueberry buckle, and the blueberry buckle is all mine."

"Actually," Helene pointed out, "since I'm the one paying, it's technically mine. Or at least a bite of it is."

She had a point there. It was Helene's birthday, and contrary to all birthday party protocol, she had insisted on hosting the five of us at the legendary Provincetown restaurant Clara's Place to celebrate. This was typical of Helene. She knew that, except for Jenny, dinner at Clara's Place would be a stretch for us. But she had couched her offer as a favor *we* would be doing *her*. "Every time I spend some of my divorce settlement on an extravagance, I feel a wonderful sense of revenge," she'd explained. Far be it from us to deny her that sweet payback.

"Okay, birthday girl," I said reluctantly, passing the plate over to her. "One bite."

Helene took one bite.

"Oh, good lord," she moaned. "This is delectable."

Helene uses words like "delectable." I use words like "yummy."

She waved over our server, Clive, who'd been hovering nearby ever since Helene had ordered two bottles of champagne at the start of the meal.

"Five more servings of the blueberry buckle, please."

"Of course," he said, as if two desserts per person was par for the course at Clara's Place.

For all I knew, it was. Nothing at Clara's Place would surprise me. I'd never before eaten at the iconic farm-(and fishing boat-)to-table restaurant. First of all, because I couldn't afford it, and second of all, because I couldn't afford it.

I was thrilled to finally be there, even if the legendary Clara Foster herself had retired. But Miles, as the purveyor of organic produce to many Cape restaurants, had told me that the new chef/owner was Clara's longtime protégé and, while making some forays into something a little broader than Clara's French country cooking–inspired menu, was mostly sticking to the dictum "If it ain't broke, don't fix it."

Certainly nothing that I'd eaten that night was broke. Not the roasted shallots on crispy polenta that I'd had for a starter and certainly not my entrée of bouillabaisse made with the freshest of shellfish and the catch of the day in a broth that I could tell was the result of hours of careful simmering until it had cooked down to literally the essence of the sea. Nope. Nothing broke there.

On the other hand, I was surprised and delighted to see swordfish brochettes with harissa, a Moroccan condiment that I happen to love. Miles had ordered the brochettes and had slid a lovely chunk of the fish off the skewer to allow me a bite or two. I savored its spicy chili hit backed by garlic and lemon, and immediately knew what I'd be ordering at Helene's birthday party at Clara's Place next year.

I had to admit, though, that the restaurant itself, having reached its much-celebrated fiftieth birthday a few years ago, was showing its age. As its popularity had grown, its dimensions had not. And I suspected that to accommodate more eager diners, the original tables had been replaced with smaller versions and placed closer together than was ideal.

If this were my restaurant, I found myself thinking, I'd buy up that sad souvenir shop next door, bump out the dining room by another twelve feet, and enlarge the kitchen to accommodate more cooks and line prep. I knew the building was a designated Provincetown landmark, so nothing about the façade could be changed, but you could probably enlarge the windows in the back of the dining room for more natural light and an enviable view of Provincetown Harbor.

But it isn't your restaurant, Sam. You don't own a restaurant, and you never will. I thought you were cool with that.

This line of thought was mercifully interrupted by Clive's arrival with a tray of blueberry buckles. He was accompanied by a vaguely familiar man of considerable heft and a mop of dark hair. From his white cotton double-breasted executive chef's jacket and black-and-white checked pants, I cleverly deduced that he was the chef.

It didn't surprise me that he'd come out to say hello to

Helene, guided by Clive's quick nod in her direction. When a customer at one of your tables is spending money like a Real Housewife, it behooves you to come out and make them feel welcome. I'd often done it myself in an earlier life. So, no, it didn't surprise me to see the chef at our table. Nor was I surprised when Miles stood and wrapped him in one of his signature bear hugs.

"Ed! How great to see you!"

He finally released the poor guy, and then held him away by the shoulders, surveying his victim's girth with a grin. "I haven't seen you since, what, thirty pounds ago?"

At this, the chef laughed and punched Miles not exactly lightly on the shoulder.

"I could say the same for you, buddy," he said. "At least I have an excuse. I cook for a living."

Miles patted his own tummy affectionately. "No excuse needed for loving good food. And I gotta say, yours is still as good as I remember."

Slinging one huge arm around the chef's shoulder, Miles turned back to the rest of us. "This is my disreputable friend Ed Captiva, the new owner of this disreputable establishment."

Ed *Captiva*. No wonder the guy had looked familiar (particularly that head of you're-not-the-boss-of-me hair). This had to be the cousin that my own sometime sweetheart— *don't go there, Sam*—Jason Captiva had told me about. The one he'd said, *unhelpfully,* was a "cook" at "that Clara restaurant in P'town." A cook. Hah. The chef, it turns out. And the owner. When Jason got back—*if Jason comes back, Sam*—we were going to have a little talk about accuracy in reporting.

Miles proceeded to introduce Ed to those of us around the table. When he got to me, he said, "And this is my friend Samantha Barnes."

Ed gave me his hand and a wide smile. "Jason's Samantha Barnes?"

I felt myself coloring. "Um, yeah, I guess," I admitted gracefully. Not.

Ed didn't seem to notice my embarrassment. "I saw him just before he left for that assignment in California. He talked about you like I never heard him talk about a girl before."

He stopped, gave me a frank look of appraisal, and then said, "Ms. Barnes, you tell him from me that Ed approves of his choice."

I was at a complete loss as to how to respond, and Miles, seeing my predicament, stepped in. "Sam's just announced that Aunt Clara's blueberry buckle is the best in the world," he said.

Aunt Clara? Clara Foster was Miles's aunt? Why was it that my friends never told me the *important* stuff?

"Clara Foster is your aunt?" I squeaked.

"Not my real aunt," Miles said, "but I've always called her that. She's a close friend of my mom's."

"And of yours," Ed added significantly.

Miles nodded, smiling softly. "Yes. And of mine. She understood when so many others didn't." I knew Miles was talking about his struggle coming out when he was a teenager. I remembered him talking about a friend of his mother's who had been supportive. I just didn't know who that friend was. "Aunt Clara and her partner, Kit, were my port in the storm."

"Clara's around here somewhere," Ed said.

At this point I think my heart actually stopped beating. The founder of Clara's Place and the author of the classic cookbook *Simply American* was *in* the restaurant? *Clara Foster was around here somewhere?*

"Clara Foster is around here somewhere?" I squeaked again.

Ed gave me a tired smile and turned to Clive, who'd managed to finish arranging the now eleven dessert plates on the now rather crowded table.

"Go find Clara, would you, Clive?" he asked. "She's probably haranguing the sous chef to double the aioli in the fish stew or something."

I thought it was interesting that Ed used the local term "fish stew" for the bouillabaisse. And that his voice was sharp with something a little more than mere irritation. *Uh-oh*. The new boss had some ideas of his own and wished the old boss would *just butt out*.

Clive hopped to it, heading back to the nether reaches of the restaurant at a fast clip. He returned in short order with a diminutive woman who looked to be in her mid-seventies, with close-cropped silver hair, deeply tanned skin, faded blue eyes, the whites a bit yellowed with age but bright with intelligence, and a determined chin. Something about Clara reminded me of my Aunt Ida the last time I'd seen her, though the two women could not have been more dissimilar in appearance. Maybe it was a shared determination not to be overlooked just because they were older. Clara was wearing a chunky gold necklace and a white linen tunic over black linen trousers, and I knew that this was a woman who, unlike yours truly, had always been effortlessly elegant.

She trotted over to Miles, who gave her a much gentler bear hug than he'd treated Ed to and then began the introductions all over again. Nobody could have been more surprised than I when, as Miles got to me, Clara Foster said, "No introduction necessary, Miles love. This is Samantha Barnes, the Cape Cod Foodie."

W ELL, SHE GOT that right. My name is Samantha Barnes—Sam to my friends—and I am the *Clarion*'s food reporter, aka the Cape Cod Foodie. Recently, Jenny and I had worked on a series of unexpectedly popular Cape Cod Foodie videos, so Clara had probably seen a few of those. Unless she recognized me from YouTube. *Please god, don't let Clara Foster have seen those YouTube videos.*

Cape Cod Foodie describes me pretty accurately. I was

born and raised in Fair Harbor, a small town on Massachusetts's Cape Cod, and I've been a foodie from forever. After high school, I went off to study at the Culinary Institute of America and, once I'd graduated, began making my way as a chef in New York City. I soon became known as a rising star in the city's food scene. That is, until my chef hubby and I mixed it up in a kind of chef fencing match unhelpfully posted on YouTube by a bystander. The video went viral, at which point I became known as the fallen star of the city's food scene.

And so I retreated home to the Cape, where I've been trying to balance my new job as the paper's Cape Cod Foodie with a complicated love life, a posse of just slightly odd friends, a falling-down house, and a ginormous puppy. Along the way, I've also discovered a new talent—a propensity for falling over dead bodies. And solving crimes. And despite my best efforts, periodically starring in some super-embarrassing YouTube clips (as in, for example, the "Santa Claus is dead" video).

But life goes on. My falling-down house, which I'd inherited from my Aunt Ida, was shaping up, thanks to Miles's DIY skills. Jason and I began stumbling toward whatever our relationship was going to be. Or at least we had been. I'd taken a huge step back last March. And here it was almost the middle of June and Jason was currently 3,000 miles away, *which I did not want to think about*.

I'd also made a trusted friend of Helene, who, as a former police psychologist, was very good at reassuring me that I was *not* crazy. At least not all the time. And I'd fallen back into my easy friendship with Jenny and was even becoming fond of her lawyer husband, Roland, and their boys, aka the Three Things.

And I'd grown to absolutely love the ginormous puppy—now a full-grown and even more ginormous dog—who had come with the house, Diogi (pronounced dee-OH-gee, as in D-O-G, which still makes me laugh).

So, yes, I was indeed the Cape Cod Foodie. And Clara Foster apparently knew me. The question was, which Cape Cod Foodie did she know—the embarrassing one or the somewhat professional version?

I THINK YOU HAVE a real talent for translating your passion for food onto the screen," Clara said. *Oh, thank god.*

Once I'd picked my jaw up off the floor, I managed to eke out an eloquent, "Um, thanks. I mean, I'm glad you like the videos."

Get it together, Sam. I tried again. "But it's really Jenny who makes the magic. I just jabber." *Jabber? Did you really say jabber, Sam?*

But it was true. Jenny was the brains behind the Cape Cod Foodie videos, and she was very, very good at her job. Which is why, in my opinion, the clips had been something of a hit and, at least locally, had restored some luster to my online reputation. And now here was Clara Foster herself saying she liked them!

"Well, you're a great team, then," Clara Foster said, shining the full beam of her smile onto Jenny before turning back to me. "I was really impressed with the latest piece on eating seasonally."

"That was a fun one," I said, all my nervousness gone now that we were talking food. "What people tend to forget is that when you eat seasonally, something like fresh local asparagus in the spring—rather than the year-round, jet-lagged specimen from Chile—becomes a special treat, something to look forward to rather than take for granted." *Says the woman who in the winter unapologetically opts for Chilean asparagus on a regular basis.* So sue me.

"You're preaching to the converted," Clara Foster said, with just a slight tone of "don't try to teach your grandmother to suck eggs." *For Pete's sake, Sam, the woman practically invented eating seasonally and locally.*

"Of course," I stammered, all star-struck again. "Sorry."

But Clara had moved on. She turned to Ed.

"That new sous chef is pretty stingy with the aioli, Ed," she said, her mouth prim with disapproval. "He's only putting in half what the bouillabaisse calls for." She gently scratched her forearm with one hand, which also reminded me of my Aunt Ida. Are all women destined to have thin, itchy skin?

"Yes, I've cut down on the aioli a bit, Clara," Ed said. I could tell he was trying to be firm, but it wasn't easy against a powerful personality like Clara. "I want the fish stock to shine."

I had to agree with him. All too often, chefs rely on the admittedly delicious garlic mayonnaise to carry the traditional fish stew, but in Ed's version the heavenly fish stock was the star, with the aioli playing the supporting role. And from the look on Clara's face, she did not agree with this approach.

I tried to change the subject. "Pairing the swordfish with harissa was brilliant."

Ed looked gratified, Clara stormy. *Uh-oh.*

Before fireworks could commence, Krista butted in. I doubt she'd even noticed the little drama playing out. I'd seen her eyes light up when Clara had said she liked the Foodie videos. Once Krista has an idea in her head, she's pretty much oblivious to anything other than getting what she wants. And Krista Baker wanted Clara Foster.

"How about we do a Cape Cod Foodie video on you, Ms. Foster?" she asked. "Sam was just saying that your blueberry buckle is the best in the world. Maybe we could do a piece here at the restaurant where you and Ed teach Sam how you make it?"

I almost dropped my teeth (as my Aunt Ida used to say). Clara Foster was maybe going to teach me how to make the blueberry buckle of my dreams? In time for the Fourth of July picnic of my dreams? Because, for me, the Fourth of July is all about the picnic. Okay, and the fireworks. And the parade down Main Street. But mostly the picnic. Which this year, Jenny had decided for me, was going to be a BYOL (bring your own lobster) clambake and would now, maybe, just maybe, conclude with the best blueberry buckle in the world.

Chef Ed also looked very pleased at this unexpected chance for some free publicity, but before he could get a word in, Clara said, "I'd be delighted, but why don't I make it at home with Sam in my own kitchen?"

That's when I realized that this was a woman who still relished the spotlight and wasn't about to share it with another chef, not even her protégé. This was a woman, I thought, who would be the star of the show until her dying day.

TWO

~~~~~

TWO DAYS LATER, the Cape Cod Foodie—wearing a cotton sundress, flip-flops, and some dangly earrings made out of little blue beads that vaguely resembled blueberries—and videographer extraordinaire Jenny Singleton—wearing her standard work uniform of black khakis and a shocking pink polo shirt—and our faithful canine companion, Diogi—wearing a fetching red bandanna around his neck—piled out of Jenny's SUV.

Diogi is what I call a Cape Cod yellow dog, a familiar mix on the Cape of yellow Lab and whatever. Maybe in his case Great Dane. Jenny thought Diogi would add interest to our little video. I thought he would add chaos. I could already tell that, just because I'd carefully brushed his coat and tied on a new bandanna, he thought this was going to be all about him. I took firm hold of his collar just to show him who was boss. As if.

The town of Fair Harbor stretches across the narrowest part of the "elbow" of the Cape, bordered on its east shore by the deep, cold Atlantic and on the west by the shallower, warmer curve of Cape Cod Bay. My house, which I'd inherited from my Great Aunt Ida, was situated on a small saltwater pond that feeds into Crystal Bay, one of the few sheltered waterways on the Cape's Atlantic side. I tend to think of Crystal Bay as pretty big, but it pales in comparison to Cape Cod Bay, which is five times as large. Clara Foster's house sat high on a dune overlooking Cape Cod Bay.

From the road, the house, set far back on the rise of the grassy dune, looked charming but not particularly remarkable. It was a typical gray-shingled full Cape with a typical gray-shingled barn behind it. The property was large, probably ten acres or so, judging from the distance to neighboring houses. Though the house itself was modest, the location was prime waterfront and I thought that the view from the top of that dune would be stunning. I wondered briefly how Clara had been able to afford what was clearly a million-dollar property. A small restaurant in a seasonal location and one bestselling cookbook do not a millionaire make. But my nosy speculation was soon forgotten as Jenny and I made our way around the side of the house as Clara had instructed us. "There will be some stairs on your left leading up to the deck on the other side of the house," she'd said. "We can talk there before we start."

Giving one of those polite hello calls as we climbed the wooden stairs to the deck, Jenny led the way with me following close behind. At the top of the steps, she stopped dead.

"Wow," she said. "Would you look at that."

We stood for a moment drinking it all in.

It was a glorious June day, warm and clear with that clarity of light that you only find on the Cape. The deep indigo blue of the bay was encircled by a miles-long curve of golden sand backed by green marshes. Looking out at the tangle of dune grass, heather, and beach roses, I was once again struck by the sheer, simple beauty of this place that I now knew, after a terribly misspent spring, I would always call home. *You might want to share that with your friend Jason, Sam, if and when he comes back to the Cape himself.*

I pushed the thought aside.

A wooden walkway led from the house to the beach below, which was completely devoid of people. Most people with waterfront property on Cape Cod Bay do not consider their beaches "private," but even if they flout tradition and post their piece of sand, that only applies up to the high-tide line. And as high tide only lasts a couple of hours each day, the beaches are essentially public. But Clara's house was at least a mile from any beach with public parking, so there was not a soul to be seen.

"Welcome," a chipper voice said.

We turned, startled out of our reverie. Clara was waiting for us at a round patio table shaded by a gaily striped bistro umbrella. A pitcher of iced tea and three glasses already garnished with sprigs of fresh mint were at the ready. Clara stood and we could see that at Jenny's suggestion ("After all, it's only a few weeks until the Fourth of July"), she'd dressed for our outing in spotless blue jeans, white Keds, and a crisp, red cotton blouse. And still she managed to look chic. Her silver hair was artfully tousled and her makeup carefully applied to bring down the carroty tones of her deep tan. This woman knew how to present herself.

"Sorry," Jenny said, "we got distracted by the view."

"Everyone does," Clara said, smiling. "That's why I almost never bring people in through the front door."

We settled ourselves around the table, and I introduced Diogi, who obligingly offered Clara his paw, a new trick he'd learned from our neighbor Helene. Diogi *wuvs* Helene and will do anything for her. Not so much me. Me, he pretty much ignores. Jenny was so entranced by this show of good manners that she made him do it again so she could catch it on film. Diogi happily obliged, ham that he is.

After a few minutes of chitchat over the iced tea, Jenny announced, "We're ready when you are, Ms. Foster."

"No rehearsal?" Clara asked dubiously.

"No need," Jenny said firmly. "Sam just asks a few questions, gets the conversation started, and the rest happens organically."

"And through the magic of editing," I added.

"And that," Jenny agreed.

Clara, as a true professional herself, knew when to let the professionals do their job. "Okay, then," she said. "Action!"

"Clara," I began, for all the world as if we'd been friends for years, "I've tried the blueberry buckle at Clara's Place, and it is, quite simply, the best I've ever had. What's your secret?"

Clara looked at me and said conspiratorially, "I suspect you already know what makes my blueberry buckle the best in the world."

I had to smile. There was no false modesty in Clara Foster. There wasn't even any true modesty. Clara Foster was a food genius, pure and simple. And she wasn't going to pretend she wasn't.

"Well, at a guess," I returned, "I would say that the secret is that you don't actually use blueberries."

Clara threw back her head and laughed, a hearty chortle at odds with her tiny frame.

"Got it in one, dear," she said. "Which is why you and I are going huckleberry picking."

Huckleberries are the small, blue-black relatives of the blueberry that grow wild on the Cape. I had been picking them my whole life. Every summer, starting in late June or early July, my grandfather would hand me a small galvanized metal bucket and off we would go to forage in the bushes behind his house. The rule was two berries for the bucket, one for me, but I had a feeling Clara wasn't going to be that generous with her helper.

Handing me the twin of my grandfather's bucket, she led me past the small barn next to the house, which sheltered a small but impressive vegetable garden from onshore winds, and then up a gentle slope that presumably led to her huckleberry patch. Diogi bounded ahead of us, nose to the ground, zigzagging to follow all the lovely new smells he found. But I could see that the trek was leaving my hostess a bit breathless, and I shortened my long strides so as not to rush her.

I could only imagine what Jenny, following us, was getting on the video camera as tiny Clara and lofty Sam (have I mentioned that I stand six feet one in my stocking feet?) wove their Mutt-and-Jeff way up through a half acre or so of wild beach plum and bayberry bushes. But truthfully, I'd stopped caring about my height about the time Krista had pointed out that the camera loved me because I was "tall like a model." Who knew? I'd always thought I was tall like an extension ladder.

When we'd reached the crest of the rise, Jenny stopped and turned to pan over the bay. From this height you could see all the way to Provincetown, the very northern tip of the Cape.

"Look!" I exclaimed. "You can see the Pilgrim Monument!"

And suddenly I was a second grader again on my very first field trip to see the 252-foot granite monument built in the early 1900s to commemorate the first landing of the Mayflower Pilgrims on November 11, 1620—facts I recited at our subsequent class play, which is why they are permanently burned into my brain. I remember that I was shocked at the time to learn that the Pilgrims almost immediately packed up and left for Plymouth. I couldn't imagine why they hadn't stayed in P'town. P'town had *amazing* fudge shops. I hadn't quite grasped that P'town didn't actually exist when the Pilgrims landed there.

But Clara, who'd had time to recover from our trek, wasn't interested in my trip down memory lane. "Sam! There's a good clump over here for you," she commanded, pointing to a few low-growing bushes thick with tiny berries.

"You're not going to help?" I asked teasingly.

Clara rubbed the small of her back. "A little stiff today," she said with a grin.

Called to order, I began plucking berries like a madwoman. It was getting hot in the midday sun, and the sooner we, as in I, got the picking over, the better.

Looking directly into Jenny's camera like the star she was, Clara said, "It's harder work picking huckleberries than blueberries. First of all, you have to know where to find them. And unlike blueberries, which grow in clumps on their bushes, you have to pick huckleberries one at a time."

As she said this, the berries dropped into my bucket with the tiny, musical pings that I remembered so well from my childhood. And suddenly I missed Grandpa Barnes, who'd been gone a good ten years, as if he'd left us yesterday.

Finally, Clara declared that we, as in I, had enough for our buckle.

"It's hard to get a big pile of huckleberries, which is why you almost never see them in pies," she said. "But they're perfect for something like a buckle, where you can stretch them out in the batter."

I took the opportunity to grab a few berries from the bush and offered them to Diogi, who'd grown bored chasing imaginary rabbits and had wandered over for his cameo role.

"You want a treat?" I asked, holding out my hand.

Diogi knows very few words in English but "treat" is one of them. In fact, next to "walk," it's his favorite. Eagerly, he snuffled my hand and then stared at me balefully and stalked away. Fruit apparently did not meet his definition of treat.

"Be that way," I said, popping a few of the berries into my mouth. "Just means more for me." I held the rest out to Clara. "And you."

Clara laughed and plucked the berries out of my hand. "What do dogs know about huckleberries anyway?"

I rolled my eyes. "Yummiest treat ever, if you ask me. The flavor is more intense than blueberries. That and the size of the berries was what tipped me off to your 'secret ingredient.'"

"You eat mindfully, as the young folks like to say," Clara noted. "That's what makes you so good at your job."

I could feel myself blushing with pleasure and was annoyed that Jenny, who never missed a trick, was clearly coming in for a close-up. I don't blush all smooth and pink. I blush all blotchy and red.

"Cut," I said. Jenny winked and turned off the camera as the three of us made our way down to Clara's house. From the outside, sheathed in silvered shingles and delineated with crisp white trim, it was a traditional full Cape, probably built in the early 1800s. Inside, though, there was nothing traditional about it.

Instead of the usual warren of small rooms that could be easily and frugally heated, we entered one open space encompassing the living and dining and kitchen areas. There was one closed door, which I assumed was to the downstairs bathroom, beside the stairs to the second floor. The dining area was next to the kitchen and consisted of a long wooden table with cushioned benches on either side and a few landscapes hanging on the wall. The living space was also furnished simply with a couch and two armchairs in matching white linen slipcovers, all facing a huge picture window looking out over the bay. The walls here were adorned with framed photos of Clara hanging out with various food luminaries such as Alice Waters and, could it be? Yes, *Julia Child*.

The personal photos were fewer, and most seemed to be of Clara and a woman I assumed was her wife, Kit Connor. Jenny had briefed me on our way over, so I knew that Kit, an artist, had died a few years ago in a car accident. In the photos, she looked to be at least a decade older than Clara. She had long, unruly gray hair; thoughtful, worried eyes;

and in contrast to Clara, a throw-on-whatever-is-clean approach to attire. I liked her on sight.

The only other personal photo was an awkwardly posed wedding shot with Clara in a navy slubbed-silk suit standing next to a bride almost swallowed by her ruffled, puffed-sleeve, Princess Di–style extravaganza of a wedding dress.

"That's my niece and me," Clara said, coming up behind me. "My sister died when Jean was just a teenager, so I stood in as mother of the bride."

"It must have been a good day for you, then," I said politely, "to see your niece happily married."

"Nah," Clara said. "Never liked that husband of hers. But Jean couldn't wait to be Mrs. Paul Wilkinson, with all the stuff that came with it."

Okay, time to smoothly change the subject, Sam.

"I, um, want, I mean, love your kitchen," I said desperately but honestly.

The kitchen, divided from the rest of the space by a long marble-topped island, made me salivate with envy. Six-burner Viking gas stove, sleek Miele fridge, acres of countertop. But the best, the absolute best, was the waist-high open-hearth fireplace with an obviously well-used grilling rack. The last time I'd seen open hearths in home kitchens was in Italy, where they are used for *cucina rustica*, or country cooking. How else would you grill your *bistecca alla fiorentina* on a cold winter's night?

Clara saw the open longing on my face, I'm sure. My open longings, as well as practically every other feeling I have, often show on my face. Once, when Jenny scolded her youngest, Evan, otherwise known as Thing Three, for a case of the sulks, I heard him say, "I didn't mean to do that face out loud." Well, that's me. I have an out-loud face. And in this case, my face was saying out loud, *Why can't I have an open hearth in my kitchen?* And Clara totally got it.

"When I sold the restaurant, I did a complete reno," she said. "Cost me everything, but hey, you can't take it with

you, right?" A shadow crossed her face and I wondered
when older people began to think about their own mortality.
"The contractor thought I was crazy when I insisted on an
open hearth for grilling my meats, vegetables, and flat-
breads."

I followed her over to the fireplace on its square brick
pedestal. It was flanked by a wooden basket of kindling on
one side and a wooden chest on the other. Clara raised the
lid of the chest, revealing a neat pile of split logs.

"Apple wood," she said proudly. "There is nothing like
apple wood for grilling."

I nodded, feeling like I'd found a soul mate. "In Italy, I
had some absolutely luscious pork chops grilled over apple
wood," I said. "They were the best I've ever eaten. Something about that subtle, sweet, fruity aroma—"

"Exactly!" Clara interrupted excitedly. "And until you've
had a fresh-caught striped bass grilled over apple wood,
you haven't lived!"

We laughed together, delighted to find a fellow enthusiast.

While Clara and I were comparing foodie memories,
Jenny had wandered over to look at the paintings hanging
behind the dining table. Then she stopped and something
about her, a kind of intensity of focus, made me wonder
what exactly had grabbed her attention. She was peering
closely at the painting closest to the kitchen, a smallish oil
of a white clapboard farmhouse. The house stood in a field
of golden grass under a darkening sky, a vast expanse of
water beyond. There was something familiar about the simplicity of the artist's style, and the slant of the light was
particular to the Cape, I thought, so probably someone local. Maybe someone Jenny knew. Jenny's mother, Sara Al-
bright Snow, was a noted painter in her own right, and
Jenny had grown up within the circle of artists seduced to
the Cape by its singular light and austere beauty.

Frowning slightly, Jenny turned to Clara, who was dumping the tin bucket of huckleberries into a colander she'd placed in the kitchen's double farmhouse sink.

Jenny pointed to the painting. "Is that a Hopper?"

I knew she meant the artist Edward Hopper. He is probably best known for his haunting views of urban loneliness, such as *Nighthawks*, that melancholy depiction of a city diner in the night's small hours. But Hopper also spent many summers on the Cape, as our art teacher, Mr. Felber, was forever pointing out. Mr. Felber had a reproduction of Hopper's *Cape Cod Evening* hanging in the art room as well as a few of his sailing paintings, such as *Ground Swell* and *The Long Leg*, which drew me like magnets. No wonder, then, that the painting Jenny was staring at seemed familiar. But the likelihood that Clara Foster was harboring an Edward Hopper was pretty slim. Even I knew that if this was a real Hopper, it would be in a museum or a private collection somewhere. Unsurprisingly, I was right.

"Well, it was a Hopper," Clara said, running the berries under a stream of cold well water. "But it isn't now. You're not the first person to be fooled."

I was confused, but Jenny got it at once. "It's a copy?"

"Yup," Clara said, shaking the colander a few times to drain it. "My wife, Kit, owned the original. She inherited the painting from her mother along with this house." *Ah, that explains that*, I thought. "Her mother was a psychiatrist Hopper visited a few times when his depression got too much to handle. He gave her the painting as payment for her services back in the forties. That wasn't unusual. Kit's mom saw a lot of struggling artists back in those days, and a lot of them paid her with sketches or paintings."

While Clara spoke, she began putting out what she'd need to make the buckle. I doubted she even needed to think about it. Two mixing bowls, one for dry ingredients, one for wet. Measuring cups. Measuring spoons. Round cake tin. Parchment paper to line it. Butter, flour, baking powder. She'd made this cake a million times. And while she worked, she talked.

"I needed money to open Clara's Place, so Kit sold it and a few others to raise the cash. But she loved that painting, so she painted a copy and framed it herself."

"Oh, yeah," Jenny said, peering more closely at the painting. "I can see now there's no signature. Hopper always signed his work."

"The others are Kit's original work," Clara said, pointing to a series of watercolors on the wall next to the copy.

Jenny studied each of the watercolors in turn. Most were the view from the house and yet each was somehow different in tone, some contemplative, others more direct.

"Your Kit was a pretty talented painter herself," Jenny said.

"Yes, I suppose she was," Clara said. "Back in the day, she made quite a name for herself. But she put that aside when the restaurant got so successful and I was so busy. Somebody had to run the home front, she said. And as long as she had something from her mother's collection to sell when we needed extra cash, she could contribute her bit."

I was starting to feel pretty sorry for the self-sacrificing Kit.

"She was careful, though," Clara continued. "She knew that money slipped through my fingers like water. She said her mother's collection would be our 'insurance' in our old age. But I had an appraiser from Hyannis come by the other day to take a look at what was left in her studio in the barn, and there was nothing left but five old oils of Kit's. They're coming by later to pack them up. They thought they might be worth maybe ten grand each. They wanted to do it first thing in the morning, but I told them my magic pills make it tough to wake up at a normal hour." Clara laughed. "I think I shocked them. Anyway," she added, "if they are worth that much, it will be nice for them and yet another disappointment for dear Jean."

I was finding Clara's flood of talk a little difficult to follow.

Nice for who? The auction house? And Jean who? Her niece? Why would she be disappointed by her aunt finding fifty thousand unexpected dollars?

But Clara was still talking, more to herself, it seemed to me, than to us.

"I wish Kit was alive to know about that. We'd talked about getting her old work appraised but never got around to it. We think we have all the time in the world, right?"

And at that, Clara's reminiscences stopped abruptly, and I realized that the woman, for all her self-absorption, still loved and missed her wife.

"I'm sorry for your loss, by the way," Jenny said, turning from the Hopper copy to Clara. This, of course, made me feel like a total heel. Why hadn't I thought to say that?

But once again Clara surprised us. "Oh, no need. Kit was much older than me and a car crash isn't a bad way to go."

What? Who actually *says* that, even if it's true? Well, apparently, Clara Foster.

"She would have hated dying from some crappy cancer or something," she said matter-of-factly. "All the tubes and doctors. People pitying you. Nope, she was getting close to her sell-by date, and that was a much better way to go."

This struck me as at once hard-hearted and funny. Which, it occurred to me, described Clara to a T.

Clara turned to me. "Do you want to see my real treasure?" she asked, wiping her hands carefully on one of the clean kitchen towels she had stacked neatly next to the sink and then tossing it into a small hamper in the cabinet below.

Jenny picked up the camera again and panned around the room before following Clara and me over to a glass-doored cabinet next to the fridge that held at least twenty cookbooks on its two shelves.

"This is my rare cookbook collection," she said. "The Culinary Institute of America approached me about leaving the books to it in my will, but I have other plans for them."

I knew about the CIA's Rare Book Collection, of course. It's a world-famous repository of rare cookbooks, including Hannah Glasse's celebrated *The Art of Cookery Made Plain and Simple*, published in 1747, and one of the first cookbooks written for the home cook, or rather, for the cooks working in other people's homes. As Mrs. Glasse, in all her eighteenth-century snobbery, says in the introduction, "If I have not wrote in the polite Stile I hope I shall be forgiven; for my Intention is to instruct the lower Sort."

And if I wasn't crazy, there was Mrs. Glasse's masterwork itself comfortably ensconced in Clara Foster's bookshelves.

"That's *The Art of Cookery*," I said faintly, reaching out to stroke the binding with one careful finger.

"It is," Clara said proudly. "That cost a pretty penny, let me tell you." As in thousands of dollars, I was pretty sure.

"I bet it did," I murmured, my eyes sliding over the neighboring bindings bearing names such as Atheneaus, Marie Antonin Carême, and—was it possible?—Auguste Escoffier. Escoffier's *Le guide culinaire*, first published in 1903, is still considered by professional chefs to be the classic work on French cuisine. This volume I didn't even dare touch. Instead I just gazed in awe at the leather binding, the words "ESCOFFIER LE GUIDE CULINAIRE" stamped in gilt on the spine. It looked like an old Bible, which, in a way, it was. At least to chefs.

"You have an Escoffier," I breathed.

Clara nodded proudly.

"A first edition," she said. "And signed by the great man himself."

She pulled the book gently from the shelf and opened it to the flyleaf to show me the signature. I turned to Jenny's camera and raised my eyebrows to indicate how impressed I was. Jenny, I could see, was less so. Irma Rombauer's *The Joy of Cooking* was all the cookbook she needed, thank you very much. And truthfully, Rombauer is a heck of a lot more useful in today's home kitchen than Escoffier. Or Hannah Glasse. For us lower Sorts.

I gazed longingly at Clara's collection and wondered how she could have afforded it. We were looking at tens of thousands of dollars' worth of rare books.

"Kit was very generous to me on my birthdays," Clara said, as if reading my mind. "Every year she sold something from her mother's collection and turned it into one of these." She waved at the books and gently closed the cabinet door. No wonder there was nothing left of Kit's inherited paintings by the end, I thought.

"Now," Clara said briskly, "let's bake that buckle."

Truthfully, there's not a whole lot of mystery to baking a buckle. Clara handed me a businesslike canvas apron and donned one herself, wrapping the ties around to the front and securing them with a neat square knot. Grabbing a red-bordered kitchen towel from the pile next to the sink, she tucked it into the waist ties, and we set to work. And by "we," I mean Clara. It became very clear that I was there primarily to hand the great chef what she needed, rather like an operating room nurse with a surgeon.

"Too much fruit can make for a heavy, gummy buckle," Clara said as she weighed and combined ingredients, "so I like a batter with a little extra structure, more like a cookie dough, so the berries don't sink to the bottom."

In short order, she whisked together the flour and baking soda and set it aside, creamed the butter and sugar, beat the eggs in one by one, and then gradually added the flour mixture. Finally, she tossed the huckleberries in a little flour to keep them separate and gently folded them in with a spatula. Equally gently, she transferred the batter to the round cake pan lined with greased parchment paper.

Making the streusel for the top took even less time, just beating the flour, brown sugar, and cinnamon on low to combine and then adding in some softened butter until the mixture looked like wet sand. I looked at the blend doubtfully.

My buckle at the restaurant had had lots of yummy, crisp-edged lumps of streusel, not this sad homogenized slurry.

Clara saw my dismay and laughed again. "Here's the other secret to the world's best blueberry buckle."

So saying, she took a handful of the streusel, squeezed it into a lump and then broke the lump into smaller pieces, which she then sprinkled over the batter.

"Brilliant!" I said, laughing, and took a handful to try it myself.

We must have looked like two kindergartners playing together in a sandbox. It kind of felt that way, too. There was something about Clara, despite her self-centeredness, that made her fun to be around.

Once the buckle was in the oven, Jenny stopped filming. Clara took off her apron and again dropped the kitchen towel into a small hamper under the sink. Chefs go through kitchen towels the way most people go through a box of tissues—once and done.

"How about some café au lait while we wait for the finished product?" she offered.

Jenny declined, but I accepted eagerly. I have never been known to refuse a cup of coffee, and I certainly wasn't going to start with Clara Foster's coffee.

Clara ground her beans fresh, of course, then emptied the ground coffee into a small French press and poured almost-boiling water over it. While the coffee steeped, she gently heated some milk in a small saucepan on the stove. After maybe four minutes or so, when some internal timer told her that the coffee had steeped just long enough, she pushed the plunger down on the press and poured the glorious brew into two fat, round café au lait cups. The milk by this point was just coming to a simmer. She snapped the burner off and poured the milk from the pan into our cups from a distance of about eight inches to make it just slightly foamy and returned the saucepan to the stove, though not to the burner she'd been using. I waited for her to sit down before I took my first sip.

"Heaven," I said.

Without taking a sip herself, Clara responded, "Yes, I know. I make the best coffee in the world, too." And we both laughed.

While the buckle baked and then cooled, we chatted, with Jenny occasionally chiming in. The talk was desultory, not particularly about food, not particularly about anything. Clara complained a bit about having to retire before she was ready ("but we make plans and God laughs") and about the indignities of aging, particularly her insomnia, which she countered with the injudicious use of her "magic pills" ("What? At my age I'm going to worry about getting addicted to sleeping pills?").

From the kitchen's bay window, I could see that the tide in the bay was ebbing, revealing long stretches of wet, rippled sandbars. Tiny sandpipers scurried across the exposed flats, probing the sand with their long, delicate bills. Farther out, the fast-receding waters had exposed an acre or so of low, square metal cages covered with seaweed. When I asked about them, Clara explained that this was an oyster farm and that each of the cages housed thousands of seed oysters.

"I like the young couple who're working that aquaculture," she said. "I'm going to take care of them, and summer can go to hell."

I had no idea what summer had to do with aquaculture, but by that point Clara had moved on to what I soon realized was her favorite topic of conversation: herself and, of course, Clara's Place, including its current incarnation under Ed Captiva. Ed, it appeared, had gotten his start at the restaurant back in the nineties and been trained by Clara as her heir apparent. He'd bought the restaurant from her when she'd retired, but he'd promised he'd never change the name, "No matter what some other damn fools say."

Our conversation ended when Clara decided that the buckle was cool enough to eat, and Jenny got some great footage of me literally stuffing my face with the Best Blueberry Buckle in the World while Diogi looked on hopefully. And in vain. When I'd finally eaten my fill, Jenny stopped filming and ate *even more* buckle than I had. Clara herself didn't indulge.

"Not much of an appetite these days," she said wryly. "The silver lining is, I've never been slimmer."

After thanking Clara profusely for her hospitality, Jenny, Diogi, and I climbed into the SUV. But as we were pulling out of the crushed shell driveway, Clara came bustling out bearing a wicker basket of produce from her garden. She handed it in to me through the SUV's window.

"This is just an excuse for you to visit again," she said. "I want this basket back."

And suddenly I realized that Clara Foster, for all her bluster, was lonely.

"It will be my pleasure," I said, meaning it. "I'll bring it back this weekend."

But I never did return that basket. Because that night a fire in Clara Foster's house took the great chef's life.

THREE

~~~

"YOU WANT ME to write *what*?"

"The obituary," Krista repeated patiently. "I want you to write Clara Foster's obituary."

Krista had sent me a text that morning, asking (well, telling) me to drop by as she had something to "discuss." I was hoping it was to talk about this terrific idea I'd had for a feature on the best lobster rolls on Cape Cod. It was not.

It was to tell me that at some time in the early hours of the morning, Clara Foster had died in a house fire apparently started from a pan left on an open flame on her gas stove.

"A neighbor saw the flames and called 911," she'd said, "but it was too late."

I was stunned. Almost as much by Clara's death itself as the thought of Clara Foster leaving a pan on an open flame. My psychologist friend Helene could probably explain why I decided to focus on that, but all I could think was, *This doesn't make any sense*.

"Please tell me she didn't . . . suffer," I'd said.

Krista shook her head. "Not from what I hear. It looks like she died in her sleep from smoke inhalation."

I still couldn't take it in. "I told her yesterday I would bring her vegetable basket back," I said numbly.

Yesterday. Had it really only been yesterday that Clara Foster had been so engagingly, outrageously alive? Did Miles know, I suddenly wondered, that his honorary aunt was dead? Did his mother know that her close friend was no more?

"Well, there's something else you could do for her," Krista had said.

I'd looked at her inquiringly.

And then she'd said it. "I want you to write the obituary."

Well, *that* snapped me out of my fog.

We were seated on opposite sides of the scarred wooden desk that had once been my father's when he had been the editor in chief of the *Clarion*. Three years ago, he'd suffered a mild heart attack, and my mother, the paper's senior reporter, had insisted that they take early retirement and move to Florida for its "healthy lifestyle." Krista had stepped in as editor in chief and saved the *Clarion* from its own early retirement by adding an online edition that had proved not only popular but profitable. And then, having saved my parents' dream, she'd offered me a job when I was at a very low ebb in my life. I owed Krista a great deal.

Not that that kept me from arguing my case in this instance.

"You want me to write *what*?"

"The obituary," Krista repeated patiently. "I want you to write Clara Foster's obituary."

I *really* didn't want to write about the death of Miles's honorary aunt. That was just too close for comfort. I also knew Krista would never understand. Krista has many strengths, including great journalistic integrity, but her emotional IQ is, well, pretty low. Better to go with a more businesslike approach.

"Krista," I said, "I write food features. I do not write obituaries. Just. Food. Features."

"Not just food features," Krista pointed out. "You wrote about a local murder, remember?"

Like I could forget.

"Yeah," I said. "And it almost got me killed."

"*You* almost got yourself killed," Krista corrected me.

I chose the universal word for *you're right, but I don't want to admit it.* "Maybe," I said.

Then, moving back to businesslike, I added, "The point is, I write about food and about its relationship to people and places. That's my beat."

Krista pounced.

"Exactly," she said, much the way a chess master says *Check.* "Who better to write about the great Cape Cod restaurateur and cookbook author Clara Foster than you, a food writer who lives on Cape Cod?"

Hard to argue that one. So apparently, I was writing Clara Foster's obituary. But maybe I could keep it to just the facts, ma'am.

"Well, I'm sure the *New York Times* and the *Boston Globe* will be coming out with their obituaries later today," I said, thinking out loud. "I guess I could just crib from them and add in some Cape stuff."

Krista stood up, put both hands flat on the desk, and leaned toward me, the sleek bell of her dark hair swinging forward.

"You will *not* rewrite the *Times* or *Globe* obits," she said with utter disdain. "The *Clarion* has followed Clara Foster's career for more than fifty years. We did a big piece on her and the restaurant for their fiftieth anniversary a couple of years ago. You can *crib* from that." She said the word "crib" the way other people say the word "steal." "And then you will talk to those who knew her and worked with her and you will make this obituary personal to Clara Foster and the Cape and the people who live here in a way that the *Times* and the *Globe* cannot."

And there it was, that darn journalistic integrity.

"Fine," I said, conceding defeat. "But just sit down, okay? It makes me nervous when you loom over me like that."

Krista barked a laugh and settled back into her desk chair. "Now you know how we short girls feel."

As I am someone who has often been self-conscious about her height, it had never occurred to me that Krista might feel insecure about her five feet three inches. I'd always thought of her as petite. Apparently, she thought of herself as vertically challenged.

For the first time I wondered what it must be like to go into a business meeting—and Krista went into *a lot* of business meetings—and in almost every case have to look up at the person, in almost every case a man, who shakes your hand. No wonder she had so carefully crafted her persona to look and act as professional and, well, intimidating as possible. The perfect hair and makeup, the sleek suits, the expensive shoes with two-inch heels, the low, modulated voice. Everything about her said, *Do not mess with me.*

With the realization that Krista might have vulnerabilities like the rest of us mere mortals, I felt a surge of compassion for my friend. But did I tell her so? Heaven forfend. It did, however, make me less likely to argue with what came next.

"But first," she continued, doing that thing she does where she talks to you while looking at the screen on her PC to see if anything more important has come up, "I want you to see if they've come up with the official cause of death. So you need to check in with Vivian Peters."

Vivian Peters. Detective Vivian Peters. I really didn't feel like checking in with Detective Peters. Not because I didn't think she was good at her job. She was excellent at her job. So much better than her boss, Police Chief George McCauley, of whom the less said, the better. Of course, McCauley set a low bar, but even if it had been high, Vivian Peters would have effortlessly succeeded in sailing over it. She'd been effortlessly succeeding at things ever since high school.

Vivvie, as everyone called her then, was one of the few students at Fair Harbor High from the Cape's indigenous Wampanoag people—most of whom live down Cape on the tribal lands in Mashpee. This had made her to my eyes beyond cool, though I realized as I'd gotten older that she must have faced challenges in ways I couldn't then begin to understand. She had been a few years ahead of me and good at everything I was not—sports, academics, debate club, you name it. Nonetheless, she had been modest about her accomplishments and genuinely friendly to all. Everyone had liked and respected student council president Vivvie Peters. Everyone liked and respected Detective Vivian Peters now. Including Jason, who'd been in her year at school and had had occasion to work with her on what I still thought of as the Case of the Dead Santa. (Which, I might add, *I* solved.)

So I knew Jason respected Detective Peters, but just how much he liked *Vivvie*, as he called her, I wasn't exactly sure. I'd never asked him, of course. And now I wondered if it was too late to talk to him about it. Once again, I had to ask myself, *How had it come to this?*

I T HAD ALL been going so well. Winter and early spring are the slow time for a harbormaster on the Cape, so Jason was for once on a fairly predictable schedule. I was writing a regular Cape Cod Foodie column once a week and doing a Foodie video maybe once a month. So nights and weekends were ours. Well, ours and Diogi's and Jason's tabby kitten, Ciati's (pronounced see-AY-tee, as in C-A-T, get it?). Because my cozy ell with its woodstove and comfy couch was infinitely more conducive to cuddling than Jason's bachelor pad over the Harbor Patrol offices, the four of us spent most of our free time there. Ciati even had her own litter box.

But no sooner had I felt secure in Jason's commitment

(because no guy renovates a boat for his girl unless he's committed, right?) than I began to doubt my own. For some reason—perhaps because I still felt some ambivalence about turning down a job at New York's hottest restaurant, Plum and Pear, to stay on the Cape—I'd agreed back in March to fill in for a month when the chef-owner, Caitlin Summerhill, had, once again, lost her latest sous chef. Back when I'd moved to the Cape, I'd sublet my apartment in the city to a friend rather than break my lease, which for some reason I had never seen fit to mention to Jason. My friend was a college professor away on sabbatical, so it had been easy for Diogi and me to move in "temporarily" while I helped out at Plum and Pear.

Jason had been nothing but supportive, but with me working nights, communication had been difficult. It only took a week for me to come to my senses. I *hated* the late hours. I *hated* that I had to hire a *stranger* to walk Diogi while I was at work. Although I still loved it, New York was nonetheless a constant assault on the senses. I missed long, quiet, contemplative walks along the beach. I missed my friends. And most of all, I missed Jason, his warmth and his understanding. And his kisses. The man is a demon kisser. But did I tell him this? Heaven forfend. I did tell him I was unhappy, but I didn't go into details. And we both agreed that I should honor my commitment to Caitlin.

Once I was back on the Cape, I was happy for about five minutes, which was about how long our welcome-back kiss lasted. And then Jason announced that he was considering an offer to be part of a twelve-week exchange program with a Harbor Patrol in Santa Barbara, California. It was a golden opportunity for him to learn more about something he called "rescue in extreme sea conditions." All I could think was, *It's our relationship that needs rescuing from extreme sea conditions*, but instead of actually saying that, I pretended to be supportive. *And look where that got you, Sam.*

Where it got me was the man that I loved living 3,000 miles away. We'd promised to talk by phone every night, but with the three-hour time difference and Jason's uncertain hours, that precious together time was a little erratic. Anyway, the program would end in a few weeks, though Jason had been a little tentative about committing to an exact date when he'd be returning to Fair Harbor. Exactly *why* he was tentative, I didn't ask. Of course. I kind of wondered, though, what *Vivvie's* future plans were.

B UT BEING JEALOUS of Detective Peters was not exactly an argument for not checking in with her in the course of writing Clara's obituary. I did need to get the official wording about cause of death.

"Okay," I said to Krista, "I'll give her a call at the station."

"Already did that," Krista said without taking her eyes off her computer screen. "She's out at Foster's house. I told them you'd be coming out to talk to her." Of course she had.

I sighed. "Why did you even pretend that you were *asking* me to write this obituary?"

At this, Krista looked up at me, a frown creasing her perfect forehead. "I didn't pretend anything. I wasn't *asking* you to write this story, I was *assigning* it to you. I'm the editor in chief. That's my *job*."

She had a point there. It was always going to be difficult for me to separate Krista the friend from Krista the boss. I tried again.

"Okay, boss," I said, giving her a mock salute as I stood up to leave.

"That's more like it," she said. "Now get to work."

FOUR

~~~~~

I MANAGED TO GET almost to Clara's house before the reality of what Krista had told me about Clara's death began to sink in. I could feel my heart rate rising, and I knew that if I took my hands off the steering wheel, they'd be shaking. To give myself some time to recover, I pulled into the empty parking lot of a small cedar swamp nature reserve about a half mile from Clara's house. I sat there for five minutes or so, gathering myself for what was ahead.

When I got to Clara's, I could barely see the house for the fire engines and police vehicles parked haphazardly on the rough grass in front as if they'd roared in at top speed and just slammed on the brakes wherever there was an open spot. The shell driveway, though, was clear. I pulled in and got my first unobstructed view of the house, which, from the front at least, showed no signs of last night's fire. But there was no mistaking the terrible smell of wet, charred wood that hung over it like a pall. The real damage, I realized, would be on the other side, where the kitchen and living space faced out to the bay.

The front door was open and a team of men and women wearing navy polo shirts, military-style pants tucked into waterproof boots, and plain tan baseball caps were tromping in and out with plastic evidence bags. Over by the squad car, a young, heavyset policeman with a very red face stood talking to a man and a woman I assumed were neighbors. As I stepped out of my truck, he frowned deeply and shouted, "Can I help you?" in that way that you know really means, *Who the hell are you and what do you want?*

"I'm, um, here to see Detective Peters," I stammered, then gathered my wits. "She's expecting me. I'm Samantha Barnes"—I almost added "the Cape Cod Foodie" but stopped myself in time—"of the *Clarion*."

Maybe I shouldn't have added that either. If anything, the cop looked even more suspicious.

"I'll check," he said, turning toward the steps to the deck, then pausing to bark over his shoulder at me, "Wait here."

Well, *that* got my dander up. *Sorry, I didn't hear you, buddy,* I said in my head. I waited until he was up the steps and around the corner to the side of the house facing the bay and then promptly followed him. And then promptly wished I hadn't.

Glass from the shattered kitchen window littered the deck. The shingled walls around the window were horribly charred where flames had licked through the splintered pane. The living area bay window was still intact but so blackened by smoke you couldn't see through it. The door on this side of the house had clearly been rammed open by firefighters and hung limply on one hinge, revealing a glimpse into a black-and-gray picture of total destruction.

The cop, his back to me, was talking to Detective Peters on the deck. Peters was wearing jeans and a camel hair blazer over a blue button-down shirt. She was, I had to admit, a very impressive woman. Her face, untouched by makeup, was smooth and bronze and enviably unlined. Her dark eyes were almost the exact same shade of rich brown as her long hair, drawn back into a sober bun at the nape of her neck. A determined chin lifted her face from pretty to striking, and her calm control as she listened to the young officer was impressive. When she saw me over the young cop's shoulder, she raised her hand in greeting. The cop whirled around, saw me, and shouted, "Hey! I told you to wait!"

"Sorry," I lied. "I didn't hear you." *Because you were so rude*, I wanted to add but didn't.

"It's okay, Joe," the detective said. "I know Ms. Barnes."

The cop nodded and turned to leave, jostling me just slightly as he headed down the steps.

"Sorry about that," Peters said. "He's new, and this thing has spooked him. I'll talk to him later."

"No need, Detective," I said, chagrined by my lack of understanding. "I'm sorry to bother you all while you're dealing with this."

"It's okay," she said. "There's not much we can do here until the crew finishes up. Why don't you and I go down to the beach to talk, stay out of their way? They're still trying to establish the fire's cause."

I nodded and followed the detective off the deck and down the long wooden walkway to the beach. The tide, though beginning its ebb, was still high, the long sand flats covered with blue water breaking in gentle waves on the beach proper. The sandpipers were off doing whatever it is that sandpipers do when there is no wet sand to pipe, but gulls swirled like white pinwheels overhead. When we stepped off the boardwalk onto the beach, I heard Peters sigh with what sounded like relief and I realized that she, too, had been spooked by what she'd seen in that house.

"We don't have to talk about this now," I said. "Krista just thought you might have an official cause of death for us . . ."

The detective shook her head. "We won't have the results of the tests for a few days, so nothing official, but it looks pretty clear that she died in her sleep from smoke inhalation. Though how she managed to sleep through that smoke alarm, I do not know. It was still going when the fire trucks got here."

"I think I know the answer to that one," I said. "She told me yesterday that she took pretty heavy-duty sleeping pills most nights."

Peters stared at me. "She told you yesterday? You were talking to Clara Foster *yesterday*?"

"Um, yeah," I said, suddenly nervous. "Well, not just me. Me and Jenny Singleton. And my dog, Diogi. Well, Diogi wasn't talking to her, obviously." *Oh, for god's sake, Sam, pull yourself together.*

I tried again. "What I mean is that yesterday Jenny Singleton and I were here filming Clara for a video segment for the *Clarion*. We got to talking and Clara mentioned that she used sleeping pills for her insomnia. Usually more than were actually prescribed."

"Yeah, that might explain why she didn't wake up."

I couldn't help myself. "But it doesn't explain how the fire started in the first place," I pointed out. "I heard that it happened in the early hours of the morning?"

The detective nodded. "A neighbor saw the flames a little after one o'clock when her dog woke her to go out. The fire chief reckons it had started maybe ten or fifteen minutes earlier. The worst damage is in the kitchen area. It's pretty clear that she forgot to turn off the burner under a pan she'd been using to cook some bacon in before she went up to bed. The grease caught fire, set a nearby dishtowel alight. The towel then fell into a basket of kindling for that fireplace in the kitchen." Peters stopped, considering. "And if you can explain why anybody would want a fireplace in their kitchen, please do."

I didn't think now was the time to explain about *cucina rustica*.

"Actually," I said, "there are a couple of other things that I think need explaining. Like why she was cooking bacon at one in the morning."

"Midnight snack?" the detective suggested. "A bacon sandwich is a great midnight snack."

I had to agree with her on that. A bacon sandwich is an awesome midnight snack. But I was not going to be deflected by food talk.

"Or how Clara, a professional chef, could have forgotten to turn off a gas burner under a pan of bacon grease," I continued. "It's Kitchen Safety 101 and second nature to any chef. Burner off the minute the food is cooked. I watched her in that kitchen yesterday. It was completely automatic. *And* I don't get how she could have left a kitchen towel on the stove top. Her kitchen towels were kept in a neat pile next to the sink, not the stove. She'd take one, tuck it into the belt of her apron while she was cooking, then drop it into a hamper under the sink when she finished with it."

"She was old," Peters offered. "Maybe she forgot. Maybe she forgot to turn the burner off. Maybe she forgot to throw the towel in the hamper."

"No," I said, shaking my head. "Clara Foster was as sharp as a tack. And anyway, turning off the burner, that's muscle memory. My father has a friend with Alzheimer's who was a golf pro. He doesn't remember who my father is, but he can still swing a mean golf club."

The detective looked thoughtful, so I decided to press my point. Thoughtful was a refreshing change from Chief McCauley. "And it *really* doesn't explain how that basket of kindling got over to the stove from the fireplace in the corner."

"I wondered about that myself," the detective said. "It seemed like the wood should have been kept by the fireplace, but I wasn't sure." She paused, then added, "Do you think you could take a look inside, tell me if you see anything else suspicious?"

"Suspicious?" I echoed.

Peters looked like she wished that particular word hadn't slipped out. I could almost see her thinking, *You don't say the word* suspicious *to a journalist*. Well, she could stop worrying about that. *I'm not a journalist*, I wanted to say, *I'm just the Cape Cod Foodie*.

What I said was, "Suspicious how?"

"Well, more like odd," she backtracked. "I meant anything out of place."

The truth was, I really, really didn't want to go into Clara Foster's burnt-out shell of a house. I wanted to remember it as it was, light-filled, full of books and art and the aroma of good things baking in the oven. Not charred and blackened, the books and art ash, the stink of smoke overlaying it all. But the truth also was that something was off here, and if I could help find out what exactly had happened last night, then I would offer that help.

"Of course," I said, "if you don't think it'll get cranky cop all mad at me again." *Oops*, I thought too late, *maybe you don't want to be making jokes at a time like this, Sam*. But I needn't have worried.

The detective let out a bark of laughter and said, "You let me handle cranky cop."

And with that, Detective Vivian Peters and her faithful sidekick Samantha Barnes set off to examine the scene of the crime. Assuming there had been a crime, of course. Which I was assuming. Because no matter what the detective said, she had used the word "suspicious" for a reason.

FIVE

~~~~~

PETERS LED ME back down the deck stairs and around to the police Ford Explorer in front of the house. Opening the vehicle's back passenger door, she pulled out a crinkly white coverall and said, "You might want to put on one of these."

I knew what it was. I'd seen the forensics team wearing them after I'd found the dead Santa last Christmas.

"I thought those were only for crime scenes," I said, very cleverly, I thought.

But the detective wasn't going to be drawn. She shrugged. "Or not," she said. "I just thought you might not want your clothes covered with ash and soot."

Chagrined, I took the suit from her outstretched hand. "Sure," I said. "Thanks."

I was even more chagrined when I saw she'd picked out a men's large for me.

Peters stepped into what I assumed was a women's medium and slipped on two booties over her shoes. Even in a shapeless white coverall, she looked official. I pulled on my own and snuck a peek at myself in the reflection in the squad car's window. I looked like a deflated Michelin Tire

Man. Sighing, I slipped on my own booties, thus completing the fetching outfit.

"You ready?" the detective asked, and I realized that she was trying to prepare me for what was to come.

I nodded. "It's probably best for us to go in through the back door on the bay side," I said. "That way I can compare what I see as I go in to exactly what I saw yesterday."

She gave me a little "you're not as stupid as you look" eyebrow raise. "Good idea."

But when I stepped through that shattered door into Clara Foster's house, all I could think was, *No, this was* not *a good idea.*

Oddly, it was not the sight of the burnt and twisted furniture or the scorched walls and soot-blackened windows that did me in. It was the smell. The house reeked of sodden, charred wood. The stench hung like a miasma over the destruction, so that even if you closed your eyes, you could not escape it. Or what had happened here.

"You okay?" Peters asked, and I realized I had stopped short at the threshold and had, in fact, closed my eyes.

I opened them and tried to look alert and intelligent. "I'm fine," I lied.

"You see anything, um, out of place?"

I looked around, trying to overlay what I was viewing now with what I had seen the day before. Most of the actual fire damage was to the kitchen area, though the open layout meant the dining area was pretty hard hit, being closer to the conflagration in the kitchen. The wooden dining table and benches were just blackened sticks and the paintings lay in charred heaps on the floor, each with its empty picture hook above like a silent witness to the devastation. In the living area farthest from the kitchen, the sectional couch, half burned and sodden, was at least still standing, and most of the photographs that had hung on the wall opposite the kitchen still hung there, although their glass was blackened by smoke.

"Anything off?" the detective asked as my eyes scanned the living and dining area.

"Not that I can see," I said. "But I wasn't paying much attention to anything but the kitchen. Jenny might notice something, though. Should I take some photos on my phone and have her take a look?"

"It's worth a try," Peters said doubtfully as I took a few shots. "But it's pretty clear where the fire started."

She nodded toward what had once been Clara's beautiful kitchen and was now a charred wreck. The marble-topped island had collapsed to the floor when the cabinets supporting it had burned through. Glass from the shattered kitchen window lay around what was once the kitchen table like some kind of bizarre confetti. Two fire investigators were picking their way through the debris, taking notes as they went. I could see a yellow evidence marker on a twelve-inch cast iron frying pan still in place on the smaller front burner of the stove. Next to the stove, another marked the remains of the woven wicker kindling basket and a half-burnt kitchen towel. All this was dispiriting enough, but it was what was on floor on the far side of the kitchen that did me in.

"Oh, dear lord," I whispered.

"What?" the detective asked sharply.

"The cookbooks," I said, pointing to the pile of burnt, twisted remains of Clara's beloved collection. The glass doors of the cabinet that had held them were hanging agape. "They're ruined. She must have been looking at one of them, maybe for a recipe, and left the cabinet open."

"They were cookbooks?" Peters asked. "Is that important?"

"Not to the investigation of the fire," I said. "But they were rare and irreplaceable."

"Well, that sounds like an insurance nightmare, but not our problem," Peters said. "Anything else look odd to you?"

I took another slow survey of the scene, my eyes catching again on the frying pan.

"That pan," I said. "That's where the fire started?"

From where we stood, I could see that the pan held the blackened curls of what looked like a pound of bacon, though not much of the rendered fat remained, perhaps burned off in the fire.

The detective was being careful now. "We think so," she said. "It looks like she'd been cooking some bacon and then forgot about it and wandered off to bed, leaving the pan on the burner, which she also forgot to turn off."

I shook my head slowly. Quite aside from the impossibility in my mind of Clara forgetting anything or wandering off anywhere, there was the problem of that particular pan on that particular burner.

"That's a twelve-inch cast iron frying pan," I said. "No chef would use a pan that size on that small front burner. They'd use the larger back burner to distribute the heat evenly across the bottom of the pan."

Peters raised her eyebrows. "Well, you're the expert," she responded doubtfully. "You think that's important?"

I nodded. "Whoever was using that pan," I said, "it wasn't Clara Foster."

There was a very long silence from the detective.

And then she said, "Okay. So tell me, you think someone else cooked that bacon and started that fire deliberately?"

I had to admit, it was refreshing to finally have someone in the constabulary who actually wanted my thoughts, but I blanched at the word "deliberately."

"Well, I'm not sure about deliberately," I hedged. "But I do think someone else started that fire, yes."

Again, the detective looked undecided about something.

"Look," I said. "I'm just here because I'm writing Clara Foster's obituary." *And because you are congenitally curious, Sam.* "Anything else we discuss is confidential. I'm under no obligation to tell Krista what we've talked about nor would she expect me to, given that the incident is still under investigation and my greater obligation is not to impede that investigation. I'm sure Krista has assigned a reporter to cover the fire, but that's not my role."

"You're not a reporter?"

"Good lord, no," I said. "I'm just the Cape Cod Foodie."

SIX

P ETERS APPEARED TO make a decision.

"Okay, then," she said. "Tell me what you think about this."

She started out the open front door, me trailing behind. She then led me over to a white Ford 350 customized with what looked like a camping unit large and high enough to walk around in but which I cleverly deduced was a fire inspection unit from the words "Fire Inspection Unit" emblazoned on its side. As we approached, one of the inspectors we'd seen in the house stepped out of the open back doors of the unit.

"Sandra!" Peters called. "Do you have a minute?"

"Sure," the woman replied and waited while we walked over to her, a friendly smile creasing her square face.

"Thanks," Peters said. "We need to see the bag the bacon came in." I was absurdly pleased that she said "we."

"No problem."

Sandra went to the side of vehicle and opened the front of one of the storage compartments that lined the outside of the unit. She then pulled out a shelf, revealing a flat eight-by-eleven plastic bag with the word "EVIDENCE" emblazoned on it. What that evidence was, though, was obscured by the bag's white write-on form labeled "Chain of Custody."

Peters reached over and carefully turned the bag over, allowing me a clear view of the contents. "Take a look at this," she said.

I stepped forward and peered closely at the bag. Inside I could see an empty one-pound package of generic super-market bacon.

"It's an empty bacon package," I offered helpfully.

"Exactly," Peters said triumphantly, as if I'd said something intelligent. "We found it in the stainless steel garbage can under the sink. The bag's empty. Why would someone cook an entire pound of bacon for what was essentially a midnight snack?"

"Maybe she didn't," I pointed out. "She might have just cooked up what was left in the package."

Peters looked crestfallen at that, and I was quick to add, "More to the point, why was Clara Foster cooking generic supermarket bacon at all?"

"She wouldn't?"

"Clara Foster was the queen of all-natural foods," I pointed out. "This brand of bacon is anything but. It's full of nitrates and is processed from industrially raised pigs. I guarantee you Clara Foster would not have had this in her kitchen."

"Duly noted," the detective said a little doubtfully.

Sandra was still standing by, clearly curious about this odd little exchange. Peters turned back to her. "Could you check to see if there's any other bacon in the victim's fridge? And do you have any of that kindling that hasn't been bagged yet?"

"I'll go check," Sandra said and headed back into the house.

"We can't open an evidence bag once it's been sealed," Peters said to me, as if that explained her request.

Sandra came back with a small stick of charred, greasy wood held gingerly in one gloved hand and a package of bacon, open and half used, proudly proclaiming itself to be organic. So, yes, whoever cooked that supermarket bacon had cooked the whole thing. Clara would have used the rest of the bacon in the fridge. Peters looked at me like I was some kind of witch or something. I tried not to smirk.

"Great," Peters said to Sandra. "You can bag that package. And could you hold that piece of kindling up so Sam can smell it?"

I don't know who was more surprised by this request, Sandra or me, but we complied.

The minute I took my first sniff, though, I understood. On top of the sweet scent of apple wood was another unmistakable odor.

"Bacon grease," I said. "It's soaked with bacon grease."

"That's what I thought," the detective agreed, giving me a look that said, *"We'll talk more about this in private."* "Thanks, Sandra," she added. "Sorry to trouble you."

"No trouble, Detective," Sandra said, smiling again. "We're here to help."

Peters cocked her head over to the hillside where, not twenty-four hours previously, Clara Foster and I had picked huckleberries. "Let's go talk."

We trudged in silence up the gentle slope and, once at the top, stood next to each other and looked out unseeingly at the curve of the bay.

"You always knew this was suspicious," I said quietly, still not looking at my companion. Sometimes, when the conversation is a difficult one, it is easier to talk to someone side-by-side rather than face-to-face. Peters seemed to feel the same way.

"I knew something didn't add up," she acknowledged, staring out over the blue water. "I don't care how delicious bacon is, nobody cooks a pound of it for a midnight snack. And why, for that matter, was that basket of kindling by the stove instead of by the fireplace? Why was there bacon grease on that kindling? Maybe, I thought, it was some kind of old wives' trick to make sure the kindling was more likely to start when lit in the fireplace?"

"Doubtful," I said. "Clara used apple wood in that kitchen hearth. The whole point is to perfume whatever's being grilled with the sweet scent of that wood, not of bacon grease."

There was a short silence as Peters absorbed this.

"Then there's only one answer, as far as I can see," she said firmly. "That grease was used as an accelerant. Somebody wanted plenty of bacon grease to start that fire. Which is brilliant, really, since fire investigators are trained to look for accelerants like gasoline in a fatal house fire, not something like bacon grease."

I thought about this for a moment. "So you're saying someone came into Clara Foster's house while she was sleeping, cooked up a batch of bacon that they brought with them, poured the grease from the bacon into that basket of kindling, dropped the kitchen towel into the basket to make it look like it had fallen there from the stove, lit the kindling, kept the empty pan on the still-lit burner until the bacon caught fire itself, *and left Clara asleep upstairs to die*?"

I could hear my voice rising by an octave as I walked through this scenario and the reality sank in.

The detective tried to calm me down. "No," she said. "I'm not saying that. Yes, that might be the scenario if someone else started that fire. But an equal case could be made, and would be made by any smart lawyer, that Clara Foster woke up a little after midnight, was hungry, and cooked that bacon herself, no matter if it was from the supermarket. Then she poured the grease on the kindling to make it light more easily the next time she used it in that fireplace. After that, she got distracted and put the pan back on the fire with the kitchen towel next to it and wandered upstairs to sleep. Then the towel did, in fact, fall into the kindling basket, et cetera, et cetera."

"But you don't think that's what happened," I said flatly. "And neither do I. Clara Foster was not a distracted or wandering type. Plus, she wouldn't have woken up at midnight. She told me her sleeping pills made her sleep like the dead." I stopped short. *Nice choice of words, Sam.*

But Peters wasn't interested in my inappropriate cliché. She shook her head. "You talked to this woman for, what, a couple of hours? How do you know it wasn't just one of her good days? For that matter, some of those sleeping pills are notorious for causing episodes of sleepwalking where a person does things they'd never do in their waking life."

I knew this was true. Miles's boyfriend, Sebastian, who is a pediatric oncologist at Hyannis Hospital, had told us about a weekend conference for physicians during which his department head, whom he described as "a very important man and serious with it," had retired to his room shortly after dinner. He'd then taken a sleeping pill and fell into a deep sleep. An hour or so later, he got out of bed and came back downstairs to the hotel lobby in nothing more than what Sebastian called "his skivvies." He'd then announced to his startled colleagues that he was considering taking tango lessons with his wife and wanted to know what they thought of the plan. The doctors had gently agreed that this sounded like a fine idea and guided the man back up to his room and into bed. The next morning he'd remembered nothing of the incident.

I nodded. "You're right. I didn't know the woman well enough to comment on her mental health or what she might or might not have done in the early hours of the morning. I'm sorry if I've overstepped here."

Peters looked at me directly, her brown eyes deeply serious. "Please don't apologize. I respect your instincts and your expertise. And I know from the Santa murder how good you are at making connections or seeing inconsistencies other people miss. You've been enormously helpful today."

I didn't know what to say. So I said, or rather stammered, "Um, thank you, um, Detective."

"No need to call me 'Detective,'" she responded. "Vivian will do."

"And I'm Samantha," I said.

"It's good to have you on board, Samantha," the detective, *oops, Vivian*, said.

She reached out a hand to shake mine and suddenly, just like everybody else, I liked and respected Vivian Peters. *Vivian Peters*, I thought, *is who I want to be when I grow up. If I grow up.*

And so we shook hands, for all the world as if we had just met. Which was, in a way, what had just happened.

FROM CLARA'S HOUSE I drove to the Tanner farm to tell Miles and his parents the news before they heard it on the radio or saw it on the *Clarion*'s website. I knew it would not be an easy visit, and it wasn't. Mrs. Tanner was stunned with grief for her friend. I thought I would be at a loss for words, but in that odd way that sometimes happens in difficult circumstances, the words came of their own accord. We talked for a long time, sitting around Mrs. Tanner's kitchen table, mugs of coffee in hand.

"Clara could be difficult," Mrs. Tanner said, "but that was because she had high standards. She expected others to meet them. And, yes, she could be self-centered. In my experience most artists are. And Clara was an artist in her own way. But if you needed help, Clara was the one to go to. She must have talked to Miles's dad for hours when Miles came out as a teenager."

Mr. Tanner nodded, his broad weather-beaten face thoughtful in remembrance. "And in the end, I understood and was proud of our boy's bravery in a way that would never have happened without Clara."

I left feeling privileged to have known Clara Foster for even a short while.

SEVEN

A FEW DAYS LATER, Mrs. Tanner called me to say that Clara's memorial service was going to be held the coming Monday at the home of Clara's niece in Shawme Heights.

"I think it would do Miles a deal of good if you were there," Mrs. Tanner said. "His Sebastian is so busy at the hospital that I doubt he'll be able to come. And Miles could do with some support."

What she didn't add, of course, was that *she* would need some support. So, of course, I'd agreed to meet the Tanners at the memorial service.

In the meantime, I needed to get through the next hurdle in the clown race that was my life. Somehow I had been bamboozled by Jenny into joining her and the rest of my so-called friends for the unhappy occasion of the airing of a *singular* appearance by none other than Samantha Barnes on the ever-popular public television show *Antiques in the Attic*.

Just how singular an appearance, my friends had no idea.

Last winter my parents had come to visit me in Aunt Ida's house, which, even with Miles's improvements, had still been in dire need of a new roof and a new boiler. Which was not likely to happen anytime soon, given my finances. But my mother couldn't resist poking around Aunt Ida's attic, which I'd been avoiding because it was the favored haunt of, *ugh*, way too many daddy longlegs spiders. But a few daddy longlegs were nothing to Veronica Barnes on a mission. In no time at all she had Jason and my dad dragging down all manner of what I considered junk, but which she, *Antiques in the Attic* addict that she was, considered treasure. And as it turns out, she was right.

Among the detritus was a very old, very dusty wooden clock that my mother insisted was something called a Massachusetts case-on-case shelf clock made by one Samuel Mulliken. All I knew was that it didn't look like it would go very far toward a new furnace. But, boy, was I wrong. My mother then showed me an *Antiques in the Attic* episode in which a twin of my clock was appraised for a jaw-dropping sum. This was the good news. The bad news was she also wrangled a ticket for my clock, accompanied by yours truly, to be appraised on the show. This, I had thought at the time, was not a good idea. And in that I had finally been right. The appraisal had taped in January. Six months later, it was finally being aired.

Well, maybe the clip wouldn't be so bad. After all, the program director had assured me that it would be edited. Even so, I'd considered not agreeing to let them use the segment, but my mother had convinced me otherwise. She'd pointed out that I'd be a fool to lose the free publicity and its attendant price premium for the clock when I eventually sold it. I, impoverished as I was, saw her point.

And now here I was in Jenny and Roland's living room with all of my closest friends—*Well, almost all, Sam. Your close friend the harbormaster is notably absent*—dreading my TV debut. I knew that the gang wanted nothing but the best for me, but they also had a really annoying habit of finding my . . . let's call them missteps . . . hilariously funny. And though they didn't know it yet, I had made quite a misstep.

Jenny insisted that I take the biggest, comfiest armchair in the living room, which she called "the seat of honor." *Hah. Just you wait. Seat of dishonor more like.* Everyone was eager to finally find out what the clock had been valued at. I'd never told them, which they assumed was just the typical Yankee disinclination to talk about money. In fact, it was because I'd been hoping that if I played it cool, like it had been no big deal, they'd forget about the whole thing. As if.

The whole gang had shown up at Jenny's and the scene was very jolly, with drinks being poured and chips and dip set out. It had been only four days since Clara's death, and I stole a glance at Miles, sitting in the corner of the couch nearest my chair, to see how he was holding up. He raised his beer bottle to me and winked as if to say, I'm okay. I realized he needed this break. And if tonight's little get-together helped with that, I was willing to do my bit.

"Okay, okay. Quiet everyone!" Jenny shouted over the din. "The show starts in five minutes."

Jenny's request for quiet went unheeded. She might as well have been talking to herself. The hubbub in the Singleton living room decreased not one jot. Which was fine by me. With any luck, we'd miss the whole disaster.

But it was not to be. I watched in amazement as Jenny's son Evan (or Thing Three, as I like to think of him), who is all of six years old but blessed with the serious nature of his lawyer father, climbed up on the coffee table in front of the couch, turned to the assembled unruly grown-ups, and solemnly began a rhythmic clapping.

Clap. Clap. Clap clap clap. Clap. Clap. Clap clap clap.

And then, as if they'd been summoned by a force larger than themselves, Ethan and Eli Singleton (Thing One and

Thing Two, respectively) ceased fighting over the last of the Cheez Doodles and joined their brother in this curious ovation.

Clap. Clap. Clap clap clap.

Miles, who'd been shoveling a clam-dip-laden Cape Cod Potato Chip (Tip: Best potato chips in *the world*) into his mouth with very little regard for the way it dripped into his beard, leaned toward me. "What are they doing?"

"Don't ask me," I said. "Ask their mom. And wipe your chin."

But even as I spoke, Jenny herself began clapping along with the boys. As did their father. That he did this without losing his dignity did not surprise me. It takes a lot for Roland to lose his dignity. Although I've seen two Johnnie Walker Reds do the trick.

Helene, on my other side, sighed and put down her glass of wine. "Well, when in Rome . . ."

Clap. Clap. Clap clap clap, the bangles on her arms clinking in counterpoint.

She gave Miles and me one of her "I am the town librarian and you will behave yourself" side-eyes. Miles ceased with the clam dip and began to clap along.

Jillian and her husband, Andre, sitting on a love seat placed at an angle to the couch, looked less bewildered than the rest of us. They'd raised two children. Apparently they knew the drill. Smiling reminiscently at each other, they stopped talking and joined in.

Clap. Clap. Clap clap clap.

Even Diogi, who had been enjoying a nice nap splayed in front of the fireplace like a doggy throw rug, took notice. He raised his head from his front paws and, slowly at first but then with what seemed to me to be enjoyment, began to thump his tail on the floor.

Thump. Thump. Thump thump thump.

Well, who are you, Samantha Barnes, to resist the herd mentality?

I gave in. *Clap. Clap. Clap clap clap.*

I looked over at Krista, who'd managed to secure the second-most-comfortable chair in the room and was surveying the scene with her usual cynical detachment. Catching my eye, she snorted dismissively and leaned over to snag the last of the boys' Cheez Doodles. Krista has never been one to miss an opportunity. Needless to say, she did not clap. Not for Krista, this weird crowd control. Nobody controlled Krista. Not even Evan Singleton. I was tempted to say something snarky to her in solidarity but found it was almost impossible to talk and clap at the same time. Who knew?

As quiet descended on the room, Jenny said, "Thank you, Evan. And now that everyone here understands the power of the Fair Harbor Elementary School Quiet Clap, maybe we can watch Sam make a fool of herself on *Antiques in the Attic*?"

I cringed inside. Jenny had no idea how accurate her description was. Even I—and I had been there—was not prepared for my latest foray into public humiliation.

EIGHT

A S THE BOUNCY *Antiques in the Attic* theme came
on, Jenny managed refills of the Cheez Doodles and
clam dip and chips and Roland refreshed the drinks all
around. I knew that my segment would probably be the final
one, but just in case, Jenny had decreed that we would watch
the whole thing. We all settled in for the duration as the announcer sang out, *"This week we're in Cape Cod, Massachusetts, famous for its beaches, its lobster rolls, the Kennedy
clan . . . and a very unexpected find in Aunt Ida's attic!"*

I sank down into my corner of the couch. *Aunt Ida's attic.* This was going to be worse than I thought.

I barely registered the rest of the show leading up to my,
ahem, star turn. Maybe it was nerves, but I found it difficult
to be absorbed in the story of how a little round man with
big ears had paid $2 at a yard sale for a mechanical Uncle
Sam bank that was actually worth $80 or to sympathize
with the owner of a thirty-piece Limoges tea set whose
worth was clearly a disappointment or even to rejoice with
the owner of a rather lovely seascape that well rewarded its
finder's good taste. In fact, I had pretty much phased out
and was concentrating instead on my second glass of wine

when my eye was caught by a vaguely familiar face on the TV screen.

A young woman, olive skin, high cheekbones, largish brown eyes, wide mouth, brown hair drawn back into a knot at her neck revealing long, dangly gold earrings. She is wearing a floaty floral dress and stands at least a half a foot taller than the appraiser next to her. She isn't beautiful exactly, but she definitely catches the eye.

"Aunty Sam!" Thing Three shouted. "That's you, Aunty Sam!"

With a start I realized that he was right. Jenny and Krista had always claimed that the camera loved me, and maybe they weren't wrong. I'd only ever looked at our Foodie videos on my cell phone's tiny screen and my impression had been that my grandfather's estimation of my looks was about right: "She's no beauty but she cleans up nice." *Well, you cleaned up nice for this one, Sam.*

"Evan, hush!" Jenny commanded. Evan hushed and all eyes turned back to the TV.

The young woman in the floaty dress is attractive, but the star of the show is definitely the timepiece on the table beside her, which the appraiser, a certain Thomas Bentley from "the renowned Hyannis auction house of the same name," is eyeing with a kind of hungry relish. You can almost see the dollar signs in his eyes.

The dark wood clock stands about three feet high and is composed of two sections: the bottom half is a dark wood cabinet that supports the clock case on top. The clock case itself—except for two brass, urn-shaped finials at the top front corners—is totally Yankee in its simplicity. The brass dial behind its glass is perfectly round, with engraved Roman numerals marking the hours. Certainly, the clock has a kind of austere charm. Anyone would like the clock. But you can see that Thomas Bentley loves the clock.

Thomas Bentley can best be described as trim. Early fifties, short blond hair with matching, precisely sculpted beard not quite disguising a slightly receding chin. Not tall, but clearly fit, wearing a close-cut double-breasted navy suit and a red-and-blue-striped silk tie. His hands are perhaps the most remarkable thing about him—long, sensitive fingers with impeccably maintained nails buffed to a fine matte shine.

"What we have here," Mr. Bentley says, resting his hand proprietarily on the top of the clock as if by we *he means* I, *"is a very rare mahogany Massachusetts case clock made by Samuel Mulliken."*

Sitting on Jenny's couch, I remembered exactly what I was feeling at that moment. I remembered Bentley raising his eyebrows at me as if to signify, *This is your cue.* I had no idea what I was expected to say. Instead I had merely nodded and tried to look intelligently interested in information I already knew.

The clock's owner gives Mr. Bentley a look of total imbecility, which is apparently reaction enough for Mr. Bentley.

"Samuel Mulliken," he continues, "came from a long line of well-known and highly respected Concord clockmakers working in the decades just after the Revolutionary War. But of them all, he was undoubtedly the master craftsman." He traces the edge of the clock with one gentle finger. "It's a wonderful piece that you've kept in very good condition."

Again, he looks at the clock's owner expectantly.

"Well, um, thanks," she says awkwardly, then, gathering steam, adds, "It's not like I actually had anything to do with that. It was my Aunt Ida who had it in her attic for all those years. It's a miracle she never threw it away."

The appraiser looks a little horrified at the idea of Aunt Ida throwing his precious clock away. "Well, thank goodness for good old Yankee thrift," he says, almost to himself, and then turns back to the business at hand.

"The mahogany case stands on these wonderful ogee bracket feet"—point to wonderful ogee bracket feet—"which are perfectly original. It has this beautiful scalloped apron

in the front"—*graceful hand movement toward the beautiful scalloped apron*—*"and it extends to the sides, as well. It's signed here on this sheet brass dial"*—*point to sheet brass dial and lower voice significantly*—*"by Samuel Mulliken himself."*

The young woman in the floaty dress seems finally to understand her role as supporting actress to Mr. Bentley's leading man. She widens her eyes to indicate how awed she is by the signature of Samuel Mulliken himself.

At about this point in the proceedings, the Three Things began a singsong "Boring, boring, boring."

"Hush!" Jenny hissed at them. "Or you're going to bed right now." They hushed. Apparently, the only thing more boring than *Antiques in the Attic* was going to bed.

"But it's these two little brass finials on the top," Thomas Bentley *continues as the camera pans in on the small brass urns, "that really put this piece into a category of its own. These clocks are exceedingly rare in themselves, but they almost never come to market with the finials intact."*

The young woman responds, in the grand Antiques in the Attic *tradition, with an absolutely meaningless "Okay," while nodding deep understanding.*

"It really is a fantastic piece," Mr. Bentley *concludes. "Do you have any idea of the value?"*

"Well," the owner of the clock is saying modestly, *"my mother did some research and thought it might be worth . . ."*

At the time I hadn't been sure I could bring myself to say what my mother's actual estimate had been. What if it was totally out of line? The last thing I wanted to be was one of those sad contestants who grossly overvalues their treasure and then has to look brave while they are told the humiliating truth. But it wasn't like I wasn't used to being humiliated for all the world to see. So I named my mother's surely overoptimistic guestimate.

Mr. Bentley smiles in triumph. "That might be slightly low," he says, chuckling at his guest's very welcome naïveté.

*"Rustic chic is hugely popular right now. Collectors would
kill for this piece."*

I remembered thinking at the time, *Don't say things like
that.* I'd learned through experience not to tempt the gods
of mayhem. Even on the screen you could see me visibly
pale at his words.

"Here we go!" Miles said with satisfaction, leaning forward in his chair and crossing his massive arms across his
massive chest. "I can't believe you wouldn't tell us the estimate, Sam." *That's not all you're not going to believe, buddy.*
All I could think about at that moment was how the show
was going to handle my little . . . slipup. I turned my attention back to the screen.

*"At auction," Mr. Bentley says, "I would estimate this
would go for three times that figure."*

I remember being utterly flabbergasted. *Three times my
mother's estimate.* Three times what I needed for a new roof
and furnace. Maybe I could buy a car that actually started.
Maybe I could even put a little bit away for a rainy day. I
couldn't wrap my head around it. I didn't know what to say.

*The young woman in the floaty dress has one of those
faces that shows every emotion. At the moment it is regis-
tering utter amazement. And then she says it. On national TV.*

"Holy BLEEP!"

My friends whooped with glee.

I couldn't believe it. Instead of simply cutting out my
little slip and leaving in my following and equally idiotic but
in no way offensive "That's, um, a lot of money," *Antiques
in the Attic* had bleeped out my naughty word and ended the
segment right there. And if the crowd in Jenny's living room
was any measure, apparently they'd made the right call.

"Oh, girl," Jillian said, wiping tears of laughter from her
eyes, "you really do have a knack."

"Always ready with the apt phrase," Roland agreed with
a wide, decidedly un-lawyerly grin.

The oldest of the Things immediately twigged to what

had gone down. "What did she say?" he demanded of his mother. "What did they bleep out?" But the glint in his eye told us he knew exactly what they'd bleeped out.

Jenny didn't even bother answering his question. "You boys go out to the kitchen and get yourselves some ice cream."

With a yell of pleasure at this unprecedented license to inject themselves with as much sugar as they could get into their greedy little mouths, the Things galloped off to the kitchen.

Their exodus meant all gloves were off.

"Well, I for one am a little disappointed," Miles said. "I like the videos where you cut somebody's finger off."

I swatted him on the shoulder, then wished I hadn't. It was like hitting a wall.

"I like the ones where you tell the kiddies that Santa Claus is dead," Helene added.

"Et tu, Helene?" I asked, dismayed. Helene was usually the one who backed me up.

"Oh, for goodness' sake," she said, unrepentant. "You have a clock worth more than a BMW and you're worried about saying a naughty word on TV?"

She had a point. *You need to get over yourself, Sam.*

"You're right," I admitted, grinning. "First thing tomorrow, I'm going out and buying me a BMW."

Roland, not known for his quick uptake on the humor front, frowned. "Do you really think that's wise?"

"When have I ever done anything that was wise, Roland?" I said, and then, taking pity on him, added, "No, of course I'm not going out and buying a BMW. I'm buying a new roof and a boiler for Aunt Ida's house."

Still with the "Aunt Ida's house," Sam? Is Jason maybe right about your commitment issues? I shook it off. Now was not the time to worry about Jason. Or my commitment issues.

"And maybe you could buy yourself something a little more professional to wear in your public appearances while you're at it," Krista said.

Krista has never been a fan of my floaty dress/dangly earrings look in the Cape Cod Foodie videos. This is a woman who wears a crisp white blouse and exquisitely tailored black pants to an informal gathering of friends to watch *Antiques in the Attic*. In the office, she dresses like a *Vogue* magazine cover.

"Sorry, Krista, not happening," Jenny said firmly. "Sam's look stays."

I blinked. Nobody said no to Krista. You tried to get around her, but defy her outright? Nope. Nobody did that except, apparently, Jenny.

"She looked absolutely right in her sundress and flip-flops in the Clara Foster video," she added.

Jenny had done a rush job on the blueberry buckle video to run alongside my obituary in the *Clarion*'s online edition, and the result, with Clara in all her feisty, funny glory, was really lovely. So much so that the *Boston Globe* had asked for permission to run it as well. Which had been a huge coup for Jenny.

"Sam's laid-back vibe is a big part of her brand," Jenny added.

I don't know what surprised me more—that I had a laid-back vibe (whatever that was) or that I had a brand. Or for that matter, that Krista was nodding agreement to Jenny's statement.

"Good point, maestro," she said briskly.

Just as I was starting to feel a lot better about the evening, the Three Things burst back into the living room, faces smeared with the remains of what appeared to be chocolate chunk ice cream. I looked accusingly at Jenny.

"You didn't tell me you had chocolate chunk ice cream," I whined.

NINE

I WOKE THE NEXT morning full of plans for how to spend my *Antiques in the Attic* windfall. Back in January, after my segment was filmed, I had placed my clock with Thomas Bentley's auction house, though he had suggested that I wait until after the segment aired to put it up for auction.

"The post-show publicity will definitely make a difference," he'd said, almost literally licking his chops.

Oh well, now that the worst was over, I couldn't help feeling that a little embarrassment was a small price to pay for a bump in the clock's final sales price. I guess I was finally getting used to making a fool of myself in public.

I climbed out of bed all ready to meet the day. Not for the first time, I blessed Aunt Ida for the large, light-filled bedroom ell that she had added to her house when it became clear that maintaining the rest of the rambling old place was too much for her.

"We're gonna be rich, Diogi!" I announced to the pooch, who was still snoring peacefully on the three-quarters of the bed that he claimed as his own.

He opened one eye lazily, decided it was too early for

conversation, and went back to sleep. Ciati, however, was delighted to have a little alone time with me and did one of those graceful cat leaps off her spot on the couch and padded over to have a good old scratch behind the ears. That attended to, I let her out so that she could pretend to hunt field mice. I've never told her that the little bell on her collar effectively makes her chances exactly nil. Let the kitten have her dreams, I say.

The morning was already warm, so I dressed in my usual very attractive summer Saturday outfit of saggy white T-shirt tucked into ancient khaki shorts. I unlatched the screen door so that Diogi could push through it for his morning ablutions when he deigned to get up, and then I padded out to the kitchen in my bare feet to make that first wonderful coffee of the day. Mug in one hand and pad and pencil in the other, I wandered out onto the so-called screened-in porch (so-called because the screens had long since bitten the dust). The only furniture on the porch was one of those super-awkward picnic tables with benches attached to it. For what reason, I could never imagine. Were the makers worried that the seating might wander off?

I managed to insert myself between one bench and the table without actually spilling my coffee, which I took as a good sign. From where I sat, I could look out toward Bower's Pond just down the hill below me. I took a sip of legal stimulant and sighed contentedly.

The morning sun sparkled on the water, and small clouds like dollops of marshmallow fluff decorated the blue sky. A mockingbird was singing his big heart out, and I was reminded of my Grandpa Barnes, a great churchgoer, who on a day like this was prone to shout, "This is the day the Lord hath made; let us rejoice and be glad in it." Well, I knew the best way to be glad in it, and that was a quick sail in my beautiful boat, the *Miss Marple*. The wind was south-southeast, which would mean an easy reach out and back. But first things first.

Is there anything more fun than spending money you don't actually have? The sheer unreality of it means you can be totally unrealistic. Flipping to a fresh page in the pad in front of me, I began to write:

1. *Get someone to actually screen in "screened-in" porch*
2. *Buy new furniture for porch in time for Fourth of July picnic, including rattan peacock chair*

All my life I had wanted a rattan peacock chair. Because who hasn't? I could picture myself, hands resting gracefully on the chair's woven arms, its back rising in a great curve behind me like a throne.

3. *Hire roofer to replace flashing*

I didn't actually know what flashing was, but Miles had told me that was what needed to be done to stop the roof from leaking, so who was I to argue?

4. *Convert oil heat to natural gas*

Which meant that I could cook with gas instead of electric, which made me so happy, I wanted to weep.

5. *Replace crappy old electric stove with gas stove*

See happy weeping, above.

6. *Buy a red car*

I don't know anything at all about cars except that I love red ones.

By the time I'd finished my wish list and reviewed it, it occurred to me that the clock probably wasn't going to cover everything on it. With a sigh, I carefully crossed out the rattan peacock chair. *There.* Fiscally conservative.

"Samantha?"

A voice from around the front of the house. For a moment, my heart leaped. But just for a moment. It wasn't a man's voice. It wasn't *his* voice. Quite the opposite. It was Detective Peters's voice.

"I'm here," I called out, forcing myself to sound cheerful. Or as cheerful as I ever sound when I am disappointed in love. "Come on around the back."

Vivian trotted around the corner of the house, a brown cardboard box tied with red-and-white string in her hand. She was wearing worn jeans, a faded Fair Harbor Oyster Fest T-shirt, and a Fair Harbor Ospreys baseball cap. If you are going to wear logoed apparel, you can't do better than the Fair Harbor Oyster Fest and the Fair Harbor Osprey baseball team. Her hair today was done in a thick braid that hung well below her shoulders, wrapped for a few inches at the end with a length of red ribbon.

"Hi," I said, standing up from the picnic table and almost falling down in the process of extricating my ridiculous long legs from the ridiculous attached bench. (Note to self: Ceremoniously burn picnic table when new furniture is in place.)

"Hi," Vivian said. "You've got a great place here." She waved the hand without the box to encompass the house and the view.

"How did you know where I lived?" I asked, and then worried that it sounded rude.

But Vivian just laughed. "I'm a detective," she said. "Plus, your address is on your statement from last year's case."

"Brilliant work, Sherlock," I said.

"Thank you, Watson."

We grinned at each other.

"Looks like you're off the clock," I said. "Unless you're undercover as a local citizen."

"As off the clock as I ever am," Vivian said wryly.

"I think I hear a 'but' in there."

"But, yeah, I did want to ask you a few questions about your conversation with Clara Foster . . ."

"Not a problem," I reassured her. "Have a seat, and I'll get you a cup of coffee."

"That would be great," she said. "I brought some dirt bombs in case you hadn't had breakfast."

"Dirt bombs," I moaned. "I *love* dirt bombs."

"Everybody loves dirt bombs," Vivian pointed out.

Which is true. Dirt bombs, for the uninitiated, are deeply moist, tender muffins with just a hint of nutmeg that have been dipped in melted butter and rolled in cinnamon sugar. One dirt bomb can hold you for an entire day.

Before Vivian had a chance to sit down, a fur tornado raced around the corner of the house, then stopped short in front of this unknown human, barking madly.

"Oh, jeez," Vivian said faintly, taking a step backward.

"Diogi," I said firmly, "shut up!" And Diogi shut up.

I recognize that "shut up" is not your standard dog command, but Diogi has been trained by Helene, and Helene is not your standard dog trainer. Helene is not your standard anything.

"Sit your butt down," I said firmly to the mutt. This was a new Helene directive and not always effective, but this time it worked. Diogi sat his butt down.

"Good dog," I said as Helene had trained me to do.

"That's a very big dog," Vivian said, standing very still and never taking her eyes off Diogi.

"Don't mind him," I said reassuringly. "The worst-case scenario is that he maybe licks you to death."

"Yeah," she said doubtfully. "If you say so." Sometimes I forget that everyone is not super comfortable with what to me is just an eighty-pound lapdog.

"Absolutely," I assured her. "But I'll take him inside while I get your coffee. Milk? Sugar?"

"Black is fine."

Diogi followed me inside, not out of any particular sense

of obedience but because he knew that breakfast was probably on offer. Also, he had saved his human from god knows what danger from the stranger on the porch *and* sat his butt down when commanded, so maybe a treat was in order.

I fixed him a bowl of kibble mixed with a hunk of leftover bread and some chicken stock I'd made yesterday and, along with a mug of coffee for Vivian, carried it outside for him. Diogi hates to miss a party.

Vivian was standing at the edge of what passes for my lawn, gazing down the hill at the *Miss Marple* tied up to Aunt Ida's rickety dock, her sail neatly furled, lines precisely coiled, deep navy sides gleaming, white deck shining in the sun. I wasn't surprised that the boat had caught Vivian's eye. Even with her mainsail furled, she was a lovely sight. Of course, I'd grown up with her, so I was prejudiced. Back in the day, she'd belonged to my parents and was called the *Nellie Bly*, a nod to my journalist mother. When they'd temporarily (I hoped) lost their minds and moved to Florida, they'd sold the *Nellie Bly*, and I'd assumed I'd never see her again, much less sail her.

But when I moved back to the Cape last year, Jason had tracked the boat down (being a harbormaster, he had his ways), taken her off her owner's hands (at what cost to himself I didn't want to think), completely rehabbed her, and given her to me as a surprise on my birthday. With a new name. The *Miss Marple*. Because he was proud of me, of my sleuthing skills, as he called them. *Oh, Sam, what have you done?*

I shook my head clear, and walked over to Vivian, the mug outstretched in my hand.

"Thanks," she said, taking a sip and turning her eyes back to the boat. "That's a pretty sailboat."

"It is," I said. "It was a present." I almost said, *from Jason*, but changed my mind at the last second. I really didn't want to talk about Jason with *Vivvie*. Not yet. Not ever. "From, um, a friend."

Vivian looked at me but just said mildly, "Nice friend."

Eager to change the subject, I said, "I'm taking her out for a little sail if you want to come along. Just for an hour or so."

"I'm not much of a sailor," Vivian admitted. "Actually, I'm not a sailor at all. But I'd like to, yes, if you don't mind having a passenger."

"Not at all," I said. "And we can talk through whatever questions you have out there. Just let me put Diogi back inside."

"I'm glad you keep him in the house when you're out," Vivian said. "You can't be too careful with that dog snatcher around."

I nodded. Fair Harbor and a few of the surrounding towns had suffered a rash of what I suppose you would call dog kidnappings (dognappings?) in recent weeks.

"Should I be worried?" I asked.

"Not if you keep him inside when you're not home," Vivian said. "The kidnapper's very careful. He never takes a dog from a public place, where he might be seen. Just from secluded homes when dogs are left outside."

"And no luck finding the creep?" I asked.

Vivian shook her head. "Hard to find him when the owners don't tell us about it until after they've paid the ransom he's asking."

I could understand her frustration, but also the owner's reluctance to take any chances with their pet's life.

"At least he always returns the animal," I said.

"So far," Vivian said ominously. "I don't want to think about what might happen if the owner can't pay up."

Nor did I.

"C'mon, Diogi," I said. "Inside you go."

TEN

~~~~~~

DIOGI FOLLOWED ME reluctantly back into the house, where I patiently explained to him that I was going out but would be "back soon," which he *never, ever* believed. Helene said that eventually Diogi would understand the phrase to mean "I will, in fact, return" instead of "I am going away forever." So far, after more than a year, it did not appear to have sunk in.

Hardening my heart, I went outside and led Vivian down the zigzag trail to the dock. She eyed the narrow, twisting saltwater river that led out of the pond to Crystal Bay. "We're going to sail through that out to Crystal?"

I laughed. "No way," I said. "She's only tied up there because I wanted to do a little work fine-tuning the mast. She's usually moored at the mouth of the river, where it comes out into Little Crystal. We'll tow her out with my pram."

I was inordinately proud of the pram and its little electric motor, which I'd bought and paid for myself out of the proceeds from my time at Plum and Pear. The motor was about the size of an eggbeater and had about that much power. But it was enough to pull the *Miss Marple* through Bower's River to the bay, which was all I needed.

While Vivian sipped the last of her coffee, I started the motor on the pram and hitched the *Miss Marple* to the boat with a tow line.

"Okay," I said, "we're ready to go."

Vivian put her empty mug down on the deck and stepped carefully into the pram. I put the engine into forward and we made our way slowly out of the river, the *Miss Marple* following nicely behind. As we putted around the final curve of Bower's River into Little Crystal, Vivian gasped.

"Wow," she said. "What a view."

What a view indeed. Crystal Bay, around which Fair Harbor is clustered, expands from Little Crystal, the smaller, more contained part of the bay where the *Miss Marple* is usually moored, into Big Crystal Bay, a much larger expanse that eventually leads out into Nantucket Sound and the ocean itself. The vista looking south from the mouth of Bower's River never fails to take my breath away. And on this golden morning it was as beautiful as I had ever seen it. Wooded hillsides formed an emerald bowl cupping the deep navy haven of Little Crystal with the occasional shingled cottage or rambling old summer place keeping watch through the pines and locust trees and pin oaks. In the distance, the narrow finger of Skaket Point marked the division between the little bay and Big Crystal, a vast waterway dotted with small, green, mostly uninhabited islands.

I glided the pram up to *Miss Marple*'s mooring, hitched it to the white float, then did the same thing for the Baybird. I climbed into the sailboat, and Vivian clambered aboard awkwardly but safely. Because the mast in a catboat is placed so far forward on the bow, the boat is mostly cockpit, lined with a narrow seat along both sides. This makes it perfect for cocktails at the mooring with friends. Miles, who is not much of a seaman, says cocktails at the mooring are his idea of a perfect sail.

"We're going to stay in Little Crystal," I said, "which means we're never more than a hundred yards from shore, but you can put on a life vest if you'd be more comfortable."

I pointed to the fancy monogrammed life jacket that Jason had given me for Christmas and his own extra-large version tucked under the boat's deck.

"Are you going to?" she asked.

"No," I said. "I wear them in rough weather and sometimes if I'm going out into Big Crystal, but not here in Little Crystal, where we're always so close to shore, and not on a calm day like this one."

"Then I'll pass," Vivian said.

"Okay," I said. "Just sit anywhere toward the bow while I get us underway." I was pleased to see that Vivian at least knew bow was forward and stern was to the rear. Sailing is full of technical terms whose origins are lost in the mists of time, but they are second nature to me and I sometimes have a hard time remembering that they can be incomprehensible and off-putting to inexperienced crew (which is what we call anyone on a boat who is not the skipper, whether they actually do any crewing or not).

But Vivian was, as I should have expected, eager to learn. She peppered me with questions from the minute I pulled the tiller out from under the deck and slid it into the boat's rudder in the stern.

"What do you call that?"

"It's the tiller," I said. "It moves the rudder, which steers the boat."

I then uncleated the sail's mainsheet.

"What are you doing now?" Vivian asked.

"I want the mainsheet to run free when I raise the sail."

"What's a mainsheet?" she asked. "Is that another word for sail?"

"You would think so," I acknowledged, "but it's actually this line. It pulls the big mainsail in or lets it out."

"So the mainsheet is actually a rope."

"No," I said automatically. "There are no ropes on a boat. Only lines."

"Why?"

How should I know, I didn't say. What I said was, "Because." *Honestly, it was like dealing with a toddler.*

I pulled the jib out of its sailbag, which had been stored under the deck, and crawled with it up to the bow of the boat. I sat cross-legged as I threaded the small sail onto the forestay that led from the top of the mast to the very tip of the boat's bow.

Before Vivian could ask, I said, "This is the jib. Most catboats don't have them, but they give the Baybird a little extra headway when you're sailing upwind."

If I hoped to stem the tide of questions with technical terms, my hopes were soon dashed. The questions as I moved around making the boat ready to go were endless. Finally, we were ready to set sail, which I had a feeling might shut my "crew" up for a bit.

"You just sit tight," I said, "while we get underway." In retrospect, I might have explained what was about to happen in a little more detail.

With the boat still attached to its mooring, I moved to the front of the cockpit, quickly raised the mainsail and jib, and cleated off their halyards while the sails flapped madly. Then I literally crawled on my belly up to the very tip of the boat's deck, slipped the mooring line off its cleat, and tossed it into the water, so that we were floating free. I hurriedly wiggled back to the cockpit and scurried back to the stern of the boat. Hooking the tiller behind one knee to turn the boat to port, or left, away from the wind, I pulled the mainsheet in hand-over-hand until we caught the wind and pulled the line through the cam cleat that would hold it fast.

Then I leaned over to pull in the port jib sheet with the other and pulled it through its cleat. With the sails set, I took the tiller in my left hand and settled back onto the cockpit seat. The boat jumped forward like a happy antelope, and we were off. As always, it felt like freedom.

I gave Vivian a smile of triumph and only then noticed that my crew was wearing the same look of alarm with which she had received Diogi's welcome.

"That's quite a little routine you have," she said. "Is it safe to move now?"

I laughed. "Perfectly safe," I said as we skimmed along the water, sails billowing in the fresh breeze. "And you were the perfect crew. You did exactly what you were told."

She smiled wryly at me. "If only I had the perfect crew in our shop."

I knew she was talking about the cranky cop. "I'm not so sure that doing exactly what you are told is the way to go in your shop."

She, in turn, knew I was talking about her boss, Chief McCauley. Honest to god, if people did what McCauley told them to do, Fair Harbor would be overrun with bad guys. But Vivian Peters said nothing, and I gave her credit for professional loyalty.

"You said you have some questions for me," I said.

"You can sail this thing and talk at the same time?" Vivian asked doubtfully.

"Not to worry," I said. "With the wind in this direction, it's one long, easy reach to Skaket Point and the beginning of Big Crystal. Then we'll tack around and do it again to get home. Pretty much nothing to do except keep the boat pointed in the right direction." I added, laughing, "And I'll thank you to call this 'thing' by her name, which is the *Miss Marple*."

"As in Agatha Christie's Miss Marple?" Vivian asked.

I nodded, a little surprised. "You read mysteries?" I asked.

"I love mysteries," Vivian said, adding wryly, "they always

get the bad guy in the end. I guess that's why they call it fiction. Maybe you should be the one asking the questions."

"Well, let's start with yours," I suggested. *It can't be any worse than the grilling you just gave me about sailing*, I thought. But I thought wrong.

ELEVEN

OKAY," VIVIAN SAID. "Let's start with this conversation you had with Clara after you filmed this blueberry babka thing."

"Buckle," I corrected her. "Blueberry buckle. The term 'buckle' comes from the way the streusel topping buckles when you cook it."

"Yeah, whatever," Vivian said. *So not a foodie, this Vivian.* "Now, this conversation, could you run through it for me?"

"I'll try," I said, thinking back. "Well, there was the sleeping pills thing, which I told you about already. And I think Clara wasn't happy about having to retire before she'd planned. And she talked about her wife, Kit, for a while and how she was going to sell some of her old paintings." I paused, not sure if this was the kind of thing Vivian wanted, but she nodded at me to continue.

"And then we talked about the oyster farm out on the bay in front of her house and how much she liked the young couple trying to make a go of it. She said she was going to help them in some way." I paused, thinking back. "That was kind of odd actually. Her exact words were, 'I'm going to take care of them, and summer can go to hell.'"

"She probably meant Summer Robinson, the neighbor that called in the fire, not summer the season," Vivian said. "Did she give you any idea why this Summer might not want her helping the shell fishermen?"

"Nope," I said, heading off the wind a bit to give a Day-sailer coming toward us a bit more leeway and returning the other skipper's wave of thanks.

"Okay," Vivian said. "Moving on. Anything else?"

"We talked a little about Clara's Place under the new chef/owner." Oddly, I didn't want to say Ed's name, so I didn't.

"And how was that going?" Vivian asked mildly.

"I'm not sure," I hedged. I was pretty darn sure it had been going badly. But I was going to stick to just the facts, ma'am. "She said she'd trained him up, and when she'd decided she had to retire, she sold it to him after he promised he'd never change the name 'no matter what some damn fools said.'"

Vivian took a deep breath, and suddenly I had a very bad feeling about what was coming.

"How well do you know Ed Captiva?"

Oh god, oh god, oh god.

To give myself a little time to think, I leaned forward to adjust the jib sheet, which absolutely did not need any adjusting.

"Not well at all," I finally said. "I'd never met him before we had lunch at Clara's Place last week. He seemed like a good guy. Very professional, very dedicated to the restaurant's mission."

"Restaurants have a mission?"

"The best ones do," I said. "And Clara's Place is one of the best. Fresh, local ingredients whenever possible, a focus on letting the flavor shine through, a certain adventurous spirit, particularly in terms of incorporating other cuisines . . ."

Vivian stopped me there. "But Clara's Place is strictly French, isn't it?"

"It was originally, from what I understand," I said. "But

there were some dishes on the menu that seemed to be reaching out a bit to other cultures." I thought back to those swordfish brochettes with harissa. And remembered Clara's reaction when I'd praised the dish.

"What?" Vivian asked, looking closely at me.

"Nothing," I said. "Just a feeling I got."

Vivian just considered me in silence.

"Like maybe Ed was being a little more adventurous than Clara would have liked," I added reluctantly.

Vivian nodded. "So maybe Ed and Clara weren't getting along so well?"

I'm not an idiot. Or at least not always. I could see where this was going. "Good lord," I objected. "You don't kill someone because they don't like you putting harissa on the swordfish brochettes."

"No," Vivian admitted. "But maybe you do if you agreed in your original purchase agreement that you would never change the name and now you need to change the name and the original owner is threatening to go to court over it."

"Ed wanted to change the *name*?"

"Not Ed so much as his investors, it appears."

I thought back to my conversation with Clara and nodded. "The 'damn fools' were Ed's investors?"

Vivian nodded. "Apparently they think Clara's Place is too 'old school'"—here she made finger quotes—"for their brand."

Again with this brand thing.

"What do they want him to call it?" I asked.

"Fish," Vivian said.

I waited for more, but nothing came.

"Fish?" I repeated. "Just Fish?"

"Just Fish. Apparently, they also have an ownership stake in a couple of other places, one called Pig, another called Cow. You get the idea."

Well, if that's branding, you can have it.

"And Ed was cool with this?"

"Ed doesn't have much choice in the matter," Vivian said. "The investors own a seventy percent stake in the place. Apparently, letting them in was the only way he could raise the money to buy Clara Foster out."

"But what about that name change stipulation?" I asked. "How was he going to get around that?"

"Well, that's not a problem for him anymore, is it?" Vivian said.

I sat stunned. "You actually think Ed Captiva *murdered* Clara Foster?"

"No, I *don't* actually think Ed Captiva *murdered* Clara Foster," Vivian said, mimicking my cadence exactly. "I don't even know if Clara Foster *was* murdered. But I can't go around interviewing possible suspects forever on the off chance. Which is why I came to you. You were there just hours before she died. You saw the crime scene, if that's what it was. You heard what was on her mind that day. If by talking with you I can come up with a strong enough case that Clara Foster's death is suspicious, I can continue with the investigation. Otherwise, if Clara Foster *was* murdered, the killer's off the hook. Do you want that?"

I shook my head. No, I didn't want that. But I also didn't want the murderer to be Jason's cousin. More particularly, I didn't want Jason to know that I was the one who got this ball rolling in the first place. Because I was pretty sure that any relationship expert would tell you that there is almost nothing more troubling to a relationship than when your boyfriend finds out you put his cousin in the frame for murder.

TWELVE

~~~~~~

LOOK," I SAID to Vivian. "You make a good point. And I want to help you bring Clara's killer to justice if she was murdered. But you have to keep my name out of it."

"Well, duh," Vivian said. "You think I don't know that you're not exactly my chief's favorite person?"

Good. This was good. She thought I wanted to stay in the background because of McCauley. But not good enough.

"Not just McCauley," I said. "You can't bring my name up to *anybody*."

She looked at me oddly, and I scrambled for a reason. "It's bad for my brand," I said desperately. "My Cape Cod Foodie brand. No more dead bodies. Not even hypothetically. Not even a whisper."

"Okay, okay," she said. "Not even a whisper."

"And in the meantime, you'll be looking at other possible suspects?" I asked.

"Of course," she said. "As a matter of routine, I'll be talking to Foster's lawyer on Monday morning about her will. I did a little research, and the *Clarion* reported her decision to leave her land to the Cape Cod Conservancy two years ago. I'm curious if that's still in effect and who gets the actual house and the two acres it stands on, which wasn't included in the gift. The lawyer did tell me on the phone that her next of kin is a niece, a Jean Wilkinson, who lives in town."

A little bell rang in my head. I wasn't sure what had triggered it or why, but I'd learned from experience not to disregard these little alarms. I tucked it away mentally to examine later.

"I'm going over to talk with Ms. Wilkinson after my meeting with the lawyer," Vivian continued. "She tried to put me off, saying she'd be busy preparing for her aunt's memorial service, but she finally agreed. I think I might just stay for that little affair, too."

"I'll see you there, then," I said. "I'm coming to provide moral support for a friend of Clara's."

"Glad to hear it," Vivian said. "Let me know if you hear anything interesting while you're there."

"Vivian," I said, "it's a memorial service. You don't go around looking for clues and pumping people at a memorial service."

"I do," Vivian said. "I'll be there and that's exactly what I'll be doing. It's my job." Honestly, it was just like dealing with Krista.

I sighed and gave up. "Okay, I'll let you know if I hear anything."

"Good," Vivian said. "I'm going to check out the insurance angle, too, on that rare cookbook collection."

"But it's the owner who collects on insurance," I pointed out. "And in this case the owner is dead."

Vivian chose this moment to avoid looking at me by gazing thoughtfully at a gull wheeling and shrieking overhead. "Which could mean that Clara Foster herself set that fire," she said finally.

I couldn't believe what I was hearing. All I could think was, *This will devastate Mrs. Tanner.*

"What? Set the fire and then went to bed while her house burned down around her?"

"No," Vivian said. "Set the fire, made sure the books were burned, thought she put the fire out, took her sleeping pills, and *then* went to bed. But the fire wasn't out."

"Okay, I guess that's possible," I admitted. "But if she needed cash, why not just sell the books like she's selling her wife's pictures?"

"What pictures?" Vivian asked.

"Her wife, Kit, was a painter. Apparently, Clara was planning to sell a bunch of them at auction for a pretty good price."

"So it sounds like she was short on cash," Vivian pointed out. "A little insurance fraud might have seemed like just the ticket."

"But she loved those cookbooks," I protested. "She wouldn't burn them. If she needed money that badly, she could have just sold them."

"Depends on what they were originally valued at and what they're actually worth now," Vivian pointed out. "Say the collection was valued ten years ago at thirty thousand dollars, but since then demand has gone down and current prices make it worth about twenty thousand, you know, like in that 'then and now' segment they do sometimes on *Antiques in the Attic*?"

Oh god, oh god, oh god.

I dipped my toe tentatively in those waters. "Did you see last night's episode?"

Vivian shook her head. "No, I was out with my boyfriend. I'll watch it online when I get a chance. I love that show."

But all I heard was "boyfriend." Vivian Peters had a boyfriend. *Vivvie* had a boyfriend. Suddenly the sun was brighter, the sky bluer.

But while I was thanking the Universe, Vivian was sticking to the matter at hand.

"So Clara might not have wanted to lose that extra ten thousand with a sale," she said.

I suppose I should have welcomed the idea of Clara inadvertently causing her own death, thus letting Ed off the hook. And I could absolutely see Clara doing an insurance fiddle. But her burning those books was to my mind unthinkable. Actually, everything about Clara's death was unthinkable. So I decided not to think about it anymore.

I glanced at my watch. "We should probably head back," I said as if I had something important to do.

Which I didn't. My Saturdays used to involve Jason and me trying to get some alone time away from the kids, as we embarrassingly called Diogi and Ciati, followed by a long leisurely breakfast, then a long leisurely walk followed by a long leisurely lunch, then a sail at some point, followed by a long leisurely dinner. That was my idea of important things to do on a Saturday. But now my Saturdays mostly involved whatever task Miles had set me to on his endless list of what needed to be done to whip Aunt Ida's house into shape. Miles himself was seldom around these days. The Tanner farm in the summer meant working long days, seven days a week. His attendance at Helene's birthday lunch had been a rare guest appearance.

"What do you have planned for today?" Vivian asked. (Note to self: Never make friends with a detective. Detectives are nosy. They can't help it.)

"My friend Helene and I are going to go through my Aunt Ida's books," I said. "She's going to help me decide which I should keep and which I should donate to the library."

But Vivian was not interested in Aunt Ida's books.

"I want to learn how to sail this boat," she said. "Can you teach me?"

WE ARRIVED BACK at the mooring utterly exhausted. Well, I was utterly exhausted. Vivian was fresh as a daisy. It wasn't enough for Vivian to learn how to trim the mainsail or steer the boat with the tiller. She had to know how everything worked. Including the physics of sailing. To give her credit, she caught on quickly. It only took us twice as long to get back to the mooring as it should have.

"That was great," she said as she plopped herself down at the picnic table on the un-screened-in screened-in porch.

I was spared answering by Diogi's joyful greeting when I opened the door from the porch into the house. As always, he was tremendously surprised that I had returned. With our happy reunion accomplished, he then turned to our guest, her earlier incarnation as possible burglar or worse long forgotten. Vivian bent down and greeted Diogi as an old friend before standing up and saying, "Well, I've gotta get going. Thanks so much for the sailing lesson. I really loved it."

"We'll do it again soon," I heard myself saying. *We will?*

Vivian nodded her thanks and then before my eyes turned into Detective Peters.

"And thanks for your thoughts on Clara Foster's death," she said formally. "Please let me know if you remember anything else, anything at all, that might have a bearing on the case."

It didn't escape me that she'd used the word "case." Vivian Peters knew as well as I did that Clara Foster hadn't set that fire herself, accidentally or otherwise.

"I will," I said. And I knew that no matter what the cost might be, I meant it.

THIRTEEN

I THOUGHT I ASKED you to dust these down before we did this," Helene complained as she grabbed another tissue from the box on the floor beside us before sneezing into it with great gusto. No little kitten sneezes for Helene. Helene does everything with great gusto.

When I first met this amazing neighbor of mine, I thought she was like no librarian I had ever known before. I was wrong. She was like no *person* I had ever known before. Maybe it was her halo of long silver curls. Or maybe it was the outfits that looked like they'd been flung on her by a fashion-crazed five-year-old who had just discovered rainbows (today's was a gauzy orange maxiskirt topped by a linen blouse in light pink). Or maybe it was the way she had of materializing and vanishing like some kind of genie. Or maybe—and this is what I suspected was the real reason—it was because before she arrived in Fair Harbor three years ago to take our library in hand, she'd spent twenty-five years as a legal psychologist with the Manhattan DA's office. That'll teach you a thing or two about human nature.

We were sitting on the floor of the tiny, disused front

parlor of Aunt Ida's house. *Your house, Sam. Your house.*
Okay, my house. The room was empty of everything except
the growing piles of books next to us taken from the shelves
that lined one wall. These piles were irresistible to Ciati,
who wove her way between them like a sleek seal, her cat
radar ensuring that she touched nothing, that the piles did
not topple. It was hypnotic to watch.

The going was slow, as Helene had found Jane Austen's
Pride and Prejudice and was prone to reading her favorite
bits aloud, including Mr. Darcy's declaration of love to Elizabeth Bennet.

"'In vain have I struggled,'" she read. "'It will not do.
My feelings will not be repressed. You must allow me to
tell you how ardently I admire and love you.'"

I sighed. "Why don't men talk about love like that anymore?" I asked. "Do you know how my ex told me he loved
me? He said, and I quote, 'You know, it would be a lot
cheaper if I just moved in with you.'"

"The fact that you accepted that as a declaration of love
perhaps says more about you than what it says about your
ex," Helene said in that no-nonsense, "let's be honest" way
of hers that can be so annoying. And insightful. Annoying
because insightful.

I considered this. "Maybe so. How pathetic is that? I
truly didn't think I had much more to offer a guy than a
rent-controlled apartment."

"But you do now?" Helene asked.

I thought about that. Then nodded.

"I do," I said. "I know now that even if I didn't go to
college, I'm smart. I can see patterns, put things together
that other people might not. And I'm brave—"

"Some might call it reckless," Helene interrupted.

I ignored her. "I'm brave," I repeated. "And I'm loyal.
And I have friends who seem to like me."

"Don't be fooled," Helene said. "We just like your
cooking."

I pretended to throw a book at her. "And, it turns out, I'm pretty good at this Cape Cod Foodie thing."

Helene looked at me, suddenly serious. "You are better than pretty good at it. You are excellent at it. You are the perfect combination of expertise and charm."

"By which you mean goofiness," I said.

"Someday, Samantha," she replied tartly, "you may even learn how to accept a compliment with a simple thank-you."

"I doubt it," I muttered.

"Whatever," Helene muttered back. I'd never heard Helene say "whatever" like that. It must be Beth Voohees's influence, I thought. Beth was the library's summer intern, a rising high school senior and Helene's devoted follower after last year's debacle with the dead Santa. She was a smart kid, but spend enough time with any teenager and even a town librarian will start saying things like "whatever."

Helene placed the open volume of *Pride and Prejudice* on the floor beside her, and Ciati promptly sat on it in that way that cats do, as if to say, *Enough about* that, *now what about* me?

"Anyway," she continued, picking up another book from the pile nearest her, "my point was that you didn't dust the books."

"I got held up," I said as I scratched Ciati under her tiny chin. "First, I had to give Detective Peters a sailing lesson, then I had to cuddle Ciati for like forever and take Diogi for a walk to make up for being gone forever for an hour. And then I had to make the *salade niçoise* for us before you got back from the library, which meant blanching the green beans and making the anchovy vinaigrette and tossing them together while the beans were still warm so they could absorb the dressing while they cooled . . ."

"Yes, thanks for that," Helene piped up. "The salad was terrific."

". . . and peel the hard-boiled eggs and slice them in quarters . . ."

But Helene was less interested in the intricacies of a *salade niçoise* than with the start of my day. "Why were you giving Detective Peters a sailing lesson? You don't even *like* Detective Peters."

Well, that shut me up. "What makes you think I don't like Detective Peters?"

"Oh, maybe by the look on your face during the Santa case whenever Jason called her *Vivvie*," Helene said. "Inscrutable you are not."

"I wish you'd stop interpreting the looks on my face," I said with what I hoped was great dignity. "It's intrusive of my privacy."

Helene snorted. "Somebody has to intrude on your privacy," she said. "Otherwise you're going to spend the rest of your days not talking to the one person you need to be talking to."

"And I suppose you think that's you," I said, still trying for the great dignity thing.

Helene snorted again. "Not even close."

I wasn't sure if she was talking about my attempt at dignity or my supposition. Maybe both.

"Jason," she said. "You need to be talking to Jason."

Helene, being a New Yorker born and bred, has never made a secret about her quest to counteract my innate Yankee conviction that one should not share one's feelings. In my opinion, it only embarrasses people. Especially the one doing the sharing, i.e., me.

"Okay, if he ever comes home again, I'll talk to Jason," I lied.

"Oh, he'll come home," Helene said with utter conviction. And I felt better.

"And anyway," I added. "I do like Vivian Peters. And I respect her. She's a good detective and open to other points of view."

"Other points of view about what?"

"About Clara Foster's death."

"I thought Clara Foster died in a house fire from a pan left on an open flame," Helene said. "That's what the *Clarion* reported Chief McCauley saying anyway."

"That is how the fire started," I said. "The question is just how that could have happened. Detective Peters wanted my thoughts on that since I'd been in Clara's kitchen the day before."

I almost mentioned the shadow over Ed Captiva, but thought better of it. Helene is the soul of discretion, but I wasn't comfortable putting Vivian Peters's suspicions into words. Words make things much too real.

Helene looked at me closely, but did not press me. How she knows when to do that and when not to always amazes me. I am convinced the woman is a witch. A kind witch.

"Anyway, tell me what to do with this," I said, holding out a copy of Agatha Christie's *A Murder Is Announced* to distract her. "Aunt Ida loved Golden Age mysteries."

I pointed to an entire row of Christies, Dorothy Sayerses, and John Dickson Carrs on the shelf next to me. "You want them for the library? I reread them all over the course of the winter."

Which was true. There is nothing like reading a Golden Age mystery in front of the fire with a dog at your feet. You feel like you are living in a game of Clue.

Helene looked doubtful. "The town library's got all the classics," she said, "in much more readable formats than the originals."

She took the book in her hand and turned a few pages gently. "You know," she said thoughtfully, "this is a first U.S. edition with the original dust cover."

She handed the book back to me. "You might want to show this to a dealer in rare books."

"Good idea." I added, "Let's start a pile for that. Maybe I'll get rich on Agatha Christie first editions."

"Let's see," Helene said, whipping her cell phone out of a skirt pocket and tapping madly with two thumbs. This new familiarity with all things technological I suspected was also down to Beth, who felt that being over sixty was no excuse for online illiteracy.

Helene tapped a few more times. "Doubt you're going to get rich," she said. "Looks like that book lists at about ninety bucks."

"I'll take it," I said happily. "I'll put the proceeds toward the peacock chair fund."

FOURTEEN

~~~~~~~~

THAT NIGHT I crawled into bed at a ridiculously early hour for a Saturday night. While I waited for Jason's call, I entertained myself watching Diogi and Ciati play the "find the kitten under the couch" game, in which Ciati sticks a paw out from beneath the slipcover and Diogi tries to shove his big head under the sofa in a vain attempt to find her, only to be utterly amazed when the paw appears in a *completely different spot.*

This was entertaining, but not as entertaining as when Jason finally called. We did our usual "how was your day" rundown, which I found a little awkward since *for some reason I didn't want to examine closely* I left out my sail with Vivian Peters and what we'd discussed. Then we moved into billing and cooing, which was always my favorite part of the conversation and shall remain private. But best of all, Jason finally gave me a firm date for his return, saying he'd be home by the Fourth of July weekend. In truth, I didn't know whether to celebrate or panic. I decided on both.

The celebrate part was easy. Get a haircut, I thought happily, maybe add a little blond streak here and there? That would mean a trip to Hyannis, because I wasn't about

to let Monica Little at Fair Harbor's one and only hair salon, Shear Delight, get her hands on me. Monica had alarm-
ing tendencies when it came to hair color. And maybe while
I was in Hyannis, I speculated further, I could go to an actual mall and by a new, super-sexy floaty dress.

I might have continued to celebrate in my mind like this
endlessly if it hadn't been for the panicking part. I had almost exactly two weeks to move the spotlight in Clara Foster's death from Jason's cousin to the real murderer, whoever
that might be. How I was supposed to do that, I had no idea.
Nada.

I may have groaned out loud at that point, because Diogi
came over to the bed and stuck his wet nose into my hand
in sympathy. I patted the bed beside me, and he galumphed
up and snuggled against his human. Ciati, never one to be
ignored, sprang up gracefully and inserted herself between
us. I felt much better.

"Well," I said to them, "maybe I'll ask Jenny if she knows
this niece of Clara's, this Jean Wilkinson. She'd be a likely
candidate for the role of murderer. I bet she's Clara's heir.
She probably got tired of waiting for that house on the dune."

Again, the little bell in my head went off. This time I
paid attention to it, sitting back, and allowing my weird
brain to find the connection it had missed before.

Jean. Something Clara had said. Something about Jean
being disappointed if Kit's paintings were worth real money.
Why would her niece, her next of kin and presumably her
heir, find that a disappointment? I needed to find that out.
And I needed to know if those paintings were actually worth
what Clara thought.

And that's when another thought drifted into view. Clara
had said her appraiser was from Hyannis. I had an appraiser in Hyannis, "a certain Thomas Bentley from the
renowned Hyannis auction house of the same name," as
Antiques in the Attic had put it. Maybe Bentley was the appraiser who'd advised Clara. How many auction houses

could there be in Hyannis? I needed to talk to Bentley anyway about finally putting my clock on auction. Maybe he would tell me his final judgment on what Kit's paintings were worth.

"But if his original estimate still holds, why would that annoy Jean?" I asked my fur buddies, who offered no response, having both fallen deeply asleep in the approximately five seconds since my last comment.

But I liked this thinking out loud thing. It was helpful.

"Unless, of course," I continued, "Clara was planning to spend that chunk of cash *before* Jean could get her hands on it," I mused to myself. *Like maybe for an expensive lawsuit to prevent Ed Captiva from changing the name of her restaurant?* I decided not to say this out loud because anything that pointed back to Ed Captiva would put me right back into panic mode.

There was only one thing that could calm me down. I got up, went out to the kitchen, and made myself a grilled cheese sandwich.

FIFTEEN

_{~~~~~}

L ATE THE NEXT morning, my ancient truck, which I'd
nicknamed Grumpy because he was, agreed to take
Diogi and me to Jenny's for a work conference. Grumpy is
on loan from Miles's mother until I can afford a vehicle that
actually starts on command and has locks on the doors that
actually work (not that anyone would want to steal Grumpy,
but still).

A front from the southwest had brought a warm, muggy
breeze and a sky washed white with thin cloud cover. Even
the leaves on the oaks and maples arching over the winding
lanes seemed to feel the weight of the weather. We arrived
at Jenny's handsome four-square captain's house just as the
Singleton family was coming back from church. The Three
Things, unusually spiffy in crisp chinos and neat button-
down shirts, spilled out of the SUV with great whoops and
shouts. The Things spend a lot of their time whooping and
shouting. Jenny followed them, looking about sixteen in a
crisp yellow sundress.

"Into the house and change!" she shouted after them as
she got out of the car.

She turned to me. "If I can get them out of those clothes

before they destroy them, I can use them again next Sunday, maybe even the Sunday after that."

"Ah, the logistics of motherhood," I said.

"Believe me," she said, "it makes the invasion of Normandy look like a cakewalk."

Roland came around the car dressed, as always, in suit and tie, which was far more formal than our loosey-goosey Episcopalian church required but was completely typical of the town's most prominent lawyer.

"Good morning, Samantha. And how are you on this fine June day?"

I can't tell anymore if Roland is just playing Lord Grantham to tease me or if it is actually Roland. The man can surprise you.

"Never better," I said. This is my standard answer to this query. I am a firm believer that nobody really wants to know how you are when they ask how you are. They just want to move on.

"Excellent," Roland replied heartily. "And how are you, Diogi?" he asked. You gotta love a guy who asks your dog how he's doing.

Diogi, who was weeing on Grumpy's back right tire, looked up at his name and wagged his tail at Roland.

"Excellent," Roland said again. "And now, Samantha, I will leave you to confer with Jennifer." Nobody calls Jenny Jennifer except Roland. And yet still she loves him.

Roland turned to Diogi. "Come, Diogi," he said. "Sadie awaits you in the backyard."

Diogi followed him happily. Diogi *wuvs* Sadie. Sadie is a very proper cocker spaniel and does not return his ardor, though she is willing to romp with him in the backyard as long as he doesn't get, well, fresh. If and when that happens, she whirls around and nips him on his nose to remind him of his manners.

"C'mon into my office," Jenny said. "The boys and Roland are going clamming." The image of Roland standing on some mucky sand bar, pants rolled up at the knees, a muddy clam rake in his hand, delighted me for a few seconds.

"Rollie loves clamming," she continued. "It's their Father's Day present to him." *Father's Day? Today was Father's Day?*

I don't know why I was so surprised that Father's Day had snuck up on me. Most holidays, unless they are food-focused, sneak up on me. I needed to call my dad, who, I was sure, had no idea it was Father's Day either. Apple, tree.

But now was not the time for that call. Jenny was in work mode and Jenny in work mode is almost as focused as Krista. I in work mode, on the other hand, am almost as focused as, say, Diogi. So I followed her meekly through the unlocked screen door to the kitchen and then into a narrow side hall to a small room that had once held all manner of junk and was now a neat home office.

We both sat down for what Jenny called a conference, even though it was only ever the two of us. "It's still a conference," she'd said when I'd pointed that out. "We're conferring." She poured us two cups of coffee from the pot she'd grabbed from the kitchen. It was stale from having sat warming on the coffee maker while they'd been at church, but I didn't complain. Even bad coffee is great.

"So this lobster roll idea of yours is a good concept," she said.

"It's a great concept," I corrected her.

I was super excited about this assignment. I'd thought it up myself and felt, in my modest way, that it was the best idea ever in the history of foodie media.

It had come to me about a week ago. The early weeks of June had enfolded the Cape in an unusually warm and sunny embrace. Diogi and I had been half dozing in the rays of the setting sun on the rock breakwater at Stone Harbor. Stone Harbor is famous for two things: its incredible view of the sunsets over Cape Cod Bay and the lobster rolls at Cap'n Tom's, its very small and very ramshackle fish market. I was idly watching the charter fishing boats chug in from the bay and hoping that if the catch had been good, I might be able to talk one of the beer-lubricated fishermen-for-a-day into selling me an extra striped bass for our dinner. Diogi was hoping dinner was soon. Diogi was always hoping dinner was soon. But our hopes were dashed when I saw the hand-lettered "Open" sign on Cap'n Tom's fish market.

In my memory, Cap'n Tom's had never opened before July 1. But the unusually warm weather had brought out the day-trippers and tourists early, and I assumed he wanted to cash in on a good thing. What this meant was that Cap'n Tom himself was going to be first in line for any spare stripers, paying a premium I couldn't match.

I had consoled myself for the loss of my fish dinner with the knowledge that I could maybe snag one of Cap'n Tom's justly famous (at least in Fair Harbor) lobster rolls instead. (Tip from Cap'n Tom himself: If you're making a lobster roll, go for an 80-20 mix of tail to claw meat to keep it moist, and mince the claw meat to keep the mixture tender.) Suddenly a lobster roll seemed like the perfect end to a perfect day. I nudged Diogi with my toe.

"C'mon, boy. Let's get something to eat."

Diogi has a chronic case of selective deafness. For instance, he cannot hear the word "sit." At least not when I say it. Helene is a different story. Helene is Diogi's General Patton. But just let me whisper "walk" or, in this case, "eat," and he's on full alert.

We had sauntered over to the fish market, a rickety, gray-shingled, one-room building with a screen door that always slammed behind you and made you jump even though you *knew* it would slam behind you and make you jump. I tied Diogi's leash to the bike rack outside, pushed through the screen door, and jumped when it slammed behind me.

Nothing ever changed at Cap'n Tom's. Not the glass-fronted display case heaped with crushed ice and featuring

a variety of local clams, oysters, mussels, and the catch
from the commercial boats that had come in earlier in the
afternoon. Not the Formica counter with a cash register
easily as old as I was. Not the blackboard listing the day's
specials. Not Cap'n Tom himself, seated on a high wooden
stool behind the counter, skinny as a grasshopper and
eighty if he was a day. And not his inevitable cronies leaning against the counter chewing the fat.

While Cap'n Tom and his buddies debated the odds of
the Fair Harbor Ospreys winning the Cape Cod Baseball
League championship this summer, I waited politely. There
was no hurry. And if there was, you were in the wrong
place. Also, I was kind of interested in the Ospreys' chances.
Collegiate summer baseball is huge on the Cape, and the
Cape Cod Baseball League pulls in some of the best college players in the country. As we like to boast, one in every six Major League Baseball players has played in the
Cape League, including the Boston Red Sox's (Go BoSox!)
Chris Sale and the New York Yankees' (Boo, hiss!) Aaron
Judge. This year, I had a personal interest as Jillian's
nephew, a first baseman from Howard University, was go-
ing to be on the roster.

While I listened to the cronies' expert baseball com-
mentary, I perused Cap'n Tom's blackboard. In all the years
my parents and I had been going to Stone Harbor, the catch
of the day at Cap'n Tom's changed frequently but never the
two specials: homemade New England clam chowder and
lobster roll. But wait, what was this? A *change*. Scribbled
on the board was "lobster roll with mango." Good lord.
Blasphemy. *But*, my foodie self reminded me, *maybe really
yummy.* (Tip: There is much to be said for a touch of fruit
in any savory salad.)

Cap'n Tom finally turned his attention to me. "What can
I getcha, Miss Samantha?" Cap'n Tom had known me since
I was a kid. He'd always called me Miss Samantha, ever
since he'd given me my very first oyster on the half shell. I

think he and his buds had expected me to gag. Instead I'd slurped it down, all briny and tasting of the sea, and greedily asked for another. This, it seemed, had engendered a certain amount of respect. Which I was just about to lose.

"A lobster roll with mango, please, Captain Tom," I said. I always called him Captain. Only the cronies got to call him Cap'n.

He looked at me like I'd grown a second head. "A lobster roll with *what*?"

"With mango," I said, pointing to the blackboard.

He squinted at the board as if he'd never seen it before.

"That says lobster roll with *mayo*," he said. "Why on god's green earth would I put mango in a lobster roll?"

I looked at the blackboard again. He was right. Granted the writing was pretty decrepit, but only some effete New York foodie would have seen "mango" in "mayo." Right then and there, I knew I'd traveled too far from my culinary roots. And suddenly it came to me. Why not do a piece for the *Clarion* on the best spots for lobster rolls on Cape Cod?

O KAY, IT'S AN excellent idea," Jenny said. "But it's going to be a challenge to keep it from being repetitive. How long can viewers be entranced by you stuffing a lobster roll into your mouth and saying, 'Yummy!'?"

I had to admit I hadn't thought about it like that. "Not long," I acknowledged.

"Right," Jenny said, "So we've got to find a way around it. Give me your list of restaurants, clam shacks, whatever . . ."

I was ready for her there. I reached into my shoulder bag and pulled out the list I'd prepared based on my own knowledge but also from some online research.

"I wanted a combination of traditional and more adventurous," I said, passing the paper over to her.

"Okay, that's good," Jenny said. "That'll keep things interesting." She looked down at the list, then frowned.

"Lobster roll with mango?" she said, looking up at me. "First, what even *is* that?"

"It's a delicious twist on the traditional lobster roll," I said, trying to sound knowledgeable, "using the sweetness of fruit to highlight the savory mayonnaise dressing."

Jenny looked unimpressed. "And who makes this concoction?"

"Actually, nobody," I admitted. "I just put it on the list because it sounds yummy to me. I thought maybe I could call around, see if anyone wants to give it a try."

"Here's a better idea," Jenny said, eyes shining with that filmmaker's zeal that I had come to dread. "We'll film you making it in your kitchen. You've never actually done a cooking demonstration! Your fans are gonna love it!"

Oh god, oh god, oh god.

SIXTEEN

$\sim\sim\sim$

BEFORE I HAD a chance to recover from this unwelcome editorial suggestion by my videographer and director, a horn tooted outside.

Jenny sighed and went to the window. Jenny hates being interrupted when she's working. I, on the other hand, like to think of work interruptions as messages from the Universe that my attention is needed elsewhere. Usually in the kitchen. Making a snack.

"It's Miles," Jenny said. "And it looks like he's got Helene and Jillian with him."

"Phew," I said to myself, silently thanking the Universe for at least temporarily shelving this cooking demonstration idea.

"Phew?"

"I mean, darn, just when we were getting to the interesting part," I lied.

Jenny narrowed her eyes at me, then turned and shouted out the window, "Are those oatmeal cookies?"

"Sure are," I heard Jillian shout back.

"Good," Jenny said. "Go around to the patio. We'll meet you there."

Jenny and I went back to the kitchen, where literally every cabinet door was open.

"Jeez, Jenny," I said, smacking them shut one by one, "your kitchen looks like it's taking off."

She looked around vaguely. "Yeah," she said, "I don't know how that happens."

She then proceeded to open one of the cabinets I had just closed, pulled out five iced tea glasses one by one and stacked them on a counter crowded with shells from a recent trip to the beach, two open tubes of kiddie sunscreen, and a paddle ball set. She then handed the stack to me, leaving the cabinet door wide open.

"It's a mystery," I agreed.

Jenny moved to the fridge to snag a pitcher of iced tea, and we went out through the living room's French doors to a rosy brick patio shaded by a wisteria-laden pergola. Helene, Miles, and Jillian had already seated themselves around a teak table, and were chomping cookies and watching Diogi and Sadie play their endless game of keep away.

I love Jenny's backyard. It is exactly my picture of what a backyard should be. An expanse of rather patchy grass, tenderly mowed every Saturday by Roland. A huge, shady old maple with a wooden swing hanging on thick ropes from a sturdy branch. Great drifts of orange daylilies and enormous purple hydrangeas blooming on fat green bushes that almost hid the split-rail fence that separates the Singletons' piece of paradise from that of their neighbors.

Once we were all seated and Jenny had filled everyone's glasses, she reached over and grabbed an oatmeal cookie and moaned. I didn't blame her. The cookies were crisp at the edges and chewy in the center, with lots of deep, caramelly brown-sugar notes and the plumpest, juiciest raisins imaginable.

Jenny reached for another. "What's your secret, Jillian?"

Jillian smiled broadly. "Lots of love," she said.

(Tip: This is not the whole truth. The whole truth is you

soak the raisins in beaten egg and vanilla to plump them up and pack them with flavor.)

Diogi and Sadie, drawn by the irresistible scent of the cookies, bounded over and sat looking pathetically at the one in Helene's hand.

"You wish," she said heartlessly.

But I noticed that she surreptitiously gave each dog a good chunk when she thought no one was looking. She just pretends to be tough.

After Jenny had swallowed the last bite of her own cookie and licked the tips of her fingers for any stray crumbs, she looked around at our guests.

"So what's going on?" she asked.

Helene, wearing a T-shirt emblazoned with the words "Not my circus, not my monkey," leaned forward. "We're here to help Sam if we can."

I almost choked on a raisin. "Help me with what?"

"With the mystery of how Clara Foster died," she said. So maybe it *was* her circus and her monkey.

I looked at my neighbor steadily. "What makes you think there's a mystery about how Clara Foster died?"

I slid my eyes toward Miles in an attempt to signal to Helene that this was *not a good idea.*

"Miles is fine," Helene said. "He came to see me this morning to talk through his feelings."

Of course he did. At some point Helene was going to have to start charging us for all this therapy she was providing.

"That doesn't answer my question," I said.

"I don't believe Aunt Clara would have left a pan on a lit gas burner," Miles said.

Well, I couldn't argue with that.

"And my mother thinks somebody killed her," he added.

Oh god, oh god, oh god.

I gulped. "Why does she think that?" I managed to ask.

"Because Clara told her recently that she was going to change her will."

"Change it how?" I asked.

"She didn't say," Miles said. "Clara had made no secret that she was leaving the bulk of her property to the Conservancy when she died, except for the house and a couple acres for her niece. But she did tell my mom recently that she wanted to make a change because, according to her, what can seem like a huge disappointment to someone is what will save them in the end."

I put my iced tea glass down slowly. Clara talking about disappointing someone. "She said those exact words?"

"Yup," Miles said. "They stuck in my mom's head because it was such a un-Clara-like thing to say. Aunt Clara wasn't one for philosophical considerations. Anyway, my mom thinks maybe somebody wanted to stop her before she could make that change to her will."

"Well," Jenny chimed in, "if that was what happened, that somebody was too late. And whoever got disappointed knows it now."

"And you know that how?" Helene asked.

"I do Rollie's books," Jenny said. Jenny is an absolute accounting whiz. "He met with Clara more than two weeks ago, which I assume was about this will-changing business, and I know he talked to all the beneficiaries yesterday."

I couldn't keep up. "*Roland* was Clara Foster's lawyer?"

"Of course he was Clara Foster's lawyer," Jenny said. "She was a highly respected local celebrity and he's a highly respected local lawyer."

Well, she was right about that. It shouldn't really have surprised me that Clara Foster's lawyer was Roland Singleton.

"Did he tell you anything about the will?" I asked.

"Of course not," Jenny said. "That's confidential until the will is probated or the beneficiaries start flapping their mouths about it."

I turned to Helene. "Why bring this information to me? Why not to Detective Peters?"

"Because if Clara Foster was killed, the police might

think it doesn't have anything to do with her will," Helene explained. "They might think it was about another little legal issue involving Ed Captiva. And that's just what we *don't* want them to think."

Oh god, oh god, oh god.

"How do you know about that?" I blurted out. *Besides you being a witch and all.*

"Everybody knows that Clara was going to sue Ed to keep him from changing the name of her restaurant," Jenny said. By "everybody," I knew Jenny meant everybody in the Snow clan, which seems to number in the millions, all born gossips.

I turned to Jillian, who'd been amusing herself passing bits of oatmeal cookies to the dogs.

"What's your role in all this?"

"I didn't have one originally," Jillian admitted. "I went to Helene's house to see if she wanted to go for a power walk on Trout's Point"—What was it with these women and their power walking? I could barely get up the energy most days to let Diogi drag me around Bayberry Point—"and Miles was there and then the three of us got to talking about Clara Foster's death and we decided that since, according to Helene, you told her the police are uncertain whether the death was suspicious, we'd help you with your sleuthing."

"What makes you so sure that I'm going to be 'sleuthing,' as you call it?"

Helene and Miles both rolled their eyes at this one in one big silent *duh.*

"Okay," I admitted, "I am interested in finding out a bit more about how Clara could have died." I refused to say "been murdered." I agreed with Vivian Peters that that had yet to be determined. "But if it is murder, you have to understand that I can't pick and choose who I want the killer to be." *Much as I would like to.*

"But you can do your best to make sure all possible suspects are considered, and we're here to help you with that," Jillian said briskly. "I'm the project manager."

I knew from experience that nobody managed a project better than Jillian. I'd seen the zillions of Excel worksheets printed out on her desk for the new assisted living addition to Shawme Manor. And I knew the contractor lived in fear of Jillian's daily briefings with him.

"Okay, I give up," I said, throwing in the towel. "What's the plan?"

SEVENTEEN

~~~~~~~~~

THE TEAM LEANED forward as one, and suddenly I loved them all so much, I could hardly breathe. But did I tell them that? I did not. Heaven forfend.

Jillian pulled a Bic pen and yellow legal tablet out of her bag.

"We're going to infiltrate the memorial service," she said. *Infiltrate?* "Of course, Helene and I will not be attending, but you and Miles and Mrs. Tanner are and, I would guess, so are Jenny and Roland."

Jenny nodded a confirmation.

"Good," said Jillian, jotting down a note. "It'd be unprofessional for Roland to tell you the contents of Clara's will, Jenny, but if the next of kin has been informed, whoever's named in it may talk about it there, especially to Clara's lawyer. You can keep your ears open while you stand by his side doing the invisible wife routine."

I have to admit, I was impressed by Jillian's thinking. The woman was even sneakier than me.

"You know how to do the invisible wife?" Jillian asked Jenny.

Jenny smiled wryly. "Oh, yeah. I've done her a hundred

times. And hated it. But this time at least it'll be for a good cause."

"Good," said Jillian briskly. "Moving on. Miles, you need to corner your friend Ed Captiva." *Corner?* "Find out, if you can, where he was the night Clara died."

"But *don't* mention the lawsuit," I added, suddenly all in. After all, I was the sleuth here. "If he brings it up on his own, that's a good sign. A murderer hardly ever points out their motive."

"Got it," Miles said, and Jillian made another note.

"Also," I continued, "if we're going to exonerate Ed"—already I'd forgotten my own warning against bias—"we need to look for other suspects with a relationship to Clara that we're not aware of. If your mother's serious about helping, Miles, she could wander around asking nosy questions like 'How did you know Clara?'" Nobody takes offense at nosy old ladies. Just look at Miss Marple."

"Florence Tanner is *not* an old lady," Helene said, clearly offended by my ageism. "She is barely a decade older than I am."

Miles grinned at that. "But she can play the old lady card when she wants to," he said. "I know for a fact that she's been pulled over for speeding on Route 6 three times since she got her new truck. And she never once got anything more than a warning. She's good at going all dithery when circumstances call for it."

"Good," I said. "Dithery works."

"And what about you?" Jenny asked.

I'd already decided that one a long time ago. "I'm going to collar the niece, Jean Wilkinson."

Once our little party broke up, Diogi and I drove home. Diogi, exhausted by his eternally unfulfilling courtship of Sadie, collapsed in a pile, and I prepared myself with a hit of iced coffee for my Father's Day call. It wasn't that I didn't want to talk to my father. I love my father and always enjoy talking with him. Just not on the phone. You'd expect a man who published a very respected regional newspaper for twenty years to be able to handle a cell phone, but you'd be wrong. There wasn't a call he couldn't cut off, a mute button he couldn't hit, a butt call he couldn't make. So I braced myself.

"Hello? Who is it? Are you there?" Honest to god, it was like Alexander Graham Bell and Mr. Watson all over again.

"Hi, Dad," I said slowly and calmly, trying to model proper cell phone protocol. "It's me, Sam. Happy Father's Day."

"Sam!" my father shouted. My father always shouts into his cell phone, due to its lack of an identifiable mouthpiece. "Is it really Father's Day? Wait! Let me get your mother." Whenever he possibly can, my father abdicates telephone responsibility to my mother. *Well, not this time, bud.*

"No, Dad," I protested. "I want to talk to *you*. On account of because you're my *father*. And it's *Father's* Day."

This got a laugh. "Fair enough, sweetheart," he said.

"So how are you?" I asked. "How's the book coming?"

Last winter my father had landed a contract with an academic publishing house in Boston for a book on legendary Cape Cod sea captains. He'd been working like the devil on it, according to my mother. "I think it's just an excuse to get out of yoga class," she'd said. In my opinion any excuse to get out of a yoga class was a good one, I didn't say.

"Honestly, sweetheart," my father said, "it's not going so well. Looking at photos of Captain Penniman's house just isn't the same as being there, you know? I need to walk under that whale bone arch to describe it properly. I need to look out over the same marshes, out to the same sea his wife would have looked out on waiting for him to come home."

I got it. I really did. It would be difficult to remember the small details if you weren't here. The young rabbits in the cool of the morning nibbling the grass. The full moon rising over the ocean, first red, then orange, then yellow, and finally silver. The wonderful funk of the mud flats at low tide.

"Yeah," I said. "I can see how that might be a problem." And then I said it, what I'd been wanting to say ever since they'd defected to the Sunshine State. "Maybe you should move back to the Cape."

Suddenly my father stopped shouting into the phone. "I'd be lying if I said I hadn't thought about that, Sam," he said, almost in a whisper. "But your mother, she loves it here. I'm not going to drag her back up there just because of some fancy of mine."

"Are you sure she loves it?" I asked. "Because she seemed pretty happy on the Cape over Christmas." *When she was trying to pin Santa's murder on the mob*, I didn't add. I was still trying to forget that. "I mean, have you *asked* her?"

"Well, no," he admitted. "I haven't actually *asked* her about it."

I sighed. Of course not. My parents talk all the time about just about everything under the sun except their emotions. My father in particular finds those kinds of conversations intensely embarrassing.

"Well, Dad," I said, "maybe you should. Maybe you should actually *ask* her about it."

Good lord, I was channeling Helene.

We chatted for a while longer about this and that, but I knew not to keep my dad on the phone too long or he got antsy. I finally let him go, though not without trying out a "love you" on him at the end. His response was a startled "Well, thank you." Which made me laugh out loud.

So the Father's Day conversation was, in my view, a success. But I had the feeling my little talk with Jean Wilkinson might not go quite so smoothly.

EIGHTEEN

～～～

I F FAIR HARBOR can be said to have an exclusive neighborhood, I suppose Shawme Heights is that neighborhood, with its noble old family "big houses" commanding fabulous views of the Shawme dunes and, beyond them, the deep blue Atlantic Ocean stretching for miles to an infinite horizon.

Like its neighbors, the Wilkinsons' house was a shingled "cottage" three times the size of Aunt Ida's house. *Your house, Sam.* It spoke quietly of old money, though it was less fastidiously kept up than most of its neighbors. The white oyster shell path up to the front door was sprouting the occasional weed and the hydrangeas that edged it needed deadheading.

As I walked up the path to the house with Miles and his mother that Monday afternoon, I realized that I was nervous. It might seem like any other summer day, but we were there because Clara Foster had died, perhaps at the hands of a killer. And if that was the case, then the odds were that somebody I would be talking to was a killer. A perfect killer if they got away with it. *Which they won't*, I promised Clara.

The memorial service was being held on the house's enormous deck overlooking the dunes and the sea beyond. A few rows of those faux-bamboo chairs so beloved of caterers everywhere had been set up facing a small lectern for the speakers. A table had been placed next to the lectern, crowded with framed photos of Clara with various luminaries of the culinary world ranging from Julia Child to Alice Waters.

With a start, I realized that I'd seen these photos before. In Clara's house the day Jenny and I had visited. And again the day after, so covered with soot they were unrecognizable. Someone had taken the time to clean them and set them up here. I was grateful that they had cared enough about Clara's legacy to do that, though I wondered how they'd managed to get access to the house.

About fifty or so people were milling around on the deck talking quietly or finding their seats as they waited for the service to start. I saw Vivian Peters among them and we nodded to each other, but by unspoken agreement we made no further acknowledgment. I noticed Krista, because it's hard *not* to notice Krista, arriving with a guy who, even in chinos, polished loafers, white button-down shirt, and navy blazer, looked like he lived on a surfboard. *Where does she find them?* I wondered not for the first time. I walked over to where Jenny was standing with Roland. With a discreet sideways nod of her head and a muttered "the niece," Jenny directed my attention to the object of my sleuthing.

Jean Wilkinson was perfect for her setting. She was tall enough to be considered elegant but not so tall that she raised eyebrows (like yours truly). And she was thin (unlike yours truly). The kind of thin that requires a lot of work at the gym and many hours on the tennis court and very little food at the table. Though she had to be in her early fifties, there was nary a wrinkle on her face or a gray hair on her head. Her ash-blond hair was perfectly colored and coiffed, and I suspected she did not have it done at Shear Delight.

Jean Wilkinson's memorial service for her aunt, however, was less than perfect. In fact, it seemed to me that it
was as perfunctory a memorial service as you could possibly have. There was no eulogy from a family member. No
friends or coworkers or luminaries were invited to speak.
In fact, there were precious few coworkers or luminaries in
attendance and I wondered if Jean Wilkinson had done any
outreach at all to her aunt's old colleagues. The officiant, a
Reverend Hardcastle, appeared to have been imported for
the occasion. He'd obviously done his research and spoke
intelligently about Clara's talent and contributions to her
field. He was vague about Clara herself, admitting frankly
that he had not known her. The only other speaker was the
head of the Fair Harbor chapter of the Cape Cod Conservancy, who spoke feelingly about Clara's love of the natural
beauty of the Cape and proprietarily about her "generous
and complete" donation of land "that now belongs to all of
us in perpetuity."

So, I thought to myself, nothing had changed for the Conservancy. If anything, the speaker seemed almost a little
surprised by the terms of the bequest. I glanced over at
Roland sitting a few chairs down from me, but his face was
a perfect mask of neutral professionalism. He was not giving anything away. I searched out Jean Wilkinson, who, as
the chief mourner, was seated at the end of the front row.
She, too, was poker faced. How do people *do* that? Wasn't
anybody feeling *anything*? Then I noticed the florid man
seated beside Jean, presumably her husband, sweat beading
his brow, his face a storm of anger. Interesting. Maybe the
news hadn't been so good for the Wilkinsons.

But wasn't anybody sad about Clara Foster's death? *I*
was sad, and I'd only met the woman once. Then I looked
over at Mrs. Tanner, sitting quietly beside Miles, tears rolling down her cheeks. Mr. Tanner, looking uncomfortable
in a suit that I imagined came out of the closet only for

weddings and funerals, sat on one side of her, holding her hand. Miles was on her other side, passing her tissues and occasionally using one himself. And I felt better.

Once the service, such as it was, ended, Jean Wilkinson stood and invited the attendees to stay for "drinks and conversation so that we can share our memories of Clara with each other." She did not seem excited about this prospect. Neither did most of the attendees, who, I suspected, had been hoping to make their escape the minute the Reverend Hardcastle gave his little blessing at the end of the service.

Most of the menfolk, with Miles leading the charge, headed for the bar that had been discreetly set up at the far end of the deck. Most of the women mobbed the catering team wandering through the crowd with trays of mini bruschetta and very small glasses of white wine.

As I grabbed a glass of wine with one hand and a soggy toast topped with store-bought salsa with the other, I watched my "team" fan out. Miles easily cut out Ed Captiva from a group of Clara's Place employees, Clive the server among them. Miles handed Ed a beer and a glass, which Ed took gratefully. Jenny, white wine in hand, was standing meekly at Roland's side while he chatted with the head of the Conservancy. Mrs. Tanner was almost indiscriminately accosting total strangers and asking them how they knew "dear Clara."

Figuring it would be a while before I could get to Jean Wilkinson, who was still accepting insincere condolences from people who were clearly perfect strangers to her, I began circulating through the crowd, hoping to overhear whatever people might be saying about Clara's death. But the conversations were benign, mostly about Clara's contributions either to the farm-to-table movement or her conservation efforts. None of the attendees, as far as I could tell, had that "avid for gossip" look on their faces that would indicate the existence of any unsavory rumors about her death. Clearly Detective Peters's efforts to keep her investigation under the radar had worked.

You can only stand around with a glass of warm and not very good chardonnay in your hand for so long before you start to feel like the most unpopular girl at the party. So I was grateful when, after about twenty minutes of eavesdropping on conversations that seemed to revolve mostly around property values, I saw a familiar face. Standing next to a table on which the caterers had set out their less-than-stellar finger foods, including a crudités platter of little more than celery and carrot sticks and a cheese platter with no fresh fruit, was *Antiques in the Attic*'s Thomas Bentley. Next to him was a woman in her early thirties, though her sensible haircut and essentially colorless clothes made her seem older. I remembered her from the show as his assistant, Barbara something, one of those beige people who somehow always seem to fade into the woodwork and whose name nobody ever seems to remember. Which made me feel bad for her.

I wandered over to the two of them. "Thomas, Barbara, how nice to see you again."

I was a little surprised by how shocked Bentley seemed to be seeing me in this context. Barbara just looked shocked that I'd included her in the greeting at all.

"Ms. Barnes," Bentley said. "What on earth are you doing here?"

"I knew Clara professionally," I explained.

"I'm sorry we had to meet again under such sad circumstances," Bentley said smoothly, having recovered himself. "She was an extraordinary woman, Clara Foster."

"I liked her house," Barbara said, unexpectedly and awkwardly, given that the house had practically gone up in flames. Bentley glanced at her sharply, and she immediately looked like she regretted saying anything. Apparently, her role was to say nothing but keep smiling pleasantly. I remembered this as her default from our time together on *Antiques in the Attic*.

"I did, too," I said, trying to smooth things over. "Actually, Thomas, I've been meaning to call you now that the clock episode has aired."

Bentley's eyes took on that hungry look I remembered from our time together in front of the camera.

"Of course," he said. "We've had a terrific response. I take it you're ready to think about selling the piece?"

"This probably isn't the time or place to discuss it," I responded, "but I'm planning to be in Hyannis in a few days. Maybe we can find a time to talk then."

"Perfect," Bentley said smoothly. "Just give Barbara a call and she'll set it up." Barbara smiled, reached into her purse, and handed me a business card. Barbara Smiley. Perfect.

I tucked the card away in my shoulder bag. "Great," I said. "I look forward to it."

"As do I," Bentley said, and from the glitter in his eyes, I knew he meant it. Barbara just smiled.

"Just one other thing, Thomas," I said.

"Of course," Bentley said politely. "How can I help?"

"It's about the fire at Clara Foster's house," I said.

"The fire at Clara Foster's house," he repeated blankly.

"Actually, not the fire," I said. "It's more about what was in her house *before* the fire."

Now Bentley was looking distinctly alarmed. "There was nothing of value in the house," he said, as if I was somehow questioning his professional acumen. "Ms. Foster assured us that all of her wife's remaining works were kept in the studio in the barn."

Barbara smiled and nodded madly, silently corroborating her boss.

"But the books," I said. "She must have shown you her cookbook collection. It included an Escoffier."

"No," Bentley said, the relief clear in his voice. "I never

actually went into her house. She took us directly to the studio in the barn. But she did mention the cookbooks to me. She wanted to know if they were still worth what she'd insured them for. I explained to her that, though of course I have some familiarity with the subject, Bentley's doesn't appraise books, that she would need a rare book dealer for that."

"Did she say why she wanted them appraised?" I asked. "Was she thinking of selling them?"

"Oh, no," Bentley said. "Unlike the paintings, she just wanted to know whether they were currently valued at more or less than the original insurance appraisal."

So Clara *had* been looking into the value of the books. In which case, it was entirely possible that the police would conclude that Clara had started that fire herself for insurance fraud. And that would break Mrs. Tanner's heart.

NINETEEN

~~~~~~~~

I THANKED BENTLEY, AND murmuring something
about seeing someone I needed to talk to, I turned to
leave, only to find Jenny at my elbow.

"C'mon," she whispered urgently. "Let's go to the bathroom."

"What? Why?"

She looked at me like I was being deliberately obtuse. "I
told Roland you knew where the upstairs bathroom was and
could show me. It was the only way I could think of to get
us some privacy. I need to talk to you."

I nodded my understanding. Together we made our way
into the house through a living room sparsely furnished in
a bland contemporary style incongruous with the house's
antique bones, and up the stairs. Sure enough, there was an
enormous bathroom just down the hall. Looking both ways
first like cartoon spies, we entered and then locked the door
behind us.

"So spill," I said, sitting on the edge of an enormous
spa tub.

"You're gonna love this," Jenny said, putting down the
toilet seat cover and making herself comfortable. "Just now,

when Rollie gave that Jean Wilkinson his condolences, she looked at him like he smelled bad and said, all snooty, 'Believe me, Mr. Singleton, if you were truly sorry about my aunt's death, you would have agreed to help me contest that will.' I thought Roland was going to choke on his scotch."

"Jenny Snow Singleton," I said admiringly, "you are the ultimate invisible wife. I can't believe she spilled the beans in front of you."

"Yeah," Jenny agreed with great satisfaction. "That woman didn't even know I was there. Better yet, when we walked away, I asked Rollie what she was talking about and he was so shell-shocked that he actually told me. Turns out, like Mrs. Tanner said, up until a few weeks ago Clara's will had most of her property going to the Conservancy except for the two acres that the house and barn sit on, which were going to go to Jean. Jean was cool with that, Rollie said, since those two acres were waterfront and the most valuable piece of the property."

Jenny paused for emphasis. She dearly loves taking her time telling a story.

"And then a few weeks ago?" I prompted her.

"Yeah, well, apparently Clara and Jean had some big fight or something and, like Mrs. Tanner said, Clara decided to change her mind and her will." Another dramatic pause.

"And Jean was out?"

"Not exactly. She still got the house and the property . . ."

"But . . ." I said as scripted.

"Drum roll, please," Jenny said.

I rolled my eyes. "This better be good."

"But she can't *sell* the house or the property. She can only live there for her lifetime. After that it reverts back to the Conservancy. And if she decides not to live there, it goes immediately to the Conservancy."

Well, that *was* a surprise.

"And Jean didn't know?" I asked.

Jenny shook her head. "Not until two days ago, when Roland went through the will with her."

There was a hesitant knock at the bathroom door. "Anyone in there?"

"Just finishing up," Jenny called back.

She flushed the toilet for verisimilitude, and I stood and ran the sink's faucet for a few seconds. As we opened the door to the rather shocked-looking woman outside in the hall, Jenny said, eyes dancing with mischief, "If you can't share a bathroom with your best friend, then she's not your best friend, am I right?"

We made our way downstairs and out to the deck, which, in the time we'd been talking, had pretty much emptied, so it was easy to find a quiet corner where we could finish our conversation.

"So, in effect," I said, leaning against the deck's railing, "Jean Wilkinson doesn't get a penny, unless she rents Clara's house out or something."

"Can't rent it out," Jenny said definitively. "I asked. The will stipulates that Jean herself has to live there or the reversion to the Conservancy goes into effect."

"Okay," I said, "but still, they could sell this place"—I waved my hand to indicate the Shawme Heights house—"and move to Clara's house."

"They could," Jenny said, "if they didn't already have two mortgages for more than this house is worth. They are totally underwater."

"Oh, Jenny," I said, honestly shocked. "Roland didn't tell you that?"

"Of course he didn't," Jenny said. "But it's a matter of public record." And with that, she pulled out her cell phone and thumbed in a few commands.

"Here," she said, holding the phone out so I could look. Sure enough, under a page headed "Barnstable County Registry of Deeds" were two mortgages in the name of Paul Wilkinson totaling a number that took my breath away.

"Which explains this sorry excuse for a memorial service," Jenny said bluntly. "Rollie says they're serving really cheap scotch."

She sounded almost as shocked by this as she'd been by Jean Wilkinson's rudeness to her husband. But she had a point. If the Wilkinsons were broke and in debt, it would explain the lack of a yard service and the very minimal furnishings in the house itself.

"But cheap booze and food might just be because Jean Wilkinson wasn't her aunt's biggest fan," I said. "She clearly only had the memorial service at all because people would talk if she didn't."

"People are already talking," Jenny said. "I've been circulating, asking a few leading questions. Word is Jean's husband, Paul, was actually fired from that wealth management company he used to work for, even though he's giving out that he 'retired early.' Apparently, he was advising his clients to invest in some high-yield financial instruments without bothering to tell them that high yield also means high risk. Now people are saying he took his own advice and ended up losing a fortune in the latest downturn in the market."

"And Jean Wilkinson doesn't work?" I asked.

"Oh, girl," Jenny said. "The only thing Jean Wilkinson has ever worked at is being Mrs. Paul Wilkinson."

"So I guess that explains why she wants to contest the will," I said.

Jenny nodded. "And good luck with that. Rollie says it's watertight, even the bit about the oyster farmers."

"Whoa!" I said. "What bit about the oyster farmers?"

"Oh, yeah," Jenny said. "I forgot to tell you about that. It just shows how petty this woman is. Last week Clara also added a codicil that deeded the contents of her house and any profits from the sale of those contents to Dave and Elisha Joy, the oyster farmers Clara told us about."

Which explained, I now realized with relief, Clara's comment that she had "other plans" for her cookbook collection.

And why she'd been curious about its current value. She wanted to know how much her bequest would be to her young friends.

"Good on her," I said. "Maybe they'll get some insurance money for Clara's cookbook collection, and for sure they'll get whatever Kit's paintings bring."

"Well, they won't get anything if Mrs. Paul Wilkinson has anything to say about it," Jenny said.

"You know, Jenny," I said, "I really think I have to meet this Mrs. Paul Wilkinson."

M RS. PAUL WILKINSON was standing quite alone at the far end of the deck, sipping her white wine sparingly, her face a mask of discontent. She was wearing a simple gray sheath that probably cost ten times as much as the vintage navy shirtwaist with white collar and cuffs that I had donned for the occasion (and which Miles calls my nun outfit). She wore no jewelry, perhaps in deference to the occasion. Or maybe because she'd sold it all to keep Cape Cod Power and Light from turning off the electricity. As I approached, I took a large gulp from my glass, just to show her how wine should be drunk at a memorial service. Or when you are about to interview someone who might be a killer.

"Ms. Wilkinson," I said, "I'm Samantha Barnes. Your aunt was something of a hero to me"—for a moment my voice faltered—"and I wanted to say how sorry I am"—I was going to say "for your loss," but couldn't bring myself to utter words that were patently untrue in Jean Wilkinson's case—"that she is gone."

"Oh, yes," my hostess said coldly. "Samantha Barnes. The Cape Cod Foodie."

She made it sound faintly ridiculous, and I felt myself color. Was what I did for a living faintly ridiculous?

"I saw your video with my aunt on the *Clarion*'s website," she added, taking another tiny sip of wine. I waited for more, but she began to move away, clearly feeling she'd done her duty toward me.

Not so fast, Your Highness, I thought.

"I saw your aunt the day before she . . . died," I said. "She spoke about you."

If I had told Jean Wilkinson that her aunt had taken off her clothes and run naked through the dunes, she could not have looked more shocked.

"She talked about *me*?"

"Of course," I said, all innocent-like. "You were her only family, weren't you?"

"Well, yes," she said, "but we weren't close. My aunt was, to put it mildly, completely self-absorbed. Other people's problems meant nothing to her."

So no love lost there, I thought. And what other people? And what problems?

"Yes," I said as if I knew exactly what she was talking about. "She said that perhaps she'd been a bit hasty in her judgment." This was a lie, of course, but it didn't count because I had my fingers crossed on the hand that wasn't holding my wineglass.

Jean Wilkinson nodded and said bitterly, "She never liked Paul."

Oh ho, now we're getting somewhere, I thought. But by this time, the woman had regained her poise.

"The restaurant was Clara's true family," she added saccharinely. Then she asked with feigned nonchalance, "What did she say about me?"

I smiled at her. "Oh, only that the appraiser had found some paintings of Kit's that might bring in some money, which sounded like good news to me, but she said 'dear Jean' would be disappointed. Again."

And at that, Jean Wilkinson looked positively livid and drained her glass of white wine in one gulp.

There, I thought. *That's* how you drink wine at a memorial service.

TWENTY

M Y SATISFACTION AT breaking Jean Wilkinson's
cool was short-lived. After wandering off with the
standard "there's someone I need to talk to," I pondered the
fact that, yes, Jean obviously hadn't known until Roland
informed her on Saturday that Clara's will now left her exactly nothing. Which made her, in my eyes, an obvious candidate for Clara's murderer. If the Wilkinsons were as short
of cash as it seemed, then the mistaken prospect of getting
their hands on a valuable piece of waterfront property
sooner rather than later might have been irresistible. And if
Jean had killed her aunt for nothing, no wonder the woman
was, to put it mildly, a little pissed off.

I was suddenly aware of Miles waving me over to where
he was standing next to Ed Captiva. Ed was wearing a blue-
and-white-striped seersucker suit, which reminded me of
my Grandpa Barnes, who always said the only suit he
would wear in summer was his seersucker.

"Ed," Miles said, "you remember Sam from the other day."

"Of course," Ed said, putting his glass of beer down on
a small table to shake my hand. "You were a fan of the
harissa swordfish."

"I was and still am," I said. "Any chance you'd share the recipe with me?"

"Not a snowball's," he said with a broad grin.

No wonder Miles and Jason liked this guy so much. He was adorable. Even if he wouldn't give me his swordfish with harissa recipe.

"I thought you'd enjoy Ed's memories of his early days at the restaurant," Miles said all innocent-like. "You guys may want to trade war stories."

I laughed. "War is a pretty apt metaphor for a busy restaurant kitchen, especially when you're just a foot soldier."

"I wasn't even that," Ed said. "I was just a pimply-faced kid fresh out of high school, hired to wash dishes. But I had Provincetown Portuguese grandmothers on both sides, and they were fantastic home cooks. I'd spent most of my childhood in their kitchens learning everything they had to teach me. So in my spare time at the restaurant, which wasn't much, I would follow Clara around like a puppy, asking questions about her cooking techniques, how she chose her ingredients, that kind of thing. The next thing I knew, she was handing me an apron. It took me ten years, and the school of Clara wasn't an easy one, the woman was fanatical about her craft. But by the end of it, Clara Foster had turned me into a chef. She was the most amazing woman I ever knew. I was so proud to be her protégé."

Here Ed's voice got a little rough and he took a last gulp of his beer as if to cover his emotion. I now knew why Miles had wanted me to hear Ed's story directly. The man seemed genuinely grieved by Clara's death. But *seemed* wasn't enough. We needed *real* proof. But before I could start what I hoped would be a subtle interrogation, Ed motioned toward the bar and said, "Excuse me. I think I need a refill." Ah, another age-old excuse to get out of a conversation at a party. Or in this case, a memorial service.

"Sure, buddy," Miles said. "Get me one, too, would you?"

Nicely played, Miles, I thought. Sympathetic or not, he wasn't going to let Ed get off that easily.

Ed nodded and headed toward the bar, while Miles and I entertained ourselves looking at the celebrity photos on the table. I pointed out the many chefs, restaurateurs, and food writers that I'd followed from a distance and the few I actually knew firsthand. One group shot of noted female chefs included both Clara and Plum and Pear's Caitlin Summerhill. I waited for the usual spasm of regret, the acknowledgment that I'd thrown away any chance of someday being in that august company myself. But it never came. All I felt was a kind of relief, a thankfulness that I no longer had to define my success in life by awards won or restaurants worked in. *So how* do *you define success in life now, Sam?* I didn't have an answer to that, I realized. Not yet anyway.

While I was getting nowhere with my personal philosophy, Ed had wandered back to Miles and me.

"I wasn't sure I'd be able to salvage those after the fire," he said, nodding toward the photographs on the table.

"I was wondering who'd done that," I said. "I'm glad you thought of it."

"Well, when I asked her niece if she was inviting some of the people in the photos to the memorial service, she said no, it was just going to be a small affair."

Ed tried hard not to sound judgmental, but I wasn't fooled. He knew as well as I did how proud Clara had been of her place in the foodie firmament. And we both knew that Jean was not going to allow her aunt that final satisfaction at her memorial service.

"But she did admit that the photos were essentially unharmed," Ed continued. "So when I asked if I could try to clean them up for the service, she really couldn't refuse. Although she did try to fob me off by saying she didn't have a key to the house. She said Clara never 'trusted' her with one. So I went to that nice police detective, who sent me off to the house with this really unpleasant cop, who made it pretty clear that he thought babysitting me was a waste of his valuable time."

"Oh, yeah," I said sympathetically. "I know the cranky cop."

"Anyway," Ed continued, "he let me in and . . ."

He paused, remembering, I suspected, what had greeted him in that house.

"I saw it, too," I said. "It wasn't an easy sight."

"No," he said, "it really wasn't. But it wasn't just the destruction and the soot and all." Here Ed looked uncertain and I knew enough not to push him, to let him fill the silence himself.

"Look," he said. "Can we maybe find a quiet place to talk?"

"Of course," Miles and I said simultaneously, which only sounded slightly weird and overeager.

"Let's take a little walk," Miles said casually, saving the day.

The three of us headed out to the edge of the Wilkinsons' lawn and pretended to be absorbed in the fabulous view of dunes and marsh and beach beyond. But that was not at all what we were absorbed in.

"There was something not right there," Ed said uncertainly. "There was something not right about how that cop said Clara died."

"Not right how?" I asked, fairly sure that Ed was going to point out what I'd already mentioned to Vivian. But maybe there was more, something I'd overlooked. After all, Ed knew, *really* knew Clara.

"Well, when I got inside, the cop told me that fire started when Clara left a cast iron pan full of bacon grease on a hot burner." Ed paused, considering what he was going to say next. "But I knew that, for one thing, Clara would never leave a pan over an open flame."

Hah. Score one for Samantha Barnes.

"For one thing?" I asked. "What else?"

"Clara wouldn't be using a cast iron pan at all."

Well, I hadn't expected *that*.

"But cast iron is the best for something like bacon," I protested. "It holds a steady heat without scorching."

"Even *I* know that, Sam," Miles said. "Let the man talk, would you?"

Suitably chastened, I shut my big mouth with a snap.

"But here's the thing." Ed paused again, but this time the wait was worth it. "Clara's arthritis made it impossible to work with cast iron. It was too heavy for her."

Of course. I should have thought of it myself. That explained why she'd retired earlier than she'd planned. And to my mind it meant that Clara Foster could not have started that fire herself. *Hallelujah.* Also, if Ed Captiva was bringing up the possibility of foul play, then in my book that was a pretty good sign that he wasn't Clara's killer. *A good sign, but not proof, Sam.*

"That's probably important," I said. "Did you mention that to the police?"

"I started to explain to him about how Clara wouldn't leave a burner on," Ed continued, "and he stopped me right there and said, 'Yeah, we know all that, and we don't think it's relevant.' So I gave up. I figure if the cops don't want my professional opinion, fine." *Ah, there's the inner diva chef coming out*, I thought.

"Well, I'm glad you told us," I said. "Because I think it is relevant. And I think Detective Peters will think so too. I could bring it up with her if you want."

"Be my guest," Ed said.

"So what do you think, Ed?" Miles broke in. "You think someone else started that fire on purpose?"

Ed's ruddy face suddenly drained of all color.

"On purpose?" he repeated. "As in, *wanted* to set Clara's house on fire? Why?"

If Ed Captiva was that someone, I thought, he was also a pretty good actor. And it was significant, I thought, that he

couldn't, or wouldn't, make the leap to the next inference—
that someone had deliberately set Clara Foster's house on
fire in order to kill Clara Foster herself.

Miles put an arm around Ed. "Sorry, buddy," he said. "I
tend to overthink things. Believe me, I know how hard it
is when someone dies suddenly and you don't get a chance
to say goodbye"—here Miles's voice shook a bit, then
strengthened—"or patch up disagreements."

Good lord, I realized, *Miles was still sleuthing*. Miles
wanted to see if Ed would bring up the lawsuit.

But Ed wasn't going there. Though he looked distinctly
uncomfortable, he just nodded and said, perhaps because
he knew we'd noticed his little tiff with Clara at the restaurant, "Yeah, like how much aioli to put in the fish stew."

I almost groaned aloud. So Ed was keeping the lawsuit
under wraps as long as he could.

We seemed to have reached an impasse. After a few mo-
ments of silence, Miles changed the subject in that way that
men do.

"So," he said, "what do you think of the Red Sox's pen-
nant chances?"

I, for one, would have asked what the final decision on
the aioli was, but okay.

TWENTY-ONE

"DIOGI, OLD PAL," I said the next morning after I'd poured about two pounds of kibble into his bowl, "that was just about the worst memorial service ever."

I settled myself at the kitchen table with my coffee and tried for a little introspection, which is not exactly my forte. What was it that so bothered me about yesterday's gathering? It wasn't just the perfunctory service or the lousy food or my encounter with the unpleasant Mrs. Paul Wilkinson. Indeed, Jenny's info on the will was, I knew, very important in terms of possible suspects with a motive for doing away with Clara Foster. And Ed's knowledge that Clara could not have started that fire herself, even if she'd wanted to, was vital evidence that could surely be confirmed by Clara's doctor.

But the whole experience had left me terribly low. I sipped my coffee, disconsolate and, let's face it, lonely. Diogi, chowing down as if he hadn't eaten for a week, was oblivious to my blue mood. But Ciati, bless her little kitty heart, jumped up into my lap and nudged my free hand with her nose, demanding that I rub her behind the ears, just the way she liked it. Almost automatically I complied, and almost automatically I began to feel better. There is something about a cat purring on your lap that makes the world a brighter place. I am firmly convinced that cats know that.

"Well," I said to her with my first smile of the day, "at least tonight I get to go to a ball game!"

There is nothing quite as magical as a summer evening baseball game. In Fair Harbor, Cape Cod League baseball is played at Thompkins Park, home to the Fair Harbor Ospreys, in a field overlooked by the Fair Harbor Elementary School. The grassy slope down to the diamond has been sculpted into four terraced levels that serve as "bleachers," with fans bringing their own folding chairs and blankets for seating. A concession stand provides the requisite hot dogs and Drumstick ice cream cones. There is also an announcer's booth, an electronic scoreboard, and an impressive array of field lights on tall aluminum poles for extra innings after sundown. The field is carefully and professionally tended, as are all the League fields. Tonight, it glowed like an emerald in the slanting light of early evening.

The other "sleuths" had agreed to meet at the ballpark about a half hour before the opening pitch of the first home game of the season. This would serve the double purpose of reviewing what we'd learned at Clara's memorial service and getting a good seat in advance of the crowd. At the season's first home game, it's always a good idea to stake your claim early. Some people go so far as to reserve their spot with empty blankets and beach chairs the morning of the game, but my family had always considered that cheating. Really, no matter where you sat, you were never going to be more than a couple of yards from the diamond anyway.

I got to the ball field first, with Helene arriving shortly after. While we waited in the parking lot for the others, I admired her choice of T-shirt, which advised the world to "Never, ever, ever give up."

"Appropriate for tonight's game," I noted.

"I thought so," said, adding, as only a librarian would, "It's a misquote of Winston Churchill, of course, but I appreciate the sentiment. So often the most important thing is to never, ever, ever give up. Particularly in baseball."

"Yeah, well, if you don't get a move on, we may have to give up on getting a good spot."

This was Jillian, who'd come up behind us and was looking more than slightly anxious about Marcel's first home game. She hurried us over to a spot close enough to first base that we could cheer Marcel on but far enough away from other early comers that we could share our findings away from curious ears.

Once the rest of the crew had gathered, we formed a circle, Helene and Mrs. Tanner on low beach chairs that they'd brought, the rest of us cross-legged on a blanket. I thought, not for the first time, that the universal adoption of jeans by every gender and age was one of civilization's great leaps forward. No one needed to worry about getting grass stains, or how to sit "properly," or if what they were wearing was "age appropriate." From Mrs. Tanner's farmer jeans to Jenny's skinny jeans to Miles's black jeans, from Helene's boot-cut jeans to Jillian's designer jeans to my whatever-was-on-sale-at-the-Gap jeans, we were united in denim comfort. Most of us had also brought a sweater or hoodie to slip on when the evening turned cool.

Jillian brought the meeting to order by whipping out her yellow legal pad and consulting what she called "the take-aways and next steps" from the meeting in Jenny's back-yard and announcing that she would now take notes on our "updates."

She wanted to start with me, as sleuth-in-charge, but I suggested that everyone else make their reports and I would take up the rear.

"Jenny should go first," I said, "since she got the real scoop."

"I thank my esteemed colleague from Bayberry Point for surrendering the floor," Jenny said.

I bowed my head in dignified acknowledgment, and she told the rest of the crew about Clara's will and Jean Wilkinson's reaction.

"Slick work, wifey," Miles said admiringly.

"I thought so," Jenny said, lowering her eyes modestly.

Jillian turned to Miles's mom. "Mrs. Tanner . . ." she began.

But before she could continue, Mrs. Tanner was shaking her head. "Florence, please," she said. "I'm just Florence. Except to Samantha, of course. I have a feeling I'll always be Mrs. Tanner to Samantha."

I smiled my agreement. No way was I calling Mrs. Tanner Florence. That would just be wrong.

"Florence, then," Jillian agreed. "You weren't at our earlier meeting about our goals for the memorial service, but I know that Miles asked you to . . ." Here she paused, obviously embarrassed.

Mrs. Tanner saved her by finishing her sentence. "To act like a nosy old lady," she said. "Not really my style, it's true. I like to keep myself to myself and like other people to do the same." *There was the Mrs. Tanner I knew and loved.* "But I have to admit I enjoyed it. If nothing else, it livened up the proceedings."

"Couldn't agree more," Miles said. "Wasn't that service deadly?"

"Miles," his mother said, frowning at him, "a better choice of words next time, please." I can't even remember the number of times I'd heard Mrs. Tanner say that to Miles when we were teenagers. Usually when he used a swear word, though.

Miles grinned. "Sorry," he said. "Wasn't it deadly *dull*?"

His mother pretended to slap him on the arm and proceeded with her update. "Anyway, I did like you all suggested and asked a bunch of folks how they knew Clara but most of them just said through the restaurant or through working with her on her cookbook or something like that. Pretty much everybody said they didn't know her well, which I kind of got the feeling meant they really didn't like her that much." Mrs. Tanner's face crumpled for a minute and my heart went out to her.

She paused to gather herself, then continued. "I guess I was lucky to know her as a friend and not a business partner or boss. But I did find one woman, a neighbor, a Summer Robinson, who knew her pretty well. She said she'd actually stopped by Clara's house earlier that night, around nine or so, to drop off a book that she'd promised to lend Clara about global warming. I said something along the lines of it was great that Clara was so environmentally aware, and this Summer woman insisted on giving me her cell number so I could call her anytime to 'talk more about the issue.' The woman's a bit of a nut. Anyway, I got her back on track and she said Clara's car was in the driveway when she got there, but the place was dark, and when she knocked, there was no answer, so she assumed Clara had already gone to bed. She tried both doors, hoping she could leave the book inside and not have to come back, but she said the place was locked up tighter than a drum. Now she wishes she'd tried harder to wake Clara up."

"Well, that's interesting," I mused. "I wonder if Detective Peters knows about this Summer Robinson's visit. Because if the house was locked up and Clara wasn't answering the door, how did the person who started that fire get in? They would have needed a key." Which, I remembered, Jean Wilkinson did not have. Or at least she'd told Ed she didn't have one.

Jillian made a note on her pad and turned to Miles.

"Were you able to talk to Ed Captiva?" she asked.

"Yup," Miles said. "Both Sam and I did. And I just can't believe that the guy would have harmed a hair on her head. He seemed genuinely sorry about her death. He said he was proud to be her protégé."

"But impressions aren't evidence," Helene pointed out. I had the feeling she'd heard that a lot in her work with the

Manhattan DA's office. "Did he mention the lawsuit?" Trust Helene to ask the tough questions.

"No," Miles said reluctantly. "I tried to give him an opening, but I didn't press it when I saw that he was clearly uncomfortable."

"That's not good," Helene pointed out. "It makes it seem like he didn't want to draw attention to any motive he might have had."

"You'd think that," Miles said, "except that he *did* draw attention to something else."

Miles paused dramatically, and after all those years in the high school drama club, he *really* knows how to do dramatically. He's even better at it than Jenny. "He *did* say he thought Clara was murdered."

Well, that galvanized his listeners.

"He actually said that?" Jillian asked.

"Well, not in so many words," Miles admitted. "What he said was he thought the whole thing was pretty suspicious. For one thing, Clara would never leave a pan over an open flame, and second, Clara wouldn't be using a cast iron pan at all. He said Clara's arthritis made it impossible to work with cast iron. It was too heavy for her."

"So," Helene concluded, "someone else was cooking bacon in that pan."

Miles nodded. "That's what Ed thinks. He thinks someone else started that fire while Clara was asleep upstairs. Though I have to say, he didn't want to believe the intention was to kill her."

"But still," Jenny broke in, "it has to mean that Ed wasn't the one who started the fire. Because if he was, he certainly wouldn't bring up the whole cast iron thing."

"I *knew* Clara didn't set that fire," Mrs. Tanner chimed in with great satisfaction. "And I *knew* it wasn't Ed Captiva. He's a good boy. He's always been a good boy."

I *really* didn't want to bring them down, but it had to be said.

"Yes, it helps his case that he volunteered information that indicated Clara's death wasn't accidental, but it isn't going to be enough to remove him from the list of suspects," I pointed out. "Not with his motive."

Mrs. Tanner looked crushed and a chorus of "Oh, come on" and "Whose side are you on anyway?" from Miles and Jenny greeted that little downer.

Jillian brought the meeting back to order with a quiet "Sam, why don't you sum up."

"Okay," I said. "To sum up, we're agreed that Clara's niece, Jean Wilkinson, seemed unaware of and was deeply unhappy about her 'inheritance' being changed from outright ownership to a life tenancy. It also looks like she and her husband are in bad shape financially. So a case could be made that the Wilkinsons killed Clara thinking they were going to inherit a very valuable property. Nor is it a stretch to imagine that Jean knew about Clara's reliance on sleeping pills. On the other hand, Jean told Ed that Clara had never given her a key to the house, so there's still the question of how they could have gotten in."

"I hadn't thought of that," Jenny said in disappointment. "I guess that's why you're the sleuth."

"I really wish you'd stop calling me that," I said. "It makes me feel like I should be wearing a deerstalker cap and carrying a magnifying glass."

"Which would be a charming addition to your already stylish wardrobe," Miles said, looking pointedly at the ripped knees of my jeans.

"I'll have you know, ripped jeans are considered very stylish," I countered.

"Not when they're covered with dog and cat hair," Miles said.

"Whatever," I muttered, taking a leaf from Helene's book.

"The game's going to start any minute," Jillian said impatiently. "Could we move on, please?"

"Right," I said. "Well, tomorrow I'll suggest to Detective

Peters that she talk to Ed about Clara's arthritis, which is probably going to turn this thing into an official investigation. And hopefully Ed's bringing that evidence forward will be a point in his favor and encourage the police to look at other suspects."

"Well, that calls for hot dogs all round," Miles announced and took himself off to the concession stand, to the delight of all the sleuths.

TWENTY-TWO

W HILE WE'D BEEN talking, the stands, or rather the hillside, had been filling up with friendly fans from the hometowns of both teams. The beauty of Cape Cod summer baseball is that because the team members are recruited from colleges all over the country, the players are not local heroes. Of course, we root for our home teams, but we don't take it personally, the way you do for your own high school or college team. The delight is in the pure sport itself.

And in trying to spot the scouts in the crowd looking for the next MLB All-Star.

I leaned over to Jillian, who was looking nervous. "Are you worried about Marcel?"

"A little," she said. "He's only a rising sophomore at Howard, so he's young for all the pressure. But I've met his host family, and they're very down to earth. They'll be good for him."

Most players in the League stay with volunteer host families whose basic responsibilities are to feed the boys, give them a bed, and make sure they get to their games on time. But everyone knows their primary role is to provide a family away from family. You can always tell who the host families are because they're the ones cheering the loudest when "their kid" comes up to bat.

"Marcel didn't want to stay with you and Andre?" I asked.

"Good lord, no," she said in mock horror. "The whole point is to have a new experience, meet new people, open your horizons. Not to live with your boring old aunt and uncle."

"Speak for yourself, woman," a deep voice boomed behind us.

We twisted around to see Andre standing there wearing an Ospreys baseball cap and a wide grin that made his high cheekbones even higher. Andre is the proprietor of Camping & Co., one of the most successful Black-owned businesses on the Cape, and is very fit. I watched Jillian's face light up at the sight of her handsome husband of more than thirty years, and not for the first time, I was hit with a pang of envy. *You're never going to have that, Sam. Not if you can't even manage a relationship for one year.*

Jillian grinned at the fielder's glove in Andre's hand and said, "You know you're never going to catch a fly ball, right? Not with all those little kids racing around."

She was right. There is intense competition among a certain cohort of very fleet-of-foot ten- to twelve-year-olds to catch the occasional pop-up fly that makes its way into the "stands." No adult, with their creaky knees and unwillingness to trample over the competition, need apply.

"There's always hope," Andre said, passing the glove to Jillian while he unfolded two snazzy beach chairs in the space of a second. I was again envious. My lengthy wrestling matches with beach chairs are the stuff of legend. Of course, I reminded myself, Andre, who made a living selling high-end hiking and camping equipment, was a pro.

Roland and the boys, also carrying the requisite fielder's gloves, found us, and Jenny moved off with them to the concession stand for "dinner." After all, you can't go to a ball game and not have a hot dog. It's the law. Everybody knows that.

All around us, families with young children were putting

down their blankets and older folks were setting up beach chairs, while the teenagers roamed in packs, constantly forming and re-forming in a kind of courtship dance that Jane Austen would definitely understand. I saw Beth Voorhees among them, her silky dark hair caught up in a high ponytail threaded through the back of the requisite Ospreys cap, her face lightly tanned with a cute sprinkle of freckles across her nose. I was pleased when she made her way over to our blanket to say hello. She's a good kid.

"Hi, Sam," she said politely. "Hi, Ms. Greenberg."

"You do realize, Beth," Helene said, "that you can call me Helene outside of the library."

Beth turned pink with pleasure. "I didn't," she said. "But thank you."

At this point, the loudspeaker boomed, "Ladies and gentlemen, please welcome the Fair Harbor Ospreys!"

A good three quarters of the assembled fans leaped to their feet and cheered madly as the boys of summer trotted out onto the field waving their caps to acknowledge the greeting. The Fair Harbor mascot capered up and down the first base line in his "osprey" costume, which Thing Three, aka Evan, announced loudly looked suspiciously like a chicken costume. Perhaps because osprey costumes are not readily available in party stores. Helene did that piercing two-fingers-in-her-mouth whistle that had brought so many taxis to a screeching halt when she'd lived in New York. It's very impressive. But Jillian managed to eclipse even her.

"There he is, there he is!" she shrieked, standing and pointing. "Third from the left. The handsome one!"

Tall, with long legs made to steal second, muscled arms that looked like they could swing a mean bat, and an angel smile white against his dark brown skin, Marcel was indeed handsome. I snuck a glance at Beth, her eyes wide, her teenage cool totally undone.

She gazed at Jillian wonderingly. "You know that player, Ms. Munsell?"

I'd forgotten that Beth's aunt worked for Jillian at Nauset Manor and that Beth sometimes volunteered to read aloud to the residents.

Jillian smiled. "I do indeed, Beth. He's my nephew, Marcel. He's a rising sophomore at Howard University."

"So he's smart and, um, athletic, too," Beth said awkwardly.

I got the distinct impression that athletic wasn't what she'd almost said. More like super cute. Jillian and I watched the girl wander back to her friends in a daze and grinned at each other. It was adorable.

The game was everything an opening home game should be. By which I mean we won. It was a great battle, but we won. Marcel, unfortunately, struck out at his first at bat, but seemed to gain confidence as the game went on, hitting two nice singles, one of which brought a runner home. At his final trip to the plate in the ninth inning, with the Ospreys down by a run, he hit an amazing triple that put him in position for what could be the tying run. And then on the next pitch, he *stole home*. I knew by this time that he had the speed to steal bases, but *steal home*? That takes nerve. Of course, some other player brought in the winning run in the tenth, but everybody knew Marcel had won the game.

Night had fallen by the time it was over, and we gathered our belongings in the glow of the field lights, the Three Things "helping" in that way that kids have of just making everything twice as complicated as it has to be.

"You carry the blanket. I carried it the last time."

"The last time was a year ago."

"It was still the last time."

"Shut up."

"No, you shut up."

"No, you shut up."

I knew from bitter experience that this could go on for hours.

And then we were saved.

"How about I carry it?"

It was as if someone had hit the mute button. All argument stopped while the boys absorbed the fact that *the guy who had won the game* was standing in front of them and *talking to them.*

"You're the guy who won the game," Thing Two breathed.

"No," Marcel said, smiling at him, "I'm just one of the guys on the *team* that won the game."

Thing One wasn't going to be fobbed off with sportsmanship-speak. "But you *are* the guy who stole home," he said.

Marcel nodded. "Yes," he admitted, "I am the guy that stole home."

Thing Three took a grubby ballpoint pen out of his jeans pocket and held it and his equally grubby fielder's mitt out to Marcel.

"Would you sign my glove?" he asked solemnly.

I doubt very much if anyone had ever asked Marcel to sign their glove before, and I was grateful that he didn't let Evan down by letting on.

"Of course, buddy," Marcel said with great grace, as if he was in the habit of signing gloves for fans on a regular basis. He signed with a flourish and handed the glove back to his fan.

"Thanks," Evan said. "And don't worry about the blanket. I can handle it." I really, really liked this kid.

Marcel turned to his aunt and uncle. "Thanks for coming out tonight," he said. "I appreciate the support."

And for just a minute he looked like the nervous kid he really was and not the guy who'd won the game.

"You hush," Jillian said. "We wouldn't miss it for the world."

At about this time, a small cough alerted us to someone standing at the edge of our little circle.

"Beth!" Helene said. "Aren't you nice to come say goodbye."

This is why I love Helene. It is no easy thing for a teenage girl to get up the courage to meet a new boy, let alone the boy *who has just won the game.*

Jillian, taking her cue from Helene, said, "Beth, this is my nephew, Marcel."

"Hi," Beth said, looking at Marcel nervously. "Good game."

"Thanks," Marcel said, equally nervously. "Glad you enjoyed it."

The silence that followed this exchange seemed to go on forever.

"Marcel," Helene said briskly. "I have to talk to your aunt for a minute. Could you do me a huge favor in the meantime? I promised Beth a hot dog earlier for helping me out today at the library."

Beth looked surprised by this out-and-out untruth, which didn't faze Helene one bit. She's used to lying for the sake of a greater cause.

"But I'm in a rush," she continued. "Could you take this"—she handed Marcel a couple of dollars—"and take care of that for me before the stand closes?"

"Sure thing," Marcel said, smiling. "Happy to help." And if his wide smile was any indication, he certainly was.

"And Beth, make sure Marcel gets some dinner, too," Jillian added, handing a few dollars to the girl, who took the money and then rolled her eyes at the way Helene and Jillian were orchestrating the proceedings.

Marcel, on the other hand, looked greatly amused.

"Your boss says I have to get you a hot dog," he said to Beth.

"Your aunt says I have to make sure you eat some dinner," she said, doing the eye roll again.

And without a backward look, Beth and Marcel left us. By the time they got to the concession stand, they were talking and laughing together like old friends. So the evening ended happily. Except that Andre had failed to snag a foul ball. Oh, well, you can't have everything.

TWENTY-THREE

~~~~~~~

MY LITTLE GOLDEN glow lasted only as long as it took me to get home; be greeted my dog, for whom, as usual, my return was a completely unexpected miracle; be ignored by my cat (*Jason's cat, Sam*), for whom my return was only what she would have expected; take a quick shower; and climb into bed. Maybe Jason would call. That would be super nice.

And then the loop started in my head.

Things were looking good, if murder can ever look good, in terms of Clara's death. There was a pretty good chance that: one, Clara had not, either accidentally or with intent, started the fire that had killed her; two, that Ed had not, either accidentally or with intent, started the fire that had killed her; and three, someone else *had*, either accidentally or with intent, started the fire that had killed her. But none of those things had been proved. I'd had a little luck figuring out whodunit with two other deaths, and my friends fully expected me to come up with the killer again. But I had no hard evidence.

Vivian Peters probably has lots of evidence.

Vivian had given me her business card before she'd left the other day, saying, "Let me know anytime if you think of anything." Wasn't Vivian going to be surprised.

Jason chose that moment to call, which made me wonder if he had some weird ESP for the name "Vivian," which made me ashamed of myself yet again. *Vivian has a boyfriend*, I reminded myself. *Which doesn't mean Jason doesn't have a thing for her*, myself responded.

All this, of course, took place in my head in the space of time it took Jason to say hello. But soon the story of his day eclipsed even my romantic paranoia.

"You'll never guess who we rescued today."

"A movie star?" I suggested hopefully.

"Kind of," he said. "Charlemagne the movie horse."

"That was going to be my second guess."

Jason laughed and said, "Really. There was a movie shoot with one of those romantic horseback-ride-along-the-beach scenes going this morning and Charlie got spooked, bucked off his rider, and swam out to sea."

"That's awful," I said. "But you saved him?"

"Yeah," Jason said. "Well, not just me. My partner Tim and me. By the time we got called, the horse had swum so far out, everyone on the beach had lost sight of him. So we coordinated a search and finally found Charlie totally exhausted about two and a half miles offshore."

"Oh, no, poor Charlie," I moaned. "What did you do? There was no way you could get him on the boat, right?"

"No way, no how," Jason said. "So Tim and I had to improvise. We rigged a support harness from a tow line, secured it to Charlie's saddle, and cleated it along the side of the boat. Then I made a kind of flotation device with a rescue buoy that we harnessed to Charlie's bridle."

"That's brilliant," I said.

"Yeah, it kind of was," he agreed. "But he was a good boy, I gotta say. He never panicked. I stayed with him, leaning over the side of the boat, just stroking his neck, you know, and talking to him, while Tim took the boat really, really slowly back to the surf line, where the handler came out and led Charlie back onto the beach."

"Oh, Jason," I said. "That's wonderful. And is Charlie okay?"

"He is," Jason said happily. "There was a vet waiting on the beach and he checked out great. Just a little tired."

"So all in a day's work," I noted.

"Yup," he agreed. "Plus, the director says he's going to give us all walk-on parts in the movie."

"Oh, boy," I said, "my guy is a movie star." At which point the conversation took a swift turn to the private.

S O THAT WAS nice, but once morning came, I was back on the sleuthing clock. Also, the Cape Cod Foodie clock. But first the sleuthing. I fortified myself with a cup of coffee, punched in the number for the Fair Harbor Police headquarters, and asked for Detective Peters.

"Peters here."

"Hi," I said. "It's Samantha Barnes. Sorry to bother you."

"Samantha," Vivian said. "That's okay. Hey, while I've got you, I've been reading *Sailing for Dummies* in my spare time. This week I've got Friday and Saturday off. You want to set up another sailing lesson?"

Not on your life, I didn't say.

"That sounds like fun," I lied. "Let me see what my work schedule looks like. But actually, I wanted to talk to you about Clara Foster's death. I've heard a few things that I thought I should share with you."

"Okay," Vivian said, suddenly all business. "Probably best if you don't come here." *On account of because my boss really, really doesn't like you*, she didn't say. "But I can be at your house in fifteen."

I hung up, a little dazed by the woman's energy. I'd barely

had a half cup of coffee. I wasn't even sure I'd be awake in fifteen.

Vivian's Jeep crunched into my shell driveway in fourteen, actually. I timed it. But she was forgiven because once again she came bearing dirt bombs.

I poured us both humongous cups of coffee, and at Vivian's suggestion, we took the muffins down to the dock to eat them. Diogi followed us with his favorite disgusting tennis ball in his mouth.

"You realize that now that you're his friend, you're going to have to play fetch with him," I warned her.

Vivian eyed the slobbery ball. "I don't think so," she said. *Hah*. Like she was going to have a choice.

At the bottom of the hill, I unearthed two ancient aluminum beach chairs with blue-and-pink webbing in what Aunt Ida had been pleased to call "the boat house." Boat shack is more like it. I wrestled them into submission at the end of the dock, and Vivian collapsed into hers with a sigh.

"This is heaven," she said, gazing out at the almost perfectly round salt pond, its shoreline edged with green-and-gold marsh grass punctuated by the occasional blue-green cedar tree. A few boats bobbed quietly at their moorings, their owners' gray-shingled cottages overlooking them like grannies watching sleeping children.

"Sitting here," Vivian said quietly, "you can almost believe in the goodness of mankind."

This shocked me. "You don't believe in the goodness of mankind?"

"In my world, it's sometimes hard to find evidence of that goodness."

"The evidence of that goodness is that *you* are in that world doing what you can to make it better," I said, and for a moment I felt like Helene. Maybe there was hope for me and this growing-up thing.

"I hadn't thought of it that way," Vivian admitted. "I'll try to keep it in mind."

Diogi, tired of all this talk, talk, talk, dropped his disgusting tennis ball in Vivian's lap. She looked at it like it was a dead thing. "What am I supposed to do with this?"

"Throw it," I said.

"Throw it where?"

"Out into the pond," I said. "He's a water dog. He loves to swim. He loves to fetch."

"If you say so," Vivian said doubtfully.

She picked up the ball, wiped off the slobber matter-of-factly on her nice clean pants, which made me like her a lot, and threw it out about twenty feet or so into the pond. In a flash, Diogi did a kind of belly-flop dive off the dock, paddled briskly out to the ball, took it in his mouth, swam back to the muddy shore, ran back up on the dock, and dropped the ball into Vivian's lap. This was Diogi talk for "Do it again." Then he briskly shook himself all over, showering us with a very pleasant combination of salt water and marsh mud.

Vivian, bless her heart, laughed and looked at me helplessly. "And this goes on for how long?"

"Until you harden your heart," I said, "or tire him out. Endurance swimming is not his strong suit."

Sure enough, by the fourth throw, Diogi decided he'd had enough and plopped himself down on the dock next to his new BFF, the Woman Who Throws the Ball, and was soon snoring gently in the June sunshine.

Vivian sighed and looked at me. "You wanted to talk to me about something?"

I hated bringing Vivian back to a world where she couldn't believe in goodness.

"I do," I admitted reluctantly. "Some friends of mine learned some interesting stuff at Clara's memorial service . . ."

"Stuff?" Vivian said. "What kind of stuff?"

So I told her. But if I expected Vivian Peters to give me something in return, like evidence, I was sorely mistaken.

"That's good intel," she acknowledged when I'd finished

my recitation. "It's really hard to argue that Clara started the fire herself, either accidentally or on purpose, given the arthritis." *Yessss.*

"And it kind of lets Ed Captiva off the hook," I suggested ever so subtly. Not. "I mean, he might have had a motive, what with the lawsuit and all, but if he was the one who started the fire, why would he make the point that it couldn't have been Clara?"

Vivian nodded. "Well, it doesn't prove anything, but it's certainly an argument in his favor."

Yessss.

"And Jean Wilkinson's response to the change in Clara's will is interesting, don't you think?" I asked.

"I already knew about the will from her lawyer," Vivian said. "But he, of course, didn't say anything about how this niece of hers reacted to the news."

"My theory is she had no idea that she wouldn't be able to sell her part of the property," I said. "I think she had great expectations and maybe got tired of waiting for those expectations."

Vivian just looked at me and said nothing.

I tried again. "I know about the two mortgages on the Wilkinsons' Shawme Heights house, but it would be good to know more about the Wilkinsons' financial situation."

Again, Vivian just looked at me and said nothing.

I pushed on. "And given what Clara's next-door neighbor said about the house being all locked up, I kind of wonder if Jean really didn't have a key to Clara's house."

And *still* Vivian just looked at me and said nothing.

"Oh, come on," I said. Okay, I whined. "I tell you everything I know, and you tell me nothing?"

"You are legally and morally obligated to tell me everything you know about an ongoing investigation," Vivian replied mildly. "I am legally and morally obligated *not* to tell you what I know about an ongoing investigation." *Well, she's got you there, Sam.*

"So it is an ongoing investigation?" I asked, just to confirm.

"It is now," she said grimly.

"That's good enough for me," I said, meaning it. I'd given her the information she needed to move forward. Vivian Peters was nobody's fool. She didn't need me to tell her how to do her job.

"There's just one thing," Vivian said.

"What's that?"

"When's my next sailing lesson?"

"When's your next day off again?" I asked hopelessly.

"The day after tomorrow," Vivian said.

Sigh.

TWENTY-FOUR

"I F YOU THINK you know lobster rolls, you'd be wrong."
Thus began "The Cape Cod Foodie: In Search of the
Cape's Best Lobster Rolls."

After my little chat with Detective Peters in which Samantha Barnes, brilliant amateur sleuth, had attempted to
advise the good detective on her investigation and been
firmly put in her place, I'd spent the next hour or so calling
the lobster shacks and restaurants on my list to make sure
they'd be ready when the Cape Cod Foodie came calling.

Though Jenny edited the video to begin with that pithy
quote, I actually said it at the end of our day-long investigation, by which point I'd discovered the truth of the statement.

Here's what I thought I knew about lobster rolls: Lobster. Mayonnaise. Hot dog bun.

Here's what I learned about lobster rolls: One, not just
any old lobster meat. This is where it pays to be picky. Find
a place that uses fresh-daily, picked-on-the-premises claw
and tail meat.

Two, for a lobster roll with mayo, you don't have to be so
picky about the mayonnaise. It's just mayo from a jar. (Tip:
It's great as long as it's labeled "real" mayonnaise, so it's

not sweet. Sweet does not make it in a classic lobster roll with mayo.) The important thing is *not too much*. You don't want that delicious lobster overwhelmed.

Three, the roll is very important. You should be picky. It should be a New England split-top hot dog bun, preferably toasted on each side, either in a pan sizzling with melted butter or on a grill after brushing the roll with melted butter.

Four, that's it. Except for maybe a lettuce leaf between the roll and the lobster to look pretty and keep the bun from getting soggy.

I also learned that I'd been right about one thing. This lobster roll round-up was the best assignment ever.

My only concern the night before as I'd drifted off to sleep after a nice chatty call with Jason—in which I had once again successfully avoided discussing the Clara Foster case—had been that the glorious weather we'd been having might not hold. A lot of what we'd be filming would be outside and gray skies do not an attractive Foodie video make. But the brilliant blue skies had held, and if the day was a little chilly, that was okay. No one wanted to see the Cape Cod Foodie all hot and sweaty.

As Jenny and I had rolled down the mid-Cape highway, we sang sea shanties to put us in the mood, merrily asking what do you do with a drunken sailor early in the morning and cheerfully admitting that Cape Cod girls, they have no combs, they comb their hair with codfish bones. Then we'd climbed out at whatever fish pier, town dock, or roadside snack shack was next on the list, including Cap'n Tom's, of course, and Jenny would pan over some incredibly scenic harbor or bay or marina or fish market, take a close-up shot of me shoving a lobster roll in my face, and finally close with a clip of me asking the proprietor what made a great lobster roll.

I'd also learned that five lobster rolls in one day (well, really two-and-a-half lobster rolls, since I split them with Jenny) is really just about enough lobster roll for anyone.

But it wasn't all fun and games. After the last roll was eaten and the last shanty sung and we were heading back home, Jenny got down to business.

"So," she'd said as we rolled toward Fair Harbor, "we might as well get that little lobster roll with mango demonstration of yours done."

"Aw, c'mon, Jen," I said. "I'm all sweaty and stuff from standing outside for hours in the blazing hot sun."

"First of all, it wasn't hours," Jenny said. Which was true. It was maybe two hours max of actual filming.

"And second of all, the sun wasn't blazing hot." Also true. It had been a nice cool day with lots of soft fluffy clouds in a blue sky.

"And third of all, you just don't want to do this cooking demonstration thing." Also true. Perhaps the truest thing yet.

"Okay," I said grudgingly. "You win."

"I always win," Jenny said. Also true.

So we swung over to Snyder's Fish Market to pick out a couple of lobsters for the Cape Cod Foodie's first-ever cooking demonstration.

Snyder's is a very different animal from Cap'n Tom's. It's a much larger establishment for one thing, with a vast assortment of fish, including blues, stripers, halibut, and tuna laid out in a beautiful mosaic on long beds of ice. It's also air-conditioned, so it's always cool and clean with the sweet, briny scent of fresh fish. At the sound of the bell over the door, Mr. Snyder came out from the back room, wiping his hands on a dish towel. He greeted me as he always has and, I hope, always will.

"Well, look who's *heeyah*," he said in his broad New England accent, "little Samantha *Bahns*." It had been a very long time since I was little, but never mind. "And little Miss Jennifer Snow," he added. It had been a very long time since Jenny had been Miss Snow, too. "What can I do for you girls?"

And for a moment, Jenny and I were kids again on the

way back from the beach with our parents, shivering in our wet bathing suits as we stood by the lobster pool picking out *the very best* lobsters.

"We need a couple of chicken lobsters," I said. Which is what we've always called the smallish, one-and-a-half-pound lobsters on the Cape. I have no idea why. Maybe because it's easier than saying "smallish one-and-a-half-pound lobster."

"You want them alive or that I should steam 'em?"

"You can do the honors," I said. I've gotten squeamish in my old age.

Twenty minutes later we were on our way, a brown bag of freshly steamed lobbies in hand.

Delicious as our lobster roll experience that day had been, neither of us could face another one, so Jenny suggested picking up the Three Things from sailing club before heading back to Aunt Ida's house to film the first-ever Cape Cod Foodie cooking demonstration.

"The boys'll be starving," Jenny said. "They'll fall on those lobster rolls like wolves."

I wasn't so sure about that. At least not in terms of the one with mango. In my experience, children have very conservative tastes in food. I once made an absolutely delicious mac and cheese with real Irish cheddar for the Things. They, having been raised by the cooking-challenged Jenny, had only ever had the kind that came out of a box. They had regarded my version with great suspicion.

"Why isn't it orange?" Thing One asked, picking at it gingerly with his fork.

"Yeah," said Thing Two, "like it's *'sposed* to be."

Thing Three, only five at the time, just dug in like the champ he was. Maybe I'd try him on the mango lobster roll.

Turns out, cooking on camera is a lot easier than cooking in real life.

First, someone else, in this case Jenny, makes you presentable. She had me put on one of Aunt Ida's circa 1952 bib aprons, this one light blue with a red cherry print, and pinned up my hair in one of those cool "messy" buns that I can never manage myself.

"There," she said, pulling a few strands forward to frame my face. "Now you match the kitchen."

Which I took as a compliment. Aunt Ida's country kitchen—with its original splatter-painted wood floor, its corner cupboard holding her collection of Blue Willow china, and its long picture window graced by a window seat covered in a cheery yellow toile print—was warm and welcoming and, yes, a little old-fashioned. I figured if I matched that description, I couldn't complain.

Second, on film you get to do this amazing thing where you don't actually wait for hours for the lobster and mango salad to chill in the fridge. Jenny just films you putting it into the fridge while you say, "So we'll put this into the fridge to chill a bit" and then two seconds later she films you taking it out again, saying, "There, all nice and chilled!"

In the space of an hour I managed to make three utterly beautiful lobster rolls, if I do say so myself as shouldn't (to quote Aunt Ida). I began by picking the lobster meat out of Mr. Snyder's freshly steamed lobbies. (Tip: Don't chop the tail meat. Tear it by hand into small chunks.) Then I toasted my three New England hot dog rolls in melted butter, in the same frying pan I use to make my famous grilled cheese sandwiches, until they were golden brown on each side.

My first lobster roll was the classic: about a quarter pound of chilled lobster meat tossed with just enough mayonnaise to coat it lightly. Then a nice green lettuce leaf—in this case from a fresh head of Boston Bibb—tucked into the toasted bun and the lobster salad lightly mounded on top. Voilà.

The Connecticut-style lobster roll had been new to me until I'd tried it that day and become an instant convert. Again, it was super easy to make, except that the lobster meat (room temperature in this case) was tossed with melted butter instead of mayo. Some places even serve it with extra melted butter on the side, an addition I can only imagine Julia Child would heartily endorse.

And finally, I made the Cape Cod Foodie's very own lobster roll with mango, because I love, love, love a touch of mango in almost any salad, where the unexpected sweetness highlights the savory dressing. (Tip: "A touch" are the operative words here. Something around a 1:4 ratio of small mango cubes to lobster works well.)

Somehow Jenny would manage to whittle all this down to five minutes of me making it all look easy. Which, actually, it was.

I put the lobster shells into the fridge to use for making stock later and cleaned up the kitchen while Jenny rounded up the Three Things, who had been entertaining Diogi by playing keep away with the disgusting tennis ball. Diogi had dominated the game, apparently, leaping up and grabbing the ball as it sailed through the air.

"He should be playing outfield for the Ospreys," Thing One said admiringly.

What does it say about me that I was inordinately pleased and proud at Diogi's prowess? Probably that I had finally succumbed utterly to the dog's charms. Next thing you knew, I'd be calling him my fur baby.

I set out the three lobster rolls on the kitchen's pine table and suggested that I cut them in thirds so they could try some of each. This was my sneaky way of maybe getting a verdict on the mango masterpiece. This suggestion, however, was greeted with great derision, as it would involve "sharing," which was apparently absolutely out of the question.

Thing One, aka Ethan, who'd turned eleven two weeks earlier, apparently had right of first refusal as the oldest of the bunch. He went straight for the classic. This almost caused dissension in the ranks, but when I pulled out a little pitcher of melted butter to pour over the lobster chunks in the Connecticut roll, Thing Two, aka Eli, happily made that his choice. That left the lobster and mango roll for six-year-old Evan.

"What are those yellow things?" he asked doubtfully, pointing at the last roll on the platter.

"Um, pieces of mango," I admitted.

"Oh, great! Mango!" Evan said. "I was afraid they were yellow peppers. I *hate* yellow peppers. Unless they're grilled. They're okay if they're grilled. But I *love* mango."

"Evan," I said, "you are a foodie in the making."

TWENTY-FIVE

~~~~~~~~~~~~

I AM NOT ONE for the setting of alarms. Mostly because I find that when I do set an alarm, I tend to wake up about five times during the night just to make sure that I remembered to set the alarm. Also, Diogi *needs* usually mean he's nosing me out of bed most mornings before eight anyway. But there are situations that call for punctuality, and this was one of them.

When I'd decided that I would celebrate Jason's homecoming with a new haircut, I'd naturally consulted with Krista, she of the Beautiful Hair. With her help, I'd managed to snag an appointment at Hyannis's Blue Door Salon to have my hair "done." Apparently you're supposed to call at least two weeks in advance for appointments with a "stylist," but Krista, who'd been going there for years, made a call or two, and suddenly I was on for eight thirty Thursday morning with Krista's very own "stylist," Marina. So there I was with my cell phone's alarm buzzing in my ear at the godawful hour of seven in the morning.

About fifteen minutes later, Krista called me. "So," she said briskly when I answered. "What are you wearing to the Blue Door?"

Krista is not one for social niceties like "Hello, how are you, etc." She figures you're fine. And if you're not fine, she figures she doesn't want to hear about it anyway.

"I hadn't really thought about it," I said. "Whatever I can find that's clean, I guess." This tends to be my approach most days, which is why most days you will find me in jeans and a T-shirt. I have enough T-shirts and blue jeans to last me almost two weeks without doing laundry. I hate doing laundry.

"No," Krista said definitively. "You need to dress how you want your hair to look. Believe me, the stylist takes their cue from what you wear."

"Really?" I asked. "Does everybody know this except me?"

"Probably," Krista said. "Anyway, how do you want your hair to look?"

I thought about that for a moment. "Um, neat and clean?"

Krista sighed.

I gave up. "How do *you* think it should look?"

She didn't miss a beat. "Long, but not too long. Long enough to pull back into a ponytail, but not so long that when it's down, it just lies there. And with some feathered layers around your face to emphasize your cheekbones. And didn't you say something about wanting highlights?"

"Highlights?" I repeated, clueless.

"Blond streaks," Krista said with a little sigh. "We call them highlights."

"Yes," I said with all the dignity I could muster. "I would like highlights."

"Okay," she said, "but tell Marina to keep it subtle. Your hair is already a beautiful color." *It is? Mousy brown is a beautiful color?* "We just want a touch of gold around the face, I think." *A touch of gold?* "How does that sound?"

I was amazed she even asked. And the truth was, it sounded fantastic.

"It sounds fantastic," I said.

"Good. In that case, wear one of those floaty dresses of yours, with sandals, not flip-flops. You have sandals?"

"Yes, Krista," I said, sighing. "I have sandals." Which was true. When you're as tall as I am, you wear a lot of flats and a lot of sandals.

"Good," she said. "Wear those. Then just tell Marina what you want and let her take it from there. You're going to wow that man of yours when he gets home."

And suddenly I realized that Krista was not being bossy. Krista was trying to help. Krista honestly wanted me to be happy.

"Thanks, Krista," I said. "I really appreciate you helping me with this."

"Just don't mess it up," she said brusquely and rang off.

"Goodbye to you, too," I said as I put my cell back on the bedside table.

HYANNIS, THOUGH TECHNICALLY one of the seven "villages" that make up the "town" of Barnstable, is a bustling metropolis of some 14,000 inhabitants. It is the commercial, legal, and transportation hub of the Cape. It has a huge natural harbor, which makes it the largest recreational boating and second largest commercial fishing port on the Cape, behind only Provincetown. The town has two main shopping districts: the Cape Cod Mall, where Marina presumably awaited me at the Blue Door, and historic downtown Main Street, home of Thomas Bentley Auctioneers, where I would be heading after getting my hair did.

I was just a tad late to the Blue Door on account of because (as Evan would say) I always get lost in Hyannis. I'd never gotten lost in all the years I lived in New York City, but I always get lost in Hyannis. This is because of the rotaries. New York doesn't have rotaries. Hyannis has several, and all of them seemed to be on the way to the Cape Cod Mall. Rotaries freak me out. I never know who has the right of way and I am never entirely sure, even with the GPS, what "take the second exit off the rotary" actually means. Is where I got

onto the rotary considered the first exit? Or doesn't it count?
Anyway, I got it wrong a few times, so I was about fifteen
minutes late pulling into the mall parking lot.

It was a chilly, gray day, which on the Cape in summer
meant it was a shopping day. But at eight forty-five in the
morning, the mall was blessedly empty except for a few folks
at the Starbucks, so I was able to turkey trot my way to the
salon without dodging the crowds. At the entrance to the Blue
Door, which of course was an actual blue door, I took a calm-
ing breath (which never works) and pushed through.

Now, I'm no expert on Zen, but the minute I walked into
that salon, I was drowning in Zen. It was like the place was
doing my deep breathing for me. The lights were low and
some kind of soothing music that was mostly soft bells and
flutes embraced me. The walls were a pale rose, matching
the actual roses on the reception desk and the sheath dress
being worn by the young woman behind the desk. I now
understood why Krista had seen fit to advise me on my
presentation. I gave her silent thanks.

"Ms. Barnes?" the receptionist asked.

"That's me," I said, and immediately wished I had said,
"Yes, that is I," as befitted my surroundings.

The young woman smiled and pressed an invisible buzzer.
"Marina is on her way," she said.

Within seconds one of those long, leggy blondes that is
all they seem to grow in Eastern Europe came marching
into the reception area.

"Come," she said. "You follow me. Your friend Krista,
she already call, tell me what you need." Of course she had.

And that was sort of the way it went for the next hour
and a half. Marina told me what Krista said I needed and
then she did it. And when I walked out of the Blue Door, all
highlighted and blow-dried, I said another silent thank-you
to Krista. I looked stupendous. It wouldn't last, I knew. I
am absolutely incapable of managing one of those fat round
brushes with one hand and a blow dryer in the other. But at

least until the next time I washed my hair, I would look stupendous.

This confidence booster came in handy at my next stop, Thomas Bentley Auctioneers. I'd never been to the Bentley offices, though they were exactly what you would expect. All Boston Brahmin and furnished in the best possible taste, with antique Karastan rugs, deep leather club chairs, and side tables amply stocked with magazines like *Antiques & Fine Art* and *Town & Country*. Well, given my new haircut, I figured I could do Boston Brahmin as well as the next girl.

"Mr. Bentley, please," I said coolly to the young woman behind the reception desk, who could have been the twin sister of the young woman behind the reception desk at the Blue Door, except her sheath was cream-colored, not pink. I was once again tempted to say, "It is I, Samantha Barnes," but resisted the urge. "I'm Samantha Barnes," I said instead. "He's expecting me."

She smiled at me and waved me over to a leather club chair. "Of course, Ms. Barnes," she said. "His assistant will be out shortly."

I was flipping through *Town & Country*, taking in a story (I am not making this up) on fox hunting, or "the hunt" as the article termed it, in Litchfield County, Connecticut, when Bentley's assistant, Barbara, came in to collect me.

I closed the glossy pages of glossy people on glossy horses, and followed her down a long hall with deep ruby carpeting and into a small anteroom with a desk on which stood a nameplate reading "Barbara Smiley" and then through the connecting door to Thomas Bentley's office.

Bentley was sitting behind his desk, a vast mahogany table so restrained in design that I suspected it cost more than the gross national product of a small island nation. He stood and came out to greet me then ushered me over to a deceptively simple chair facing it. I didn't want to think what the chair cost.

"Please," he said, "have a seat." He paused. "And may I just say how well you look today."

Which I took as polite-speak for "You look stupendous, for once." But before I could say something self-deprecating in response, like "Take a picture because you'll never see me like this again," Helene's voice came back to me. *"Someday, Samantha, you may even learn how to accept a compliment with a simple thank-you."*

"Thank you," I said simply. *There, how hard was that?*

The rest of our conversation was all business. Not that it was much of a conversation. Bentley did most of the talking, and I did most of the listening. I'd already signed the contract for his auction house to handle the sale of the clock (which he insisted on calling "our" clock, which annoyed me), so all we had to do at this point was agree on a minimum below which we (by which Bentley meant *he*, as *I* was prepared to take anything) would not go.

"Not that I am at all worried about our clock reaching that minimum," he said. "Not after the very helpful publicity engendered by your appearance on *Antiques in the Attic.*"

As if somehow I should be proud of my part in that fiasco. It was like talking to Krista. Apparently, even in the rarified world of antiques, all publicity is good publicity. Well, at least I'd be getting something out of it, i.e., money.

Once we'd worked out the details of when the clock would come up in the auction rotation, Bentley stood to signal the end of our conversation, saying, "Well, thank you for your time, Samantha." In a nanosecond, Barbara was at the door to escort me out, and I realized she was trained to listen for these cues.

"Just one more thing, Thomas," I said. A shadow of annoyance crossed his face, but he sat back down behind his desk. Barbara disappeared discreetly.

"Of course," he said politely.

"You said at the memorial service that you recommended a rare book dealer to Clara Foster. I have some of my Aunt

Ida's books that I should probably have someone take a look at before I decide what to do with them," I said.

"I suggest Abraham Beame of Beame's Rare and Used Books in Wellfleet," Bentley said. "I recommended him to Ms. Foster. He's very good."

Of course. I should have thought of Beame's Books in the first place. I knew Beame's from once-a-summer pilgrimages made to the bookstore with my Grandpa Barnes. He would park me in the children's book section, where I would pore over classics like the original *Wizard of Oz* books or Robert Louis Stevenson's *Treasure Island* with its thrilling Wyeth illustrations. If I was very good and did not disturb my grandfather while he made his usual perusal of what seemed like hundreds of books on Cape Cod history, he would allow me to buy any book that took my fancy as long as the price soft-penciled on the frontispiece was under two dollars and fifty cents. My Grandpa Barnes took old-fashioned Yankee thrift seriously.

"Thank you, Thomas," I said, rising. "You've been very helpful."

"Not at all, Samantha," Bentley said, rising in turn. "It's been a pleasure."

And in a nanosecond, Barbara was there once again to escort me out of Bentley Auctioneers.

I was feeling pretty good as I drove back to Fair Harbor. I'd got my hair did, and I was a big step closer to being financially secure.

"Grumpy, old boy," I said, patting the truck's cracked plastic dashboard, "you may be back on the Tanners' farm sooner than you think."

TWENTY-SIX

~~~~~~~~~

THAT NIGHT I fell into bed exhausted and was almost glad that Jason didn't call. He seldom missed more than one night, so we'd catch up tomorrow. Maybe I'd send him a selfie of my new stupendous self.

I was wakened the next morning by Ciati and Diogi loudly demanding to be let out for necessary personal reasons. Ciati had a litter box, but clearly found it inferior to the privacy of Aunt Ida's tangle of bayberry bushes. She was an outside cat to her tiny core, though she seldom strayed farther than twenty feet from the front door. Diogi was even less prone to travel, finding his half-hour sniff-check of the property's perimeter more than enough excitement for the morning and requiring a nice little nap on his human's doorstep until she deigned to open it.

As usual, I used my morning window of alone time to make a cup of coffee and quickly peruse the *New York Times* and *Boston Globe* on my cell. I also checked the *Globe*'s hit rate for the Clara Foster video and had to blink twice to make sure I was reading it right. Well, that was gratifying.

I took a quick shower (wearing a seldom-used shower cap to protect my stupendous hair) and got dressed. In honor of my new hair, I even went so far as to pull on a white sleeveless cotton blouse and a really cute pair of shorts in a greeny-blue Hawaiian print pattern that I'd bought the year before at an end-of-summer sale and then never worn because, as it turned out, it really had been the end of summer. A quick look in the mirror assured me that, yes, those shorts were pretty darn short, but hey, there are a few advantages to being a very tall girl and very long legs tops the list.

As I was making the bed, I heard a car crunching into the driveway, followed by a moment's silence after whoever it was shut off the ignition, and then the slam of a car door. I was a little surprised that Diogi wasn't barking his head off. I wasn't expecting any of my friends, who are the only intruders into Diogi's domain who are afforded that courtesy. Everyone else is loudly warned off until his human commands him to shut up. But not this visitor. In fact, this visitor was being greeted by yelps of joy.

All was made clear when I peered out the door of the ell. It was Jason.

Jason being greeted with doggy abandon by Diogi, whose wagging tail was a blur of joy. Jason holding Ciati in his arms while she meowed with pleasure and sniffed his ear lovingly. My Jason. My first thought was, *Thank goodness I look stupendous.*

"Jason!" I cried. Well, maybe shrieked. I ran out to add myself to the group hug, though the animals weren't giving us a chance to do much more than a quick peck. Which was probably a good thing. I'm good for nothing once Jason gives me a proper kiss.

"This is such a great surprise! I thought you weren't supposed to be back for another week!" I grabbed the hand that wasn't holding Ciati and tried to pull him toward the ell. "Come on in!"

But Jason didn't move from his spot. And that was when

I realized that Jason had so far said exactly nothing in greeting to me. *Uh-oh.*

"What is it?" I asked, stopping short and looking at him closely for the first time. Jason did not look stupendous. Jason looked awful. His clothes were rumpled, he was unshaven, and his hair looked, well, like it always looked—a mess. He also looked like he hadn't slept all night. In fact, he looked like someone who had taken the overnight red-eye flight from California. Which no one in their right mind does without a really good reason.

"I got a call," he said dully.

"A call?" I repeated idiotically.

"Yes. From Vivvie Peters. Late last night your time. I took the red-eye from LA."

Vivian Peters called Jason late last night?

"Why did she call you late last night?" I asked. My brain was simply not taking any of this in.

"To tell me that Ed Captiva was under arrest."

"Oh, Jason, no," I gasped. "He can't be. I told her . . ."

I stopped myself just in time. I'd almost said, "I told her why it couldn't have been him." And that would have led to all sorts of questions along the lines of why I was talking to Detective Vivian Peters about *anything* connected to this case. Which would lead back to the fact that I had started the whole investigation into Clara's death in the first place and now, it seemed, in getting Ed accused of her murder.

I needed time to think. And Jason needed time to calm down. I did the only thing I could think of. I made us some grilled cheese sandwiches.

B ETTER?" I ASKED as Jason pushed himself away from the kitchen table.

"Much," he said.

I had been sitting across from him, silently watching

him devour two grilled cheese sandwiches to my one. We'd literally not said a word to each other since I'd steered him into the kitchen and put a bowl of my famous (not) honey-roasted walnuts in front of him to munch on while I made the sandwiches. The man had been in a kind of shock that, in my experience, could only be countered by highly caloric sustenance.

He looked at me across the table and smiled, and the icy fear in my heart began to melt.

"I'm sorry, Sam," he said. "This wasn't the homecoming I had planned."

Was it wrong that I was quietly happy that Jason had had a nice homecoming planned?

"Don't be silly," I said softly, reaching across the table and twining my fingers with his. "I'm just glad you're back."

Jason pulled his hand gently from mine. "I'm not back," he said quietly.

"You're not back," I repeated dully.

He shook his head. "I fly back to Santa Barbara tomorrow at the crack of dawn. I'm only here for the day, to talk to Vivvie."

Not back. Not here to see you, Sam. To talk to Vivian about Ed. And once again, I was ashamed of myself. *His cousin is in deep trouble and you want a romantic reunion?*

"Of course," I said, trying not to sound disappointed.

"Not that she can tell me much," Jason acknowledged. "But she has agreed to let me see Ed and talk to his lawyer. It's important that he knows he's not alone in this."

Jason pushed himself back from the table and stood. Diogi scrambled up from his patch of sunlight hopefully. There is nothing Diogi enjoys more than whizzing around in the Harbor Patrol Grady-White, sitting forward in the bow, nose into the wind, ears streaming back, and what I can only describe as a smile on his big, goofy face. Maybe the Man with the Boat was going to take us for a ride? *Not gonna happen, boy.*

Jason went over and rubbed Diogi gently on the head. "Not gonna happen, boy," he said with a rueful smile. Jason knows Diogi as well as I do.

"Okay," he said, turning to me, "I'm off. I've got a lot to do today. But can I stay here tonight? The exchange guy from Santa Barbara is still in my apartment at the Patrol building."

You have to ask? I wanted to wail. What I said was, "Of course." Then I added, "I'll make dinner." Because apparently Jason might not expect that either.

"Thanks," he said tiredly. "Sounds good." He walked over to the kitchen door, then stopped and looked back at me.

"Sam?" he said.

I just looked at him.

He shook his head and clearly decided not to say whatever it was he'd been going to say. "Tonight," he said. "We can talk tonight, Sam. We need to talk."

Oh god, oh god, oh god.

TWENTY-SEVEN

~~~~~~~~

I RESOLVED NOT TO think about the scariest four words in the history of relationships. I reminded myself that at least twice in the short conversation Jason and I had already had, I'd made it all about me, about us, when it had been all about something much more important—a man's life. *Time to grow up, Sam*, I told myself.

Aside from providing Jason with another sustaining meal that evening (Steak on the grill, maybe? With corn on the cob and a tomato salad?), I determined that the best thing I could do to help him, to help Ed, was to stay out of the case altogether. I'd done nothing with my meddling but put Jason's cousin at risk.

And, I admit, I was rather stunned by what felt like Vivian Peters's betrayal. Yes, I had been the one who'd shared the information with her that strongly suggested that the fire in Clara's house had been deliberately set by someone else. But I had thought that because it was Ed who'd offered that information, she would agree that it made him an unlikely candidate for the role of Clara's killer. And then she'd gone off and a day later arrested him. Without even letting me know she was going to do so. So yes, I was feeling a little betrayed.

Which I knew was irrational. You don't share information in a murder investigation with the caveat that it can only be used to advance your own agenda. As Vivian herself had warned me, it had been my obligation to share that information. And hers *not* to share the results of her investigation with me, though she had seen fit to let Jason know. *That Vivvie's gonna be waiting a long time for her sailing lesson.*

So much for growing up.

B EAME'S RARE AND Used Books is the kind of bookstore that dreams are made of. Occupying a central spot on Wellfleet's Main Street, it is housed in a three-story white clapboard building that, according to a plaque on the façade, had for over a century served the town as Ketchum's General Store.

As I walked into the bookstore that day, I gazed around me and was pleased to note that nothing had changed. Not the scarred pine floors, not the pressed tin ceiling with its incongruous fluorescent lights, not the acres and acres of bookshelves covering every conceivable subject from art to zoology.

I'd called ahead to see if it might be possible for Mr. Beame to look over Aunt Ida's Golden Age mysteries. The phone had been answered by Abraham Beame himself, and though his voice was not young, it was exceedingly energetic. When I'd asked if it might be convenient to meet that day, Mr. Beame had said, "Of course, anytime, anytime. I'm always here. Just toddle along to my office in the back of the store. Always in. Always in."

Encouraged by this welcome, I'd asked if dogs were permitted in the store. As long as I was going to Wellfleet, I was hoping to take Diogi through the town's beautiful White

Cedar Swamp, with its wooden boardwalk winding through one of the few cedar forests left on the Cape.

"Of course, of course," Mr. Beame said cheerfully. "I'd lose a lot of walk-in business if I didn't allow dogs, wouldn't I? Yes, a lot of business."

I wondered if Mr. Beame repeated everything he said. As it turned out, he pretty much did.

I'd packed up my books in an old cardboard box, and Diogi and I headed over to Mr. Beame's shop. After wandering through a maze of shelves stuffed with books and the occasional surprise nook set up with an old armchair and rickety table for comfortable browsing, Diogi and I finally stumbled upon a door marked "Office." I knocked and the same cheerful voice from our phone call called out, "Come in, come in!"

Whatever I had been expecting after wandering through the store itself, Mr. Beame's office was not it. No precarious stacks of dusty books on chairs, no overflowing, haphazard shelves. No pigeonhole desk with untidy piles of paper. No. This was the office of a man of business. Glass-fronted bookcases with carefully lettered subject labels inserted in brass holders housed hundreds of books, many of them leather bound, their titles stamped in gilt on the spines. Mr. Beame's desk was a sleek Scandinavian number, with an equally sleek Aero chair behind it. Seated in that chair was Mr. Beame himself, who did look like I'd expected. Early seventies, I guessed, rather tall and quite trim, with fluffy gray hair that stood up in odd cowlicks here and there, and sharp gray eyes behind half-moon reading glasses teetering on a long nose. He was wearing an ancient blue blazer over a checked shirt and polka-dot bow tie.

He smiled, stood, and came around the desk to greet me.

"Ms. Barnes," he said, shaking my hand. "It's a pleasure to meet the Cape Cod Foodie in person. A pleasure. I so enjoy your food videos. So enjoy them. I always learn something, and you always make me laugh."

"Thank you," I said. Gosh, I was getting good at this simple thank-you business.

He bent down and politely offered his hand for Diogi to sniff. Diogi, equally politely, did so. Mr. Beame smiled up at me.

"He's a grand fellow," he said, rubbing Diogi's head at just the right spot between his big, floppy ears and earning my dog's forever love. "Absolutely grand."

Mr. Beame motioned me to one of the two wooden captain's chairs in front of the desk. Diogi settled himself at my feet, gave an enormous yawn, and promptly fell asleep. Mr. Beame sat opposite us and proceeded in the space of about fifteen minutes to go through the dozen or so mysteries I'd brought, muttering quietly to himself ("a little foxing here, but not too bad . . . original dust jacket, pristine") and placing each book carefully on one of two piles on the desk, one rather taller than the other.

Placing a hand on the taller pile, he said, "These can go into the used book section. They're only worth a few dollars each, just a few dollars, but they'll sell like hot cakes. Mysteries always do. Always sell like hot cakes."

Then, putting his hand on the other pile, he said, "These first editions, though, I could sell tomorrow for a few hundred dollars, yes, a few hundred, I think, to my Golden Age collectors. Particularly your first U.S. edition of Dorothy Sayers's *Whose Body?* Yes, particularly that one. I think you might do quite well with that one, quite well. It seems your aunt was quite the collector."

"Actually, she was quite the hoarder," I said.

Mr. Beame laughed. "Often the same thing," he said, nodding. "Yes, often the same thing."

Once Mr. Beame and I had dispensed with the necessary financial details about Aunt Ida's hoard (or collection, depending on your point of view), he walked over to one of his glass-enclosed bookcases, opened it, and lifted out a slim volume, which he then handed to me.

"I hope you will accept this, Ms. Barnes," he said shyly, "as a token of my esteem for your work and your wit." My *wit*? He made me sound like Dorothy Parker.

He held out the original 1960 edition of Peg Bracken's classic *The Compleat I Hate to Cook Book*.

And now it was my turn to laugh.

"I accept it with pleasure, Mr. Beame," I said. "This was, I kid you not, my mother's favorite cookbook." I did not add that it was also her only cookbook. "I will add it to my collection," I said, grinning. "Right next to my Escoffier."

That was supposed to pass as wit but failed utterly. A shadow passed over Mr. Beame's face. "I appraised an Escoffier recently," he said. "A beautiful book. Beautiful. Unfortunately, it is said to have perished in a house fire."

Said to have perished?

"You mean Clara Foster's Escoffier?" I asked.

Mr. Beame looked at me in surprise. "You knew Clara Foster?"

"We met," I said. "She showed me the Escoffier." I decided to take the bull by the horns. "But why did you say 'said to have perished'?"

Mr. Beame sighed. "Well, you see, Ms. Barnes, a week before her death, Ms. Foster called me. Apparently, Thomas Bentley had recommended that I appraise her cookbook collection. I was happy to do so. It was a fine collection, and I told her then that the value of most of the books was about the same as the original appraisal, done some ten years ago, but that the Escoffier was currently in great demand. I'd heard there was a private collector very much interested in acquiring a good copy, and if she was interested, I could try to find out more. But she said no, she had other plans for the books. And then, two days later, well, you know what happened."

It was a measure of Mr. Beame's distress, I thought, that not once had he repeated himself throughout this explanation.

"But why did you say the book 'is *said* to have perished'?" I persisted. "I saw the collection after the fire, Mr. Beame, and believe me, there was nothing left but a pile of ash and wet pulp."

"Ah," he said. "But are you very sure that the Escoffier was part of that pile? Because the word now is that the collector is off the market. He apparently has his Escoffier."

TWENTY-EIGHT

~~~~~~~~~~~~~~~~

WELL, I HADN'T seen that one coming.

"Sorry, Diogi, old buddy," I said as we climbed back into Grumpy. "No scenic tramp through the cedars today. I've got some serious rethinking to do."

My best serious rethinking has always been done walking along a beach. Today, the westerly breeze would be blowing onshore over the waters of Cape Cod Bay, which would be welcome on this warm day. It would have been nice just to hit Quanset Beach, Fair Harbor's public bay beach, but I had Diogi with me, and, quite sensibly, dogs are not allowed on Fair Harbor's crowded public beaches during "the season." So instead we headed, with only a twinge of guilt, to Clara Foster's house. Or rather, to Clara Foster's beach.

I considered parking at the nature reserve and walking the half mile or so down the road to Clara's path to the beach. It would take only ten minutes or so. But I'm never really comfortable walking Diogi on the side of the road, so I scrapped that idea and just pulled into Clara's driveway. If the Conservancy wanted to sue me for trespassing, so be it.

As I'd hoped, the house was empty, the police tape gone. The soot-blackened windows had been cleaned, though, and great lumpy garbage bags were piled next to the driveway ready for their trip to the dump. So the cleaners had come and gone, sweeping out Clara's life. I shivered in spite of the warmth of the day. Diogi seemed to feel my mood and stuck so close to my side as we made our way across the dunes to the beach that I took him off his leash. He wasn't going anywhere.

The tide was dead low, with literally half a mile of sand flats reaching out into the Bay before finally reaching the ebbed waters. About 400 yards out, I could see two figures bending over the oyster beds. I assumed these must be the Joys doing whatever it is that oyster farmers did. Otherwise, the beach proper, well away from any public access, was empty except for a flock of whimbrels scurrying along the flats on toothpick legs.

This was too much for Diogi, who suddenly made a break for it. Diogi considers it his sacred duty to, at all times and in all places, try to catch shorebirds. Not that he ever does. First of all, they can outrun him on the soft, wet sand. And they can fly if need be. Second of all, he is easily distracted, as he was in this case by a fiddler crab side-walking along the edge the marsh grass. A quick yelp told me the crab had bested him.

Suitably chastened, Diogi returned and agreed to walk sedately with me up and down the edge of the beach proper as I did my serious rethinking.

Had I, in fact, seen the Escoffier in the pile of ruined books in Clara's house? It had been the only leather-bound volume in the collection. Of all the bindings, it would have been the likeliest to survive, at least in part, even if its pages had been destroyed by fire or water damage.

I tried to picture the sad heap of ruined books in my mind's eye. It seemed to me that there had been no twisted scraps of leather, no traces of gilt lettering sparkling through the gray ashes. But I couldn't be sure. I supposed I could ask Vivian Peters if any of the books on that pile had been saved as forensic evidence, but I doubted very much that they had. And besides, I was still in no mood to talk to Vivian Peters. And, I reminded myself, I'd vowed to stay out of the Clara Foster case. At least for today, at least while Jason was home.

In my distraction, I had not noticed Diogi trotting out over the sand flats toward the oyster farmers and those wonderfully smelly oyster cages. I hurried after him, my sneakers sinking into the soft, wet sand.

"Diogi," I shouted, "you come back here."

Needless to say, Diogi did not come back.

"Not to worry," the larger of the two figures called to me. "He can't do any harm."

I waved my thanks and walked a bit more sedately toward my goal, my now-soaked sneakers squelching attractively. I could see upon closer inspection that the two figures were indeed male and female, though both wore rubber deck boots and the yellow waterproof overalls known as fishing bibs over sun-bleached olive T-shirts. The woman had straight brown hair pulled back at the nape of her neck and a friendly, if not beautiful, face. Her husband had a shaved head, a full beard, and kind eyes. Without even talking to them, I could understand why Clara had a soft spot for the young couple, who looked to be still in their twenties. They seemed to be delighted with Diogi's company and he with theirs if his rapidly wagging tail was any indication.

"Sorry about that," I said as I finally got close enough to grab Diogi's collar.

"Don't be silly," the young woman said. "He's a sweet fellow."

"But your oysters . . ." I began.

The man laughed. "If he can get into those cages, more

power to him," he said. The two dozen or so low metal cages draped with seaweed looked like they would withstand a man with a crowbar let alone a sniffing dog.

"I'm Samantha Barnes," I said. "And you must be the Joys."

"Yes," the young woman said. "Elisha and Dave." There was just a little question in her voice, a little surprise that I knew who they were.

"I knew Clara Foster slightly," I said by way of explanation. "She thought very highly of you."

A shadow passed over their faces.

"And we thought very highly of her," Paul Joy said.

"We were so sad to miss her memorial service," Elisha added softly.

"We didn't miss it, Leesh," her husband said with a shade of bitterness. "We weren't invited."

Elisha looked at him and cocked her head slightly toward me as if to say, *Not in front of a stranger.*

"It's okay," I said. "You didn't miss much. It seems like there wasn't a lot of love lost between Clara and her niece."

"Between her niece and anyone," Paul muttered. So they knew about Jean Wilkinson's little plan to contest Clara's will.

"*Anyway,*" Elisha said, "we're sad to have lost Clara. She was a good friend."

"And she was a real cheerleader for what we're doing here," Paul added.

"I'd like to know more about it," I said. It wasn't for nothing that I was known as the Cape Cod Foodie. "All I know about oysters is that Cape Cod has the best."

Paul laughed, a good, throaty laugh, and said, "That's a good place to start. Cape Cod oysters have a unique flavor profile because they tend to grow in waters that are a mix of salt and fresh. So they are justifiably popular and always have been." He paused.

"I hear a 'but' there," I said.

He nodded, "But that popularity has often led to over-fishing of wild oysters."

"And shoreline development that destroys their habitat hasn't helped," Elisha chimed in.

"On top of that," I added, not wanting to sound like a complete know-nothing, "oysters filter our waters."

"Exactly," Elisha said. "An adult oyster can filter up to fifty gallons of water a day."

"At any rate," Paul said, "we've got a tremendous opportunity here to overturn the effects of overfishing. But the upfront costs are huge. Clara understood that. It looks like now we'll be able to add another acre of seed beds this season, probably in flip beds, which we've never been able to do before. She was a real friend."

So Roland must have outlined the possibility of the proceeds from the sale of Kit's paintings and possibly an insurance payout for the cookbooks. But the Joys made no explicit mention of Clara's bequest to them, of course. Cape Codders do not talk about their finances. It is considered slightly more unseemly than talking about the state of your bowels. This, I understood, was as close as they could come to acknowledging Clara's generosity in front of a relative stranger. I was touched that they felt that obligation.

Diogi by this time had grown bored and had started back toward shore, having spotted a woman walking along the shoreline with two golden retrievers, who, in his opinion, would definitely want to play with him.

"Argh," I said. "Looks like I'm going to have to go after my dog again."

"Oh, that's just Summer," Elisha said, waving over to the woman on the shore, who, I noticed, did not wave back.

"Summer?" I asked. "Summer Robinson?"

Clara Foster's neighbor, Summer Robinson. The Summer that Clara had said could "go to hell" if she didn't like

Clara helping the Joys. The Summer who by her own admission had been at Clara's house the night of the fire and later, when it was too late to save her neighbor, called in the alarm.

Here was a suspect made in heaven.

TWENTY-NINE

_{~~~~}

Y ES, SUMMER ROBINSON," Elisha said. "Do you know her?"

I shook my head. "Clara mentioned her, that's all," I said.

No way was I going to tell the Joys that Summer had apparently objected to Clara's plan to help them.

"Anyway, Summer won't mind the pooch," Elisha said. "She's a big dog lover."

"To put it mildly," Paul muttered under his breath.

Nonetheless, I said a hurried goodbye and dashed off to collar Diogi, who was already at the butt-sniffing stage of doggie introductions.

"I'm sorry about that," I said as I pulled Diogi away from his new friends. "I usually like to ask the owners before allowing my dog to play with their pets."

I tried to smile ingratiatingly at Summer Robinson. But my smile had no discernible effect. The woman looked to be in her late sixties, tall and thin, almost bony, with long, straight salt-and-pepper hair parted in the middle and hanging limply around a weathered face bearing what I suspected was a permanent look of discontent.

"I am *not* Bear and Alba's owner," she said primly. "I am their companion and caregiver."

I was confused. "So they're not your pets?"

"Certainly not," she replied waspishly. "They are *my* companions and caregivers."

Uh-oh. I was beginning to understand.

"Yes, of course," I stammered. "I'm sorry if saying 'owner' and 'pet' might not feel right to you."

I was doing my best, and fortunately Summer seemed to be somewhat mollified. Her face softened and I could almost see a nice person in there.

"We are all on a journey of learning," she said, nodding her head graciously. "By all means, free your companion to play with Bear and Alba. Ever since that horrible person started kidnapping canine companions, we've decided it is best for them not to wander freely outside the house without my oversight, so they are eager to play."

So I freed my companion, which meant I was going to have to stand there and chat with this woman while the dogs had a playdate. Might as well do a little discreet pumping while I was at it.

"Do you live nearby?" I asked. Like I didn't know.

"Yes, just back there behind that dune," she said, turning to point about 500 yards down the beach. "You can just see my house."

Sure enough, I could just see the twin of Clara's house in a little hollow behind the rough dune grass waving in the breeze.

"So you must have been the one who spotted the fire at Clara Foster's house," I said.

She nodded. "Bear had been having a restless night, which I now realize must have been because his sensitive nose had detected smoke, and woke me whining to go out about one o'clock in the morning. That was when I saw the flames in Clara's kitchen window."

"It was such a tragedy, Clara's death," I said.

Curiosity got the better of Summer. "You knew her?"

"Oh, yes," I said, as if we'd been friends forever. "In fact, I saw her the day before she died. We were talking about the Joys." I nodded toward the young couple out on the flats. "She said she was going to help them. I wasn't sure that was such a good idea . . ." Again, fingers crossed behind my back.

"It absolutely was *not* a good idea," Summer said, the discontent back on her face. "I told her that. Leave that house and the land it's on to those, those *kids*? They're nice enough, but I knew they'd just sell it to some spec builder who'd tear down the house and put up an energy-hogging McMansion on some invasive grass lawn covered with fertilizer that will poison the bay, just like that niece of hers wanted to do."

Good lord. Was that what Summer thought Clara had been planning? To give the house and the two acres it sat on to the Joys?

"She told you that was what she was going to do?" I asked.

Summer backtracked awkwardly, as if she wished she hadn't said anything. "Well, no, she wouldn't tell me exactly *how* she planned to help them, no matter how hard I pressed her."

I could just see Clara quietly enjoying driving this busybody neighbor crazy.

"Clara and I weren't close," Summer continued, "not like Kit and I were. I think she resented our friendship. She wouldn't even give me something to remember Kit by after she passed on."

Ah, now we're getting to the crux of the matter, I thought. But to get her back on track, I prodded her a bit. "So you thought Clara was going to help the Joys by giving them the house?"

"What else did she have to give those kids?" Summer said, then paused and added, with what I thought was very inappropriate satisfaction, "At any rate, she didn't have time to do it. All the land, including the house and its lot, goes to the Conservancy, just like it was supposed to."

I couldn't help myself. "She never intended to give the Joys her property," I said. "All she wanted was to leave the Joys some books and artwork."

Summer looked stunned. Nobody, I thought, likes to find out they aren't the know-it-all they thought they were. *Note to self, Sam.* But Summer really did look stricken, and suddenly I felt sorry for the woman.

"Most people don't like to talk about things like wills," I offered as explanation. "Nobody likes contemplating their own death. I'm surprised she told you about it."

Summer looked uncomfortable at that, but said nothing.

"She didn't tell you about her plans, did she?" I said, taking a shot in the dark. "So how did you find out?"

Summer's face crumpled.

"I saw an e-mail," she admitted miserably. "I was bringing her a brochure about dune remediation to prevent coastal erosion." Suddenly Summer's eyes began to gleam with missionary fervor. "It's so important. Sand dunes are natural barriers against powerful waves and storms and they're a rich habitat for coastal vegetation and wildlife. We need to defend them like the national treasures they are, especially against their biggest threat, continued residential construction."

I didn't disagree with her on any of this, but it seemed to me we were getting off topic.

"And did you give her the brochure?" I asked.

"Well, no, not exactly," Summer admitted. "I knocked at the back door, but when she didn't answer, I figured she was upstairs napping—she'd been napping a lot lately—so I just let myself in—nobody locks their doors around here during the day—and put the brochure on the kitchen island next to her laptop. And then I saw it, this e-mail to her lawyer that I guess she'd been working on. It said she wanted to make a change to help the Joys. She didn't say what exactly, but I knew. I knew she was angry at her niece about wanting to sell the house and its part of the property. She'd been so mad the day they had that fight that she told me about her plan to only allow Jean life tenancy. But I do a lot of work with the Conservancy and I know you can't do that for anyone other than family members. For the Joys to have the house, she'd have to leave it to them outright, figuring those kids wouldn't sell. But I knew they would and . . ." Clara caught herself and stopped.

"And?" I said.

"I didn't mean to read it. But the laptop was open, and I saw the words 'change my will' in the e-mail, and I just couldn't help reading the rest."

My mother the investigative journalist has this theory that confession is a vastly underappreciated human need, except perhaps by the Catholic Church. Well, far be it from me to deny Summer that need.

"Of course you couldn't," I hastened to reassure her. *Because you're a nosey parker*, I didn't add. "I understand."

"Well, Clara didn't," Summer said bitterly. "She found me there, looking at the e-mail. I didn't even hear her come down the stairs. We had a big fight. She called me a snoop and I called her a fool. I thought she was betraying our commitment to the environment. I thought the worst of her and she let me think it," she finished miserably. "And now it's too late."

Too late for what? I wondered. Plus, something else was nagging at me. Why all this concern about Clara's will? Even if Clara changed it, it might be decades before she died. Why had Summer been so worried about something so far down the road? For that matter, if Clara Foster had been so keen to help the Joys, help that they clearly needed sooner rather than later, why leave them the artwork and the cookbooks when she died? Why hadn't she sold them herself and given the proceeds to the Joys immediately?

She could have sold them in a minute, but she'd decided to hold on to at least the cookbooks until she died. *Until she died.*

And that's when I realized why, the first time I'd met her, Clara had reminded me of my Aunt Ida. The yellowish cast to her skin and the whites of her eyes. The breathlessness after the short walk to the huckleberry patch. The frequent naps. The loss of appetite. The back pain. The itchy skin. All symptoms my Aunt Ida had had in the last few months before she succumbed to pancreatic cancer.

Now I understood the shadow that had passed over Clara's face when she'd said, "You can't take it with you, right?" And her words about Kit's death, which had seemed so callous at the time. "She would have hated dying from some crappy cancer or something," she'd said. "All the tubes and doctors."

I couldn't be sure, but it seemed to me that Clara Foster had been dying and that she knew it. She hadn't sold the Escoffier because she wanted to hold on to that precious possession, to have it close to her until she died, which was perhaps only a matter of months away. I was comforted by the fact that on the day she died, she'd been lovingly turning its pages.

But something else was bothering me. Why had Summer been so worried about Clara changing her will when, as far as she knew, Clara had a long life ahead of her? I doubted that Clara had told her about her diagnosis. Clara, in her pride, hadn't confided her illness even to her friend Florence Tanner. Clara had a dread of "people pitying you."

"How did you know Clara was dying?" I asked her gently. "What else did you see? Did you look at a few other e-mails?"

"No!" Summer said, genuinely shocked. "I told you, I saw that e-mail by accident."

"So how did you know?" I asked again.

"There was a brochure on the kitchen island next to the

laptop," Summer admitted, almost in a whisper. "It was called 'Living with Stage Four Pancreatic Cancer.' I know about pancreatic cancer. A cousin of mine died from it. There's no going back from stage four. I knew that at the most Clara had maybe a few months left."

Summer paused, then added in bitter self-recrimination, "And all I could think about was her leaving that house to those kids."

And without another word, Summer Robinson turned and walked away, her canine companions following her faithfully.

Diogi, abandoned by his new friends, returned to my side, and looked at me questioningly.

"That's right, bud," I said. "Walk's over."

THIRTY

M Y CONVERSATION WITH Summer Robinson was buzzing around in my head like a persistent house-fly, but I'd promised Krista the copy for a feature that she insisted on calling "Clambake Confidential" by the end of the day, and for Krista a deadline means exactly that. You meet it or you're dead.

Usually my work is totally absorbing. I can sit for hours typing away on my laptop, happily choosing just the right words to describe a charming, homey restaurant or a particularly pleasing dish. I literally have nothing else on my mind. But that day I had a lot on my mind. Nonetheless, I managed to describe and send off to the boss lady my vision of the perfect Bring Your Own Lobster Cape Cod Clambake, crowned by the Best Blueberry Buckle in the World for dessert.

Which reminded me of Clara, which reminded me of something I didn't want to think about. Which was Vivian Peters, who was probably at this very moment telling Jason about my role in making his cousin a prime suspect in Clara's murder.

But maybe I could fix that. Summer had believed that Clara was going to leave her property to a young couple who, she also believed, would sell the land to developers. Summer knew that Clara was dying. Had she convinced herself that she had a small window of opportunity to stop what she believed would be an environmental disaster for her little corner of the Cape?

I needed to talk to Vivian Peters about my conversation with Summer. But more than that, I needed Vivian Peters to talk to me. I needed to know what evidence she had on Ed. Maybe she'd tell me in exchange for what I'd learned about Summer. But Vivian had made it clear that I couldn't expect her to spill about an ongoing investigation. I needed something I could give her that would encourage a grateful exchange of information. But all I had to offer were a few hunches about some environmentally concerned woman. *Oh wait. You do have something else to offer her, Sam.* Tomorrow was Saturday and Vivian's day off. If the fine weather held, it would be a perfect day for a sail. And Vivian wanted another sailing lesson.

A quick text, an equally quick response, and it was all arranged.

Now all I had to worry about was what Jason had meant by "We need to talk."

To avoid thinking about that, I turned to distractions Number Two and Three, home improvement and retail therapy. The Fourth of July picnic was coming up fast, and I was obsessed with the idea of having the picnic on the screened-in porch. Now that I was (almost) flush with cash, I thought it was time to give Miles a break from fixing up Aunt Ida's house. (*Your house, Sam.*) First I called the handyman Miles had recommended and arranged for him to come by the next day for an estimate. Then Grumpy, Diogi, and I chugged over to Taylor's Hardware, where I intended to buy the best picnic table they had.

Over the years, Taylor's Hardware had morphed into much more than the original jumble of plumbing supplies and stacks of paint cans I'd known as a kid. To compete with the big box stores in Hyannis, it had grown into a full-fledged "home and garden shop" where customers from all over the mid-Cape came for everything from Le Creuset pots to, yes, picnic tables. In fact, now the store's official name was Taylor Home and Hardware. Of course, nobody in Fair Harbor calls it that. To us it will always be Taylor's Hardware.

Wandering through the outside space that now housed the garden center and what was rather grandly termed "patio furniture," I was greeted and advised by Andrew Taylor himself, an old fishing buddy of my father's and about as contrary a man as you would ever want to meet. When I told him I wanted a picnic table with two benches but that the benches shouldn't be attached, he said flatly, "Then that's not a picnic table."

"Not a picnic table?" I said blankly.

"Nope," Mr. Taylor said. "That's just a table and two benches."

"But I want to use it outside," I said, "or actually on a porch, where it's going to be exposed to some weather."

"Then that's an outdoor dining set," Mr. Taylor informed me.

"Okay," I said, giving up. "I want an outdoor dining set."

"We got those," Mr. Taylor said.

The conversation went on along those lines, but by the end, Mr. Taylor decided that I wanted an acacia wood outdoor dining set consisting of an eight-foot-long table and two benches. With a couple of chairs at each end, I figured it could seat ten people, so I said okay. Not that I really had a choice.

"You want this delivered?" Mr. Taylor asked as he wrote me up.

"How much would that be?" I am, after all, a true daughter of the Cape.

"Free for you, Samantha," he said without looking at me. No sense in embarrassing everybody.

"Then, yeah, thanks," I said, equally matter-of-fact.

"Okay," he said, making a note. "You live in Ida Barnes's old place, right?"

"Right," I said.

And then Mr. Taylor surprised me. "The wife and I like those Cape Cod Foodie videos of yours," he said, looking up from his notepad. "That one where you made the lobster rolls was a hoot. We made the one with the mango. It was real tasty."

"Thanks, Mr. Taylor," I said, trying not to sound surprised. "I'm glad you liked it."

He nodded and moved on. "The table and benches will be out to Ida's place by three today."

Try getting that kind of service at a big box store.

And finally, distraction Number Four, menu planning. Once home again, I took a yellow legal pad and my companions and caregivers, aka Diogi and Ciati, down to the dock, where I sat cross-legged on the sun-warmed wood jotting down ideas while the animals entertained themselves playing hide-and-seek in the marsh grass. For the clambake itself, in addition to everybody's lobsters, we'd have a mess of longneck soft-shell clams, known locally as steamers, which would be dunked in individual ramekins of melted butter. In honor of Jason's heritage and Jenny's conviction that meat must be had, I'd also serve several large coils of Portuguese linguica sausage. Of course, we'd have corn on the cob slathered with butter, and steamed potatoes from the clambake, also slathered with butter. And then, to finish, the Best Blueberry Buckle in the World. I almost swooned over the perfection of this menu.

The arrival of my "outdoor dining set" at three o'clock

as promised was the cherry on top of my afternoon, to use a culinary metaphor. It fit perfectly along the back of the porch, leaving plenty of room for my imaginary peacock chair and the future "outdoor lounge furniture" I'd seen at Taylor's Hardware and now coveted.

S O I WAS feeling somewhat better when Jason rolled back into the drive in his rental car around six that evening. The good news was that he looked somewhat less stressed than when he'd arrived at six that morning. The bad news was that he greeted Diogi and Ciati with significantly more enthusiasm than he greeted me. Or at least that's how it felt.

Giving me another one of those quick pecks, he said, "You mind if I take a shower?"

"Be my guest," I said, trying hard to sound casual. He gave me a quick, puzzled glance, which made me suspect that it had come out sulky instead.

I tried again. "Steak and grilled vegetables sound good?"

"I'll take the steak," he said with a ghost of his old grin. "You can have the vegetables."

I smiled back and he trudged toward the house, Diogi and Ciati following closely lest he disappear again and never return. I had to admit, I kind of felt the same anxiety.

While Jason made himself presentable, I went into the kitchen and got the steak out of the fridge. (Tip: For a perfect medium to medium-rare steak, bring the meat to room temperature before grilling it. The major cause of those burned on the outside, bloody on the inside steaks is cold meat slung on a hot grill. Room temperature meat on a medium grill should give you a nice char on the outside and lovely deep pink meat shading into a line of ruby in the middle.) Then I pulled my dog-eared copy of Clara Foster's *Simply American* off the cookbook shelf in the corner cupboard so I could check her recipe for grilled vegetables. Just looking at the familiar cover twisted my heart a little. I hoped Clara was somewhere looking down at me and disapproving of the way I sliced the zucchini. While I prepped the vegetables, Diogi snored softly and Ciati did that endless cat-grooming thing with her little pink tongue.

I found Sade on my music app and drifted along to the world's most romantic songs while I sliced the eggplant and zucchini. I was softly crooning "he's a smoooth operator" off-key to myself when I felt Jason's arms encircling me from behind. I forgot all about the eggplant and zucchini. That's how hot Jason is. I leaned back against him, and we swayed silently together until the end of the song. I realized at that moment that there was no place I'd rather be, nothing I'd rather be doing, than dancing with Jason in my Aunt Ida's kitchen.

"Mmmmm," I murmured.

"You want me to start the fire?" he whispered softly into my (stupendous) hair.

"Yes, please," I whispered back.

"Great," he said in his normal Jason voice. "I'm hungry!"

If there is any man less romantic than Jason when he is hungry, I have yet to meet him. And if there is any man more adorable, I have yet to meet him either.

I smiled to myself as we disentangled ourselves. Jason, barefoot, was wearing an old pair of blue jeans on his slim hips and an equally old but spotlessly clean white cotton shirt, unbuttoned and the sleeves rolled up to the elbows. I found myself staring at the tantalizing glimpse of his lovely tan chest and flat belly. Embarrassed, I pulled my eyes away, only to find him staring at my shorts. Or rather, my (stupendous) legs in those shorts.

"I'm glad to see you dressed for dinner," I said, grinning at him.

"You too," he said, never taking his eyes off my legs.

This day was looking up.

"The charcoal's in that galvanized can by the grill," I said. "And there's a beer for you in the fridge."

"You," Jason said as he opened the fridge and peered inside, "are the girl of my dreams."

Yup. Definitely looking up.

THIRTY-ONE

AS JASON HAD predicted, he ate most of the steak and I ate most of the vegetables, but both of us were happy with that division of eating labor.

We ate in the un-screened-in screened-in porch, sitting across from each other at the new picnic table. I mean, outdoor dining set. Jason didn't talk much, and I gave him his space. The man was jet-lagged, and I knew he must have had a tough day. Which I didn't want to think about. So instead, I contented myself with watching him eat. Chefs (*ex-chefs, Sam*) like watching people eat the food they've cooked. And I liked looking at Jason pretty much anytime. I liked the way his mop of unruly black hair, even freshly washed and presumably combed, did that thing called whatever it wanted, to paraphrase Helene's T-shirt. I liked the way his dark eyes were fringed by thick lashes that my nonna would have said were "wasted on a man." I liked the way the muscles of his forearms slid under his bronze skin, perpetually tanned by long hours spent on the water. The list went on and on.

"Coffee?" I asked when we'd both pushed our plates away.

"Probably a good idea," Jason said. "We do need to talk."
Oh god, oh god, oh god.

"Okay," I said. "I'll bring it into the living room."

Aunt Ida's living room is my second-favorite room in the house after the ell. And the kitchen. Okay, so it's my third-favorite room in the house. I love its original whitewashed shiplap walls, wide-plank pine floorboards, and beautiful rag rug in faded blues and greens. An old roll-top desk graces one corner, and a supremely comfy couch, its back draped with an antique blue-and-white coverlet, faces two wooden armchairs on either side of the original fireplace with its simple white-painted mantelpiece.

Coming back with the coffee, I found Jason stretched out on the couch, arms tucked behind his head, eyes closed.

My first thought was, *Oh, good. No talking tonight. And*, I realized with a pang, *no anything else.*

Which was when Jason cracked open his eyes and sat up, swinging his long legs off the couch. I wasn't sure whether to be relieved or disappointed.

I put the mugs on the old wooden sea chest that serves as a coffee table and sat down next to him.

"Oh, jeez, thanks for this," Jason said as he took a sip. And still he said nothing.

Suddenly I was very tired of waiting for this talk Jason had decided we needed to have.

"What's on your mind, Jason?" I asked.

I maybe asked it a little sharply because he looked at me with surprise over the rim of his coffee cup. "Ed," he said, putting the mug down on the chest. "Ed's on my mind, of course."

Was talking about Ed better or worse than talking about our relationship? Both had their possible downsides. And the one could definitely affect the other.

I looked closely at Jason's exhausted face and felt a wave of pity.

"How did it go today?" I asked gently.

"Some good, some bad," he said. "On the plus side, the evidence against him is all circumstantial. On the downside, it's pretty strong. He knew Clara's house, so he'd know about the kindling basket in the kitchen. And there's no doubt that he's got a strong motive, given the lawsuit Clara was threatening him with. But the clincher, apparently, is that he did have a spare key to the house. Clara came by the restaurant shortly after her wife died last year, saying he was the only person she trusted to keep her spare. Ed admits it and there were plenty of other people who heard the conversation."

"But he told me that when he'd wanted to get photos of Clara from the house, he'd had to get one from the police," I pointed out.

"Yeah," Jason said. "He claims he'd lost the key Clara had given him."

"You didn't hear this from Detective Peters?" I said.

Jason shook his head. "No," he said. "Ed told me most of this. Vivvie called me as a courtesy, but it would be inappropriate for her to talk to me about an ongoing investigation. She wasn't giving anything away."

Including that your girlfriend was the one who started the whole ongoing investigation thing, I thought. God bless Vivian Peters's professional standards.

"So no specifics?" I asked.

Jason shook his head. "No. No specifics. But still, I've known Vivvie a long time and I got the feeling she'd been pressured into bringing Ed in. I don't think she really believes he's the guilty party."

Jason's own professional standards kept him from saying who might be pressuring Vivian. But I could take an educated guess. Police Chief McCauley had a decided penchant for the obvious suspect and the quick win in the cases that came under his purview.

"I wouldn't be surprised if she wasn't keen on Ed as primary suspect," I said. "Seeing as he was the one who gave us the information that clinched Clara's death as suspicious."

Jason raised his eyebrows. *Oops.*

"Us?" he asked mildly. "What us?"

"Well, me," I admitted. "Or actually, Miles."

If anything, the eyebrows went higher.

"At the memorial service," I explained. "Miles was talking to Ed, and Ed said Clara couldn't have been the one using that cast iron frying pan because of her arthritis so it had to be someone else. So I told Detective Peters . . ." I trailed off.

"You've been involved all along, haven't you?" Jason said. Not accusingly, just wonderingly. "Why didn't you tell me? You hardly mentioned anything about this in all the times we've talked on the phone."

I decided to come clean. "Because it was me and my big mouth that got Detective Peters thinking Clara's death was suspicious," I said, adding, "Well, actually she already thought something was off. But I was the one who confirmed it. I was the one who started this whole thing. And now your cousin is the prime suspect and it's *all my fault.* I'm never going to learn to stop sticking my nose into police business."

Jason just shook his head tiredly. "And I hope you never do, Sam," he said. "You're good at this stuff. And you know as well as I do that the important thing is getting to the truth. I can't believe you don't trust me enough to know I'd never blame you for doing the right thing."

"I do trust you," I said miserably. "But I thought if I found the real murderer before you got back, we could avoid the whole thing."

"But why?" he asked. "Why did you want to avoid it?"

"Because," I said, "I thought that deep down inside, on a strictly personal rather than professional level, you might blame me, and given the state of our current relationship, it might not survive the strain."

If I'd surprised Jason with my involvement in Clara Foster's murder, that was nothing compared to the astonishment I saw on his face now. "The state of our current relationship?" he echoed. "What state of our current relationship?"

"The state where I go off to New York City for a month because of my commitment issues and then you go off to California for three months because of your commitment issues," I said miserably.

Jason leaned toward me, his dark eyes, those beautiful dark eyes, on mine. "I don't have any commitment issues, Sam," Jason said. "I am totally committed to you."

I swallowed, the sudden lump in my throat making me unable to speak. *Jason was totally committed to me.*

"Do you have a commitment issue, Sam?" he asked, his eyes clouded by doubt.

How could I explain? I wanted to tell him that, yes, there once might have been some fear of the overwhelming emotion I felt for him. That, yes, there once might have been some regret over the career and the life I'd left behind. But I also wanted to explain that our separation had proved to me how groundless that fear was and how insignificant that regret. But I still couldn't speak, so I just shook my head, hoping my eyes were saying what my voice could not.

Jason grinned at me. "I'm glad to hear it," he said.

And then it wasn't necessary for me to say anything at all because Jason Captiva was kissing me.

THIRTY-TWO

~~~~~~~~~~

THE SNOGGING, AS Helene would term it, went on for some considerable time. It was only Diogi in the kitchen whining to go out that managed to break us apart.

"You stay there," I said to my love. "I'll take care of that."

Jason settled back happily into the soft down cushions of the couch. "Hurry back," he said, his voice lazy with promise.

But Diogi, of course, chose that night to mark virtually every corner of the yard just in case any dogs might come by in the night and not realize that this was his domain.

"I'm baaaack," I said in my best Arnold Schwarzenegger imitation when I finally returned to the living room, only to find Jason once again stretched out full length on the couch, snoring lightly, Ciati snuggled next to him.

Smiling to myself, I tucked a throw pillow under his head, draped the blue-and-white coverlet over his sleeping form, and went off to my lonely bed somehow as happy as I'd ever been in my life.

* * *

THE BED WAS still lonely and I was still oddly happy
when I woke in the morning. Turning on my side, I
saw the piece of paper on the pillow next to mine.

"Off to the airport," Jason had written. "You looked so
peaceful, didn't want to wake you. Sorry I conked out last
night. Promise to make it up to you (wink wink). Love you.
Jason. PS: Your hair looks stupendous."

I got up and tucked the note away in the little Shaker box
that I keep for my precious things. Like this. My first love
letter from Jason Captiva.

I got up and took my first cup of coffee out to the porch,
where I watched the kids playing tag in the yard. The
morning sun was making short work of burning off the thin
wash of clouds in the pale blue sky, and a warm breeze
from the southwest was already rippling the surface of
Bower's Pond below.

Despite the perfection of the day and my relief that Jason and I were once again in harmony, my worry about
Ed's situation had not diminished. I was glad I'd arranged
the sailing lesson with Vivian, whom I'd decided to forgive
for arresting Ed now that Jason had told me in so many
words that it hadn't been her decision. Plus, I was impressed
that she'd taken me seriously when I'd begged her not to tell
anybody (by whom I meant Jason) about my involvement
in the case. On top of that, I didn't even care anymore that
Jason called her Vivvie. Because Jason was committed
to me.

So I was pleased when Vivian pulled into the driveway
at nine on the dot, just as we'd arranged. Ten minutes later,
I was explaining to a crestfallen Diogi that the Woman
Who Throws the Ball and I would be "back soon." As I
closed the kitchen screen door behind us, he phlumped
down on the kitchen floor with a sigh of despair.

"He can't come with us?" Vivian asked.

"Not unless you want to try getting an eighty-pound dog out of a tippy pram into a tippy sailboat," I said. "We tried it once with him swimming out to the boat, but its deck sits almost two feet above the water line. It was the saddest thing you ever saw, me trying to drag him up out of the water, him slipping back."

"Don't worry, buddy," Vivian said through the screen door, "we're going to have some amazing ball throwing when I get back."

Diogi's tail thumped happily on the floor in response, and Vivian and I trotted down to the dock with lighter hearts.

I WAS RIGHT ABOUT it being a perfect day for a sail. The breeze was steady but not too strong, just right for a nervous novice. Not that Vivian appeared to be in any way nervous.

"Do you want a life jacket?" I asked.

"Nope," she said. "It's only kids who are required to wear them, right?"

"Yup," I said.

"Plus," Vivian added with an impish smile, "even if it was required, *you* could always bribe the harbormaster."

I stared at her. So she did know about my relationship with Jason. And she thought it was funny. I let out a bark of laughter. "I have been known to do that," I said.

And we grinned at each other like naughty kids.

I took Vivian through the basics, with her asking questions nonstop.

"Why can't you always just sail straight to where you want to go?" she demanded.

"Because sooner or later where you want to go will be straight into the direction the wind is coming from," I explained patiently. "The wind needs to be coming at least at a slight angle toward the sail."

To illustrate, I pushed the tiller toward the sail and the *Miss Marple* pointed her nose directly into the wind until the whole mainsail started flapping like a bedsheet hanging out to dry and the boat slowed to almost a complete stop.

"Now we're what's called 'in irons,'" I said. "Which is good for nothing unless someone falls overboard and you want to stop and pick them up."

Vivian caught on right away. "But what if you need to change your course? How do you turn the boat without losing all your wind?"

"If you push the tiller hard all the way toward the sail and hold it there, you can turn the bow of the boat through the wind fast enough to catch it on the other side of the sail. That's called tacking."

"Why is it called tacking?"

I sighed. "Because."

Vivian just grinned at me.

"So this is how it works," I said. "When I as the skipper want to tack, I let you as the crew know by saying 'Ready about.' Then you say 'Ready,' meaning you're all set to handle the sails for the tack."

"Got it," Vivian said. "But I don't have to do anything with the mainsail, right? The little thing that holds its rope, sorry, the mainsheet, just twirls itself around."

"The cam cleat, right," I said. "So the mainsail will take care of itself and all you have to do is let the one jib sheet loose and tighten the other once we're through the tack."

"Got it," Vivian said again.

"Okay," I said. "Ready about."

"Ready," Vivian responded.

I pushed the tiller hard over until the mainsail moved to the other side of the boat and began to fill. Vivian meanwhile set the port jib sheet free, and once the jib was over, cleated the other jib sheet.

"Now we're underway again," I said, "and we just keep tacking back and forth until we get where we want to be."

We tried tacking a few times, with Vivian trying both roles, that of skipper and crew. I had to admit, the woman was a natural. She was also indefatigable.

"Okay," I finally said, "that's enough for today. Next time we'll try jibing. Jibing makes tacking look like a walk in the park."

"Great!" Vivian said. "When's next time, then?" Honest to god, the woman exhausted me.

THIRTY-THREE

A NICE BIG GLASS of iced coffee on the un-screened-in screened-in porch revitalized me. (Tip: To keep the ice from watering down the coffee as it melts, make a tray of ice cubes out of coffee and keep them handy in the freezer.) If Vivian thought she was getting away with no tit for tat again, she had another think coming, as my Aunt Ida would say. I gave her a sail; she was gonna give me info.

"What's happening with Ed Captiva?" I said abruptly as she threw Diogi's disgusting tennis ball across the yard for about the hundredth time.

She turned to look at me, and after a thoughtful pause during which I imagined she was trying to decide just how much she could or could not tell me, she finally said, "Nothing. We're still holding him."

"But why?" I protested. "I mean, Ed was the one who gave you the information that turned this into a murder investigation in the first place. Why would he tell you about Clara's arthritis, if he was the one who used that cast iron pan?"

"Well, there are some people," Vivian said diplomatically, "who think he was afraid that one of his colleagues would bring it up sooner or later, so he preempted them to make himself look less suspicious."

"That's ridiculous and you know it," I said. "Except in books, nobody who's killed somebody uses that kind of crazy logic to divert suspicion from themselves."

Vivian just shrugged. She wasn't going to bad-mouth another law enforcement officer, let alone her boss, to a civilian no matter how thick he was.

"And he has no alibi," she added. "He lives alone, it was his night off at the restaurant, so he went to bed early. And he had a key to the house at least at some point. On the plus side, he's now got the best criminal lawyer on the Cape, thanks to Jason."

I didn't even mind Vivian talking about Jason. What a difference a day makes.

"Well," I said, "in case it's helpful, I learned a few things yesterday that might open up the investigation a bit."

"Do tell," Vivian said. Which I thought was encouraging.

So I told her about my conversation with Summer Robinson and what I'd learned about Clara's cancer diagnosis. But if Vivian found my sleuthing impressive, she managed to hide that fact.

"Well, that's interesting about Clara knowing she was going to die soon," she said. "That didn't show up in our tests, of course, which only measured the soot in her airways and the level of carbon monoxide in her blood so that we could be sure that smoke inhalation was the cause of death. But still, it doesn't make much difference to the case unless someone found out about her diagnosis and wanted to kill her before she changed her will."

"Like Summer," I pointed out helpfully.

But Vivian wasn't having it.

"Maybe," she said doubtfully. "Although that's a bit of a stretch. I interviewed her early on, and I've got to say, I find it hard to believe that that sad little woman would murder someone because she *thought* they were dying and she *thought* they might give away two acres of land to people who she *thought* wouldn't use it properly."

I hated to admit it, but she had a point. I sighed.

"What about the Wilkinsons?" I reminded her.

Vivian shook her head. "They have an unshakable alibi."

I really wanted to know what that alibi was. "No alibi is unshakable," I said provocatively.

It worked. "Well," Vivian said dryly, "attending the annual fundraiser for the Police Athletic League of Cape Cod with a number of local luminaries from Fair Harbor, including the chief of police, is the exception that proves the rule."

"Yes," I said, conceding defeat. "I can see that it would be."

And so the day, which had started out so encouragingly, was suddenly on a downward slide.

ONCE VIVIAN LEFT, I considered my options and finally decided I didn't have any. There didn't seem to be anything else I could do to help find Clara's killer. I wandered into the kitchen with every intention of making myself yet another grilled cheese sandwich when I was distracted by the sight of Clara's cookbook on the kitchen counter. As I slid it back onto the shelf next to the rest of my much-loved cookbooks, I had a sudden vision of Clara's cookbook collection. Clara's collection and her beloved Escoffier. *Clara's Escoffier.* Was it possible that Clara's death had nothing to do with her house and property but with the Escoffier? Had someone who knew the Escoffier's worth stolen it to sell to a private collector and set the fire to cover the theft?

I could only think of two people who had that kind of knowledge and those kinds of contacts—Abraham Beame and Thomas Bentley. And, as Abe Beame was the one who'd told me in so many words that he thought Clara's Escoffier had been stolen, that left Thomas Bentley.

Obviously, I couldn't just go to Bentley and accuse him of stealing Clara's Escoffier. But it might be interesting to hear his reaction if I pointed the finger at Beame. I checked my watch. It was eleven thirty in the morning. I knew that Bentley Auctioneers did its major auctions on Saturday afternoons, so the chances were that I could find Bentley in the office prepping.

"Bentley Auctioneers," a familiar voice said, "Thomas Bentley's office. How can I help you?"

"Hi, Barbara," I said, "Samantha Barnes here. Is Thomas in?"

"Just a minute, Ms. Barnes," the assistant said, "I'll check." Which, of course, is assistant-speak for "I'll see if he wants to talk to you."

Apparently, he did, because Bentley was on the phone in a matter of seconds.

"Samantha," he said, "how can I help?"

I could tell we were on speakerphone by the slight echo-chamber effect and by the distinct sound of papers being shuffled around while Bentley multitasked. I hate being part of someone's multitasking.

"Just very quickly, Thomas," I said. "You remember Clara Foster's Escoffier cookbook, the one I mentioned at the memorial service?"

"Yes," he said with a distinctly wary tone to his voice.

"Well, I heard that there had been a collector looking to add an Escoffier to his collection but that he'd apparently filled that gap recently."

"And?" he said, no longer trying to hide his, what, annoyance? Displeasure? Anger? "What are you trying to say, Samantha?"

So I crossed my fingers and let him have it. "I'm trying to say that I think somebody, maybe Abe Beame, stole the

Escoffier and set the fire to cover the theft." *There, Bentley, is that clear enough for you?*

There was dead silence on the other end of the phone. Even the rustling of papers had stopped.

"Thomas?" I said.

"I'm here," he replied coldly. "And no, I do not think Abraham Beame stole Clara Foster's Escoffier and set her house on fire to cover the theft. The idea is preposterous. You do not set fire to someone's house for a book, not even a rare book. You need to think twice before you make false statements about a professional in our field, Samantha. There are laws against reputational slander. And now, if you don't mind, I really do have to go."

And without further ado, Thomas Bentley hung up on me.

THIRTY-FOUR

Nicely played, Sam. Now the man responsible for the health of your bank account either thinks you are a horrible person or, if in fact he did steal the Escoffier, probably suspects that you are on to him. Terrific. The day was going from bad to worse.

I went into the kitchen and refilled my glass with more cold coffee. Then I added a healthy dollop of milk for good measure, mostly because I like the creamy swirls it makes when I pour it in.

My animal companions followed me hopefully into their favorite room in the house, where their human often dropped yummy things on the floor while she was cooking and depended on them to vacuum them up and thus do their bit toward kitchen upkeep. Which reminded me that it was lunchtime. Animal companions have an uncanny sense of timing when it comes to meals.

I had nothing particular in mind for lunch, so I thought I'd make my standard go-to, tuna salad with a little chopped sweet onion piled high on a toasted slice of the homemade sourdough bread that I always keep at the ready in the freezer. I drained the oil from the can over the kibble in Diogi and Ciati's dishes.

"There," I said. "Knock yourselves out."

I, in turn, munched away at the kitchen table, pondering that phone call with Bentley. Had he just threatened me with legal action? Had he suspected that I wasn't doubting Abe Beame, but him, Thomas Bentley? Or was I imagining things? *I need someone sensible to talk this through with*, I thought.

So I wasn't really surprised when Helene materialized at the kitchen window. Yes, it was lunchtime, and yes, she usually worked in the library on Saturday mornings and then came home for lunch, and yes, she knew that my lunches were much yummier than hers and that I was always willing to share. But mostly I wasn't surprised because Helene somehow always knows when I need her. I had long since given up trying to figure out how. Or how she does that magical appearing-disappearing act. Probably best not to inquire, I thought.

By the time I had smiled at her and pointed over to the screen door, she was already beside me.

"Ooh, delectable," she said, eyeing my sandwich. "Got any more?"

"Help yourself," I said, cocking my head toward the leftover tuna salad on the kitchen counter. "Bread is in the freezer."

"First some hellos are in order, aren't they, gang?" Helene said to Diogi, who was greeting her enthusiastically but politely (i.e., not licking her to death) as she had trained him, and Ciati, who was twining herself between the librarian's legs in ecstatic figure eights.

As always with Helene, treats were produced miraculously from one of the many pockets of her eclectic wardrobe. Today's outfit was slim black capri pants, topped by a lavender tunic. On her right shoulder, she'd pinned what looked like a refrigerator magnet reading: "The only thing that you absolutely have to know is the location of the library. —Albert Einstein." Her long silver curls were held back by a tortoiseshell headband, revealing a pair of earrings in the shape of miniature dream catchers.

She brought her sandwich over and sat across from me. "So," she said after a few bites, "how did things go with the books?"

For a minute, I wasn't sure what she was talking about. So much had happened since we'd been sitting on the floor of the front room discussing Golden Age mysteries that I'd completely forgotten about the appraisal.

"Oh," I said when I'd figured it out, "good. It was good. He was nice, Abe Beame. He said about a half dozen might bring in some peacock chair money."

"Excellent," Helene said. And then looking at me with those piercing blue eyes of hers, she added, "And what else?"

So I told her. About my encounter with Summer Robinson. About Ed's arrest. About Jason's literal flying visit. About my suspicions regarding Thomas Bentley. Through it all, she sat quietly eating her tuna sandwich, those eyes of hers never leaving my face. I sometimes think she's not so much listening to my words as reading my mind.

"So what do you think?" I asked when I was talked out.

"I think that people with only one truth can be very dangerous," she said enigmatically.

"Care to explain?" I asked.

She leaned toward me. "We all know people who believe strongly that 'war is bad,' right?"

"Right," I said. "And they're not wrong."

"No, they're not," Helene said. "But if it is their *only* truth, if there are no circumstances in their mind when war, as awful as it is, *might* be necessary, the consequences can be unfortunate. If nothing is more important than peace, it allows the holder of that one truth to justify any inaction—like not standing up to fascism—or, conversely, any action—like committing a heinous crime—to prevent war."

"So you think whoever killed Clara Foster was in the grip of one inflexible truth?"

"I have no idea," Helene said frankly. "But I do think that most murderers have what they consider one overarching 'truth' that allows them to kill another person in defense of that truth. Sometimes it's a conviction that they've been treated unfairly, or that money will, in fact, buy happiness and wholeness, or that family always comes first. There are any number of one-truths that can push a person to kill. Only sociopaths kill for no reason. And most murderers are not sociopaths, in my experience."

And Helene's experience was extensive. For more than two decades, the woman had evaluated people facing criminal charges, talked with witnesses, and consulted on murder investigations. I trusted that experience.

"Okay," I said, "what do you suggest I do next?"

"I know you," she said. "You'll do what needs to be done." *Not super helpful.*

Then she added, "But whatever you do next, I think you should be very, very careful."

Which I should have expected.

W HAT I DID next had absolutely nothing to do with Clara Foster's demise, so I didn't have to worry about being very, very careful. What I did next was meet with the handyman I'd called about my porch.

I have to admit, I was a little taken aback when Nat Pomeroy pulled into my driveway. The guy looked like my idea of a meth dealer, with long, stringy hair, a two-day growth of beard, and one of those skinny bodies that seem to thrum with internal energy. But when he smiled, it was the smile of an angel, and I instinctively liked him.

Our discussion about screening in the un-screened-in porch took quite some time. First, we had to talk about what a wicked good guy Miles was and how Nat's dad knew my dad and said he was a wicked good guy. Also, Aunt Ida's house was a wicked nice house and the porch would be wicked nice once he, Nat, got done with it. Then he marched around the porch, taking endless measurements and jotting them down neatly in a beautiful leatherbound notebook with a little silver pen. So definitely not a meth dealer.

When he'd finished, Nat gave me his estimate. Which came to much less than I'd expected. "That sounds, um, good," I stammered. "If you want, I can write you a check for half now."

"Nah," Nat said. "You just pay me when the job's done."

Also unexpected. "Um, okay, if you're sure," I said. Then I asked the fateful question. "When can you start?"

I steeled myself for disappointment.

"The job's pretty straightforward and I got everything I need in my shop," Nat said. "Tomorrow's Sunday. I can make the screens on, say, Monday and Tuesday, then install them on Wednesday."

I blinked. Four days. Never in the history of mankind has a contractor offered to start and finish a job in four days.

"Um, okay, sure," I said.

Nat made another neat notation in his little book, tucked it away in his back pocket, shook my hand, and got into his spotlessly maintained truck and left.

Nat's leather-bound notebook had reminded me about something I'd wanted to check with Jenny. Maybe I shouldn't give up on my Escoffier theory yet.

where u, I texted her.

home. trying to keep kids from killing each other. too soon for wine?

I checked my watch. Five fifteen.

nope.

come now. bring food. fridge empty. except for wine.

I laughed. be there in a half hour.

"C'mon, Diogi," I said. "We have to run an errand of mercy."

Ten minutes later, I was at Mayo's clam shack at Shawme Beach. The clam shack sits on the beach just next to the parking lot. Because Shawme is a town beach, dogs aren't allowed on it during high season, but Diogi was used to waiting for me in the truck. He tended to consider it prime nap time. The lot wasn't particularly crowded at that hour, so I could have parked near the clam shack, but because I had Diogi with me, I drove down to the far end, where I could park in the shade of a couple of locust trees and leave Diogi in Grumpy with the windows cracked open.

"Back soon," I said to Diogi, who, of course, whined miserably as I left him to his lonely fate.

I was walking back to the truck with two grease-spotted white paper bags of yummy fried food in hand when I heard a hesitant voice behind me say, "Ms. Barnes?"

I turned, and it took me a minute to place the non-descript young woman behind me, her own grease-spotted bag in hand, as Thomas Bentley's assistant, Barbara.

"Barbara," I said. "I almost didn't recognize you outside of the office. What are you doing in Fair Harbor?"

"I left work early," she said. "Not long after you called. My grandmother lives out in Crystal Bay and she's been sick, she's dying actually, so I take off when I can. Mr. Bentley has been very understanding."

"I'm so sorry," I said inadequately.

Barbara shrugged her shoulders slightly and said, "What can you do? I thought I'd come over and pick up some food for dinner. She doesn't have much of an appetite anymore, but I thought some fried clams might tempt her."

For a moment, the conversation seemed like it was going to languish. Then Barbara blurted out, "I heard you and Mr. Bentley talking today on the phone. He had it on speaker and he almost never closes the door between our offices." Her face was a study of worry.

"I'm sorry if that upset you," I said.

"It did," she admitted. "You see, Mr. Bentley and I know Abraham Beame, and Mr. Beame would never take advantage of an old lady like that. No reputable antiques dealer would. If it ever came out, they'd be ruined."

What she was saying made sense, actually.

"Well, I wish Thomas had explained that to me," I said. "I wasn't accusing Mr. Beame. I just wanted to know if it was a possible scenario."

"Trust me," she said, firmly for her, "it isn't."

"Well, I appreciate the information," I said.

"You can call me anytime with questions," she said.

But I wasn't listening to Barbara anymore. We'd reached my truck. My empty truck.

THIRTY-FIVE

～～～～

DIOGI WAS NOT in the truck. Diogi was, in fact, sitting next to the truck, the passenger side door wide open, surrounded by a circle of kids, maybe ten years old at most, who were calmly feeding him French fries.

"What are you doing?" I asked. Okay, shouted.

"Feeding the dog," one remarkably self-possessed little girl said.

"How did he get out of the truck?" I demanded.

"He was whining," she said. "He was hungry. He didn't like being in that stinky old truck. So we let him out. You should have locked the door if you didn't want anyone to let him out."

Well, she was right about the stinky old truck. The stinky old truck with the broken door locks.

"The lock is *broken*," I found myself saying defensively. *Defending yourself to a ten-year-old, Sam. Does it get any more humiliating?* I gave up. Okay, so maybe I'd overreacted. Maybe I'd forgotten that Vivian had said the dognappers took dogs only from very private homes, not very public parking lots. So sue me.

Diogi in the meantime had transferred his affections to Barbara, who had offered him one of her French fries.

"What a great dog," she said, patting him on the head as he looked at her soulfully. I could have told her that look was all about the fries, not her, but I didn't.

"Get in the truck, Diogi," I said firmly, pointing to the passenger seat of my stinky old truck. And Diogi got in.

As we drove away, I realized that in all the excitement, I'd forgotten about Barbara. That made me feel bad. She had said more in those three minutes of conversation than I'd ever heard her say before. The woman was, I suspected, very shy. And I hadn't even had the good manners to say goodbye.

My take-out dinner was gratefully received by Jenny and the Three Things. After we'd pigged out on all sorts of delicious fried food, including more French fries for the insatiable Diogi, the boys retired to play some kind of incomprehensible video game involving cartoon frogs hopping from lily pad to lily pad and bopping each other on the head with cartoon caveman clubs. Diogi and Sadie went out to the backyard to resume their endless courtship, and Jenny and I retired to the living room with our glasses of wine.

Despite Barbara's excellent defense of Abe Beame (or unbeknownst to her, Thomas Bentley), I still thought I should try the stolen Escoffier idea out on Jenny. I went through my scenario with her, but she wasn't impressed.

"I don't know," she said doubtfully. "I think that assistant person may be right. It does seem like a pretty big reputational risk for a pretty small payoff. And certainly, it wouldn't be worth killing anybody for. Besides, how can you even be sure whatshisname's fancy cookbook wasn't in that pile of burnt books?"

"I can't," I admitted. "I only had a quick look and the cleaners have already cleared the place out."

"Then you're out of luck," Jenny said, "unless you have a photographic memory."

How could you be so stupid, Sam?

"I do!" I said. "Or at least my phone does. I took some photos of the damage that day. Detective Peters wanted me to ask you if you saw anything significant in them. And then I completely forgot about them. I took a photo of that pile of burnt books, I'm pretty sure."

I pulled out my cell and began scrolling past the zillions of pictures that I'd taken of Diogi to send to my parents, who insisted on calling him their "grandpuppy." Not to make a point or anything, I'm sure.

"Yup!" I said at last. "Here's the pile of burnt books. Or at least I think it is. It's kind of hard to tell." In truth, it was impossible to tell.

Jenny squinted at the tiny screen, then tried zooming in with two fingers.

"This is crap," she said, handing the cell back. "Forward it to me, and I'll see what I can do."

So I forwarded it to her and we went into her office and Jenny did a bunch of professional photographer magic tricks on her huge desktop monitor, muttering incantations like "resampling" and "interpolation." And the next thing I knew, I was looking at what was to me a truly horrifying image of Clara's beautiful cookbook collection reduced to a pile of blackened rubble.

"Now we go through it up close," Jenny said and, zooming in, began examining the pile inch by inch.

And then I saw it. A glimpse of gold.

"Stop there," I said, leaning forward over Jenny's shoulder. Yes. A tiny scrap of charred leather, the gilt letters "A. Esc" clearly visible.

"That's it," I said, stepping back. "That's the Escoffier."

I didn't know whether to be disappointed or pleased. On the one hand, I hated to think of that beautiful book gone, ruined in that fire. On the other, so much for my suspicions about Thomas Bentley.

"You might as well take a look at the rest of the photos,"

I said, sighing. "I told Detective Peters I'd share them with you and there's only three, one of the dining area, one of the living room, and one of the kitchen."

I shared the files and watched as Jenny did her magic again. She looked at the living room shot, shook her head no, then moved on to the dining area photo. She squinted at it, then peered even more closely.

"What's all this?" she asked, pointing to the charred heaps on the dining room floor, each with its sad, empty picture hanger on the wall above.

"Those are, or were, the watercolors that fell off the dining room wall," I said.

"Right," she said. "So what's going on here?"

She zoomed into an empty section of the wall closest to the kitchen. "There's a hanger here," she said. "So where's the painting that should be under it?"

She was right. Where there should have been a twisted mass of frame and canvas, there was absolutely nothing.

Jenny turned to me. "Where is it?" she asked. "Where's the fake Hopper?"

I stared at her. "Someone started that fire to steal a fake Hopper?"

Jenny just looked at me steadily.

"No," she said finally. "Someone started that fire to steal a real Hopper."

THIRTY-SIX

A ND IT ALL fell into place.

"Kit didn't make a copy of that painting," I said slowly, working it all out in my head. "She just kept the original and said it was a copy."

"I *knew* it," Jenny said. "I *knew* that painting was a Hopper. I bet the signature was hidden under that frame that Kit made. But Clara was so convincing that I told myself I was wrong."

"Clara was convincing because she really thought it *was* a copy," I said. "Because that's what Kit told her."

"But why?" Jenny said. "Why would Kit lie to Clara about it?"

"Because it was going to be their 'insurance' for their old age," I said, my voice rising in my excitement. "Kit knew that if Clara had any idea that she hadn't sold the Hopper back when she'd sold those other paintings from her mother's collection to buy the restaurant, that she'd insist on selling it to finance the expansion she'd always wanted. So Kit didn't tell her. I bet she was going to wait until Clara retired, until the restaurant was no longer an excuse for 'spending money like water.'"

"And then she never got the chance," Jenny said, now

equally excited. "She died in that car accident before she could tell Clara."

She smiled broadly at me. "By George, I think she's got it!" Jenny is very fond of quoting from the plays we'd worked on in the high school drama club.

"Henry Higgins, *My Fair Lady*," I responded automatically.

"Got it in one," she said back automatically, and we both high-fived automatically before getting back to business.

"So where do we go with this?" Jenny asked me.

"I'm not sure," I said. "It all makes a certain kind of crazy sense, but it's complete speculation. I mean, how do we prove that what we were told was a copy was really an original, when we don't have it?"

"Good point," Jenny said, suddenly downcast.

We both sat silently for a minute.

"Wait! I have an idea," Jenny said.

She turned back to her computer and began typing away, clicking on websites, pulling up photos of what even I could tell were real Hoppers, most of them showing Cape Cod scenes.

"It's not here," she said finally.

"What's not here?"

"The real Hopper," she said. "If Kit had sold a Hopper back in the seventies, it would be in the catalogue raisonné of Hopper's works. And it's not."

"What's a catalogue raisonné?" I asked.

"It's a comprehensive listing of all the known works of an artist," Jenny explained. "I'm not surprised that Kit's Hopper doesn't show up, since it was a private gift from the artist to her mother. But if Kit had sold it on, a record of that sale and the painting itself should now be on that list."

"So she didn't sell it," I said.

"Exactly," Jenny said. "*We* know there was a real Hopper. And it appears nobody now owns it. Which means that Kit never sold it."

"And nobody ever realized Kit's 'copy' was an original?"

"Well, *somebody* did," Jenny said grimly.

"Don't you have a nasty, suspicious mind," I said. Not that I hadn't been thinking the same thing myself. "How much do you reckon *somebody* thought it was worth?"

Jenny typed something quickly into Google search and hit Enter. A least a dozen news headlines popped up, all variations on the same theme:

Edward Hopper's *October on Cape Cod* Sells at Auction for $9.6 Million.

If I could whistle, which I can't, I would have whistled.

"Holy . . ." I gasped, stopping abruptly when I realized what I'd almost said.

Jenny laughed. "Samantha Barnes, *Antiques in the Attic*."

I smiled ruefully. "Got it in one."

I HAD ONCE TOLD Jason in all innocence that I did some of my best work in bed, and he'd laughed and laughed. When I finally figured out what was so funny, I said, all flustery, "No, I mean some of my best *thinking*." And it's true. About the some of my best thinking part anyway.

As I lay there in the dark that night, free from any distractions, I let the little fragments of things that I'd heard, things I'd seen, things I'd sensed, float around in my head until they lined up in some kind of order.

Bentley's proprietary attitude to Aunt Ida's case clock; the way he kept calling my clock "our" clock. Bentley's overreaction when I'd questioned the possibility that the fire had been started to cover the theft of the Escoffier. Bentley, who knew everybody and everyone in the art and antiquities field, and would surely know how to quietly dispose of a stolen painting. Particularly one that might be worth as much as ten million dollars.

Bentley, the expert in American antiques—and art.

Bentley, who could have seen Kit's "copy" and known immediately what it was. Bentley, who could easily check the art world's extensive catalogue of all known Hopper works and confirmed that "his" was an unknown original.

Bentley, who had scoffed at the idea of killing someone for a mere five figures. But perhaps he would feel differently about killing someone for ten million dollars. *Was Bentley capable of murder if the price was high enough?*

It all added up. And then it all fell to pieces.

I'd forgotten. Thomas Bentley had never been in Clara Foster's house. He'd never seen the Hopper "copy." Or so he said. Well, that could be checked. After all, my new BFF Barbara Smiley had said I could call her anytime with questions. And I had a whole lot of questions for her. Which, I realized, would have to wait for Monday, when presumably she would be in the office. Dang. Oh well, pretty soon I'd have some information for Vivian that should definitely change the course of her investigation.

W HILE I WAITED, I tried to occupy myself with giving Aunt Ida's house a good scrubbing. I hate to admit it, but I love cleaning house. But even waxing and polishing and sweeping and dusting couldn't stop my brain from pondering questions that only Barbara could answer. So it was with glad heart that I heard her now familiar voice at the other end of the line at precisely 9:01 a.m. on Monday. All I said in explanation when she'd picked up the phone was that I wanted to ask her a few questions about Clara Foster's art collection.

"Of course," Barbara said. "Just let me shut the door to Mr. Bentley's office."

I thought it was significant that she didn't want her boss to hear her talking to me.

"Thanks, Barbara," I said. "I really appreciate it. It's just a few questions, mostly about how stolen art is handled in the art world."

There was a short silence on the other end of the line.

"You think Bentley Auctioneers traffics in stolen artworks?" she asked. Her voice had lost all its initial friendliness.

"No, no," I said. "I'm just curious about how the, um, sale of something like a rare book"—let her think I'm still focused on the Escoffier—"or any work of art, really, if it were stolen, would be handled. Is there some kind of collector's black market?"

Barbara sniffed dismissively.

"Only in James Bond movies," she said. "Not in real life. There are thieves who think there are people out there who want stolen art on their walls or stolen books on their shelves. Then, to their dismay, the criminals find out that collectors aren't stupid. Collectors don't buy stolen goods. First of all, it's illegal. And second, most are buying books and art as investments. And pieces that you can't sell, because they have no paper trail of legal provenance, are worthless."

Now I was honestly curious. "But I've read news stories about stolen artworks," I said. "So how do the thieves make their money?"

"Either from ransoming the artwork back to the original owner, usually a museum," Barbara said, "or by selling it to other criminals for a fraction of its real value."

"And the other guy sells it on?"

"No," Barbara said. "The other guys are professional criminals. They hang on to the artwork to use as a bargaining chip with law enforcement if they're ever arrested for another crime."

"As in, 'I'll tell you where that stolen Picasso is in exchange for a reduced sentence'?"

"I'm afraid so."

"So there really wouldn't be any advantage for someone in the art world to steal an artwork and then try to sell it privately?"

"That's what I've been trying to tell you all along," Barbara said, a little waspishly.

I didn't blame her. As far as she was concerned, I was asking a lot of stupid questions about a cookbook. A rare cookbook, but still a cookbook.

"Sorry," I said. "I know I'm being a pain. I'm just trying to figure out what might be a motive for killing a harmless old woman like Clara Foster."

If I thought I was going to get to Barbara by playing the sympathy card, I was wrong.

"I understand," she said, "I really do. But I honestly think any reputable dealer simply wouldn't do anything like what you're suggesting. First of all because, as I said, it's professional suicide, and second because there's probably more to be made on commission than on selling into the criminal black market."

"I'm sure you're right," I said, completely discouraged.

"And Ms. Barnes," Barbara added almost apologetically, "if you still think Abraham Beame was in any way involved in Ms. Foster's death, I think I should tell you that the night she died, Mr. Beame was at a charity auction for the Police Athletic League. I know that because Mr. Bentley mentioned it today."

My heart sank. "How would Thomas know that?" I asked, already knowing the answer.

"Because Mr. Bentley was the guest auctioneer that night," Barbara said.

W ELL, SPANK MY bottom and call me Judy," I said to Diogi after I got off the call. "Samantha Barnes is wrong again."

Not for the first time I wished I could do my sleuthing the proper way, where you flash your police ID like they do on TV and ask, "Where were you the night of the murder?" before going off on some wild-goose chase. Oh well, at least

I'd had the good sense to talk to Barbara before I presented my latest theory to Vivian.

Diogi made it clear that we would both feel better after a nice long walk. I let Ciati out to pretend hunt while Diogi and I set off for our new favorite beach walk. As I pulled into Clara's driveway, I wondered how long I was going to be able to get away with trespassing on Conservancy property but decided not to worry about it. This deserted stretch of beach was the only place I knew where I could safely let Diogi run free in the high season. I stuffed a poop bag in my pocket, and we hopped out of the truck.

There was a fresh onshore breeze coming across Cape Cod Bay, so what was already shaping up to be a very warm day was for the time being a perfect eighty degrees. The incoming tide was still half low, so I slipped off my sneakers and Diogi and I wandered along the water's edge as shallow waves lapped our toes. I felt my tired brain emptying out into the vast dreamscape of water and sky, and once again sent a little note of thanks to Aunt Ida for bringing me home.

But no respite lasts forever. Not in my busy little brain anyway.

If not Bentley, who?

THIRTY-SEVEN

I T CAME TO me when I saw Summer Robinson's laundry fluttering on the clothesline next to her house. I love the sight of clothes on a line. And, of course, Summer would eschew a dryer if she could. Probably even in the dead of winter. Well, good for her, I thought. Given what we'd all learned about climate change, you really couldn't be too environmentally conscious.

Or could you?

I thought about what Helene had said about one truth crowding out all others. I thought about Summer and her commitment to protecting the environment. Maybe Vivian and I were wrong. Maybe that "sad little woman" had at some point moved from commitment to zealotry.

I thought about Summer's reaction when I'd told her that Clara hadn't been planning to leave her property to the Joys. *"I thought the worst of her and now it's too late."* Too late for what? Too late to undo Clara Foster's murder?

Clara had liked shocking people by talking about her "magic pills." If I knew about them, there was a pretty good chance that Summer did, too. Had she found a way into

Clara's house and started that fire knowing that Clara was virtually unconscious from sleeping tablets?

It all made sense. At least until that snarky little voice in my head asked, *And then stopped to take the "fake" Hopper away with her for no good reason?*

Okay, so that was maybe a sticking point. If I knew anything, I knew that whoever started that fire also took the Hopper.

And then I remembered something else. Summer saying that Clara had been jealous of her close friendship with Kit. That Clara would not even give Summer "something to remember her by." What if at the last minute, Summer had seen what she knew only as Kit's "copy" of an artwork that she'd loved and decided to take it as something to remember her dear friend by?

Of course, none of this was in any way supported by any evidence. And the only way to get that was to talk with Summer again and hope that she would give something away. This approach has had mixed, not to say dangerous, results for me in the past, but this time I thought I had a plan that even Helene would approve of. This time I was going to be very, very careful. If Summer Robinson was a possible murderer, it probably wasn't a good idea to talk to her on a secluded beach. But a crowded beach—that was another thing entirely.

I herded Diogi back to the truck and drove down the road to the parking lot of the nature reserve to make a few calls. The last thing I needed was Summer seeing my unmistakable vehicle in Clara's driveway.

First, I called Mrs. Tanner. I thought I remembered her saying something about Summer giving her a phone number, and it turned out I was right. "I feel bad that I haven't gotten back to her," Mrs. Tanner said. "But we've been so busy on the farm."

Then I called Summer and told her that Mrs. Tanner had given me her number and I was interested in talking with her about the Conservancy but didn't have a lot of free time. However, I was on my way to Mayo's clam shack at Shawme Beach and maybe we could talk over my lunch break? I almost felt bad at how eagerly she accepted my invitation.

"I'll leave right away," she said. "It won't take me ten minutes."

I'd been planning to drop Diogi at home so I wouldn't have to leave him in the truck, but now there was no time for that. We hightailed it to Shawme, and fortunately, the shady spot at the far end of the lot was open. I looked around and saw no troublesome children in sight. "You stay in the truck," I said sternly.

Diogi looked at me, all innocence.

"I mean it," I said. "If you stay, I promise I'll bring you some fries."

I swear the dog smiled. Apparently "fries" was another one of his vocabulary words.

I barely had time to get over to the clam shack and get in line before Summer was at my side. I ordered my usual fried clams, onion rings for me, and fries for Diogi, and asked what she'd like.

"Oh, no, nothing for me," she said, holding up a glass jar full of what looked like sludge with bits of green things floating in it. "I've brought my own raw vegetable soup made with potato peel broth."

I looked away before she could see the horror in my eyes.

We sat at one of the clam shack's picnic tables, all of which are so rickety as to make my old one look like a masterpiece of carpentry. The conversation at first was fairly general. I glanced through the pamphlets she'd brought to give me about the Conservancy and we talked about the many environmental dangers faced by the Cape—warming sea waters as a result of climate change, residential and commercial pollution of the groundwater, overbuilding encroaching on precious marshlands.

I actually kind of hated what I had to do next. But I did it.

While little kids raced around our picnic table chasing seagulls, and harried parents tried to convince them to sit down and eat their hot dogs, I subtly, I hoped, suggested that I would understand if Summer Robinson might have wanted to kill her next-door neighbor.

"You know," I began, "I can see how it must have been a bit of a relief to you that Clara died when she did. I mean, given that you thought her land might go to those kids. After all, Clara was going die soon and this way what you thought would be an environmental disaster was averted."

Summer's reaction to all this was to stare at me in alarm and then burst into tears.

The little kids' reaction was to run back to their parents yelling, "Why is the lady crying?"

The parents' reaction was to throw all the hot dogs back into the cardboard box they'd come in and hustle the kids off to another picnic table.

This gave Summer a little time to compose herself.

"I know that because I care deeply about the earth, a lot of people consider me crazy," she said, wiping her eyes with a crumpled paper napkin. "But never before has my concern for our planet inspired someone to think I might be a *murderer.*"

I guessed I hadn't been as subtle as I'd hoped. Well, there was nothing for it but to throw all my cards on the table.

"I wasn't accusing you," I sort of lied. "I was just saying I would understand if you had done it. And it wasn't just your activism that made me think of you," I added. "It was the missing painting."

Summer looked at me blankly. "What missing painting?" she asked. *Uh-oh.*

"Kit's copy of the Hopper," I said weakly. "It's missing."

"Why would I take *that*?" she said. "Why would I want some copy Kit had made of somebody *else's* painting? I'd wanted one of her *own* paintings." And then she started to cry in earnest. "And even if I'd wanted to stop Clara that way, *which I didn't*, it couldn't have been me. That house was locked up tight."

Okay, so I knew when I was beaten.

"I'm sorry, Summer," I said sincerely. "I had it all wrong."

"Yes, you did," she said, sniffing, "but I can't blame you for trying to find whoever killed Clara."

Now I felt worse than ever. "Well, thank you," I said. And then as a peace offering, "Is it okay if I keep the brochures?"

"Of course," she said with a watery smile as she gathered up her Mason jar and I gathered up the brochures and Diogi's now stone-cold French fries.

We went our separate ways, and as I wandered back to Grumpy, all I could think was that once again I'd failed. I'd failed to find a credible suspect for Clara Foster's death. I'd failed to save Jason's cousin Ed. I had no more options, no more likely choices for the role of Clara Foster's killer.

I wasn't particularly concerned when I didn't see Diogi's big yellow head hanging out of the truck window. He often took a snooze while I was running some errand or another. But my world changed forever when I opened the driver's side door. The truck cab was empty, completely empty. As was the pavement outside the truck. No Diogi in the truck. No Diogi outside the truck.

My first wild hope was that those kids had come by again and Diogi had followed them off somewhere. But when they'd opened the truck door yesterday, they'd left it wide open. No kid shuts a car door unless a parent tells them to. And this time the door was shut. So, okay, somebody had let Diogi out, shut the door, and he'd wandered off, I told myself.

I told myself that even as I was staring in horror at the sheet of paper on the passenger seat, weighed down by a rock.

He's wandered off, I told myself as I scrambled into the cab, grabbed the paper, and read the words printed on it.

He's wandered off, I told myself even after I'd read the words and put the note down carefully on the seat beside me.

But saying it wouldn't make it so. Because Diogi hadn't wandered off.

"If you ever want to see your dog again," the note read, "do not say a word to the police. Bring $1000 tomorrow for the exchange. You will be contacted with instructions."

Diogi hadn't wandered off. He'd been taken.

Oh god, oh god, oh god. Please no.

I felt the panic rising in me like a hot flood. Diogi kidnapped. Diogi frightened, maybe even hurt. This couldn't be happening. Not to my sweet boy.

Calm yourself, Sam, I told myself firmly.

Calm myself? I shrieked inwardly. *How do I do that?*

Think about what you know about these dog kidnappings. Vivian said the owners have gotten their pets back safely. All you have to do is wait.

Wait?! I don't know how to wait.

It was true. Patience was not one of my virtues. When faced with a dilemma, I charged ahead, wisely or not. But I would listen to the voice in my head this time. I would wait. I would do as I was told.

And you will not go to the police. Not even to Vivian. The person who has your dog could be watching you.

Right. I will not go to the police. Not even to Vivian.

So it was quite a shock to find Vivian in my driveway as I pulled in.

THIRTY-EIGHT

~~~~~~~~

F OR A MOMENT my heart leaped. Vivian had found
Diogi! She'd brought my dog home!

But I knew it wasn't so. This wasn't Vivian the cop wearing her neat detective blazer and her hair back in a bun. This
was Vivian in jean shorts, the end of her braid wrapped with
a leather tie, idly checking out her cell phone while leaning
against her old Honda SUV. This, I realized, was Vivian all
ready for a sailing lesson. Which I'd completely forgotten
we'd arranged for her next day off. Which was today.

Don't tell Vivian.

I tried to compose myself.

*Just act normal. Don't let on. She wants to go for a sail,
you go for a sail. Better that than the sicko who stole your
dog sees her here with you.*

I was actually encouraged to find that I'd moved from
shocked despair to a kind of cold anger. Despair was a giving
up. Anger was a looking forward. *Yeah. Looking forward to
paying that sicko back for putting my dog through this.*

Vivian looked up from her phone and gave me a little
wave. I tried to arrange my features into a semblance of my

normal self. It was a measure of how serious the situation was that I actually managed to do so.

"Vivian," I said as I climbed out of the truck. "Sorry I'm late. Just give me a second to get ready."

"Sure," she said, "take your time. I'll throw the ball for the mutt in the meantime. Where is he?"

Do not tell Vivian.

"At the vet's," I said, and searched wildly for a possible cause. "Getting his glands expressed."

Vivian scrunched her nose up in distaste. "I don't even know what that means, and I don't wanna know."

Which was a good thing, because I didn't know either. I just knew it was something disgusting that vets did.

"Be right back," I said and hurried into the ell before I was forced to tell another ludicrous lie.

I slapped the brochures down on the bed, promising the Universe that I would read them cover to cover if only I got Diogi back safely. *Please, please, please.*

Then I rushed into the bathroom and splashed cold water on my flushed face until I looked only halfway crazed.

And finally I went and sat on my couch and breathed deeply. *This time you're going to do it right, Sam.* And it worked. Long, slow, deep breaths, in and out, in and out, just like Helene had taught me (much against my will) until I could feel my racing heart calm.

A sail would do me good, I told myself as I pulled my hair into a ponytail and threaded it through the opening in the back of my old Nauset Sailing Club baseball cap. At least it would fill a few hours with a kind of focus that might keep me from obsessing over the nightmare I'd found myself in.

Please, please, please.

"Let's go," I called to Vivian as I walked out of the ell.

She slid her cell back into the pocket of her shorts, saying, "Great. Time to let someone else catch the bad guys for a while."

Don't tell Vivian.

"Let's try Big Crystal today," I said.

Normally, I would not suggest that a beginner take on Big Crystal. At low to mid-tide, its shallow waters can be treacherous for those who don't know them well. And gusts from an ocean breeze out of the south or southeast could be a little scary. But Vivian was not your average beginner and a trip out to Big Crystal and back would fill at least a couple of hours. Plus, we were going out at high water, so we'd be able to sail without worrying about staying in the channel. And the wind was a perfectly manageable offshore breeze of about five knots or so. We'd be doing an easy reach both ways. I would take the tiller on the way out, we decided, and Vivian would skipper on the way in.

Unfortunately, an easy reach means just that. It's easy. A few long legs, the sail halfway out, requiring almost no attention, and the skipper with little to do but point the boat in the right direction. It is one of those rare points of sail when skipper and crew can have a conversation that consists of more than "ready about" or "jibe ho." And a conversation was just what I didn't want to have.

But not Vivian, it appeared. Ever the detective, that Vivian.

"So what's wrong, Samantha?" she asked.

Don't tell Vivian.

"What makes you think something's wrong?" I hedged.

"Um, you've got a face like a storm cloud and you didn't even pat the *Miss Marple* on her deck and say, 'Hello, old thing' like you always do when we come aboard."

"I do that?" I asked, amazed. I had no idea.

"Yup, every time," Vivian said. "So I figure you've got something on your mind. Maybe something to do with Clara Foster's murder?"

I grabbed it like a life raft. "Yeah," I said. "I've had a busy couple of days getting absolutely nowhere. I just really don't want to think it could be Ed Captiva. But I've decided it's time to leave it to the professionals."

"Probably," Vivian said. "But tell me what you've been up to anyway. You always have something valuable to contribute." As my mother always says, *You can't flatter people too much*.

I fell for it totally, even though I knew I would just come out looking like an idiot. I explained about finding the remains of the burnt Escoffier in the photo on my phone and not finding the remains of the Hopper "copy."

"So you thought maybe someone started the fire to disguise the theft of a copy of a painting?" she said doubtfully.

"Not exactly," I said. "We did some research, and as far as we could see, there was no original Hopper painting on record. But it definitely existed. Hopper gave it to Kit's mother."

Vivian was quick, I'd give her that. "So you think the painting on the wall was the original," she said. "Kit lied. She never sold the painting, never made a copy."

"Right," I said, and explained my fruitless quest to prove that Thomas Bentley knew the painting was an original and had been planning to sell it on some mythical art black market.

"And this assistant person told you Bentley never went into the house, so he couldn't have seen the painting, and besides, it would be professional suicide, not to mention illegal, not to mention unprofitable to do what you'd suggested."

"Yup," I said. "And here's the kicker. Guess who was the auctioneer at that charity gala for the PAL?"

Vivian let out a bark of laughter. "Man, all the bigwigs were there that night!"

"We don't get a lot of galas on the Cape," I said. "My folks used to get roped into that one, too."

Vivian gave me a look, the kind of look that says, *must be nice to be the daughter of bigwigs*, and for the first time I wondered what kind of obstacles she, a girl from the

Mashpee reservation, had to overcome to get where she was. As the daughter of two journalists, I knew about the prejudice that the Wampanoag had long faced and still faced. I knew about their struggle to control their own land and culture. But before I could apologize for my insensitivity, Vivian had moved on.

"So I'll check out his alibi, but it looks like this Bentley character is off the table," she said. "Who was next?"

Even more shamefaced, I told her about my attempt to cast a perfectly harmless environmentalist in the role of crazed killer.

"Yeah, I could see that that might have been an awkward conversation," Vivian acknowledged. "Might have made sense to come to me first with that one."

"It was all moving so fast," I said. "And I wanted to make sure I was on the right track before I wasted your time."

By this point, we'd reached the channel markers into Big Crystal, an enormous curve of blue water protected from the Atlantic Ocean to the east by a narrow, five-mile-long barrier bar of sand and dune grass known by locals as the Outer Beach. To the west, Big Crystal was bound by the curve of the Fair Harbor shoreline. Straight ahead of us, the bay seemed to stretch endlessly, which in a way it did, as eventually, slightly beyond the horizon, it emptied out into the ocean itself. A few small islands floated in the blue like green oases.

"It's beautiful," Vivian breathed. "And nobody lives on those islands?"

"Not on most of them, unless you include ospreys and peregrine falcons and sharp-shinned hawks. Although a few are privately owned, like Bartholomew's." I pointed to one of the larger islands in the distance. A long, weathered dock stretched out to the channel that skirted the island, a battered Boston Whaler tied up to it. "But the families usually only use them in the summer. Looks like the caretaker is getting it ready."

"Wait, wait, wait!" Vivian yelled, pointing toward the water near Bartholomew's Island where something that looked amazingly like a dog's head was bobbing in the waves. "What's that?"

THIRTY-NINE

~~~~~~~~

I COULDN'T HELP IT. My heart leaped. And then came crashing down to earth.

"Are those *seals*?" Vivian exclaimed.

I squinted out to where she was pointing, where I could just barely make out about a dozen black heads bobbing on the water.

"Yeah," I said. Not a dog. Seals. Whose long square heads look remarkably like the head of a large dog.

Normally, I would have been equally excited. I mean, who doesn't love seals (except fishermen, but that's another story). But not today, not with my terrible, aching worry. "Those are their heads. You want to go take a look?" I asked listlessly.

"How long will it take to get there?" Vivian asked, looking at her watch. "I've got to be at my parents' house for dinner by five."

"Maybe another twenty minutes," I said.

"Then let's go!" Vivian said.

"You got it," I said, heading the boat closer to the wind in the direction of the island. "That's an upwind course, so we'll have to tack back and forth, but it shouldn't take us too long."

The new point of sail required a little more concentration on our part, but not so much that we couldn't continue our conversation, thank goodness. Because my worry about Diogi had come slamming back at me, almost as punishment, I thought, for losing track of it for a while. It was actually a relief to occupy my brain with the puzzle of Clara Foster's death.

"So you've got no more ideas about who might have set that fire and taken that painting?" Vivian asked.

"None at all," I admitted. I told her about my various conversations with Barbara, saying, "Aside from Bentley, there's nobody else likely to know what that painting really was. And if you didn't know what it was, why take it? Plus, if you were expert enough to know what you were looking at, you'd also know that, because it was stolen, you'd never get more than a fraction of its worth."

"Okay," Vivian said, suddenly very serious. "Point one, there *is* somebody aside from this Bentley guy who might know what that painting really was."

I looked at her blankly.

She sighed. "That assistant person, Barbara whatever."

"Barbara Smiley?" I asked, incredulous.

"Yeah, her," Vivian said. "Why not?"

"No reason why not," I said doubtfully. "It's just that she's so, well, invisible. I can't see her as a murderer."

I paused, thinking it through.

"But it might make sense," I mused. "She seems to know her stuff. Clara said that 'they' thought Kit's oils might be worth something. Not 'him.' 'They.' As in Bentley *and* Barbara. And I know Barbara's been in Clara's house. She told me that herself at the memorial service. She said she liked it. And then she'd looked like she wished she hadn't said anything. At the time, I thought it was because Bentley likes her to stay in her place, which means not talking to *his* clients."

"But now you think she realized she'd just admitted being in the house itself, not just the barn," Vivian said.

I nodded. "Maybe she asked to use the bathroom in the house when she and Bentley were in the studio looking over Kit's paintings. And maybe while she was in the house, she noticed the Hopper and asked Clara about it." I paused, remembering back, then added excitedly, "Actually, when Clara was talking to Jenny about the painting, she said, 'You're not the first person to be fooled.' Barbara must have asked Clara about the painting."

At that moment the wind shifted slightly. "Pull the sail in a bit," I said to Vivian. It might take us a second tack to get to the island now, but we'd still make it in time to see the seals and get Vivian back in time. Vivian expertly pulled in the sail to exactly where it needed to be. She really seemed to have a sailor's sixth sense for wind direction, which was pretty impressive for only her third time out.

And then I remembered something else. Something Clara had said to me. *"They're coming by later to pack them up."*

"Oh lord," I said, almost in a whisper. "Barbara was there that day."

"What day?"

"The day Jenny and I were there, the day of the fire."

"Are you sure?"

"Pretty sure," I said. "Clara said 'they're coming by later' to pack up Kit's paintings. It had to be Barbara. Bentley wouldn't waste his precious time packing up a few paintings by some local artist."

But Clara had said more than that. *"They wanted to come by first thing in the morning, but I told them my magic pills make it tough to wake up at a normal hour."*

"Oh god," I said. "And on that first visit Clara said she'd told 'them' about her sleeping pills knocking her out. And by 'them,' I bet she meant Barbara. Barbara does all the arrangements."

Vivian's eyes lit up. "So let's assume Barbara uses the

bathroom in the house and sees the painting. She asks Clara if it's a Hopper, which explains why Clara says that your friend Jenny's not the first person to think that. Barbara knows Clara uses sleeping pills. Barbara arranges to come back in a few days to pack up Kit's paintings. On the way she stops and buys a package of bacon, puts it in her shoulder bag. She carries a shoulder bag?"

"Yup," I said.

"Good," Vivian said. "And how about that bathroom? Did you go in there? Do you know how big the window is? Big enough to climb through?"

Honestly, the woman made my head spin with her staccato questions.

"I did go in," I said. "And the window was your normal window, plenty big enough to climb through."

"Good," Vivian said again. "So this Barbara person spends some time in the barn packing up the paintings, then goes in to say goodbye to Clara. Uses the bathroom again and unlocks the window. Then she leaves, drives over to, say, that public lot at the nature preserve. Parks there. Then she walks back to the house, sneaks in through the bathroom window, and hides . . . where?"

"In the bathroom," I said. "It's the only separate room downstairs."

"Boy, that's a long time to wait in a bathroom," Vivian said doubtfully. "We're talking, like five or six hours, until Clara goes upstairs to bed and then a couple more until Barbara's sure she's asleep."

"I guess she figured eight hours waiting in a bathroom was worth ten million dollars," I suggested.

"But that's where we hit another wall," Vivian said. "She'd know she'd only get a fraction of that amount because the painting was stolen."

Dang. But Barbara was my new favorite suspect and I wasn't giving her up without a fight. *Think, Sam, think.* And then it came to me.

"But she'd get it *all* if the painting *wasn't* stolen," I said.

Vivian looked at me like I'd lost my wits. "So now you're saying she stole a painting that wasn't stolen. "Is there a universe where that makes sense?"

"Think about it," I said. "Yeah, it's hard to sell a stolen painting. But what if you found a lost original? Barbara's grandmother is dying. What if, after she dies, Barbara plans to 'find' the original Hopper in Grandma's attic? She's probably rich. Barbara told me she lives on Big Crystal and waterfront like that costs money. Thanks to Clara, a lot of people know, or think they know, that Kit sold an original Hopper at some point. Why not to Barbara's grandmother? So all Barbara's got to do is get that painting out of Clara's house without anyone wondering where it's gone or why."

Vivian looked at me steadily.

"That's good," she said, "but you've forgotten one thing."

"What?" I asked, somehow dreading the answer.

"She knows that *you're* interested in how somebody would dispose of a stolen artwork. If we're right, this woman's not stupid. She's probably figured out that *you're* wondering where the painting's gone and why."

Oh god, oh god, oh god.

"Any chance this Barbara person has made plans to meet you in some out-of-the-way place?" Vivian asked.

I stared at her. *This Barbara person* who knew that I couldn't lock my truck. *This Barbara person* who knew that Diogi was a sucker for French fries. *This Barbara person* who just happened to meet up with me at Mayo's clam shack, and who, for all I knew, had been following me around for two days, telling Bentley she was tending to her sick grandma while waiting for her chance. Her chance to snatch Diogi. And then to meet me in some out-of-the-way place ostensibly to pay a ransom.

Barbara Smiley had my dog. A killer had my dog.

Tell Vivian. Tell Vivian now.

FORTY

~~~~

WHAT'S THIS?" VIVIAN asked, taking the crumpled piece of paper I'd pulled from my pocket and holding it out to her.

"Just read it," I said dully.

Vivian scanned the note. "Somebody snatched your *dog*?" she asked, incredulous. "And you didn't *tell* me?"

"They said not to," I said miserably. "You told me yourself that the dog snatcher gave the dogs back once they had the ransom money. You told me that nobody told the police until after." I felt the tears I'd been holding back all afternoon begin to well up. "I couldn't take the risk. Not with Diogi."

Vivian nodded. "No," she said, "I get it. Of course you couldn't."

I felt marginally better.

"But," she added, her face grave, "this isn't how the dog snatcher works, Sam." She rattled the note in her hand. "He doesn't leave a note. He calls on a burner phone, tells the owners to leave the money in their mailbox, comes by in the early hours of the morning, takes the money, and drops the dog."

"I didn't know that," I said hollowly. "I thought it was the dog snatcher."

"So now you know who sent this," Vivian said. "You know what this is. This is not about your dog. It's about someone out for you."

I nodded. "I know. It's Barbara Smiley getting me to meet her somewhere so that she can get rid of the only person she thinks knows about the Hopper."

And then, as the tears finally spilled over, I said, "But I don't care about that, Vivian! I care about Diogi. She's got *Diogi*."

Vivian slid along the narrow seat closer to me. She reached out with her free hand and put it over mine. "We'll get him back, Samantha. I promise you, we'll get him back."

"How?" I wailed.

"You'll set up the meeting," she said. "You'll meet this Barbara and my team will be hidden nearby. We'll get her, don't worry."

"But I won't even hear from her until tomorrow," I said. "We can't wait that long! It might be too late."

Vivian nodded, silent. Neither of us was going to say what we really feared. That it was already too late to get Diogi back.

"Okay," she said. "I'll sail. You call that Bentley guy, find out where this Barbara's grandmother lives."

"Can't be done," I said. "There's no cell service out here."

"Then we'll use my police radio," Vivian said, reaching into one of the pockets of her shorts and pulling out a kind of scary-looking mobile unit. "It's got RBX."

I just looked at her blankly.

"Sorry," she said. "It's what we call telephone interconnect. You can make a call to any phone in the radio's coverage without relying on cell service. Just give me this guy's number."

I nodded, pulled my own useless phone out of my pocket, and wiping away my tears, read out Bentley's number from my contacts. Vivian punched it in and handed the radio over to me as she cleated the mainsheet and took the tiller.

"Thomas Bentley's office." An unfamiliar voice, probably the temp.

Thank you, thank you, thank you.

"Hello," I said, trying not to sound as insane as I felt. "This is Samantha Barnes. I have an urgent question for Thomas about the Mulliken case clock. I'm thinking I might not go ahead with the sale." *There, if that didn't get Thomas Bentley on the phone, nothing would.*

"I'll put you through directly, Ms. Barnes," the voice said.

Within seconds, Bentley picked up. "Samantha," he said, his voice worried. "What's this about not going through with the sale?"

"It's an issue I'm having with your assistant, Barbara, actually," I said channeling my grandmother on my father's side, a redoubtable Boston Brahmin herself. "I feel that she's behaved unprofessionally"—Bentley made a little strangled sound, but I didn't give him a chance to respond—"and I'd like to speak with her directly before I decide what to do about your firm handling the sale. I need to speak to her face-to-face. I'd like her grandmother's address in Fair Harbor, please."

"I want to help, Samantha," Bentley said, his voice desperate, "but I don't know it. I don't even know her grandmother's name. She's from the mother's side of the family, I think. But I can call Barbara, tell her to call you."

"Absolutely not," I said firmly. "Please do not speak to her and make matters worse. I will wait to talk to her until she returns. In the meantime, if you can refrain from contacting her, I'm sure we can move forward with the sale once Barbara and I have spoken."

"Of course," Bentley said, the relief in his voice palpable. "I'll say nothing to her until you've had a chance to do so yourself."

"Thank you, Thomas," I said. "I knew you'd understand."

I ended the call and handed the radio to Vivian as I took the tiller back.

"You lie pretty good," Vivian said.

"For all the good it did us," I said miserably. *Diogi, where are you?* "We still don't know where Barbara's grandmother lives."

"Okay," Vivian said. "Go through that conversation again with me, word for word, where she talked about her grandmother. You're good at that."

I shook my head. "It wasn't much. She said her grandmother lived in Fair Harbor, somewhere on Big Crystal."

"Think," Vivian commanded. "What were her exact words?"

"What does it matter?" I said hopelessly. "There's got to be at least a hundred houses along the shore."

"Try anyway," she said.

I stared out toward the blue horizon, willing myself to remember. I'd asked Barbara why she was in Fair Harbor. *My grandmother lives out in Crystal Bay.*

"Oh my god," I whispered, almost to myself.

"What? *What?*"

"She said her grandmother lived out *in* Crystal Bay," I said. "Not on Crystal, not on the shoreline, *in* Crystal!"

Vivian got it right away.

"On one of the islands, you think?" she said.

I nodded.

"How many have houses on them?"

I ticked them off on my fingers. "Bartholomew's, Villeroy's, Taylor's," I said. "Only three."

"Where are they?" she said, looking out over the bay. "Other than Bartholomew's, I mean."

"Villeroy is out there, almost to the Sound," I said, pointing to an island that was hardly a speck on the horizon. "Taylor's is beyond that, I think. I've never sailed that far."

"Okay," Vivian said. "Here's what we're going to do. I'm going to call back to headquarters, get them started on identifying the families that own those islands. In the meantime, you and I are going to take a closer look at Bartholomew's."

By this point we were only about 500 yards from the island, the seals' heads clearly visible now.

"What if she's on the island?" I asked, alarmed. "What if she sees us?"

"The chances are only one in three," Vivian responded. "And do you really think that this Barbara whatshername is up in some tower somewhere scanning Crystal Bay for suspicious characters in sailboats? And besides, we're not going ashore or anything, just scoping it out."

I had to admit she had a point. Plus, it was action of some sort, and when in doubt, Samantha Barnes always prefers action. To the eternal dismay of Helene Greenberg.

"Yeah, okay," I said. "Let's aim for that little beach next to the dock. It's directly upwind, but we can tack up toward it, then sail parallel to the shore. There's probably a break in the trees somewhere along there to give them a view of the bay. Maybe we'll be able to see up the hill to the house."

"Sounds like a plan."

I nodded. "We're about a quarter mile out. Maybe less. I'm going to tack now, and then I figure it'll take us two more short legs to get us in the channel in front of that beach."

"Got it," Vivian said.

"Ready about," I said, and waited automatically for Vivian to give me the usual "ready." Nothing. She was staring at the island.

"Vivian," I said, "ready about."

"Not ready," she responded absently, still staring at the island.

Never in my sailing days had I ever had a crew say not ready. "Ready about" is not so much a request as a courtesy. If the skipper wants to tack, that's kind of their call, not the crew's.

"Not ready?"

"Nope," Vivian said distractedly, then pointed with her free hand toward the path that led down the hill to the dock. "What's that?"

And then I saw it. A blur of yellow fur charging down the path. No, not a blur of fur. A dog. And not just any dog. I knew this dog as much by heart as by sight. It was Diogi.

FORTY-ONE

〰〰〰

H E STOPPED SHORT at the end of the dock.
Even at that distance I could see, almost feel, his quivering intensity as he lifted his broad nose to the breeze. *Oh no*, I prayed silently. *Don't do it, Diogi.*

I'd once read about a study that found that dogs could identify their owners by smell from as far away as twelve miles if the conditions were right. We were much closer, maybe the length of four football fields. And something had brought Diogi barreling down that hill. Even with wind blowing offshore, Diogi had obviously smelled something. Me? Sound, I knew, was heightened over the water because the air is dense with water molecules. Perhaps, then, smells were as well.

"What is he doing?" Vivian said, and I knew that she, too, had recognized Diogi.

"I think he knows I'm out here," I said, almost in a whisper. "I think he's caught my scent."

"Should we call him?"

"God, no," I said. "He'd never be able to swim this far. And keep your voice down. Sound carries over water, too."

"Okay," she said, speaking more softly. "So what do we do?"

"We try to get to the dock before he decides to swim out," I said.

"But what about Barbara?" Vivian asked. "What if she sees us? You know, it's pretty clear she was planning to, well, deal with you in some way. What if she's got a gun?"

Which was entirely possible. A lot of people kept shotguns on the Cape to defend their gardens against pesky critters like groundhogs.

"I don't *care* about Barbara," I hissed. "That's *Diogi* over there. And like you said, she's probably not on the lookout for cops in sailboats."

Vivian nodded her understanding. "Okay," she said. "Let's do it. But I'm going to call Harbor Patrol, tell them to get some police backup out here ASAP."

"It won't be ASAP enough," I said. "It'll take them at least a half hour. But it's worth a try."

To this day, I don't know what she said to the Patrol. I was totally focused on getting to that dock as fast as the *Miss Marple* could take us.

Which wasn't fast enough.

We'd only gone maybe fifty feet, when I saw Diogi's back haunches lower themselves as he prepared to spring.

"Diogi!" I shouted, heedless of any danger from Barbara. "No! Stay!"

But it was too late.

Diogi hurled himself off the dock. And began swimming out to the *Miss Marple*.

Vivian stared at me in horror, the radio forgotten in her hand. "What do we do now?"

And suddenly, my mind was coldly clear. "It's like a man overboard drill," I said. "You're going to watch him, never let him out of your sight. I'll sail. If he starts to go"—and here my voice caught in my throat and it took all my control to continue—"starts to go under, you mark that spot against a landmark on the shore and you never take your eyes off it. Understood?"

"Understood," Vivian said.

The next few minutes felt like hours. Slowly, incredibly slowly it seemed to me, the boat made its way toward Diogi, who continued swimming resolutely, occasionally lifting his nose and checking his course toward the boat like the wonderful, smart, brave dog he was.

Please, please, please.

But I could see that he was flagging. He'd never make it. We'd never make it. Not with our zigzag course.

"Change of plan," I said to Vivian. "You take over. I'm going to go get him."

Again, Vivian did not question me. "Okay," she said as I stood and handed the tiller to her.

"Just keep tacking toward us," I said as I pulled my life vest out from under *Miss Marple*'s deck and zipped it on. I'd never actually worn it before or bothered to adjust it properly to my chest with its three straps, so it was loose on me, but never mind, it would have to do. "When you get within twelve feet of us, head up into the wind to stop the boat. Got it?"

"Got it."

And with that, I kicked off my sneakers and slid off the side of the boat into the water. The vest was loose, but I could maneuver in it and it would keep me afloat. I began to swim toward my dear, brave dog.

Please, please, please, I prayed as I struck out with all my strength, face upright so that my eyes never left that golden head, my arms and legs propelling me forward in a desperate crawl. And though I'd never swum so fast in my life, I knew in my heart of hearts that it was hopeless. *Don't be ridiculous*, a voice in my head said. It sounded remarkably like Helene. *The most important thing is to never, never, never give up.*

And so I kept going, swimming faster than I would ever have thought possible. Diogi, though, with at least another hundred yards between us, had slowed considerably, and I knew he was badly tired.

"It's okay, Diogi," I shouted over to him, desperately hoping he could hear me over the sound of his own breathing and the frantic splashing of his front paws. "It's okay, boy. You can do it."

Was I imagining things, or had his ears perked a bit? Was his paddling stronger now?

And so we continued, me tearing at the water with frantic strokes, shouting encouragement to Diogi.

One hundred yards, fifty yards. Twenty feet.

And then, suddenly, I couldn't see him. He'd gone under.

Please, please, please, I prayed as I flew through the water. And then his head bobbed back up again. His beautiful brown eyes stared into mine as I grabbed for his collar, pulled him toward me, then swam around so that I was next to him, both facing the same direction. I wrapped my arms around his heaving chest.

And realized that our combined weight was more than my life vest could support.

With my legs treading water madly to keep both our heads above water, I looked around frantically for the *Miss Marple*, found the boat about two hundred yards and maybe two tacks away. Even at a glance, I could see that Vivian was doing a good job sailing the boat as close to the wind as possible. But she'd never make it to us in time. I knew I wasn't the one in danger. Even without a life vest, I could float on my back for an indefinite amount of time. But a dog will just keep trying to swim until, well, until they can't anymore. It didn't bear thinking about. It couldn't happen. It wouldn't happen. Not if I had anything to say about it. If Jason could save a drowning horse, I could save a drowning dog. And suddenly I knew how. Or I hoped I knew how.

"It's okay, boy," I said gently to Diogi.

I suppose it was a good thing that Diogi was too exhausted to panic. I knew what I had to do and it would never work if Diogi struggled against me. Still treading water furiously and with one arm around Diogi's chest, I used the other to unzip my life vest. I knew that most standard adult PFDs were sized for thirty- to fifty-inch chests. There was a chance, just a chance that this would work.

I shrugged off the life vest and, holding it tightly with one hand, pushed it down under the water. It took a few tries, but I finally managed to snag the forepaw closest to me with one armhole. Pulling the jacket up so that the arm-hole was now where his leg met his chest, I took a desperate chance and let go of him with my other arm. I would need both hands for this.

To my enormous relief, the brief respite that he'd had while I'd been supporting him seemed to have given Diogi a second wind. I knew it wouldn't last long though.

I swam around in front of him to his other side, still holding the life vest up with one hand, trying to keep it tight enough that it wouldn't slip off the one leg I'd managed to get into the armhole and yet not impede Diogi's ability to paddle.

But getting his other leg into the other armhole was not going to be as simple as the first attempt. With the back of the vest now across Diogi's back, I couldn't simply pull it down under the water to snag his foot. Instead, I had to grab his paw and thread it through the armhole, which would mean going underwater myself. I could only imagine the panic he would feel as I slipped under the waves. And this was not going to work with a panicking dog.

"Diogi," I said as calmly and firmly as I could. "I will be *back soon*." And I will swear to my dying day that he understood me.

Still holding the life vest with one hand, I took an enor-mous breath and let myself sink down until my face was level with Diogi's chest. I could see his legs working like pistons. As quickly and gently as I could, I grabbed his right forepaw and threaded it through the vest's right arm-hole, which meant tipping him about forty-five degrees. If the dog was ever going to panic, now was the time. But Diogi didn't panic. Diogi just kept swimming with three legs. Diogi knew I would be coming *back soon*. I guided his leg all the way through the armhole and kicked myself up to the surface, gasping for air.

"Be back soon," I gasped again to my startled dog before taking another gulp of air and diving back down again.

Because I needed to zip that jacket up. *Please let it fit*, I prayed as I sank down. *Please, please, please.* As quickly as I could, I swam down below his belly and pulled the vest together with both hands. *Yesss.* It was tight but they met. Trying to avoid Diogi's paddling legs, I fumbled at the zipper. One try, then another, and then—*thank you, thank you, thank you*—I felt the two sides of the zipper come together. I pulled the slider up, and with one last kick, I came up to the surface.

Where my dog was bobbing like a cork. A big, beautiful, doggy cork.

"Yo! Samantha!"

I looked around and saw the *Miss Marple* making good time toward us, Vivian standing in the stern, the tiller tucked behind one leg, as she hailed me. In just a few minutes, she'd be close enough to throw me the other life vest. We'd figure out what to do next from there.

"Okay, boy," I said, "you and I are just going to wait here until Aunty Vivvie comes and picks us up."

And with that, I took hold of Diogi's collar and floated spread-eagled on the water like an exhausted starfish. Everything was going to be all right.

That was when I heard the shout from the shoreline.

"Hey, you! You bring that dog back here!"

I SPLASHED UPRIGHT AND turned toward the small beach on the island behind me. I knew who I was going to see, of course. Barbara Smiley. I'd been somewhat prepared by Vivian for the shotgun dangling from one hand at her side, but no one is *really* prepared for a shotgun. My heart began to hammer. *At least she isn't pointing it at you, Sam.*

And then she was.

"I mean it," Barbara shouted as she raised and pointed the gun at me. "I want my dog back."

Her dog? Was she going to shoot me and claim she'd just been trying to scare me into bringing *her* dog back?

And then Vivian Peters did one of the bravest things I have ever witnessed.

Still standing with one leg hooked around the tiller, she shouted across the water at the woman with the gun, "Barbara Smiley, I am Detective Vivian Peters of the Fair Harbor Police. You are under arrest for the murder of Clara Foster. The Harbor Patrol backup is right behind us. You cannot win. You will lower that gun immediately and throw it at least ten feet out into the water."

It was as if time itself slowed.

Barbara Smiley turned toward Vivian, the gun still in the ready position. Then slowly—much too slowly, it seemed to me—she lowered it and, as if she'd come to a decision, finally threw it violently into the bay. The fight was gone. She bent at the knees and collapsed, kneeling, onto the beach, bending her head into her hands and slowly rocking back and forth in a wordless keening.

"Good," Vivian shouted. "I want you to stay exactly there, Barbara. Do you understand? You are not to move."

The bowed head nodded silently. Barbara Smiley was vanquished.

FORTY-TWO

~~~~~~~~

I T MAY SEEM odd to those who do not sail themselves, but what was almost as amazing as Vivian Peters's bravery in the face of Barbara Smiley's shotgun was her handling of the *Miss Marple* through it all.

The woman had judged the swiftest course toward me while I was frantically trying to reach Diogi, had kept the boat sailing true while she talked a killer into dropping her weapon, and then, when she was six feet away from Diogi and me, had thrown the *Miss Marple* into irons to bring the boat to a gliding stop. While the mainsail and jib flapped, she threw me the other life vest and, once I'd slipped it on, helped me get Diogi up and into the boat. That took some doing, with me pushing and Vivian pulling and Diogi, who had finally decided to panic, yelping and scrabbling and generally taking as much paint off the topsides and deck with his big, doggy nails as he possibly could.

Of course, the minute he was actually in the boat, he was super happy. Because there is nothing that Diogi likes as much as being in a boat. Just not climbing into a boat.

I was scarcely more coordinated in getting onto the *Miss*

Marple than my dog, but eventually I managed to flip-flop my way into the cockpit, where I took the tiller and, at Vivian's suggestion, sailed us over to the dock and tied up next to the motorboat moored there.

"You wait here," she said when we landed. She snatched up a length of corded nylon line from under *Miss Marple*'s deck and headed over to Barbara, who had not moved from her place on the beach.

The detective walked across the sand and, without saying a word, firmly helped Barbara to her feet, tied her hands behind her back, and gave her the standard caution. Then she led her to a weathered wooden bench next to the dock, where they sat side by side in absolute silence until Barbara suddenly looked over to where Diogi and I sat huddled together in the *Miss Marple* and said, very calmly, "I'd like to apologize."

My first reaction was, *Yeah, well, I don't care what you'd like.*

My second was, *But I can't stand it. I need to know why you did what you did. What was your one truth that blinded you?*

I looked at Vivian and she nodded. Barbara had been cautioned. She knew the consequences of any statement she might make now.

I stroked Diogi's head and said, "Stay. I'll be back soon." And Diogi understood. Diogi stayed.

I climbed out of the boat onto the dock, walked over to the bench, and sat down as far from Barbara Smiley as possible.

"I don't want an apology," I said. "You cannot apologize enough for what you've done. But I do want an explanation."

"Okay," Barbara said dully. "If I explain it to you, maybe you'll accept my apology." *Doubt it.* I just waited.

"I had to save the island," she said.

You killed a woman for an island? You kidnapped my

dog for an island? You were going to kill me for an island?
I wanted to ask. What I asked was, "Why?"

"My mother was a Bartholomew," she said. "I'm Barbara Bartholomew Smiley."

She stopped there, as if that explained everything. Which in a way it did. I knew about the Bartholomews. It would be hard to live in Fair Harbor and not know about the Bartholomews. Frederick Bartholomew had founded the village of Fair Harbor in 1657, and his increasingly wealthy progeny had produced one of the great Cape Cod clans, now much diminished but for some three hundred years extremely influential pillars of the community. My Grandpa Barnes once told me that his grandfather remembered the first automobile that had braved the rutted roads of Fair Harbor, owned, of course, by a Bartholomew. Fair Harbor was still dotted with the Bartholomew name, including the town square, known as Bartholomew's Green, and Bartholomew's Point, a great swath of land along Big Crystal, once the site of Frederick's original cattle farm and now owned by the Conservancy. The island we were now unhappily visiting sat just off Bartholomew's Point. Over time, the family had faded out as more and more of Frederick's descendants moved to the mainland, primarily to Boston. I hadn't even realized there were any Bartholomews left in Fair Harbor.

"Bartholomew's Island has been in my family for more than nine generations," Barbara continued, her voice unconsciously swelling with pride. "Our name *meant* something," she added, her voice almost pleading with me to understand. "The island is all that we, my grandmother and I, have left. And now they want to take it away from us."

"They who?" I asked. "And why?"

"Lawyers," she said with disgust. "When my pathetic father died five years ago, it turned out he'd squandered what was left of my mother's trust trying to prop up some kind of small-time financial Ponzi scheme. When the thing went bust, he swallowed a handful of sleeping pills and a bottle of vodka, leaving my mother to face the defrauded investors who wanted their money back. Even though my father was a Smiley, my mother felt he'd disgraced the Bartholomew name."

Oh dear, I thought snarkily, *we can't have that.*

But the words were spilling out of Barbara like water that had been dammed too long. "She was determined to pay off the people my father had scammed. Not that she had any choice. The lawsuits never stopped coming. It's taken everything we had, and we still owed hundreds of thousands of dollars. We moved in with my grandmother out here on the island. It was the only thing we had left. The town select board knew, of course, what was happening with us and began pressuring my mother to sell the island to the Conservancy at a ridiculously low price. Enough to pay off our debt, but leaving us essentially penniless. Like they cared. My mother began talking to developers instead, but she died last year before she could move forward on that. I'm convinced she died of a broken heart. Then my grandmother got sick. I'd had everything taken from me, the last of the Fair Harbor Bartholomews, and now I was going to lose my home, my patrimony, unless there was some kind of miracle."

"And the Hopper was that miracle," I said.

"Exactly," Barbara responded excitedly.

I raised my eyebrows at Vivian in mute question. Did she want me to keep asking the questions? Vivian nodded toward me. Barbara had decided that I was the one she wanted to talk to, so the interrogation, such as it was, was in my hands. But good cop that Vivian was, she gave Barbara the standard caution again. Barbara acted as if she wasn't even there.

"Can you imagine how I felt when I saw that painting? All those years trailing around behind Bentley, keeping my mouth shut like he wanted, watching him glad-hand the rich clients while I did all the work. Well, it paid off. You get an eye for the real thing. And I knew that painting was the real thing."

"But you didn't tell Clara Foster that," I said.

"I did, though," Barbara said. "Before I stopped to think, asked if it was a Hopper. And she actually laughed at me." Barbara's face went stony. "She was a mean old lady, all wrapped up in herself. You should have heard her talking to Bentley about giving her land to the Conservancy because she wasn't going to be one of those 'rich fat cats' who sell their land to the highest bidder. Like she had any idea what it was like to *be forced* to sell your land to the highest bidder. So I figured, if she doesn't have the sense to know what she has and if she doesn't want to listen to me, fine. I won't tell her."

"But you could have told Bentley," I pointed out.

"Oh, sure," Barbara scoffed, "and have him take all the credit *and* the commission? I don't think so."

"But you knew that if you stole the painting, Clara would immediately realize that you'd been right, that the Hopper was an original. And you'd never be able to sell a stolen painting with that kind of history."

"You're right," Barbara said. "My only hope was to cover up the theft of the painting in some way and then 'find' the original in my own house. A house fire seemed like the best answer."

"But why kill Clara?" I asked. "Why not just wait until she was out of the house?"

For the first time Barbara looked uncomfortable, maybe even a little guilty.

"If I hadn't blurted out my suspicion that what she had was an original, I could have done that. It was clear that I was the first person to mention that possibility to her. But as it was, I couldn't be sure that she wouldn't put two and two together and realize that the fire was to disguise the theft of the painting. But if she wasn't around to say anything . . ."

"So you decided to make sure she wouldn't be," I continued for her. "You decided that she should die in that fire."

"Hey, look," Barbara said defensively, "the lady was going to die soon anyway."

"How did you know that?" I asked sharply.

"That first appraisal, the one where I was there with Bentley and Clara at the studio?" I nodded. "I asked if I could use the bathroom in the house. The barn didn't have one. Clara said sure, there was a powder room downstairs, and I went back to the house alone. While I was there, I thought I'd look around. I liked her house. I was getting myself a glass of water in the kitchen when I saw this brochure about living with pancreatic cancer on the kitchen island. My grandmother has liver cancer, so I thought it might be helpful. I was standing there reading it when Clara Foster came in. She looked at it in my hand and said, 'I'd appreciate it if you didn't wander around my house reading my private papers.' I felt like a fool, so I said, 'No, no, I just wanted to take a look at those watercolors over there.' And I put the pamphlet down and started to walk over to the watercolors on the dining room wall and then I saw the Hopper."

She paused, clearly back in the moment, the moment when she'd seen the answer to all her troubles.

"And then?" I prompted her.

She shook her head a bit, as if to bring herself back. "And then I went home and looked up Hopper's catalogue raisonné and stage four pancreatic cancer and I knew what I had to do. And that I had to do it quickly, before she died of cancer, before her estate and the contents of her house were appraised and someone else figured out what was hanging on that wall."

She knew what she *had* to do. She *had* to kill an old lady.

Who, because she was cranky and critically ill, deserved to die before her time in defense of Barbara Bartholomew Smiley's one truth—the family name, the family patrimony.

Vivian cleared her throat warningly, and I realized that my feelings, as usual, were written all over my face. Which was not going to help us any. With an enormous effort of will, I kept my temper.

"And it worked," I said in what I hoped was a measured tone. "You knew Clara knocked herself out at night with sleep aids, you knew if you left the bathroom window unlocked you could get into the house and hide while you waited. You thought you could start a fire so that it would look like the result of a forgetful old woman, then take the Hopper and nobody would be the wiser because nobody would even notice the painting was gone. Nobody would suspect that the fire was set to hide a theft."

Barbara looked at me accusingly.

"But *you* did," she said. "Even though at first you thought it was about some old cookbook. I tried to head you off, tell you what a stupid idea it was. And then you wanted to know about the black market in stolen artwork, and I had to tell you how stupid that idea was, too. But I knew where you were headed. This wasn't about any cookbook. It was about the painting. And if you'd figured out that much, I was pretty sure you'd figured out that a lost original was much easier to sell than a stolen one."

"So you followed me around until you could get your hands on my dog," I concluded, "and you held him for ransom." And this time I couldn't hide the disgust in my voice. "Except the ransom was going to be my life."

"Well, I couldn't risk it, could I?" Barbara asked as if I were the one being unreasonable. "It would be easy to ask you to meet me on the island, easy to shoot you—I'm a good shot, my grandmother and I used to shoot skeet up on the hill. I'd wait until you were off the dock and standing on the beach, so any blood would just be on the sand. Later, I'd shovel the sand into the water, bury your body on my property."

There is nothing quite like the sensation of listening to someone coldly describe the anticipated manner of your murder. I felt like I was in one of those awful dreams where you can't wake up. Except it wasn't a dream. It could, in fact, have been a reality.

"And Diogi?" I asked, my voice almost a whisper. *Please let her say she was planning to let him go. Please, please, please.*

"Yes, that's what I wanted to apologize for," Barbara said. "I'm sorry for taking your dog. We always had springer spaniels at the big house when I was a child. I love dogs." *Yeah, just not people.* "I know how awful it must have been for you when you got that note from me. But I swear I was never going to hurt your dog. He's a nice dog. He's been sad with me, but I thought once you weren't around, I could keep him and he'd forget about you."

That did it. *Once I wasn't around? Keep him? Forget about me?*

I'm not sure what I would have done next. I know I leaped to my feet, that I walked over to Barbara and leaned down until my face was only inches away from hers, that I barely registered Vivian putting a steadying hand on my arm.

"The Patrol's coming up to the dock, Samantha," she said quietly. "We're done here."

I turned, still dazed, and saw the Harbor Patrol's Grady-White, piloted by someone—*who wasn't Jason*, I thought miserably—zoom up to the dock. Three police officers jumped out with guns drawn. Vivian waved the cops over, who by this time had seen that the situation was under control, and handed over her prisoner. As Barbara Smiley was being bundled into the Grady-White by the officers, Vivian walked me back to the *Miss Marple*.

"How do you want to get home?" she asked. "We can give you a tow, if you'd like."

"If you don't mind," I said, "I think I'd rather sail."

I needed to empty my mind. I needed to sit with my dog at my side and find some kind of peace.

But Vivian didn't have that option. "I don't blame you," she said as she turned back to the Grady-White and a world that made her doubt the goodness of mankind.

FORTY-THREE

<hr>

A S FOR ME, I had my doubts about the goodness of mankind, too. Until my friends showed up. Every last one of them, one at a time, staying just a few minutes each, as if to reassure themselves that I was in one piece and Diogi back where he belonged. Hogging the bed.

We were in bed because Helene had come over first, somehow knowing I needed her. Because she is a witch. Diogi and I had pulled into Aunt Ida's driveway around five that afternoon to a frantically mewing Ciati, who (also witchlike) knew something was off. Usually we were greeted with silence and a haughty sniff, as if to say, *About time you got back.*

I stripped off my wet clothes, pulled on my ratty old robe, and did the next obvious thing: I made grilled cheese sandwiches for Diogi and me. Helene apparated at the kitchen door just as I was using my thumb to wipe up the last delicious crumb on my plate. Without asking, she walked in, took one look at me, and said, "You need a bath and bed and brandy."

People always want to pour brandy down my throat when I've had a shock. I don't even like brandy, but apparently, it's the law.

"Don't you want to know what's happened?" I asked.

"Not until you're clean and tucked up in bed," she said.

So she drew me a bath in Aunt Ida's claw-foot tub, put some clean jammies on the stool next to it, and waited in the ell, Ciati curled in her lap, while I soaked out all the horror of the day. Diogi, however, followed me into the bathroom as if he did not want to let me out of his sight, poor fellow. When I came out of the bathroom all rosy clean and comfy in my PJs and feeling much, much better, Helene pointed at the bed, where she'd turned the covers down and fluffed the pillows.

"In you go, both of you," she said. So I slid in under the covers, Diogi hopped up on top of them, and once I'd propped myself into an almost seated position, Helene handed me a small tot of brandy.

"Now you can tell me what's happened," she said.

So I did, sipping the brandy and ending with, "I swear I tried to be very, very careful."

She smiled at me. "Of course you did." I felt as if she'd conferred some sort of blessing on me.

"Now," she said. "What do you think you should do next?"

Without even answering her, I picked up my cell and called Jason. I didn't even see her disappear. Of course I never do.

The conversation was not long. Just long enough to go through the day's events, and then finally begin to sob, while Jason said things like "Everything's okay" and "Don't cry" and all those other things that men faced with a crying woman say because *they don't know what to do.*

Eventually, I took pity on him and quit my blubbing, instead ending my recital with, "And I hated it when the Patrol boat came and it wasn't *you.*"

WHILE I WAS falling to pieces on my phone, Helene was filling in the team on hers. I found out later that

Jillian had helped her put together a *conference call*, for Pete's sake, so she wouldn't have to repeat herself. Then they came to check on me, one by one, or two by two in some cases, in twenty-minute intervals, following Jillian's timetable.

First Miles and Mrs. Tanner, who scolded me roundly for risking my life for what she called "some damn fool dog." At which Diogi, who had previously been deep into an exhausted sleep, lifted his head and gave her what can only be described as the stink eye.

"You did it, though, Sam," Miles said, leaning down to give me a big hairy kiss on the cheek. "You proved that Clara couldn't have set that fire herself, either by accident or on purpose."

"No," I said. "It was Ed who did that when he brought up her arthritis."

"But *you* were the one who figured out that this Barbara Smiley was the killer," Miles insisted.

"Wrong again," I said. "That was Detective Peters. I thought it was Barbara's boss, Thomas Bentley."

"But you solved the case," Mrs. Tanner insisted. "You started it and you solved the case."

And then, in an unconscious echo of Jillian's Marcel after the home game, I said, "No, I was just part of the team that solved the case."

Then came Jenny and Roland bearing a bottle of what even I knew was very expensive brandy. They'd stashed the Three Things at a neighbor's house, for which I was grateful. I like those kids, but this was not the time for questions like "Did the bad lady really have a gun, Aunty Sam?"

Jenny skootched Diogi over so she could sit next to me on the bed, where she sat patting my hand as if somehow that could make everything all better. Which, oddly, it almost did.

"I understand you are to be congratulated for apprehending yet another member of the criminal class," Roland said.

I decided I was tired of trying to explain my role and would just go with Helene's suggested approach. "Thank you," I said.

Roland poured some of the very expensive brandy in my glass. I grimaced and took a sip. Actually, the stuff was almost drinkable.

"There," he said. "That's better. I know how much you enjoy brandy." He might have been kidding. It's hard to tell with Roland.

And then came Krista, who couldn't seem to decide whether to be furious with me for "nosing around a murder case that belonged to another reporter" or to be delighted with me for my "scoop."

"And, oh yeah," she added. "I have a great idea." *Uh-oh.* "I thought maybe Jenny could film you and the dog"—Krista almost never called Diogi by his name. She thought his name was silly—"doing a re-creation of you saving him."

I just looked at her. Sometimes it helps to have a face that does the talking for you.

"Too soon?" she asked.

"Krista," I said, "it will always be too soon."

"Okay," she said breezily. "We'll work out something else tomorrow."

Sigh. *Whatever.*

And finally, there was Jillian bearing a plate of brownies still warm from the oven.

"Child," she said, "I didn't know when I met you that I would end up worrying about you more than my own grown kids."

"Sorry," I said through a mouthful of brownie.

"Hold on," she said. "You can't eat a brownie like that."

Then she disappeared into the kitchen and came back with a nice, tall glass of cold milk. This is what happens when you make friends with someone old enough to be your mother. It's great. I took a big swig and wiped the milk mustache from my upper lip with the back of my hand.

"There," she said. "Better?"

"Much better," I agreed.

"Okay," she said. "I'm the last one on the roster, so it's my job to tell you that you have to call your parents."

This is also what happens when you make friends with someone old enough to be your mother.

"Really?" I asked. Okay, whined. "I'm tired. Can't I call them tomorrow?"

"No back talk," she said firmly. "You call your momma."

It wasn't my momma I was worried about as I punched in their speed dial. I knew my investigative journalist mother would consider everything I'd done perfectly reasonable. And I was right.

"There was a mystery to be solved, you solved it," she said. "It's the job."

I didn't bother trying to convince her that, in fact, it was neither of our jobs. It was just our nature.

It was my father I was worried about. Though we tended to play down any health issues in our family, ever since the heart attack that had sent my folks scurrying down to Florida, I had worried about him. Mostly I worried that my shenanigans might give him another heart attack. Not that I'd ever told him that. Heaven forfend.

But I needn't have worried.

"You did all the right things, Sam," he said calmly. "In extreme circumstances, you were sensible and practical." This, from a man who was sensible and practical to his Yankee core, was high praise indeed. "I'm proud of you."

"Thanks, Dad," I said, and, when I realized my voice was wobbling, hastily added, "Gotta go."

"Me too," my father said.

And we both hung up, somehow both knowing we were loved.

And then, with the 'rents informed and last of the team out the door, I fell asleep.

And woke the next morning to Jason standing beside my bed.

It was like some kind of weird replay of the morning he'd arrived after Ed's arrest. He was bleary-eyed, unshaven, rumpled. But this time he was beautiful. Easily the most beautiful sight I'd ever seen.

"You look terrible," I said.

"You look beautiful," he said.

"You do, too," I amended.

"Which is it, terrible or beautiful?"

"Terribly beautiful," I said.

And then I got up and made the man a grilled cheese sandwich.

FORTY-FOUR

I WAS NOT THE only one rejoicing at Jason's return. While he munched on his breakfast grilled cheese, Ciati said hello, loudly and repeatedly, to her human, who was the only human in the world who knew exactly the best spot to scratch under her chin. Then Diogi had to say hello, with much slobbering, to his human's human, the Man with the Boat. Then, once I had fed my human and convinced him to take a shower, I had to persuade him to take my place in bed—without me.

"Stay with me," he said, pulling me close. "We've got a lot of catching up to do."

It is extremely difficult to resist a man all fresh and damp from a shower and wearing nothing but a towel. Especially if that man is Jason Captiva. Who is universally acknowledged to be the hottest harbormaster in the history of harbormasters.

"Save your strength for later," I said as I pushed him toward the bed and danced out of his reach.

"Mmmm," Jason said sleepily as he pulled the covers up to his chin. Within seconds he was out like a light.

"Big talker," I whispered.

* * *

M Y NEXT PORT of call was the Fair Harbor Police Department. Vivian had texted me that morning asking me to come by to give an official statement and I, of course, agreed. I had a few questions of my own to ask, and if we could circumvent Chief McCauley, I might get some answers to them.

Luck was with me. McCauley, Vivian told me, was off doing some course in Bourne on "Improving Community Relations." This made me laugh. "Just not having the man in the community improves relations, if you ask me," I said.

"Which nobody is," Vivian said severely. But I'd seen the little smile she hadn't been able to hide in time.

The Fair Harbor Police headquarters sits across the street from Thompkins Park. A few years ago an enterprising food truck vendor had recognized that the Fair Harbor cops, whose canteen was notoriously bad, were his for the fleecing. He did a very brisk business in coffee and donuts from the park's parking lot. While we waited for my statement to be typed up, Vivian and I walked across the street and spent a few minutes perusing the choices. As I am a donut purist, I asked for the simple glazed option. Vivian, who apparently views a donut as merely a vehicle for as many sugar-laden toppings as possible, went for something called a double chocolate cream with rainbow sprinkles.

"That," I said as we walked back to her office, "is not a pastry befitting your professional dignity."

"Hey," Vivian said, "we just cracked a high-profile murder case. My professional dignity can withstand a little hit from a donut."

I was glad to see her in such good spirits. I was also ridiculously pleased that she had said "we."

"How did it go with Barbara?" I asked, taking a tiny sip of my coffee in its brown paper cup. It was good but very, very hot.

"Well, like you saw, all the fight was out of the woman," Vivian said. "I'm glad you got as much out of her as you did, though. Because once she had a lawyer in her corner, she wasn't doing a lot of talking. Your statement is going to be crucial."

"But will it be enough to convict?" I asked.

"It'll help," Vivian said. "Even without a formal confession, which isn't enough to convict by itself anyway, we've got motive, opportunity, and method. All thanks to you."

She took an enormous bite of her sugar bomb, followed by a huge gulp of steaming hot coffee.

"How do you do that?" I said.

"Do what?"

"Drink coffee hot enough to cause third-degree burns."

"It's a required course at Police Academy," she said.

Not to be outdone, I took a slightly larger sip of my brew followed by a couple of frantic breaths to try to cool it down in my mouth. When I was able to speak, I asked, "And what about the Hopper?"

"We're searching the house on the island for the painting. Once we've found it—and we will find it—we're golden."

I had no doubt that Vivian Peters would find that painting.

"You realize, of course," I said, "that the Hopper belongs to the oyster farmers, the Joys. They're going to want it to get it authenticated."

"I hadn't thought about that," Vivian said. "I gotta talk to that lawyer, Roland Singleton. I don't want to complicate this thing right now. It'll probably take some time for Clara Foster's will to go through probate. Maybe he'd be willing to hold off on telling the Joys about the painting until then. I don't care if it is by some famous artist; it's crucial evidence and we need to keep the chain of evidence clean. It's got to stay in our hands."

"Tell you what," I said. "When you do find it, why don't you ask an expert to come out from Boston's Museum of Fine Arts and take a look? When Jenny was looking for that particular painting, she went to their online archives first. They've got something like fifty Hoppers in their collection. They can at least tell you what you've got. I think Roland would be willing to hold off getting the Joys' hopes up until he has a better idea of what their hopes should be."

And what would obviously be yet another huge disappointment for Jean Wilkinson, I thought. Honestly, I was beginning to feel sorry for the woman.

Vivian, after one final swipe at the chocolate on her face with the food truck's totally inadequate tissue-paper napkin, stood up.

"Okay," she said, "time to get back to catching bad guys."

"Or bad girls."

"Or bad girls," she agreed.

I handed her my napkin, which I had not had to use because I had eaten a grown-up's donut.

"You've got more chocolate on your chin."

She took the napkin and scrubbed her chin.

"Thanks, Samantha," she said.

"Why don't you just call me Sam?" I suggested.

Vivian looked unaccountably pleased. "Well, sure, Sam," she said. "And maybe you could call me Vivvie?"

Vivvie. Suddenly the name had a good sound. Like the name of a friend.

"You got it, Vivvie," I said.

FORTY-FIVE

THE NEXT STOP for me was the Fair Harbor Farmer's Market, one of my favorite places in the whole world. Every Sunday from May to October, local purveyors set up their wares on the town square, which I was now trying hard not to think of as Bartholomew's Green. You can wander to your heart's content admiring amazing produce like white radishes so pretty you hated to eat them and sampling yellow cherry tomatoes so sweet that you were reminded that tomatoes are indeed actually a fruit.

I picked up some banana nut bread for Jason's breakfast/lunch if he ever woke up, plus a jar of homemade beach plum jelly for me to slather on my sourdough toast. At the Fur Buddies Bakery stand, I stopped for Diogi's favorite peanut butter dog biscuits and Ciati's salmon "goldfish" crackers. Then I picked up a pound of scallops fresh off the boat and some early baby zucchini with their blossoms still attached. (Tip: If you can get your hands on fresh zucchini blossoms, dip them in a light flour-and-water batter and then deep-fry them in a couple inches of sunflower oil. They make a great appetizer.) I grabbed a head of Boston Bibb lettuce so fresh, it still had the morning's dew on it for a salad that would include the halved cherry tomatoes and sliced white radishes. There. Dinner done.

I didn't bother with dessert. Dessert was going to be ice cream at Dream Cones. Tonight, I thought I'd go with a crisp classic waffle cone topped with a double dip of salted caramel swirl and coffee chocolate chip. Jason would, I knew, stick to one scoop of vanilla and one of chocolate. He claims it's because he's a purist, but I think it's because he's a Puritan. He once told me he thought my ice cream choices were "decadent." And when I'd protested, he'd said, "But that's great. I like decadent in a girl." Which made me all flustery.

Jason was still sleeping when I got home, so I went into the kitchen to put the groceries away and gave the kids a few treats while we waited for him to wake up. Then I toasted a couple slices of sourdough, slathered them with butter and beach plum jelly, and indulged myself happily. After all, I'd had a tough day yesterday. Then I gave Diogi some more treats because, after all, he'd had a tough day, too. Then I gave Ciati a few more goldfish because, even though her day had been pretty good, she was now protesting so loudly at Diogi's preferential treatment that I was afraid she'd wake Jason up. I had never met a cat so vocal. Or so argumentative.

While we were chowing down, Jason wandered into the kitchen wearing nothing but those faded blue jeans and that fine California tan. You don't get that kind of tan on the Cape. He looked like one of the guys on the covers of those steamy romances that I'm always too embarrassed to buy at Fair Harbor's bookstore because the owner, Madeline, is kind of judge-y. "But not so judge-y that she doesn't stock them," Jenny had once pointed out to me as she pulled one called something like *Love's Manly Messenger* off the shelf and added it to her pile by the cash register.

"What's wrong with that cat?" Jason asked as he reached over to snag my last remaining piece of toast.

"Good morning to you, too," I said as I swatted his hand away from my grub.

In response, the man leaned down and gave me a kiss that made me glad I was already sitting down. I handed him my last piece of toast.

He grinned, took a huge bite, and said, "See? The kiss worked."

"It always works," I admitted. "You're a first-class kisser. That's the only reason I keep you around."

"Well," he said, taking my hand and pulling me up from the chair and into his arms, "let's see if we can find another reason."

It was a long time before Jason got back to that piece of toast.

W HAT *is* WRONG with that cat?" Jason asked.
      We were sitting next to each other on the porch, Jason sipping a Sam Adams and I a glass of wine, enjoying the end of the day as it slid into a rose-and-gold evening.

"She wants more of her special goldfish," I said over Ciati's wails. Maybe she was part Siamese?

"You're feeding my cat goldfish?" Jason asked, sounding slightly horrified.

"Goldfish crackers," I explained. "All natural, made with salmon from the Fur Buddies pet bakery."

Jason rolled his eyes. "A pet bakery," he repeated. "When did Fair Harbor get a pet bakery?"

"While you were off rescuing horses with the Santa Barbara Harbor Patrol," I said.

Jason's face got serious at that.

Uh-oh.

"They offered me a job," he said abruptly.

Oh god, oh god, oh god.

I didn't say a word. I couldn't. Even Ciati had gone quiet at that.

"I don't have to decide now," he said, looking down at his beer bottle as if reading the label required all his concentration. "The opening isn't until September, and I don't have to give them an answer for a couple of weeks."

"Are you considering it?" I finally asked.

He looked up at me, and I could see the uncertainty in his eyes. "I don't know," he said at last. "But if I do, I'm hoping you'll come with me."

And then I couldn't help myself. Leave the Cape? Leave my life, my friends, my house, my job?

"Oh, but Jason," I cried before I even knew what I was saying, "I'm the Cape Cod Foodie."

I T IS A measure of the man that he understood what I was saying.

"Of course you are," he said, smiling at me, trying to lighten the mood. "You're a Cape Cod girl, born and bred. I'm surprised you don't comb your hair with codfish bones."

Despite the lightness of his tone, I knew what he was saying. Better than anyone other than Helene, Jason understood how I had struggled with my choice—not that it had even been a choice in the beginning—to make a new life on the Cape, to leave my old life, my old dreams, behind. I doubted, though, that he understood that now I had new dreams, new dreams that included him and a life together in this place that both of us loved, me once reluctantly, him always wholeheartedly. I hadn't told him about this dream. I'd thought I had time, once he was home. And even now I didn't tell him. Even now, when it seemed to be slipping out of my grasp. But not because of my usual reticence about talking about my feelings.

Jason had always made it very clear that he would never stand in the way of my ambitions, even when I had wanted him to (or thought I wanted him to). And I was not going to stand in the way of his. I'd listened to him on the phone for weeks, listened as he talked about his work in Santa Barbara, his voice vibrant with discovery and the joy of learning new skills. I knew the Patrol there was four times the size of Fair Harbor's, its remit much larger, its budget substantial. I knew what kind of prospects it could offer to a man of Jason's ability and dedication. And I was not going to stand in the way of that.

"Please," I said. "I wasn't saying, no, I won't come if you decide to take the job. I honestly don't know what I'll do. But I'm not going to be the deciding factor, Jason. I'm so proud that they've seen your worth, and I want you to have every opportunity a job like this could offer you. You need to come to a decision based on your goals, your dreams."

And then I added, "And if I do go, I can always be the Santa Barbara Foodie." I hoped I'd said it with a light touch. But just saying it made my heart sink.

Jason looked at me, doing that very, very still thing he does when he's trying to master some emotion.

"Well, we'll see," he said finally. "Like I said, there's no rush to decide."

Then he changed the subject in the way he knew was most likely to divert my attention from the subject at hand.

"C'mon," he said, "let's go get some ice cream."

FORTY-SIX

B Y MUTUAL UNSPOKEN agreement, Jason and I shelved the Santa Barbara discussion in favor of simply enjoying the five days we had left before he went back to work at the Fair Harbor Patrol on Monday. It was, in an odd way, an idyllic interlude, perhaps because we both knew it might be our last truly happy time together. Since Jason had cut short his stint in the exchange program to come back after my latest encounter with a murderer, his apartment over the Patrol offices was still the domain of his exchange buddy, so he moved in with me and the animals, where we played happy family on our little piece of paradise.

The weather held fine, so in the morning we'd take a long walk around the sandy roads of Bayberry Point or dive into the clear, cold water of Bower's Pond and swim laps out to the channel marker and back. Then we'd lie on the dock's sun-warmed boards before heading back up to the house for lunch and what Jason insisted on calling—delicately, I thought—a "siesta." Apparently, people in Santa Barbara thought a little nap after lunch was perfectly normal. Not that we napped.

Afternoons were dedicated to work. This consisted on

my part of some Foodie features for Krista with titles like "Summer Salads for When It's Too Darn Hot" and "Grilling for Dummies." (Tip: Not that you're a dummy or anything, but if you're grilling chicken, try skinless, boneless chicken thighs. They've never met a marinade they didn't like, and unlike chicken breasts, they are almost impossible to overcook, so they never dry out.) Jason's contribution was to sample my test recipes and rate them yea or nay. To my certain knowledge, he never rated a single one nay.

Not that we didn't have the occasional excitement. On Wednesday, Nat came by as promised to screen in the unscreened-in porch. He did a beautiful job. Each screen had been inset into a wooden frame painted a soft blue-green that almost exactly matched the original paint of the posts and beams of the porch. Within a few hours Nat had pieced the screens into place, and Jason held them steady while Nat adjusted the brass butterfly latches that held them firm against the porch framing. When it was all finished and Nat had driven off after refusing Jason's offer of a beer ("Been sober ten years," he'd said. "Be a shame to ruin my record now."), I sat at the picnic table, that is, the outdoor dining set, and marveled at my screened-in screened-in porch. Samantha Barnes was now the proud owner of what those fancy magazines called "an outdoor living space."

This milestone was only surpassed by the delivery later that afternoon of my peacock chair and a wooden porch swing, all paid for by the proceeds of the sale of my Golden Age mysteries by the lovely Abraham Beame. Miles took some time off to come over and help Jason hang the swing, much to my delight and Diogi's disapproval.

Diogi did not like the porch swing. It was Diogi's opinion that furniture should not move. For the first few hours he barked madly at it every time it swayed in the breeze before finally giving it up as a lost cause. Jason and I spent a lot of time on that swing for the next few days, leaning against each other like some kind of old married couple, completely content.

But when I was on my own, I sat in my peacock chair. I *loved* my peacock chair. It made me feel like royalty.

At night after a latish dinner, Jason and I would settle into the soft down cushions of the old couch in the living room to read, Jason happily engrossed in a history of some civilization I'd never even heard of, me devouring some mystery by a writer that he'd never heard of. Nights can be chilly on the Cape, even in late June, so we'd light a fire and Diogi and Ciati would plop down on the floor in front of the fireplace, where they would curl around each other and promptly fall asleep. When the flames had died into embers and our eyes were too heavy to read another word, we'd retire for the night, happy with our day's labor and each other.

And we did labor. Or at least Jason did. The man was obsessed with preparing the clambake pit so that everything would be ready for my Fourth of July BYOL clambake. I have honestly never seen a man so happy. First, he had to scout out the perfect spot on the little sand beach next to Aunt Ida's dock, making sure it would be above the high tide mark on the day. He wouldn't dig the actual pit until Sunday, the morning of the Fourth, but over the next three days, he and the Three Things scoured the shoreline for the grapefruit-sized rocks that would line the bottom of the pit. These they piled in an ever-growing cairn that was so beautiful I almost didn't want it trashed for the clambake. Almost, but not quite.

Next came the collection of the driftwood for the fire that would heat the rock layer. This became Diogi's favorite game ever. The boys would run up and down along the shoreline vying with each other to carry back the most pieces of silvered, twisted wood. Then Diogi would pick out the largest, heaviest piece, grab it firmly in his teeth, and drag it backward to the Man with the Boat, who would praise him lavishly. Then later that night Jason would sneak down to the beach and return Diogi's offerings to the main pile so as not to hurt his feelings.

I N ALL THE excitement about the preparations for the big day, I hadn't really thought about what was happening in the case against Barbara Smiley. I assumed it was going according to plan, that they'd found the Hopper, but I hadn't heard a peep from Vivian since our conversation over the donuts. I was even curious enough to ask Roland if he'd heard from her about the Hopper, since he was the one who would have the happy task of telling the Joys the news that they were now in possession of a painting worth millions.

"We did talk," he'd said. "I agreed with her that it was prudent not to raise their hopes until such time as this alleged painting is recovered and authenticated."

Alleged painting. Roland is, indeed, always prudent.

"But you haven't heard if the painting's been found?" I asked.

"Not a word," Roland said.

I tried not to look as worried as I felt. But really, what was the holdup?

FORTY-SEVEN

I TRIED TO PUT the case against Barbara Smiley out of my mind. *Not your circus, not your monkey, Sam*, I reminded myself. Not particularly successfully. Something was wrong. The only thing to do was concentrate on my Fourth of July clambake picnic. What my picnic needed was more people! Because, as things had turned out, my bank balance could handle it.

Bentley had actually auctioned off what he continued to call, annoyingly, "our clock." Not so annoyingly, he had upped the minimum bid significantly, given what he called my "online exposure." Which sounded dirty but just meant the ridiculous number of hits on my *Antiques in the Attic* YouTube clip, which were now in the six digits. But if the payback for cussing on-screen was a nice juicy check for Aunt Ida's clock, I'd figured I could bear the embarrassment. And I was right. It was a super-nice payback. I could invite as many people as I darn well pleased to my Fourth of July picnic.

So Diogi and I headed over to Clara's beach, where the Joys were working out on the flats in their matching mud-streaked rubber overalls, to invite them to the party.

"We'd love to come," Elisha said. "We've got some good news to share."

I assumed the good news was what I'd already heard from Thomas Bentley, who'd been quick to call me after Barbara's arrest to make sure I understood that he'd "known nothing about that dreadful woman's plans." I'd assured him that that was the case, and he'd added that given the publicity the case was going to generate, he was considering upping the estimate for Kit's paintings to a minimum bid of fifty thousand dollars and had discussed that with the couple. So, though I said nothing to the Joys, I had some idea of what their good news was.

"That's great," I said. "We can celebrate together."

I left them standing there, their arms around each other's waist as they waved goodbye. I was suddenly very aware of how happy they were in their work, in the modest, fulfilling life they were living. And for the first time I wondered if and when they finally got possession of the Hopper, becoming millionaires might not be a good thing at all for them.

Well, there wasn't much I could do about that, but maybe there was something else I could put right. I'd been wrestling for days with guilt for what I'd put poor Summer Robinson through.

"C'mon, Diogi," I'd said. "We've got some bridges to rebuild."

We found Summer pinning laundry onto her line. It took some thorough groveling on my part, but eventually she thawed enough to offer me some herbal tea. While Diogi, Bear, and Alba chased one another in delighted circles, we sat in ancient Adirondack chairs in her garden surrounded by a sea of orange daylilies and found common ground in our love for the Cape, dogs, and surprisingly, murder mysteries.

"I've got Deborah Crombie's latest Duncan Kincaid/ Gemma James novel," she said. "You're welcome to borrow it."

Understanding that with that offer I had been officially pardoned, I responded by inviting her to my picnic.

"I'd be delighted," she said. "Could I perhaps bring a new friend?"

"The more the merrier," I said. "Just bring your own lobsters if you want them."

At which Summer blanched and said, "I am not in the habit of eating crustaceans such as lobsters or shrimp."

Which, in retrospect, I might have expected. "Of course you aren't," I amended hastily.

"But," Summer added with a smile, "I consume shellfish such as clams and oysters with abandon." *Well, everyone has their little inconsistencies.* "I assume you're having steamers?"

"You bet we're having steamers," I said.

"Good," Summer said with great satisfaction. "I look forward to the feast. And I will bring some home-brewed beer as my contribution to the festivities."

Uh-oh.

My next invitation went to Abraham Beame, who was, he said, delighted to come. In fact, he said it twice. He would be delighted, yes, delighted to come. I really, really liked Abraham Beame.

And last, but certainly not least, I asked Vivvie. I'd run into her at the post office, and though I was pretty sure it was going to be all hands on deck for the Fair Harbor Police Department on the Fourth (beer and fireworks never being a good combo), I was so happy to see her again that I mentioned it just in case she'd be free.

"Any chance you could come by for a little Independence Day picnic with Jason and me and a few other friends?" I asked.

"Well," she said as we walked out of the post office, "it's not really *my* Independence Day, you know."

I was stricken. Once again, I'd been insensitive to her Wampanoag heritage.

Vivian took one look at my face and burst out laughing. "I'm teasing you!" she said. "Sure, I'm Wampanoag nation but obviously I'm also American. It's kind of like dual citizenship. I'd love to come to your picnic, but I'm taking July third off for our tribe's annual paw-wah, so I'm on call for the Fourth."

I felt marginally better. "Couldn't you just drop by?"

"I'll try," she said.

"That would be great if you could," I said. Then I added, because I just couldn't help myself, "How's the case coming against Barbara Smiley?"

Vivvie looked distinctly uncomfortable. "It's complicated," she said. "Maybe I'll have more to tell you by the Fourth."

From the all-business look on Vivvie's face, I knew I'd have to be satisfied with that. But driving back to Aunt Ida's house, I worried. Had something gone wrong?

I comforted myself with the thought that the important thing was that Ed Captiva was a free man. Second only to that good news was Ed's offer, when Jason invited him to our clambake, to take charge of the actual clam baking, as he called it. But only, he'd added, "if Sam wouldn't mind."

Mind? Mind giving over the responsibility for tending a driftwood fire for two hours until the rocks below it were glowing red while I went to the Fair Harbor Fourth of July parade? Mind not lining those red-hot rocks with a thick base of wet seaweed, then layering in the potatoes, clams, lobsters, sausage, and corn, then adding another blanket of seaweed? Mind not wrestling with the heavy cotton tarp that had been soaking overnight in the pond and topping the whole thing with it to seal in the steam generated by hot rocks and wet seaweed? And finally, mind not keeping watch for another hour or so while everything cooked? Mind giving that little job to Ed? No, I said to Jason, I would not mind giving clambake kitchen duty to Ed Captiva.

"But in recognition of Ed's service," I said, "I insist that we provide our chef with a massive cooler filled with enough Sam Adams to get him through the gig."

"I love how thoughtful you are," Jason said, suddenly serious.

Any other man might have said that line lightly. Any other woman might have taken it lightly. But Jason was not one to talk about love lightly. He was never going to end a phone call with a casual "love ya." In the year that we'd been more or less together, he'd never actually said, "I love you." But he was completely unembarrassed to say, with absolute sincerity, things like "I love the way you laugh" or "chop an onion" or "look in those short shorts" or "always stop to talk to dogs."

Oh, Sam, Sam, Sam. What are you going to do?

FORTY-EIGHT

WHAT I DID was nothing. At Helene's suggestion, I might add. It had taken me almost a week to finally talk to her about my dilemma. Our dilemma, actually. Jason's and mine. I knew that Jason was as conflicted as I was. He was pure Cape, born and bred. His life had been dedicated to preserving our fragile peninsula. It was hard, as I knew from experience, to leave the Cape behind, no matter how far away you went. Yes, Jason had liked his time in Santa Barbara. What wasn't to like? I'd seen the pictures. It was a beautiful town on a beautiful coastline filled with beautiful people living in beautiful houses and sailing beautiful boats in California's beautiful weather.

But Santa Barbara wasn't the Cape. It was that simple. Or not that simple. It had taken me an entire year to figure that out for myself. And now Jason had to figure it out in a couple of months. And I didn't know how to help.

So one night, as Jason and I were reading after dinner, I said, trying hard to sound casual, "I haven't seen Helene in like forever. I think I might go over and have a chat with her, see how she's doing."

"Oh, she's fine," Jason said, looking up from the enormous tome on African history he'd been reading. "I saw her a couple of days ago at the library. She recommended this book on the Mali Empire to me and it was lunchtime so we got a couple of lobster rolls at Stone Harbor and watched the fishing boats for a while."

"Well, I miss her," I said. "I'll be back in a little bit."

"Have fun," Jason said vaguely, already back to the Mali Empire. Whatever that was. He'd told me, but I'd already forgotten everything except that incredible amounts of gold were involved.

And so Diogi and I trotted over to Helene's house to ask her what to do.

And she said "nothing." As in, "Do nothing." In fact, those were her exact words. "Do nothing," she said.

"Do nothing," I repeated, raising my eyebrows. "I should do nothing."

"That's my advice," Helene said. "Jason gave you the space you needed to make up your own mind about what you wanted to do, where you wanted to be, *who* you wanted to be. And from what you've told me, you've made it clear to him that you're going to give him that space, too. I'm impressed. And I think you should do exactly that. Which means do nothing."

Helene was impressed. Which was kind of like impressing the Dalai Lama.

"Okay," I said. "But what if he decides to go? What do I do then?"

"Oh, Sam," Helene said, sighing. "I don't know."

Helene didn't know. Which was kind of like Ken Jennings throwing in the towel in *Final Jeopardy*.

"If you don't know," I said, okay, moaned, "how am I supposed to know?"

"Sam," Helene said severely, "you're a grown-ass woman." A *grown-ass* woman? Helene had definitely been spending too much time with Beth. "Do not cross that bridge until you come to it. Enjoy this golden time with your man. If and when you have to face that question, you will know the answer. Trust yourself."

Trust myself. *As if.*

The next day, to distract myself from doing nothing while Jason made maybe the biggest decision of his life, of *our* life, I did the final shop for the big event, armed with a nice wad of cash contributed by my sweetheart.

First, I made my way to Snyder's Fish Market, where I picked up the order I'd put in for the steamers and two chicken lobsters for Jason and me. (Tip: Live lobsters and clams can keep happily in the fridge overnight. But it is very important that they be allowed to breathe. Always make sure the bag they are in is open at the top.)

Then a quick stop at Nelson's Market, where I stocked up on several large coils of Portuguese linguica sausage, vast quantities of butter, and a bag of lemons. Finally, I finished up at a local farm stand, where I scored eight pounds of new red bliss potatoes, two-dozen ears of corn, and four pints of fresh blueberries. Because no way was I picking huckle-berries for the four blueberry buckles that I, with Jillian's expert help, was going to bake that afternoon.

You'd think all this would take my mind off Jason for at least a little while. But you'd be wrong. The only thing that was taking my mind off Jason was Vivvie's unexpected "It's complicated."

I couldn't stop wondering what she'd meant by that. Complicated how? Had Barbara confessed officially to the murder of Clara Foster? Had her confession, or lacking that, my statement about what she'd said to me on the is-land, been backed up by the forensic evidence? And most important, had they found the Hopper and confirmed Bar-bara's motive for Clara's murder?

Oh, for the good old days of Golden Age mysteries when the story simply ended with the unmasking of the murderer by the brilliant detective.

FORTY-NINE

WHEN THE FOUNDING Fathers invented the Fourth of July, they were not thinking about dogs. Not that I blame them. I know they had other things on their minds. But still, the Fourth is tough on the doggies.

Last summer, when Diogi was just a pup, I'd tied a red, white, and blue bandanna around his neck to match my own blousy red top, navy blue jeans, and white high tops and taken him to the town's Fourth of July parade. The Three Things had promised Diogi they would save him a spot on Main Street just in front of the Penny Candy Store. This sugar wonderland was essentially the only store in Fair Harbor on their radar screen. It had long since ceased to sell candy for a penny apiece but did have the best homemade fudge *in the universe*, according to the boys. Who were probably right.

The Fair Harbor Fourth of July parade forms in the parking lot behind Taylor's Hardware, then proceeds down Main Street, turns right after the town green onto South Fair Harbor Road, and ends at Thompkins Park. The Penny Candy Store is about a block from Taylor's, so once I'd squeezed my butt onto the curb between Thing One and Thing Two, my ginormous six-month-old puppy firmly tucked between my knees, we could hear the high school marching band tuning up. This had amped the boys' excitement level considerably. Jenny and Roland were standing behind us, with Roland saying things to his unruly progeny like "Remember, you are to remain seated during the parade" and "Above all, you are not to run out into the street." Which I thought showed just how much he really believed these little hellions were going to stay seated during the parade.

At first all was well. The parade was led, as always, by the town's vintage 1945 police car, which looks like nothing more than a huge, shiny black beetle. It was being driven by none other than Sheriff McCauley, waving with one hand to the crowd lined up on the sidewalk. The crowd had cheered and waved back. I had not. McCauley and I had a history. My puppy had been a little confused by the shouting and waving, but was not overly concerned. He had his human and his three best friends with him, so what could go wrong?

I'll tell you what. The fire engine is what. It had been almost ten years since I'd been to Fair Harbor's July Fourth parade. I'd forgotten about the fire engine. The fire engine always came next, after the vintage police car. The fire engine's job, in my opinion, is to bring the kids along the route to a fever pitch of excitement by blasting its siren *every single block* of the route. Well, it had taken only one klaxon blare to lift the Three Things to their collective feet, yelling and cheering—or from Diogi's increasingly panicked point of view, screaming—and to send my puppy diving for cover, which, in this case, was up my blouse.

I'm sure we made quite a picture as I scurried back to where Grumpy was parked behind the library, carrying my ginormous shaking puppy (most of whom was still inside my clothing), his leash trailing behind us like a sad tail.

S O DIOGI WASN'T going to the parade this year. And neither were Jason and I if we didn't get this party started pretty soon. The day dawned bright and crisp, and Jason, bless his heart, was down at the beach at the crack of dawn, digging his fire pit and lining it with the stones his young cohorts had collected over the course of the week. I wandered down a little later with a thermos of coffee and two plastic mesh laundry baskets that I'd picked up at the dollar store in Hyannis. These we proceeded to fill with seaweed we gathered from the rocks exposed by the low tide. Jason did something fancy with some line that he found in the old boathouse and lowered the baskets from the dock into the water to keep the seaweed fresh and moist for later.

That rather fun chore accomplished, we sat on the dock taking turns sipping coffee from the thermos. Diogi and Ciati, having finished their morning routine, then wandered down to join us. The four of us sat in silence, watching the sky turn from a pale blush pink to a light blue the color of a robin's egg. I was as quietly happy as I had ever been in my life.

"Ahoy, mateys!"

The chef had arrived. Ed looked as jolly as I had ever seen him. Jason had told me that the brouhaha about changing the name of Clara's Place had finally been put to bed when Ed's investors had realized, like Bentley, the advantages of notoriety. Clara's Place it was and Clara's Place it would stay. Ed was resplendent in chef's whites covered with a vast red apron and a red Boston Red Sox (Go Bo-Sox!) baseball cap over his wild Captiva hair. He was lugging a plastic milk crate filled with tongs and oven mitts and other assorted chef-y paraphernalia, so Jason hustled over to help him while Ciati stood by offering helpful hints at the top of her little cat lungs and Diogi ran in circles around the two men, making every effort to trip them up. I figured they didn't need me adding to the chaos, so I went back up to the house, where maybe I could find some peace and quiet.

What, or rather, who, I found was Krista. Krista in a red

miniskirt, white sleeveless top, and blue espadrilles, stepping out of her sleek black convertible sports car, her matching sleek black hair barely mussed even though the car's top was down. I, on the other hand, was wearing saggy chino shorts and an old T-shirt all raggedy around the collar. My bare feet were muddy from the seaweed gathering, and my hair had not yet seen the ministrations of a brush. The mental comparison did not make me happy.

"What are you doing here?" I asked rudely. Fortunately, Krista doesn't recognize rude. She sees it as straightforward.

"Well, first of all, I thought you'd like to know that they caught the dognapper," Krista said.

I let out a whoop. "That's great!" I said. "How?"

"Apparently, one of the dogs he carted off took offense and bit him up so bad he had to go to the emergency room, but he wouldn't tell the doctor on duty how it happened or where the dog was. The doctor has a dog herself and knew about this dog-snatching thing, so she called the cops."

"I love it!" I said. "Thanks for coming by to tell me."

"Yeah, well, I thought you'd like to know," Krista said. "But really, I wanted to know if you've heard anything about the holdup on the Foster murder, now that I know you've got a source in the police department."

"Detective Peters is not my 'source,'" I said, all huffy. "If anything, I was *her* source."

"Yeah, well, she's gone all silent on my reporter," Krista said. "So I thought asking you was worth a try."

I shrugged. "Haven't heard a word either," I admitted.

"Don't you think that's a little weird?" Krista said. "My source said it was all wrapped up."

"Well, if your source is McCauley, that's what he always says," I pointed out.

She nodded. "True."

Then she added innocently, "Any chance Vivian Peters is going to be at this little jamboree today?"

The woman really has a nose for news.

"She may stop by," I admitted. "And you are not, I repeat, *not* to badger her. This is a purely social occasion."

Krista acted like she hadn't heard me. Which is one of the reasons I like her. There are a lot of people in her business who would have promised whatever I asked and conveniently forgotten that agreement the minute opportunity knocked. Not Krista. Krista never lies. She just doesn't respond.

"As long as you're here," I said, "you can help me carry that down to the dock." I pointed to Aunt Ida's ancient blue Coleman cooler, which I'd already filled with the fortifying beers I'd promised Ed.

"Jeez," Krista said as she grabbed a handle and hefted her side, "what's in this thing?"

"A case of Sam Adams for the chef."

"Who's the chef?"

"Ed Captiva," I said. "You met him at Helene's birthday lunch."

Krista's eyes lit up. "Oh, yeah," she said, "I remember him. He's one big hunk of man."

Uh-oh.

Together we hoisted the cooler down the hill to where Jason and Ed were lighting the driftwood fire that they'd laid over the stones in the pit. The plan was that Jason would go do his harbormaster thing in the parade while Ed stayed behind tending the fire. If Krista's eyes lit up at the thought of Ed Captiva, they were nothing compared to Ed's when he saw Krista Baker.

Jason and I took one look at each other and left them there to get further acquainted. The last thing we heard as we started up the hill was Ed asking Krista if she liked to cook and Krista responding, "God, no. The only thing I make in my kitchen is reservations." Ed's booming laugh followed us all the way back up to the house.

After a quick shower, I ran a comb through my hair (which through the magic of a great haircut still looked stupendous, even when all I did was wash it and let it dry naturally) and put on my traditional Fourth of July outfit (yes, the same one that Diogi had climbed into the year before), and Jason and I headed out for town.

This year the parade was super fun. Diogi stayed behind to "help" Ed with the fire by bringing him stray pieces of driftwood so I was unencumbered by my scaredy-cat dog. Which made me wonder why the phrase is scaredy-*cat*, when in my world, the dog was the scaredy one and the cat could totally care less.

I had a grand time with the Three Things. We cheered loudly for the Nauset Sailing Club's homemade float bearing its traditional Sunfish sailboat with a red, white, and blue striped sail and, as was traditional, the club's youngest sailor at the helm. We oohed and aahed at the Uncle Sam on stilts and clapped along with the high school marching band playing John Philip Sousa's "Stars and Stripes Forever." And we totally lost it for the Shawme Manor float, a long flatbed truck on which a dozen older ladies and gentlemen were doing an enthusiastic Electric Slide led by none other than Jillian herself. But best of all, in my opinion, was the Harbor Patrol's Grady-White being towed on a trailer behind the Patrol's Ford Explorer. The boat was draped with red, white, and blue bunting, and at the helm was the hottest harbormaster on Cape Cod (and maybe the world) waving to his adoring (on my part anyway) fans.

"Aunty Sam!" Thing Three, otherwise known as Evan and my favorite of the hellions, exclaimed, "That's Jason! That's Jason being the harbormaster! I've never seen Jason be the harbormaster! How wicked cool is that?"

I agreed with all my heart that Jason being the harbormaster was wicked cool. And for a moment I felt that my heart would break.

FIFTY

~~~~

"SO YOU GUYS are going to follow me back to Aunt Ida's house?" I asked Jenny as we made our way to the library parking lot after the parade. I was waiting for the little irritating voice in my head to say, *It's* your *house, Sam*, but the voice remained silent. The voice knew that I was no longer of two minds about whose house it was. It was *my* house. But I was always going to call it Aunt Ida's house; that's just how it was. That was its name.

"We've got to stop back to pick up our lobbies and a cooler of soft drinks," Jenny said, "but then we'll be right over."

The minute they arrived, the boys ran down to observe the progress of the fire after a stern prohibition from their father about staying at least three feet away from the fire pit. *Yeah, dream on, buddy*, the little voice in my head said.

Jillian and Andre pulled in not long after the Singletons, both looking like an ad for the good life in tan linen shorts and long-sleeved Breton fishermen's tops—hers red-striped, his blue—and bringing with them a long folding table to hold the overflow that couldn't be handled by my table.

"Great!" I said, leading them around to the porch. "We'll

set it up in here, making a T-formation with my outdoor dining set."

Jillian looked at me, eyebrows raised. "Your *outdoor dining set*?" Somehow, she managed to make it sound all ohh-lah-lah. "Girl, call it what it is. That is a picnic table."

I laughed. "Well, don't tell poor Mr. Taylor that. But I agree. Picnic table it is."

I covered both tables with a couple of Aunt Ida's red-checked tablecloths; filled some dollar store polka-dotted kiddie sand buckets with reusable bamboo forks, knives, and spoons; plunked down a couple piles of paper napkins topped with a few rocks to keep them from becoming giant confetti; and set out a leaning tower of heavy-duty paper plates. Voilà, table set.

Helene materialized shortly thereafter, wearing white capri pants and a red T-shirt with "Life, liberty and the pursuit of happiness" printed on it. Behind her came Beth and Marcel pulling an extremely large cooler filled with many lovely bottles of rosé on ice. Being teenagers and thus way too cool to dress in holiday-appropriate gear, they were wearing blue jeans and sun-faded T-shirts and somehow looked fabulous.

Even more fabulous and magical, Mr. Abraham Beame arrived virtually within seconds of Helene, which I took as a sign from the Universe of, I don't know, something. He came bearing the latest cookbook from the Cape Cod Fishermen's Alliance, which he presented to me with a flourish.

"Just published," he said. "Just published and I thought you'd like to have a copy."

"How incredibly thoughtful," I said. "I had no idea it had come out. I'll add it to my collection."

"There's an excellent recipe in it for monkfish that you won't want to miss," he said. "Excellent."

This was a guy who talked my language. Twice.

I took the cookbook into the kitchen for safekeeping, but not before I'd introduced Abe to Helene and left them discussing the next Fair Harbor Library book sale in their own little book nerd heaven.

A little while later Miles pulled into the crushed shell driveway with Mr. and Mrs. Tanner and his boyfriend, Sebastian. A Sebastian sighting is a rare treat, as his practice is all absorbing, so I gave him a big hug, which embarrassed me a little. But I think that Sebastian and Miles are great together, for all that they live such different, busy lives, and I'm convinced that my delight when I see the elusive doctor serves as positive reinforcement.

Mrs. Tanner was resplendent in a red blouse tucked into navy Bermuda shorts and white knee socks decorated with little American flags. Miles was wearing his usual jeans and white T-shirt, but had a fake tattoo of a star on each cheek, one red, one blue. Sebastian was wearing his usual spotless chinos and a blue polo shirt but, to my delight, had allowed Miles to give him matching stars. Mr. Tanner was wearing work pants and a short-sleeved tan button-down shirt.

"I'm not so into silly," he said.

Next came Dave and Elisha Joy in a battered old truck that made Grumpy look positively glitzy. This was the first time I'd seen Elisha in anything other than her rubber overalls. She was wearing a loose, crinkly cotton shift over what looked to me distinctly like a baby bump. When she caught me staring, Elisha smiled and did that thing that pregnant women do where they cup their belly with both hands and look angelic. Then Dave did that thing that husbands of pregnant women do where they put their arms around their wives protectively and beam. They were adorable.

"You've guessed our good news," Elisha said.

"I'm thrilled for you," I said, giving her a very careful hug. "I am putting you in the seat of honor."

And I led her into the screened-in screened-in porch and handed her into my peacock chair.

Last to arrive was Summer Robinson. What with the joyous doggy reunion of Diogi, Alba, and Bear, I almost didn't notice the other woman getting out of Summer's Prius. And when I did notice her, I almost didn't recognize her. Was this really Jean Wilkinson?

Because this was not the Jean Wilkinson I'd met at Clara Foster's memorial service. This was a very different Jean Wilkinson. The woman walking toward me looked a good ten years younger than the one I'd met at the service. She wore no makeup and her hair danced in loose waves around her lightly tanned face. Instead of designer clothing, she was wearing a pair of soft chinos and a faded L.L.Bean polo shirt. And instead of an angry scowl, she had a friendly smile on her face.

"Ms. Wilkinson," I said lamely, trying to not sound or look as flabbergasted as I felt.

I obviously failed miserably, as Jean Wilkinson laughed (*Jean Wilkinson laughed*) and said, "No need to look so alarmed. I promise I won't bite. And please call me Jean."

"Of course I'm not alarmed," I lied. "I was just, um, surprised."

"Which is to be expected, seeing how I behaved the last time we met," Jean said. "Summer told me about your visit and how you'd apologized. She thought I'd benefit from doing the same."

I glanced over at Summer, who, *and I am not making this up*, winked at me.

"Well, let's consider the apology made and accepted," I said, eager to get past the moment. Feelings and all that. "But I should let you know that the Joys are here today."

"Good," Jean said firmly. "I need to apologize to them, too."

"Great," I said faintly. But what I really wanted to say was, *Who are you and what have you done with Jean Wilkinson?*

As if she'd read my mind, Jean said, "I've had a bit of a change of heart, no, a complete change of heart since we last met. I'd like to tell you about it."

"Of course," I said. "I just need to check in with the guys

tending the fire first. In the meantime, can I get you a beer or a glass of wine?"

"I'd love a nice big glass of wine," Jean said, just to keep surprising me.

"Me too," Summer said with enthusiasm. Will wonders never cease.

And so I led the ladies over to Helene's cooler, where Beth and Marcel were dispensing paper cups of Helene's rosé.

"A hefty pour for my friends Summer and Jean," I said.

THE MENFOLK, AS it turned out, didn't need my oversight. Instead, I joined Krista in watching the whole operation from the dock. In my absence the fire had burned to embers, and Ed and Jason put down the first layer of wet seaweed that would steam our food over the glowing hot rocks. Miles and Sebastian brought down the potatoes, corn, lobsters, steamers, and sausage, which Ed placed on the seaweed in tidy layers. Finally, he added the second layer of seaweed, covered the pit with the wet canvas, and sealed the edges with sand and rocks. All of this accompanied by the requisite Sam Adams.

"That'll take about an hour while the whole mess steams to briny perfection," he said. He lifted the top of the cooler and said in all innocence, "Who drank all the beer?"

Krista snorted and said, "It's anyone's guess, Hot Stuff, but why don't we go up to the house and see if we can find you some more."

While the gang waited for the food to cook, Roland brought the boys and the dogs down to the dock to swim, and Mr. and Mrs. Tanner played a rousing game of horseshoes with Jillian and Andre. Jenny and the Joys sat on the porch and talked babies, while Abraham and Helene pretended they knew how to play badminton. And Jean Wilkinson and I had our little chat.

"You've probably heard about my husband's money troubles," she said, taking a nice hefty swallow of her wine.

I took my own hefty swallow and nodded.

"Well," she said, "what you also may have heard but what *I* certainly hadn't heard was that a lot of those troubles were because Paul had a girlfriend who insisted on being kept in the style to which she wished to become accustomed."

I took another swallow of my wine and shook my head. "Hadn't heard that," I said.

"I only learned about it at the memorial service," Jean said. "As people were leaving, I overheard two of my so-called friends laughing about Paul's 'fancy woman' in Boston."

"That must have been hard," I said.

"Actually," Jean said, "it was oddly liberating. I'd been doing everything I could think of to get us out of the hole that man had dug, including infuriating my aunt and considering a lawsuit against those nice Joys, while he'd been buying tasteless jewelry for his girlfriend."

I wanted to ask her how she knew it was tasteless but didn't. That will forever remain a mystery.

"Anyway, I started going to Aunt Clara's house to oversee the cleanup, which insurance covered, thank god. And every day I would sit on that deck and look out at the bay and every day I started to feel a little bit better. I started divorce proceedings and put the house on the Heights on the market, and all I could think was 'good riddance.' One day this nice neighbor came over with her dogs and brought me some early zucchini from her garden. We got to talking, and I realized how far I'd wandered from the path I thought my life would take when I got married. Those talks helped a lot, but it didn't take me long to realize that it was Aunt Clara's house, the location, the *place* that was healing me. All in the space of two weeks. Can you understand that?"

"I do," I said. "I totally do."

"Then you can understand why I've decided to move

into her house permanently," she said. "You can understand that what I thought was a disaster was, in fact, a great gift."

The wisdom of the elders, I thought.

At this point, a whooping and hollering from the Three Things down on the shore alerted me and my assorted guests that the whole mess had steamed to briny perfection. Then began a quick pilgrimage down to the beach carrying bowls and platters to collect the food and another, much slower, pilgrimage back up the hill with said food.

Soon we had settled ourselves around the *picnic* tables on the *screened-in* porch, where we started our feast with steamed clams dunked in melted butter. This was followed by the lobster, also dunked in melted butter, and the potatoes and corn, both drizzled with melted butter. In fact, the only foodstuff not served with melted butter was the linguica, which I presented with a nice grainy French mustard and which Jason and Ed ate vast quantities of, calling it, only half jokingly, "the food of our people."

And finally, once the table had been cleared—at their own insistence—by Beth and Marcel, the *pièce de résistance*: the blueberry buckles that I'd made the day before. Jillian and I brought them out with the boys following behind, each bearing a blue bowl filled with whipped cream like some kind of kiddie version of the Three Kings bearing gifts. There were great cheers from the crowd, with Helene giving one of her ear-splitting two-fingered whistles and Miles declaring, "Ladies and Gentlemen, I give you the Best Blueberry Buckle in the World."

It wasn't Clara Foster's blueberry buckle. For one thing, I hadn't used huckleberries. For another, I'd added a whisper of cinnamon, because it is my opinion that there is no baked good that is not improved by a whisper of cinnamon. But it was still the Best Blueberry Buckle in the World because it was dedicated to the memory of Clara Foster.

FIFTY-ONE

B Y THE TIME Vivvie Peters rolled in, the guests had said their goodbyes, Jason had ensured that the fire in the clambake pit was well and truly out, I had managed to put the kitchen to rights, and Diogi and Ciati were conked out in the ell.

Jason and I were sitting on the porch in a kind of exhausted haze of happiness when I heard Vivvie calling around the corner of the house. "Please tell me there's some dessert left."

"In the kitchen," I yelled back. "I saved you a piece. The whipped cream is in the fridge."

Vivvie came out on the porch bearing a triangle of buckle almost drowned in whipped cream.

"Have some buckle with your whipped cream, why don't you?" Jason said.

"Have some respect for an officer of the law, why don't you?" she said.

"Children," I said, "no squabbling."

"He started it," Vivvie muttered. Then she took a bite of her buckle. "Oh," she moaned, "now I can die happy."

I managed to contain my impatience while Vivvie polished off her buckle, but it wasn't easy. As far as I was concerned, there were still a lot of loose ends to tie up around Clara's death.

Jason came out with coffee for the three of us and said to Vivvie, "Okay, Detective Peters, spill."

And spill she did. Yes, Barbara had officially confessed to Clara Foster's murder. Yes, the forensic evidence backed up her version of the events.

"Which," Vivvie added, "was also your version of the events, Sam."

"Maybe it was my version of 'howdunit,'" I admitted, "but you were the one who came up with 'whodunit.'"

"I am feeling distinctly out of the loop here," Jason complained.

"Well, that's what happens when you go gallivanting off to California instead of staying here on the Cape with Sam where you belong," Vivvie said.

The silence that greeted her quip was deafening.

"Oops," Vivvie said. "Awkward."

I was speechless, but Jason sprang into the breach. "No, no," he said, "it's a fair point."

Which did not make it any less awkward.

"Anyway," Vivvie said desperately, "there's actually some rather surprising news that I wanted to share with you."

"Do tell," I blurted out gratefully. "Did you find the Hopper?"

"Well," she said, "we did find a painting hidden under the floorboards of the attic of the old Bartholomew place that matched the description you gave us. So we had a Hopper expert come out like you suggested to confirm that this was the Hopper original."

"And?" I asked.

"And it wasn't."

I was floored. I was gobsmacked. Call it what you will.

"Not the real Hopper?" I said. "How did they determine that?"

"It wasn't very difficult," Vivvie said. "She took the painting out of the frame. And just as you and Barbara Smiley suspected, the artist's signature was under it."

"But she still didn't think it was the real Hopper?" I asked. "Why on earth not?"

"Because the signature on the painting was Kit Connor's."

Not the real Hopper. Kit's *copy* of the real Hopper. Just as she had always claimed. Barbara Smiley had been wrong. Jenny had been wrong. Except in her estimation of Kit's own talent, even as a copyist.

"You know what this means, of course?" I said.

"That the Joys aren't going to be millionaires," Vivvie said. "That's gotta hurt."

"They never knew they might be millionaires," I said. "Roland Singleton agreed with you that it would be 'prudent' not to tell them until the painting had been found and verified."

"Smart guy, that Singleton," Vivian said.

"But that wasn't what I meant by what this means," I said.

Jason got it immediately. "It means the original Hopper is still out there somewhere," he said.

I nodded. "Exactly."

Jason looked at me. "And you're going to try to find it?"

"Nah," I said. "Not my circus, not my monkey."

"Good," Vivvie said, grinning and standing up to leave. "Because if I never go to one of your circuses again, it will be too soon."

FIFTY-TWO

~~~~~~

T HAT NIGHT I opted out of the Fair Harbor fireworks
display. Not because I don't like fireworks. I *love* fireworks. Diogi, on the other hand, considers loud booms fair
warning of the coming apocalypse, which he then prepares
for by cowering in Aunt Ida's claw-foot bathtub. Fortunately, the fireworks were being held off Stone Harbor, so
hopefully the booms wouldn't be loud enough to spook him.

Jason, who also loves fireworks, had opted to stay with
me and my lily-livered dog. Because that's the kind of guy
he is. The kind of guy who takes the red-eye home from
California because his cousin needs him. The kind of guy
who, two days later, takes the red-eye home again because
his girl needs him. The kind of guy who spends almost a
week making a clambake pit because his girl wants to have
a real Cape Cod clambake. The kind of guy who agrees that
because they had a huge picnic lunch, there's no need to
make dinner even though he knows he's going to get really
hungry again at some point. The kind of guy who gets an
incredible job offer but is willing to walk away from it if his
girl doesn't want to move. The kind of guy who has always

wanted his girl to live her own life, her own dream. The kind of guy who is not afraid of the word "commitment."

And what about you, Sam? I asked myself as I snuggled up next to that guy on the porch swing, one of Aunt Ida's quilts tucked around us to ward off the evening chill. *Are you afraid of the word "commitment"?* That one was easy. I was absolutely *not* afraid of the word "commitment." Not as it applied to Jason anyway. If I knew anything, I knew I was totally committed to Jason Captiva. And not just because he was an excellent kisser. Although that helped.

And what about the rest?

There I still wasn't sure. Jason had made it clear that he'd give up the job in Santa Barbara if I wasn't prepared to go with him. And I wasn't sure if I was prepared to go with him. I also wasn't sure that I could bear to be the reason that he couldn't live his life, his dreams. This, I believe, is what is called being between a rock and a hard place. I tried to put the dilemma out of my mind, to be grateful that no booms disturbed the peace of the night, to simply feel the beauty of the shimmering reflection of the full moon on Bower's Pond as it began its rise behind us, of Jason's strong arm around me. This was enough. For now, this was more than enough. It was perfect.

So I was a little disappointed when Jason pulled his arm away and turned to face me. We'd lit a few of Aunt Ida's old oil lamps and put them on the porch table, and I could see in their warm glow that the man had something serious on his mind. *Uh-oh.*

"I've been thinking," he began. There was a long pause, during which I realized I was holding my breath. "About us," he added. And paused again. This was going to take a while.

"Me too," I said, if only to move the conversation along.

"Have you come to any conclusions?" he asked.

"No," I admitted. "Other than that I am totally committed to you."

Another long pause.

"That's about how far I've gotten, too," Jason admitted.

"Maybe that's enough for now," I said. "Maybe we just have to trust ourselves. Trust that we'll make the right decisions when the time comes. That's what Helene thinks anyway."

Jason nodded, his dark eyes thoughtful. "Helene's advice is usually good."

I looked at him. "You go to Helene for advice?"

"Of course I do," Jason said. "*Everybody* goes to Helene for advice."

"And what was her advice?" I asked.

"She said I should trust myself," he said. "That I'd know the answer when the time came."

"Well," I said, "the woman's consistent anyway."

Jason smiled. "And then I asked her what I should say in the meantime."

"And what did she advise?" I asked softly.

"This," Jason said, leaning toward me and taking my cold hand in his warm one.

"'In vain have I struggled,'" he began.

I couldn't help myself. I started to laugh. "Oh, Jason," I said. "You're channeling Mr. Darcy!"

"Don't laugh," he said, even though he was now grinning himself. "I'm not done."

"Okay," I said, wiping tears of laughter from my eyes. "Pray continue, kind sir."

"'It will not do,'" Jason said, suddenly serious, the rough edge back in his voice. "'My feelings will not be repressed. You must allow me to tell you how ardently I admire and love you.'"

I wasn't laughing anymore. I was completely and totally undone. This sweet, sweet man ardently admired and loved me.

"Oh, Jason," I breathed, "I ardently admire and love you, too."

I still had no idea how we would build our future together, but build it together we would. And, I thought, it would be wonderful. And then I wasn't thinking anything at all. Because Jason Captiva was kissing me.

I HAVE NO IDEA how long we sat there, wrapped in Aunt Ida's quilt, whispering lovers' nonsense to each other as the moon rose ever higher in the night sky.

Eventually, though, Jason pulled away from me. I waited for more terms of endearment.

"I'm hungry," he said. "Is there any of that blueberry buckle left?"

AUTHOR'S NOTE

I AM FREQUENTLY ASKED what town on the Cape Fair Harbor is based on. None. It is completely imaginary. Ha-ha. Only kidding. Fair Harbor is a mash-up of several mid-Cape towns, including Orleans, Chatham, Brewster, and Wellfleet (and their waters), depending on what I need for the story.

I should add that there is no such organization as the Cape Cod Conservancy, though it is loosely based on the Cape Cod Conservation District, whose good work preserving the Cape's fragile ecosystem cannot be overstated.

ACKNOWLEDGMENTS

If you have read this far in the Cape Cod Foodie series, you will have noticed how important family and friends are to Sam. Well, the apple doesn't fall far from the tree. The Universe has smiled on me with its gift of a large, bumptious, and loving family, and a lunatic bunch of understanding and loyal friends. How wonderful it is to be able to thank you all here.

Let me start with dear friends. Endless thanks to Jenny, BJ, Simon and Ling, Ada and Ronald, Trish, Susie and Ed (and Hugo and Delia, of course), Sarah, Jan and Phil, Santiago and Ethel, Belinda, Nancy, John and Pat, Pierre, Paula and Gary, and Erika. And, of course, the BNYM gang (you know who you are). I don't know how or why you all put up with me, but I am forever grateful.

And my family . . . oh, what a wonderful family I have! There are my lovely brothers John, Tim, and Dan, and big sister (and all-time top Cape Cod Foodie booster), Megan. Not to mention my wonderful in-laws—Robin, Fran, Jacquie and Margie, Guy, Laura, and Julia. How very lucky I am to have you all as my posse.

You may have noticed that this book is dedicated to Nick and Quinn, who, as you might have guessed, are my kids. Okay, so they're not kids anymore. In fact, they are incredibly funny, smart, successful adults. I love you more than the world. Now, go clean up your rooms.

And finally, there's my wonderful husband and soul mate, Bill, who was the cutest, funniest, smartest guy in the room when we were sixteen—and still is. Thank you for somehow managing to retain your optimism and sense of humor through two years of virtual isolation with Yours Truly. You are my rock.

RECIPES

A Simply Delicious Summer Picnic

You don't need to have a clambake to enjoy a mouth-watering summer picnic. Here's one that incorporates all the major picnic food groups: chips and dip, grilled everything, and decadent baked goods. This starts with a classic clam dip, followed by skewers of grilled shrimp, sausage, and corn and ending with a scrumptious blueberry buckle. You're welcome.

KEEP IT SIMPLE CLAM DIP

The only trick here is to make sure the cream cheese is softened to room temperature, which makes the blending much easier.

(MAKES: 2 CUPS)

1 3-ounce package cream cheese, softened
1 7-ounce can minced clams (drained but reserving 2
    tablespoons of the clam liquid)
1 cup sour cream
⅛ teaspoon Worcestershire sauce (or more to taste)
1–2 tablespoons lemon juice

Drain the clams, reserving 2 tablespoons of the liquid, and mash into the softened cream cheese. Add the clam liquid, sour cream, Worcestershire sauce, and lemon juice, and blend well.

Serve with a good strong potato chip, like Cape Cod Potato Chips.

SHRIMP, LINGUICA, AND CORN SKEWERS

As the vast majority of us are not going to find ourselves at a real Cape Cod clambake anytime soon, these yummy skewers are easily grilled in your own backyard or under a broiler and are a lovely meal in their own right. (Tip: If you can't find linguica at your local supermarket, feel free to substitute another smoked and pre-cooked sausage like andouille or chorizo.) And do make the aioli for dipping—it's super simple.

(MAKES 4 LARGE SKEWERS OR 8 SMALL ONES)

For the skewers:

16 jumbo or 20 extra-large shrimp, deveined but with
    shell on

½ cup extra-virgin olive oil

2 tablespoons chopped fresh oregano or 1 teaspoon
    dried

Coarse salt

Lots of freshly ground pepper

3 ears corn, shucked and cut into 1-inch-thick rounds

½ pound linguica, cut into 1-inch pieces (16 pieces)

Lemon wedges for serving

Aioli for serving

Combine the oil, oregano, ¾ teaspoon salt, and pepper in a large, shallow bowl. Add the shrimp and corn and toss to coat.

Preheat the grill to medium-high or, if you are using a charcoal grill, until you can hold your hand 5 inches above the grill for just 3 to 4 seconds. If you are using your oven's broiler, let it preheat for about 5 minutes.

Divide the shrimp, corn rounds, and linguica among the skewers, making sure you skewer the shrimp at their top and tail to hold them firmly.

Grill, turning every two minutes or so, until the shrimp are opaque, 5 to 7 minutes. Don't worry if the corn begins to brown a bit—that caramelization is delicious.

Serve the skewers with lemon wedges for squeezing over the shrimp, and the garlic-infused aioli for dipping. And do encourage your guests to eat with their fingers!

For the aioli:

5 medium garlic cloves, pressed or minced

1 tablespoon lemon juice

Salt

1 cup mayonnaise

1 tablespoon Dijon mustard

In a small, shallow bowl, combine the pressed garlic and lemon juice, spreading the garlic in an even layer. Sprinkle lightly with salt and let it rest for 10 minutes to infuse the lemon juice with garlic flavor.

Pour the lemon juice and garlic into a fine mesh strainer over another bowl, and press down on the garlic with a spoon to get all the lemon juice into the bowl. Discard the garlic.

Stir the mayonnaise into the lemon juice, add the mustard, and refrigerate until ready to serve.

DARN FINE BLUEBERRY BUCKLE

Far be it from me to claim this as the world's best blueberry buckle, but it's pretty darn fine! If you can find huckleberries, that's great, but regular blueberries are fantastic in this recipe. A couple of tips: Note Clara's suggestion about squeezing the streusel before breaking it up in clumps for the topping. Also, tossing the blueberries with a bit of flour before folding them into the batter will keep them from clumping. And, finally, placing your cake pan on a small baking sheet can help to keep the bottom of the cake from over-browning.

(SERVES 8)

Streusel:

⅓ cup all-purpose flour
½ cup packed light brown sugar
2 tablespoons granulated sugar
¼ teaspoon cinnamon
4 tablespoons butter, cut into 8 pieces and softened
Pinch of salt (if using unsalted butter)

Cake:

1 ½ cups all-purpose flour
1 ½ teaspoons baking powder
10 tablespoons butter, softened
½ teaspoon salt (if using unsalted butter)
⅔ cup granulated sugar
1 ½ teaspoons vanilla extract
1 large egg, room temperature
½ cup whole milk
1 pint (about 2–2½ cups) blueberries
Optional: Whipped cream to serve alongside

To make the streusel:

Using a mixer at low speed, beat the flour, both sugars, cinnamon, and salt (if using) to combine and break up any brown sugar lumps.

Still on low, add the softened butter and beat for 2 to 3 minutes until the mixture looks like wet sand.

To make the cake:

Preheat the oven to 350 degrees.

Butter the bottom and sides of a 9-inch round cake pan.

In a small bowl, whisk the flour and baking powder together.

In another larger and heavier bowl, beat the softened butter, sugar, and salt (if using) at medium speed until light and fluffy, about 3 to 4 minutes.

Add the vanilla and the egg, beating well.

With the mixer on low, add the flour mixture in three parts, alternating with the milk.

Toss the blueberries in a separate bowl with 1 to 2 tablespoons of flour and then fold them gently into the batter with a spatula.

Pour the batter into the cake pan and use the spatula to spread it into an even layer.

Top with the streusel: Take a handful of the streusel and squeeze it into a clump. Break the clump into smaller pieces and sprinkle them over the batter. Keep this up until you've used all of your streusel.

Bake the cake for about 40 to 45 minutes or until the streusel is golden brown and a toothpick inserted into the middle of the cake comes out clean.

Transfer the cake pan to a wire rack to cool for about 15 to 20 minutes.

Run a thin knife around the edge of the cake, top it with a plate, and gently invert the cake onto the plate, streusel side down. Using another plate, invert the cake again, so that it is streusel side up. (This is easier than it sounds.)

Serve in wedges with whipped cream on the side (optional, but really, who doesn't want that option?). Ta-da!

Ready to find
your next great read?

Let us help.

Visit prh.com/nextread

Penguin
Random
House